THE EARL NEXT DOOR

THE EARL
NEXT DOOR

The Bachelor Lords of London

CHARIS MICHAELS

AVONIMPULSE
An Imprint of HarperCollinsPublishers

EPub Edition MARCH 2016 ISBN: 9780062412928

Print Edition ISBN: 9780062412942

Avon, Avon Impulse, and the Avon Impulse logo are trademarks of HarperCollins Publishers.

AM 10 9 8 7 6 5 4 3 2 1

For my mother.
Whose spirit of selfless caregiving inspired
the theme of this book.
And who knew I was a writer before I did.

CHAPTER ONE

No. 21 Henrietta Place
Mayfair, London, England
May 1809

Nothing of record ever happened in Henrietta Place.

Carriages did not collide. Servants did not quarrel in the mews. No one among the street's jowly widowers remarried harlot second wives. No one tolerated stray dogs.

Families with spirited young boys boarded them in school at the earliest possible age.

A calm sort of orderliness prevailed on the street, gratifying residents and earning high praise from Londoners and country visitors alike. It was a domestic refuge. One of the last such sanctuaries in all of London.

Certainly, the stately townhome mansion at number twenty-one was a sanctuary to Lady Frances Stroud, Marchioness Frinfrock, who had been a proud and attentive resident since her marriage in 1768. With her own eyes, Lady Frinfrock had seen the degradation and disquiet that had become prevalent in so many London streets: noble-born men fraternizing with ballet dancers in The Strand; week-long ramblings in Pall Mall. And the spectacle that was Covent Garden? It wasn't to be borne.

What a comfort, then, that Lady Frinfrock would always have Henrietta Place, where nothing of record ever happened. Where she could live out her final days in peace and tranquility.

"It looks to be fair for a second day, my lady," said Miss Breedlowe, the marchioness's nurse, crossing to the alcove window that overlooked the street.

"A fog will descend by luncheon," said the marchioness, frowning.

"If it pleases you, we could take a short walk before then," the nurse said. "To Cavendish Square and back? Spring weather is so unpredictable, we should take advantage of the sun before it disappears again for a month."

"Cavendish Square is not to be tolerated," said Lady Frinfrock.

Miss Breedlowe looked at her hands. "Only so far as the corner and back, then?"

"Not I," said the marchioness, pained.

A sigh of disappointment followed, as it always did. How unhappily accustomed Lady Frinfrock had become to her nurse's chronic sighing. It was obvious that Miss Breedlowe endeavored to be patient, although, in her ladyship's view, not nearly patient enough. In return, the marchioness rarely endeavored to be agreeable enough.

And why should a woman of her age and station be prodded through an inane schedule of someone else's design? To be forced to engage in robust activities intended for no other purpose than to move her bowels? If her inept solicitors felt that her alleged infirmity warranted the nurse-maiding of sullen, sigh-ridden Miss Breedlowe, then so be it. They could cajole her to compensate and house the woman, but they could not force her to abide her. Or to walk to Cavendish Square when she hadn't the slightest desire to do so.

Miss Breedlowe cleared her throat. "Perhaps tomorrow, then."

Lady Frinfrock made a dismissive sound. "If you wish to walk to Cavendish Square, Miss Breedlowe, pray, do not let my disinterest detain you."

The nurse turned from the window and studied her. "I had hoped to discover an activity that we might enjoy together."

"A vain hope, I fear. I am a solitary soul, as the tyrants at Blinklowe, Dinkle, and Tuft, would comprehend if their service to my estate extended beyond calculating my worth in shillings and pounds and subtracting their yearly portion. Instead they have shackled me to you."

To her credit, the nurse did not blanch, but she also did not reply. The marchioness looked away. If such frank language could not elicit some measure of honesty from the woman, perhaps it would scare her into not speaking at all. Either would be preferable to her current trickle of disingenuous small talk, not to mention the incessant sighing.

"I dare say your planters are the most beautiful for several blocks, my lady," Miss Breedlowe said after a moment. "Do you direct your gardener in their care?"

"They are not the loveliest on their own accord, of that you can be sure."

"How talented you are."

The marchioness snorted. "You can but see what becomes of a garden when left unattended, even for a week. Just look at the deplorable state of Lord Falcondale's flower boxes and borders, if you can bear it. Such an eyesore."

"Oh, yes. The new earl. Which house is it?"

"Number twenty-four. There. Directly across the street. It's been in his family for an age." She gently tapped the window with her cane. "His late uncle, the previous Lord Falcondale, paid fastidious attention to the upkeep of those planters. Tulips and ivy mostly, this time of year. Simple flowers, really. No effort to maintain, but perfectly lovely if kept headed and weeded, which he did. Not to mention his staff swept the steps and stoop several times a day, even in the damp. But now his far-flung nephew has inherited, and I fear the entire property will fall into disrepair."

"Hmmm," said Miss Breedlowe. "That would be a great shame."

"Doubtless it seems like a small thing to you, but this sort of irresponsibility can bring about the demise of order and calm in a quiet street like our Henrietta Place. It doesn't help that number twenty-two," she gestured again, "next door to Falcondale's, has been unoccupied and for sale these last five years. The house agents keep it up, but there's no substitute for the loving care of a devoted owner and staff."

"Indeed."

"To make matters worse, the new earl is completely unresponsive to neighborly suggestion. I dispatched Samuel to speak to his gardener, only to be told that the man has let him go, the careless sod."

"Dismissed his gardener?"

"He sacked the whole lot. I've since learned that every servant has been turned out. Now I ask you, how is a house of that size to be maintained without staff?"

"I can only guess, my lady, but do take care. It would not warrant you to become overset." She ventured small steps toward the marchioness.

"The demise of order and calm." Lady Frinfrock tsked, waving her away. "The demise of order and calm."

As if on cue, a carriage, buffed to a sun-sparkling sheen, whipped around the corner, thundering down the cobblestones from the direction of Welbeck Street.

"Who the devil could this be?" the marchioness whispered. She drew so near to the window, her breath fogged the glass. The carriage careened toward them at a breakneck pace, slowing slightly as it neared Lady Frinfrock's front window. With eyes wide, the marchioness watched it jostle past her house and well beyond the weed-ridden planters of Falcondale's front door. Only when it reached the unoccupied house at number twenty-two did it lurch to a stop, the coachman yanking the reins as if his life depended on it.

"Such traffic in the street today," Miss Breedlowe said.

"Nonsense." Lady Frinfrock pinned her gaze on the carriage. "There is no *traffic* in Henrietta Place. Not on this day or any day. Such recklessness? A conveyance of this size? It's wholly irregular!"

"Indeed. Perhaps a neighbor is expecting out-of-town guests?"

"No relation to the occupants of this street could afford a vehicle so grand," she said. "Except, of course, for me. And I have no relatives."

"Not even the new earl, Lord Falcondale?"

The marchioness harrumphed. "He cannot afford even a gardener."

The carriage door sprang open, and Lady Frinfrock leaned in.

"Oh, look," said Miss Breedlowe, cheerful interest in her voice. "It's a young woman. How beautiful she is. And her gown. And hat. Oh, she's brought someone with her. A companion. Hmm. Perhaps a servant?" Her voice went a little off, and she crooked her head to the side, studying the two women collecting in the street.

"Is that an *African?*" Lady Frinfrock nearly shouted, planting both gloved palms on the spotless glass of the window.

"I do believe her companion is an aboriginal woman of some sort," Miss Breedlowe said, her voice croaking, as she moved herself closer to the glass.

"But whatever business could they have in Henrietta Place?"

Miss Breedlowe reached out a hand to steady her. "Do take care, my lady. Perhaps we should return to the comfort of the chairs."

"I shall not be comfortable in chairs," said the marchioness, swatting her away. "But has the young woman come alone?" She tapped a bony finger on the glass. "Where is her family? Her husband or parents?"

"Perhaps the men who have accompanied her are her—"

"Servants, clearly," interrupted the marchioness. "Look, Miss Breedlowe. Trunk after trunk. Crates and baskets. Oh, God. They are conveying it to Cecil Panhearst's old house. It's been sealed like a tomb since 1804."

"So they are. Perhaps you're to have a second new neighbor."

"A lone young woman and an *African?*" She placed her hand on the window with no mind to the smudged glass.

"Highly likely, I'd say. It would appear they are...Yes, they are unpacking."

"Well, that cannot be," Lady Frinfrock declared, shaking her head at the street. "I won't stand for it. Not without knowing who she may be or where she came from. And why she is accompanied by an African."

"Oh, do not worry," Miss Breedlowe said. "The servants will learn her story soon enough. If she has any staff at all, they will talk with the other servants on the street."

For the first time since the carriage arrived, the marchioness lifted her eyes from the window and turned to stare at the nurse.

"Why, what an excellent idea, Miss Breedlowe." She raised her cane and jabbed it in the direction of the startled younger woman. "How resourceful you are. *The servants will talk.*" She raised one eyebrow. "*They will learn her story soon enough.*"

As Miss Breedlowe stared in disbelief, the marchioness scrunched her face and then swung the tip of her cane in the direction of door.

"Oh, no, my lady," said Miss Breedlowe, backing away. "You cannot mean me."

"Oh, yes, 'tis exactly what I mean. Finally, a suitable application for your indeterminate hovering and resigned sighs. We shall devise a reason for you to approach her, and you will discover her business in my street. It is our duty as mindful, responsible residents to know."

"But I was speaking of the maids, my lady. The kitchen boys."

"The maids are unreliable. The kitchen boys are inarticulate. You, however, are ideal for this sort of thing. Steel yourself, Miss Breedlowe. We cannot know what manner of objectionable thing she may say or do. Better fetch your gloves. And your hat."

CHAPTER TWO

No. 24 Henrietta Place
Later that same morning

Bored, tired, and cagey, Trevor Rheese, Earl of Falcondale, hunched over the chessboard, ignoring the game, and wanted.

Wanted privacy, wanted freedom, wanted *out*.

It was a sin to want—scripture was very clear on it: *Thou shall not covet*—but Trevor had been only loosely adherent to scripture in his life, and generally when it aligned with whatever his first inclination might be.

At the moment, he was inclined to want.

It was not broad, his list of wants. He did not wish for wealth or possessions, fame or prestige. Honestly, he did not even care about bloody respect. No, the things he wanted were trifling, bordering on humble. A scant duo of circumstances, nothing more.

Firstly, he wanted to go. To leave. To depart the sodden, sullen, perpetual chill that hung over the islands of Britain like a shroud and to arrive anywhere else in the world. Anywhere except, he was careful to add, the scab-like string of baking rocks known as the Grecian Isles. Even more than he wished to depart England, he wished never to return to the crumbling shores of the Ottoman Empire's *island paradise*, ever again. Leaving Athens had been only temporary fix; his enemies would search for him in England next. True freedom, he knew, lay anywhere else.

After Trevor left England, his second burning desire was to be *left alone*.

Utterly, entirely, completely alone.

He didn't want to mingle with people of his own class. He didn't want to mingle with people of his own country. He didn't want to mingle with people of *any* country.

He did not want a mistress or a wife or an heir—or even a bloody house cat.

Truth was, he didn't even want to be earl, but his uncle had succumbed to lung fever before ever taking a wife. It had been his mother's dying wish that, if it fell to him, he would make some effort toward the estate.

How ironic, then, that when Uncle Peter cocked up his toes, the old goat had been neck-deep in debt. Trevor spent his first month as earl selling his uncle's assets—the last of which (assuming he could find a buyer) was the Henrietta Place townhouse.

Not much longer, he hoped. Two weeks. Perhaps a month.

Until then?

Until then, he would keep a close watch over his shoulder and pass the time playing chess.

"You are forcing me to think, Joseph." Trevor gazed at the chessboard, scrutinizing his defense. "Ah, moved the knight? Clever. Remind me not to leave you alone to strategize for longer than five minutes."

"Who was at the kitchen door?" Joseph asked, smiling. "Cook?"

Trevor shook his head. "No, it was a boy from the market. The cook, I'm assured, has finally come to terms with the fact that he needn't return, ever again, regardless of any fresh rage that might rise to the surface of his wounded pride."

"You look for vermin in the market crate?"

The earl sat back. "I did actually, not that it's any of your concern. I didn't see you leaping up to receive it." He slid his queen's rook across the board. "I think you're the laziest manservant ever to survive a house-wide sacking."

"Oh, I'm a manservant now? As in a paid valet?" He smiled again.

"Right. I've spoken too soon. A valet would require a pension, holidays, an afternoon off."

The boy laughed. "I'd claim a proper salary before I bothered with that."

"Ah, yes. Now I remember why I can't get rid of you. I don't pay you." He advanced his king's pawn, angling for a kingside castle.

He was just about to tell the boy that he would take the first turn in the kitchen, when a noise split the air. A loud noise. Shrill. The sound of wood scraping against stone.

"What the devil was that?" Trevor's head snapped back.

"Sounds like something's split in two," said the boy, wide-eyed.

"It's coming from upstairs. The third floor—no, the second." Trevor stared at the ceiling. "The *empty* second floor. Where there's nothing left to split." He shoved from his chair and crossed to the stairway, looking up.

He'd grown accustomed to this during his years in Greece—sounds, scrapes, things that went bump in the night. Barely a week went by without the sleep-robbing sound of an argument, the shrieks and clatter of a raucous party, or, perhaps loudest of all, the *clunk-clunk-clunk* of something heavy and stolen being dragged up the stairs.

But they were in Mayfair now. Unexpected, jolting noises were out of place. Likely, it was nothing—a rodent or a bird flying against a window—but the hairs on the back of Trevor's neck still bristled. He frowned at the ceiling, straining to hear.

"Perhaps you missed one of the maids," Joseph said, trailing him to the stairs. "When you sacked everyone."

"We've been alone in this house for nearly a week, Joe. No one has been missed."

An unsettling second sound screeched from above. Next, a bump.

"Bloody, bleeding bother," Trevor said under his breath, climbing the stairs, while keeping his eyes on the landing. "What now?"

"I told you the house would be haunted," Joseph said.

"Yes, and I told you I couldn't think of a less likely dwelling for the supernatural. Ghosts, I've been told, seldom congregate in light-filled rooms, swept clean, and devoid of all furniture. Nowhere to hide."

A new noise—this one, unmistakably human—wafted from above. A sigh. Followed by a whimper. And then laughter.

Brilliant. Someone was *laughing* on the second floor.

Someone female.

He paused and held out a hand. The boy stopped.

"Maybe this was the spirit's home, before we stripped it," Joseph whispered, "and now it's cross because we carried away all its possessions." He crept up another step.

"Yes, and how bitter it now sounds. Laughing in the…I believe it's in the music room." He shoved off the top step and walked lightly down the landing, poking his head into each room as he went.

The noises, now a clatter of footsteps and banging—Was someone opening a window?—were loud and most certainly coming from the music room. The *fully enclosed* music room. One of many rooms with no direct access to the outside. Because they were thirty bloody feet off the ground.

He swore, cursing this burden, the newest in the long line of burdens he'd encountered while settling his uncle's estate. The sounds and ruckus had stopped, naturally, now that they had bothered to have a look, but he motioned for Joseph to stay behind him.

Moving deftly, he fell against the wall behind the door. He nudged his head around the jamb. He scanned the room.

Nothing.

Four walls. Dusty floorboards. No furniture, because they'd hauled it off to auction last week. Not even a footstool remained.

Slowly, he edged back. Had they imagined the entire thing?

A window was open, he saw, its drapes fluttering in the morning breeze. That was odd and suspicious.

He stepped toward it.

And collided squarely with a girl.

No, not a girl.

His scrambling fingers felt a fully formed woman, curved and supple. She stilled under his grip for half a second, feigning docility. He craned to get a look at her, and she darted to the right. He grunted and lunged, snatching her back.

They tangled—arms against elbows, her hair in his face, her hands swatting—until finally he clamped down. He jerked the two of them back behind the door, muzzled her mouth with his palm, and scanned the room again.

Still vacant.

She'd been standing behind this very door; it was why he hadn't seen her before. He'd have lost his thumb for such carelessness in Greece.

"Joseph! It's a woman. Doubtful she's alone. Check every room in the house. Mind yourself."

The boy appeared in the doorway, wide-eyed, and Trevor jerked his head. Joseph nodded and darted away.

Trevor checked the room again. It was empty and silent except for her muffled struggle and the drapes snapping in the breeze. Carefully, he loosened his hold to crane around and have a look at her.

Bad idea.

In one glance, the room blurred and blinked and then dissolved entirely away. His whole consciousness became a pair of alarmed green eyes staring back at him.

He stumbled backward a step, taking her with him, and bumped into the wall.

She had hair the color of honey. The struggle had pulled it from a complicated knot on the top of her head, and now it fanned over them both. He felt it against his cheek.

She was young, but how young? Twenty-four? Twenty-five? No older than that, certainly. Well cared for, too, with a creamy complexion and small nose, long lashes, smooth hands. She smelled like a florist's cart. She looked him directly in the eye without a moment's hesitation.

"If there are others," he managed to say, "do not think of alerting them. *Not. One. Word.*"

She tried to speak, soft lips moving under his palm, but her words were muffled by his hand.

"A simple nod of the head will do," he told her. "Are you alone?"

Instead of answering, she bit him. Not deeply, but hard enough to startle. His hand jerked, and she used the moment to yank her head to the side.

"If you please," she said, breathing heavily, "you're suffocating me. I'm not at all given to screaming. It is not necessary to—"

"*Are. You. Alone?*" he ground out, leaning over her.

"I've come with my maid," she said to the wall.

What sort of intruder was accompanied by a maid?

"If you please," she said, "you're hurting my shoulder."

"Where is she?" he demanded.

"Where is who?"

"The maid."

"My maid is not dangerous. She's barely five-feet tall and nearly sixty years old. And she is nowhere. She has gone back into my house."

"Your house? How did she manage that? This is *my* house, or did you lose your way and break into the wrong one? Ow!"

Her boot made piercing contact with his instep. "Look," she said, struggling, "clearly, there has been a misunderstanding, but you cannot possibly think that I can harm you; you're twice my size. Please, sir!" She ground her sharp heel deeper into the side of his boot. "You really can let me go. When I am unrestrained, I absolutely can explain."

Let her go? He looked down at his hands. His brain had been so preoccupied with her face that he had nearly forgotten about her body.

Nearly.

She felt warm and soft and alive. The fabric of her jacket was stiff, but he clearly felt contours. Firmness here, softness elsewhere. Dainty elbow, delicate wrists and fingers.

Reluctantly, he released her, his fingers skimming the expensive wool of her traveling suit as they took the long route to fall away.

"Thank you." She gasped, stumbling out of his arms. She yanked down the hem of her jacket and whipped her hair over her shoulder.

"Who are you?" he demanded.

"I am Piety Grey," she said, recovering enough to offer a dazzling smile. "Of New York City. Recently relocated to London. To Henrietta Place. I have bought the house next door."

She stuck her hand out, like a man intending to shake.

He stared at it, not quite sure what to do. She quickly retracted it. "But perhaps you don't shake hands upon first meeting in England."

"Falcondale," he replied, reaching out his hand. Her glove-less palm felt small and cool. It was, perhaps, the first time he acknowledged the quality of the palm of someone else's hand. He shook.

"We do, actually, shake hands in England, although typically not... Well, I can't really say. I've been away for quite some time, and even before I left, it was never my focus."

"Falcondale?" she asked. "As in the earl? *Lord Falcondale?*" She flung her arms wide. "But I was led to believe you resided in your country home this time of year."

"You were led to believe what?" His voice cracked.

"It was in the contract," she said. "Surely you remember. The solicitors went back and forth in order to get the dates correct. My arrival in London was to be timed with your departure for the country."

He stared at her blankly.

"It is *me*, your lordship," she prompted. "The woman who will be renovating the house next door? What a pleasure to meet you! And on my very first day in London."

While he struggled with that statement, she affected more smiling, solicitous head nodding, and hand clasping. All of it was a little too joyous and felicitous and delighting. Trevor took an uneasy step back.

"I suppose it is obvious that I have found the doors and the shared passage." She gestured to the wall behind her. "I'm sorry I didn't introduce myself first by way of your front door. I never would have stumbled to your side of the wall if I had realized what I had found. I thought it was a closet."

"Closet?" he repeated.

"There," she said, pointing again.

Trevor swiveled his gaze like a tourist, sightseeing in his own home. In a far corner, a small door stood ajar in the shadows. She crossed to the small door, explaining, "It appears exactly the same on my side. Like storage, no? I thought, how lucky for me, another closet. But it wasn't. It was the passage." She smiled at him. "Our passage."

Our passage?

He gaped at her. "I've never seen that door before in my life."

"Oh," she said, and her smile went a little off. "Well, it's inconsequential, really, compared to our larger agreement. By the time I vacate your house, it'll be nailed up, tight as a tomb, and you may go on ignoring it."

Trevor stared, trying to mince through confusion so deep, his ears had begun to ring.

"This little door," she explained slowly, soothingly, "leads from *your house*," she patted the plaster beside the door, "through a small, tunneled-out passageway to *my* new house. See? It goes back and forth, between the two homes. Of course the buildings share this wall, as most row houses do."

He ran a hand through his hair, scrambling to keep up.

"The passage connects to a room in *my new house*. It's an odd, unexplained sort of fluke in the masonry," she continued. "Well, not a fluke, really, as someone, at some point, must have planned for it, and tunneled it out, and installed doors on both sides. But it's hardly typical and largely unnecessary; however, in the case of my renovations—"

"Stop." Trevor closed his eyes and pinched the bridge of his nose. "If you please, *do stop*. Miss...?" He squinted at her. "What did you say you're called?"

"Piety Grey."

"*Please, stop, Miss Grey*. I grasp that there is a passage. This I can plainly see. However, the bit that bears repeating, if you please, was your mention of an 'agreement.' Or, 'contract,' was it?"

She opened her mouth to answer him and then closed it, eyeing him critically. He stared back, raising an eyebrow.

"The *agreement*," she began pointedly, "stipulated in our— yours and mine—*paid, binding contract*." She eyed him. "It grants me the right to temporarily board in your home while carpenters make crucial repairs next door."

Oh, God.

Trevor said nothing—there was too much, perhaps, in that moment to say—and she finished, "I have paid you a fee to reside here in your house during the months you take up residence in your country estate."

"A *paid* contract?" Trevor repeated hoarsely.

"But this was the most crucial piece, my lord. I cannot believe you have no memory of the fifty pounds I paid to let this house."

Trevor gasped. "Fifty pounds? Surely you're joking."

"Surely *you're* joking," she laughed, but it was a strained, nervous sort of laugh, frantic and panicked. She began to pace.

"This...this was all finalized," she said, "signed and sealed and notarized." She gestured to the right and left. "My lawyers in New York, your solicitors here in London." She stopped and turned to face him. "You cannot mean that you have no memory of it? The money? The payment's been issued and gone for months. Even before I sailed from New York. I know we have only corresponded via solicitors until now." Miss Grey pressed on. "But surely you cannot say that you don't recall *any* of this. I have a document signed by your own hand..."

"Not by *my* hand."

"But you agreed."

"I agreed to nothing," he said. "Even if it made sense, which it does not, I would never agree to lease out my home to a—" He ran his hand through his hair again. "To anyone. But especially not to—" He ended abruptly, overwhelmed suddenly by the urge to do as he had done in Greece and simply give the order, *Get out*. He walked to the small door instead and slammed it shut.

"Sorry," he said, reaching for calm. "Let me begin again." He looked at her. "Are you married, Miss Grey? Are we saying, *Miss* Grey, or *Mrs.* Grey?"

"It's *Miss*." She raised her chin.

"Of course," he said. "Very well. What of your father, where is he?"

She blinked. After a long moment, she said, "My father is deceased."

"Your guardian, then? Who looks after your affairs?"

"I, alone, have moved to London and purchased the house, sir. I am in control of my own affairs."

Rather than grapple with that statement, Trevor found words for what he should have said from the very start. "*Miss* Grey," he began, grabbing the back of his neck, "I am the new owner of this house. I have only just inherited it, the title, all of it. The previous earl, my uncle, has died. Some six weeks ago. Any arrangement you made would have been with him."

Miss Piety Grey gasped. "Died? I'm so sorry for your loss, my lord."

"Don't be. Be sorry that you made a deal with a dead man."

Another gasp. "I beg your pardon, I have a docume—"

"Look," he interrupted, "I'm selling the house. As soon as possible. I'm not sure of the sum it will fetch, but, assuming my solicitor confirms the legality of your arrangement with the late earl, perhaps I can repay your family some part of it."

"If I wanted to reverse the settlement," she said, "which I do not, the money would go to me, not my family."

"That makes no sense, but very well," he said. "The repayment would go to you, but this house will be put up for sale next week. In the meantime, *I* live here. You cannot, you shall not, reside inside it. Legal, binding documents or no. It's entirely out of the question."

Miss Grey narrowed her eyes. "I see. Of course, I could not predict your uncle's untimely death, but I do wonder why you were not informed of our arrangement when you inherited? The paperwork to finalize the settlement was, at least on my end, oppressive. Did your uncle leave you no will, no ledgers? Did he not speak of it?"

"We were not familiar," Trevor said. "I am still sifting through his, er, ledgers. My first priority was to take stock and sell everything of value."

Miss Piety Grey crossed her arms over her chest. "Sixty?" she said.

"I beg your pardon?"

"I am offering you ten pounds more. To honor the agreement I made with your uncle."

"You're mad," he said. "Even if I could move out so that you could move in, which I have no intention of doing, you could enjoy an extended stay at one of London's finest hotels for that sum. Why not book a proper suite of rooms in St. James and wait out the repairs?"

"No," she said quickly—too quickly.

He studied her. "Why in God's name not?"

She drew breath to answer but then looked away. She was revising, taking care with what she said. Everything else had come out in a veritable gush, but now, she edited. It was, perhaps, her most revealing tell. Revealing what, he couldn't say, but he knew when someone was withholding. Or lying.

"If you please, Miss Grey?"

She glanced up and offered a grim smile. "A hotel would never do," she said quietly, almost shakily. "My circumstances require that I set up house immediately. I must move in," she said, ticking off the list of "musts" on her fingers, "hire a staff, buy furnishings, establish myself in the neighborhood."

When she looked at him again, she was emphatic. "I cannot appear transient," she said. "I am *not* transient."

Before he could respond, Joseph trooped into the room. The boy glanced quickly at Trevor but stared at the young woman. "They're empty," the boy said, his voice cracking. "The other rooms."

"Yes, Joe. She is alone," Trevor said, turning to look out the window. "And, you'll be relieved to learn she is neither ghost nor forgotten maid. She is…" He looked at her.

"Piety Grey," she provided again, reviving her smile.

"This is my serving boy, Joseph."

She nodded and turned her smile on defenseless, impressionable Joe. "But you must meet my maid," she said, darting to the passage.

"Tiny!" She shouted the word through the doorway. "Do come and meet our new neighbors!"

No, we must not meet your maid, Trevor thought, even as the sound of frustrated effort rustled from the other side of the tiny half door.

From the mouth of the passage crawled a petite, middle-aged woman with brown skin. She was dressed in the plain uniform of a servant, except for the bright-orange turban securing her hair. Her expression registered somewhere between diligent retainer and perturbed relation. Before she spoke, she looked at Trevor squarely in the eye.

"Missy Pie," she said, "all the house trunks are inside. They finished ten minutes ago and then invited themselves in, right through the front door. Wandering around like company. Swarmed the ground floor, looking for Lord-knows-what. If you don't get them outside, they'll break something or steal it. They're thick as ants on your jewelry trunk right now."

"Yes, of course," said Piety Grey, looping her arm around Tiny's and patting the top of her hand.

"Lord Falcondale," she said, "this is my companion and maid, Tiny Baker. As you can see, I was not exaggerating about her harmlessness."

To the maid, she said, "Tiny, the earl next door has died, and this is his nephew. The situation, I'm afraid, is not as we expected."

The woman narrowed her eyes at the earl, studying him shrewdly, looking back and forth between him and her charge.

Miss Grey went on, "If you'll excuse us, my lord, we hired hostlers in South Hampton, and they have agreed to help us with the unpacking. I'm afraid they are more accustomed to horses than people."

She nodded to her maid and released her, and the woman ducked through the passage.

Piety went on, "Of course, we have yet to unload our personal trunks because we planned to reside here." She looked around. "I traveled from New York with very few fixtures, but it appears what I brought might be useful here. Have you no furniture?"

"The house is empty by design," he told her impatiently. "The furniture has been sold—and hopefully the house will soon follow. It is empty except the bare necessities for the boy and me."

"Very well." She scanned the room like someone of a mind to provision. He cleared his throat and stepped in front of her view.

Miss Grey snapped her gaze to his face and went on, "My English solicitor has been notified of my arrival, but I do not expect to meet him for a day or so. No one could venture a guess as to precisely how many weeks it would take us to reach London from New York." She paused, rubbing two fingers back and forth over her brow. "In the meantime, please think over my offer of an additional ten pounds. I'd like to discuss it more."

Before his next denial, she added, "In future, of course, I will apply to your front door. Please do forgive my intrusion here. You have been most kind."

"Right." Trevor mumbled the word even while he thought, *No, no, no, and no.*

Before he could say the words out loud, she smiled again, gave a small wave, and ducked into the passage to trundle through.

CHAPTER THREE

Piety Grey waited a full hour before she approached the earl with a revised offer.

It was, for Piety, an exercise in extreme restraint.

It was also time well spent. She dashed off letters to her solicitors, to the staffing agency that would supply maids and footmen and grooms, and to the builder she would hire to restore the house. All the while she allowed her brain to reorder the impression of the man next door, who would, it seemed, crush her dream.

No, she thought, not crush it. The man who would *block-ade* her dream. It took considerable effort to suppress the surge of queasy anxiety that flooded her belly at the thought of falling weeks behind schedule, and she reverted to her original impression. He was a crusher of dreams.

Of course he was absolutely nothing like her lawyers in New York had led her to expect. He wasn't old, for one, not even a little. Not old, not infirm, and most annoyingly, not absent.

He was strong enough to pounce on her and restrain her. If he wished, he could pick her up and carry her around, which certainly he did not wish. He wished to be rid of her; he made that perfectly clear. Rarely, in fact, had she met a man so steadfastly disinterested to the point of rudeness, and again, how lucky. Preoccupied men didn't have time to make assumptions, correct or otherwise, about her unique circumstances, and better still, they didn't have time to "improve" said circumstances by insinuating themselves into her affairs.

So what if he seemed a little unyielding? Piety could manage men who wanted nothing to do with her. It was men who wanted too much who became a problem.

And *management* is exactly what he would require. Luckily, she had planned for this. Well, if not exactly for this, she had forced herself to anticipate any manner of setbacks or false starts. She would discover some solution and make him see rather than accept defeat. God forbid, she turn back now.

It was in the spirit of this—*not* turning back—that she and Tiny clipped down her steps after one, long hour; strode to his front door; and knocked. Stridently.

"Hello again!" Her beaming smile greeted him when he opened the door.

The earl blinked. It was clear that he had not yet become accustomed to the sight of her.

"I was not sure if you lived alone," she said tentatively, craning around him, "or if we would have the pleasure of meeting the countess?"

He narrowed his eyes. "There is no countess," he said, stepping onto the stoop and slamming the door behind him. "Which is to say..."

And so it began. Piety watched him descend. Deny and descend.

She retreated to the first landing, giving him plenty of room. She smiled, she nodded, she forced herself to listen. He made valid points, strong points. He was sarcastic and ironic and wry.

"So let me be very clear," he said, taking a step down to the landing, "in no way"—he stepped down again—"am I amenable to"—another step—"the so-called agreement that you had with my uncle, the previous earl."

Clearly, he tried to crowd her, to intimidate. *I'm a man. I'm tall, solid, broad-shouldered.*

The aggressive display was unnecessary; she knew this much from being tackled by him. Now, he loomed. While the tackle had demonstrated his strength and agility, the looming invited her scrutiny of the little things.

His tan, for example. He as far too tan for a gentleman. His face and neck were as brown as the sailors on the ship that had conveyed her to England.

And his hair. It was thick and brown with hints of auburn. Lighter on top from the sun. Too short to be stylish, but long enough to curl. Long enough to flop.

He was not, she thought, *unpleasant* to look at. If not traditionally handsome, then certainly he was compelling in a weary-warrior-left-out-in-the-sun-too-long sort of way.

Piety wondered if he was a warrior.

Or if he was weary.

She wondered how he came to be so very tan.

He could be a reclusive, asthmatic father of eight for all she knew, but it appeared that he lived alone. It appeared there wasn't even a staff. Only the boy, Joseph. If so, another stroke of good luck to counter all the bad.

"I have no plans to move out until the sale," he said, oblivious to her scrutiny. He stepped down again. "You cannot move in. Not for an extra ten pounds. Not for any amount. Unless you intend to buy my house, too."

Now he was one step above her, looking down.

She stared up, shading her eyes from the sun. "I've come with a new deal," she said softly. He was so close. There was no need to shout.

"The answer will remain no."

"But you haven't even heard my offer."

He sighed. "Make no mistake, Miss Grey. This house will be put up for sale next week. Prospective buyers will visit. House agents will tour. Creditors will appraise. None of this can happen, you understand, with *you* installed in a bedroom, or elsewhere—with you anywhere at all."

She rose to the same step. "Forget the bit about me letting a room or moving in at all. Of course you are correct, it would be wildly inappropriate for me to share this house with you, and I understand how disinclined you are to accommodate me. Instead," she stoked up her smile, "what I really want is use of the passage."

"What?"

Piety worked to replenish her patience. "My house is rustic and out of date," she explained, "but I *can* live there. I am not afraid of a little dust or damp." Behind her, Tiny cleared her throat dramatically, making the sounds of strangled shock, but Piety ignored her.

"It's not what I had planned," she went on, "but it will do. What will not do, however, is the stairs."

Trevor nodded. He swore. He turned away. She heard him mutter words to the wall: "I don't want to know. I do *not* want to know." He turned back. "*What* about the stairs?"

Piety shook her head with remorse. "Rotted through." She gestured heavily. "Apparently, there was a leak, and the damage nearly crumbled the entire stairwell from the first floor to the next."

"Why not use the servants' stairs?"

"Fire," she said simply. It was the truth. Unbelievable, but true. The situation required no embellishment.

"If there are no stairs," he asked slowly, incredulously, "how did you find yourself on the second floor and able to make your way through the so-called passage and into my house?"

"Oh, there is scaffolding," she said, waving a dismissive hand. "It will do for now, but it is tenuous at best." She looked calmly down the street. "And it would never support the weight of carpenters."

"Carpenters? What is your intention for carpenters?"

"What do you think? The will restore the house. They will access the upper floors by using *your* stairs, and *our* passage."

"You intend to trail through my house with carpenters?"

"I cannot allow renovations on the upper floors to be postponed until a new staircase is put up. Workmen, supplies, furnishings, they all must be conveyed up. Every room *must* see improvement right away. Not to mention, I, myself, will be settling in. Unpacking. Bringing in tapestry, carpets, art. I'll need access as well."

He drew breath to tell her an obvious, *No*, but she rushed on. "My new offer is this: Lease me access to the passage and permission to slip in a back door of your house, up your stairs, and through the passage when I need to reach my upper floors. *That* is what I want." She drew breath to finish. "It is a fraction of what I paid for, but essential to what I need."

He hesitated only a fraction of a second. "No."

Piety screamed internally but pressed on. "Did you hear the bit about the back door? We wouldn't be traipsing through the main hall."

"*Absolutely* no."

She tried again. "You will find that I am perfectly willing to work around the business of your daily life. I'll forestall access for the carpenters until any time you name. Myself as well. We'll all stay away. An hour or two each day to get to the top, that's all we'll really need."

"And what of my sale?" he said, leaning on the banister. "I'm advertising the house as vacant and available to buy. I ask you, Miss Grey, how will this arrangement appear? With your team of workmen trooping up and down the stairs? With you, dragging carpets through the kitchen door?"

"Unbelievable," he answered for her. "And strange. And gossip-inducing. Not to mention, it would emphasize the fact that the second floor conceals a giant hole in the masonry and a phantom closet."

"It's a passage."

"It's yet another problem that I must solve."

"Yes, I see your point. What if I forestall the workmen for a time, and I restrict the use of the passage to myself alone? In the evenings? So I may settle into the upstairs. So I may unpack."

"You coming and going is worse than the workmen."

Piety raised one eyebrow. "I'm sorry, my lord, that you find me so unpleasant."

"It is merely your proposal that I find offensive," he said, running his hand through his hair and looking at the sky.

"Not a proposal, a settlement. Paid in full. For a fraction of what I may actually receive."

"Paid in folly," he countered, "if the payment even exists."

"But my money is gone, just the same. As you will see." She took a shallow breath. Her composure was slipping; her smile was barely in place. "Your lordship, please. You are making this unpleasant when it does not have to be."

He narrowed his eyes, studying her. She felt his slow perusal of her face. For better or for worse, she let her smile slip and allowed some of her weariness to show. But would he see her resolve? Her determination or desperation?

She opened her mouth to say more, but he cut in, his voice low and even. "Have your solicitor be in touch." He backed toward the door. "Mine will review the documents. Some concession may be made. I cannot imagine what, because there is no circumstance wherein I will become involved in sharing a *hidden trap door* with you or with your workmen. If so much as an insect from your property scurries into my music room…"

She was about to simply tell him about her mother. And the money. About her need to insinuate herself into this house and this street. Instead, she was cut off by footsteps, padding up behind them. Piety bit her tongue and turned around.

It was a woman, thin and straight-backed, her steps careful and tentative. She admitted herself through the front gate as if stepping into a morgue.

The earl groaned. "Good God, what now?"

"Good morning, my lord," the woman said nervously, her voice soft with humility. "I apologize for disturbing you. My name is Miss Jocelyn Breedlowe, and my employer, the Marchioness Frinfrock, is your neighbor directly across the street." She gestured weakly to the towering mansion behind her.

The earl looked at the property and waited.

Piety did the opposite. She smiled broadly and descended the steps to extend a hand.

"So pleased to meet you, Miss Breedlowe. I am Piety Grey, and this is my maid, Tiny." The woman shook Piety's hand awkwardly and glanced to Falcondale, unsure.

Piety continued, "We are from America."

The other woman smiled cautiously, nodding.

"From New York City," Piety went on, "but we have relocated here. To Henrietta Place." She gestured broadly, indicating the street. "And I've bought the house next to the earl. Number twenty-two."

"How do you do?" the new woman managed. "Are you...will you...Has your family had the privilege of meeting the earl?"

Piety considered this a moment and defaulted to honesty. "I have moved to London alone, Miss Breedlowe. My father was lost to pneumonia in the autumn of last year. My mother has started a new life with a new husband. And this," she indicated the street again, "*this* is my new life."

Miss Breedlowe made a strangled sound.

The earl appeared beside Piety, suddenly animated. "Miss Grey," he told the startled Miss Breedlowe, "was just explaining that she and I may be required to work together. To work *closely* together. To see repairs made to a wall shared by our two properties."

The older woman blinked. She stared at Piety and back at the earl. She looked over her shoulder at the house of her employer. She coughed.

Piety shot the earl a disgusted look and weighed her choices. Well, she could hardly leave it at that. He was trying to scare them both away. He insinuated an impending scandal where there need not be. Not if they were mindful. Not if a handful of influential people could be made to see.

Miss Breedlowe clasped her hands before her, clearly trying to understand. She repeated the earl's last words. "Work together?"

"Would you believe that the stairs in my new home are sorely damaged?" Piety raised her eyebrows.

"I hope you do not mean unsafe?"

"Gravely unsafe, I'm afraid." Piety confirmed her words, following with a quick rendition of the stairs and scaffolding and the rot.

"You know, my intention was to become acquainted with all of the neighbors—it's why I've called upon the earl—and I should like to meet your marchioness as well. My situation is unconventional, to say the least, but it is not wrong-minded." Piety slid a glance at the earl. "It is not *bad*.

"Do you think," she continued, "that I might call on her ladyship and explain?"

"Well…" Miss Breedlowe seemed at a loss for words.

Piety forged on. "I haven't had the time to order cards, so may I impose on you to implore her? I can call whenever it suits her, including, well, including right now."

The other woman nodded and cleared her throat. "Might I suggest you wait for an invitation from her ladyship? Likely, she will wish to *summon* you."

"Lovely, but this is even better." Piety clapped her hands together. "I'll wait for her summons. Thank you, Miss Breedlowe."

The woman's face turned red, and she nodded but then looked at the earl. "I beg your pardon, Lord Falcondale?" she asked.

"Yes?" he answered, although his tone said, *please—no.*

"Forgive me," she continued, "but the purpose of my...that is, the reason I approached you and the young lady was to—" She cleared her throat. "Lady Frinfrock wishes to extend one or two neighborly suggestions regarding the care of your flower boxes." The woman cringed. "If you would be so obliged."

"My what?" He grabbed the back of his neck. "No. Wait. Do not answer that."

"I never wished to intrude on your business with the young lady," she said.

"I have absolutely no business with the young lady." He glared at Piety. "But you may tell the marchioness that the flowers should be the least of her worries. Oh, and the planters are only going to get worse."

With that, he turned and climbed the steps, entered the house, and slammed the heavy door behind him.

CHAPTER FOUR

The summons from Lady Frinfrock was not long in coming. A uniformed butler rapped upon Piety's door within an hour and escorted her and Tiny across the street.

Miss Breedlowe waited in the vestibule. "How good of you to come," she said, her smile thin. "Her ladyship will receive you in the library."

Piety nodded, trailing behind her lead.

This is the future of my house, she thought, taking in the gleaming marble floors and golden fixtures, both reflecting the glow of a dozen fresh candles.

Although perhaps a little less fussy, she amended, noting the lace doilies and elaborate porcelain figurines crowding every surface.

And less dark. Heavy, velvet draperies sagged in folds and rosettes from the windows.

And less coddled smelling.

Their procession took a sharp right turn at a marble statue of a koi, and Miss Breedlowe sped up, shooting Piety another inscrutable look.

"What is it?" whispered Piety.

She shook her head and shrugged. "I apologize in advance."

Piety wanted to laugh. "If you grew up sitting audience for my mother, Miss Breedlowe, you would not worry on our behalf. We are not afraid, are we, Tiny?"

"Did you see the statue of that big, fat fish?" Tiny asked, marveling at the scrolled molding around the ceiling.

Piety smiled. "You see, not scared at all."

They came to a stop at the end of the hall where the butler waited to announce them. "Her Ladyship, the Marchioness Frinfrock." He intoned the introduction with emphasis and swung open one side of a towering double door. "Your guests, my lady," he said to the room beyond the doors.

Piety, who had been forcing a smile all day, suddenly had the very real urge to giggle. It was all so formal and earnest. Beside her, Tiny ran a hand over the chair rail, checking for dust. Miss Breedlowe seemed frozen in place. Piety gently nudged her in the direction of the door.

The room was a library in the truest sense—an homage to books, to quiet study, to solitude. Spindly furniture crowded a grate; a drinks table hid in a dark corner; a massive desk weighed down the far wall. The desk reminded Piety of her father's, and she was halfway to it, anxious to run an appreciative hand over the smooth mahogany, before she realized that it was occupied.

"I beg your pardon," she said, snatching her hand back. She smiled at the short, stout woman behind the desk. "Hello."

Silently, the old woman stared back.

This was the marchioness? But she was so little. And old. And entirely out of sorts. Although, how regal she endeavored to look.

Piety cast a questioning glace back at Miss Breedlowe, who hovered near the door.

"Lady Frinfrock," Miss Breedlowe began, "may I present Miss Piety Grey, recently relocated from America."

Piety smiled. "How do you do, my lady?"

Silence reigned.

Piety searched her brain for what, if anything, Miss Kembleton-Wise may have instructed them in school about the proper address of an English aristocrat. All she could remember was that Europeans were known to take their supper very late in the night, and it was passing rude to discuss money or enterprise. Money, she knew, was not appropriate polite conversation in America or anywhere else for that matter; but how would Piety explain her current situation without it? Regardless, she vowed again not to lie. If the marchioness led conversation beyond the usual pleasantries—if she demanded answers to the questions why, and how, and when—Piety would tell her. Conceal nothing. Well, almost nothing.

Piety tried again. "It is an honor and a pleasure to meet you, my lady." She extended her hand to shake.

The old woman did not move. Piety checked over her shoulder, and Miss Breedlowe shook her head. Piety retracted her hand.

"What a lovely home you have, my lady," said Piety, determined now.

Slowly, with a voice far deeper than one would expect from a woman so small, the marchioness spoke. "What business do you have with Cecil Panhearst's former home?" A cane emerged from below the desk, and she jabbed the air in the direction of the street.

"I am the new owner," Piety said. "I have bought Mr. Panhearst's former house."

"Young ladies do not *buy* houses," she replied. "Where is your family? Your husband or your father?"

"I am not yet married, my lady, and my father is deceased."

The marchioness stared. "Very well. What of your mother? Also dead, I presume?"

Piety did not blink. "My mother enjoys very fine health. She has remarried. To a man in New York City, which is my former home." She looked deeply into the old woman's suspicious scowl, carefully choosing her next words.

"I received a large, er, settlement in my father's will," she said.

"No male heirs?" asked the marchioness. "None at all?"

"I was my father's only child."

"Yes, but you are a female. As you surely know, females do not inherit money, nor do they own property. If not a brother, then a nephew? An uncle? A cousin? There is no male relation to manage the spoils of this will?"

Piety quietly shook her head.

"No man at all to buy this house, at the very least, on your behalf and install you properly inside it, along with someone to look after you? Surely you do not contend that you, yourself, are the sole owner of this home? That you will live there alone?"

Piety let out a breath and stood straighter. "Yes, I do contend that, my lady." After a beat, she bolstered her nerve and added, "I should like to ask, do you own this house? Do *you* live here? Alone?"

The marchioness's head snapped up. "I do in fact, although I am the octogenarian widow of an esteemed marquis, not a young, unmarried American of whom no one has ever heard. Furthermore, the circumstances of my ownership are very rare, and my late husband, may God rest his soul, toiled scrupulously for years with the solicitors to make it so."

"Well, then you will understand." Piety rushed on, remembering to smile. "Because my father went to the same lengths before he died." She raised her chin. "It is for the very concerns that you now raise—no brothers or male heirs to see to my best interests—that I seek to safeguard his fortune by...by..."

"Spending it?" guessed the marchioness.

Piety sighed. It was the truth. "Yes. Some of it. It went to buy the house."

The marchioness was silent for a moment, studying her.

Piety forged on, "I had always dreamed of living in England, you see. My father's family can trace our ancestors to Cornwall. It is believed we still have cousins there."

"I have no interest in your Cornwall cousins, Miss Grey, unless they, too, intend to relocate to Henrietta Place. Continue."

Piety cleared her throat. "After my father's estate was settled and my mother remarried, I needed a change. So I approached my father's solicitor, a close family friend, with the idea to move abroad, and he happened to have an associate here in London who could arrange the purchase of a property that would suit my needs. There was paperwork, signatures, bank drafts posted across the sea."

The marchioness harrumphed. "Do I look like an office clerk, Miss Grey? I don't care about your business transactions. Either you own the house or you do not; that is not for me to determine. However, I do make judgments about the common decency and proper behavior of the people on this street. And considering what I have seen of you, the pressing question may be: What sort of person are you, Miss Grey? Will you introduce suspect morality into our quiet and orderly street?

"You have told me about your dead father and remarried mother, but what of a guardian or companion for yourself? From what I can collect, you intend to reside in a four-story townhome mansion completely alone. Unchaperoned. A single young woman. No husband. No guardian. No family whatsoever."

"Oh, I intend to employ a full staff. I will begin hiring domestics as early as tomorrow."

"Butlers and footmen do not qualify, Miss Grey. Who is to protect you from them? I will not abide a clandestine lack of convention in the street, my girl. No resident of Henrietta Place will abide it." She thumped her cane loudly on the floor.

There was a pause, and then the marchioness asked, "What is your business with the Earl of Falcondale?"

"I beg your pardon?"

"The earl. Next door. When I finally persuaded fearful Miss Breedlowe here to insinuate herself into your carryings on, you had already conveyed yourself to his front door and lured him into the street."

This, too, was not unexpected. The old woman had clearly been taking careful note of her arrival.

Piety proceeded slowly, choosing her words carefully. "I've only just met his lordship. We are neighbors to the side, obviously, and there are one or two construction issues pertaining to the adjoining wall of our homes. I will hire workmen to make repairs throughout the house immediately. It was on this matter that I called on him today."

"And I suppose it is your American sensibilities that regard this sort of contact with a bachelor as appropriate? Setting up house next door to a young, unmarried gentleman—and I use that title with generous speculation, you should know. You, with no chaperone to advise you against pounding on his door in the broad light of morning, carrying on, up and down the steps, without even a proper introduction.

"You are an American," she went on, "but even an American must know better than to comport herself in this manner—at least one dressed as finely as you, who claims to possess the resources to buy homes and ocean passages, with education in her speech and at least some notion of proper address."

Piety sucked in a breath to explain, but the marchioness cut her off. "It begs the question, young lady: the money, and the property, and the voyage all alone. There is a large portion of this narrative that is conspicuously absent." She raised one bushy eyebrow.

"Absent?" Piety repeated. If she failed to fill in the missing pieces, whatever they may be, the marchioness would surely make up her own.

"Out with it," continued the marchioness. "It is clear to me you are *running away*; I want to know *to whom* or *from what*. Why have you come?"

Piety blinked. Behind her, she could feel Tiny drift across the room to stand at her side.

"Think on it." Lady Frinfrock's tone held a clear warning. "Weigh your answer carefully, and do not conjure up falsehoods to me—not after I've indulged you this far. The direction we all take from here depends very much on what you have to say for yourself in the next moment."

Piety nodded, breathed deeply. *Oh, that.*

How foolish and short-sighted she had been to circumvent her real purpose. But the truth, she knew, could fall one of two ways: Either it would endear the marchioness to her situation, or...

Or what?

She would be shocked and drive them from her home? Fine. They would go. They would proceed directly across the street and do as they as they pleased. It was her house, bought and paid for, just as Piety had said. Certainly, London was different than America, but not so different that a demanding neighbor, marchioness or not, could force her from her own property simply because she had not taken a liking to her situation.

"I stand waiting, Miss Grey." The marchioness watched Piety expectantly.

"Yes," Piety nodded. She cleared her throat. "My mother and father were estranged for much of their marriage," she began. "They did not suit—fiercely, they did not suit—mostly due to my mother, whose personality may be most charitably described as volatile. Primarily, I was raised by my father, to whom I was very close."

"His name?" cut in the marchioness.

"I beg your pardon?"

"Miss Grey, so far I have learned only that your name is Piety Grey and that you hail from New York, but this is all that I know. Who are your family?"

"Of course. Hyatt. William Hyatt Grey." She watched as the marchioness took up a quill and began scribbling notes. "He owned a bank, er, several banks—nearly a dozen—throughout the states of New York, New Jersey, and Pennsylvania. He was a brilliant man and a loving father." She felt her throat begin to ache, her voice grow high and thick. She cleared her throat.

"When he died quite unexpectedly, from a horrible onset of pneumonia, last November, his will stipulated that the banks be sold and that a significant fortune go almost entirely to me. The terms of the will were not a surprise, and yet, my mother was enraged. The will provided for her in high style, but I...I received far more. The money set me free. She quickly remarried."

"How fortuitous for a woman whose own daughter describes her as volatile."

"Yes, well, I said that she was volatile; I did not say she was ugly. She is a striking woman who moves briskly through the social whirl of New York."

"I assume this new marriage has bearing on you and your arrival in London?"

"Quite. She married a man named Owen Limpett."

"Limpett." The marchioness repeated the name, writing it down.

"Yes, Owen Limpett, a widower, and the so-called stocking king of New York."

"I beg your pardon."

"Stockings, my lady. Socks. Hose. He owns a mill that manufactures stockings and such. Thousands of pairs, according to my mother. What my mother did not tell me, but what has become plainly obvious these last six months, is that the fortune with which he dazzled her during their brief courtship is either substantially smaller than expected or entirely inaccessible to her—and to his five sons."

"Five sons?"

"Yes. Mr. Limpett has five grown sons who remain at home, and, for whatever reason, they have aligned themselves with my mother, or she with them, because together they have become tireless in hounding me."

"Hounding you in what way, precisely?"

"Hounding me for my inheritance."

The marchioness squinted at her. "What claim could stepbrothers, or even a mother, assuming the will is as explicit as you claim, have over your inheritance?"

"Their wish is for me to marry one of them."

"Who wishes this?"

"All of them."

"Which one are you meant to marry?"

"Any of them."

"Well, that makes no sense at all."

Piety took a deep breath. "One of the brothers in particular— Eli, he's called—seems to be my mother's preferred choice, and he is the most aggressive in pursuing me, but it has been made clear that a match among any of them would do."

The marchioness paused for a moment and then rose to stand. "I see," she finally said. "You are fleeing an undesirable match."

"Please believe me," Piety said, rushing to the edge of the desk, "when I say that this so-called match is far, far more harrowing than 'undesirable.' " She blinked and felt her throat close again.

"Do not smudge the blotter, if you please, Miss Grey," the old woman said, reclaiming her own perch. "We shall revisit the topic of your ghastly mother and the avarice of your randy stepbrothers soon enough. At the moment, I wish to know: Who is this woman?" She pointed her cane at Tiny.

Tiny, bless her, had hovered protectively throughout the interrogation, quietly lending support but saying nothing. Without hesitation, Piety said, "Tiny, let me introduce you to our new neighbor."

Chin high and shoulders back, Tiny stepped to the front of the old woman's desk.

"Please meet Tiny," said Piety. "Tiny Baker. My personal maid."

"You mean your slave."

Piety immediately shook her head. "Absolutely not." She draped a secure arm around Tiny's thin shoulders. "Tiny is a free woman and has been since I was a girl. She is paid a salary for her work, and I provide her with a growing pension, just as my father did."

"Is this true, Miss Baker?" the marchioness demanded.

"I am no slave, misses," Tiny said. "Mr. Hyatt paid for my freedom years ago, and I've had a real salary—a decent, living wage—ever since."

Piety squeezed her.

"Fascinating," whispered Lady Frinfrock, wiggling out of her chair again and scuttling around the side of the desk. She marched up to Tiny and looked her up and down. "I would not have believed it if I had not heard it with my own ears, seen it with my own eyes. Absolutely fascinating."

Piety's smile turned hard. "No disrespect, my lady, but Tiny is like a member of the family—quite the only family I have left—and by no means is she a spectacle. I understand that Negro servants are not typical to England, but we had hoped to find a more generous attitude toward equality and respect here than in America, not less."

"Oh, and you shall find it, Miss Grey, of that you can be sure. I am not gawking at Miss Baker, I am marveling at her. Tell me, if you please, Miss Baker: What is your age?"

The two women exchanged glances, and Tiny shrugged. Piety would not speak for Tiny. If the maid wished to share personal details with the marchioness, she would do it. If not, then Piety would defend her privacy until the last.

Piety waited, smiling gently at her old friend. After a beat, Tiny stepped forward. "I do not rightly know how old I am, marchioness."

"We celebrate Tiny's birthday on the eleventh of June, Lady Frinfrock," Piety said, and she rushed to add, "but I hope you'll respect my protectiveness of Tiny and her privacy. I am happy to share the details of my unconventional journey to your street, my lady, but Tiny's experience is her own to tell or not tell. I believed this introduction was meant to—"

"This introduction," interrupted Lady Frinfrock, "was meant to gauge the amount of calamity you may ultimately bring to the peace-loving residents of Henrietta Place." She hobbled back behind the desk.

Piety watched her climb into her chair, hoping to God that openness had been the right play. The marchioness was shrewd and plain-spoken, but was she cold-hearted? Selfish to the bone? Piety had years of experience with petty domination, and she did not detect jealousy or control for controlling-sake.

Lady Frinfrock went on, "You cannot possibly conceive of calamity in a street, but I have passed a quiet, orderly life in Henrietta Place for some thirty happy years. The very last thing I wish to endure in the twilight of my life is a scandal-seeking, caution-to-the-wind *bohemian* setting up house next door."

Miss Breedlowe gasped, and Piety opened her mouth to say more, but the marchioness raised a quelling hand. "I do not wish to hear it, if you please! I am not a gossip monger; I have no taste for your lack of convention or your arduous journey. My sole regard is for how you will comport yourself in my street." She took a deep breath and snatched up the quill again, making notes as she spoke.

"To that end," she said, "this is what I intend. Miss Breedlowe? I am temporarily relieving you of your duties as my paid companion and relocating you to the position of chaperone to my neighbor, Miss Piety Grey."

"But, Lady Frinfrock." Miss Breedlowe stepped forward in protest.

"Do not trouble yourself, Miss Breedlowe. The salary will remain the same, as will the references when you, thankfully, depart. You shall simply provide companionship for someone new, and I shall enjoy some blessed peace—and don't pretend that this arrangement does not appeal to us both."

"But, your ladyship," asked Miss Breedlowe, "what of your health?"

"My health will remain unchanged with or without you—ill, fine, properly exercised or no. I can easily get along without you, as I did, happily, before my sodden lawyers insisted that you hound my ever step for an astronomical monthly fee. I believe we can both agree that I do not live or die by your hand. However punctual you may be, you are not a physician nor a worker of miracle healing."

"Perhaps," Miss Breedlowe said, sputtering, "but neither am I a chaperone. I have no idea how to adequately chaperone Miss Grey, nor do I believe she wishes to employ a chaperone."

"I don't care how adequate or inadequate you may be and, if you take the same stance, then I suppose Miss Grey can hardly object, can she? My concern is that she remains mostly out of sight. No more knocking on the earl's front door, for God's sake.

"What say you, Miss Grey?" The marchioness paused to assess Piety. "Would it be so awful to have a proper Englishwoman sharing your new home, helping you get settled into town, advising you on the customs, the geography, the climate? In time, you may search for your own companion, but what I propose is immediate protection and counsel. Beginning now. To tarry could jeopardize your entire future, make no mistake. Think of your future life as an outcast if you do not. Received nowhere and making the acquaintance of no one of quality or breeding? A pariah, very near."

Her eyes wide, her face flushed, Miss Breedlowe said, "But, my lady, you—"

"I would *adore* her companionship, my lady!" Piety cut in quickly. "How thoughtful you are. But really, I insist on paying Miss Breedlowe's salary myself."

"We shall see about that, won't we? I will believe the bank drafts conveyed from over the sea when I clap eyes on them. You don't object, do you, Miss Breedlowe?"

"I suppose, if it's really what you wish, my lady," Miss Breedlowe finally said.

"Excellent. It is precisely what I wish. Since the day you first arrived, in fact. When we adjourn, you may proceed upstairs and begin to pack. Shouldn't take long, considering you wear the same beige dress every day."

"As for *you*," she went on, turning her gaze to Tiny.

Good lord, what now? Piety grabbed Tiny's hand and held on.

"You," the marchioness repeated, "I should like to invite to remain here. In my house. With me. As my guest."

"*As what?*" Tiny and Piety said in unison.

The marchioness eyed Piety and then turned a softer expression to Tiny. "If Miss Baker is truly a free woman, then I would like to give her the opportunity to stay here, with me. In my comfortable home. With a suite of her own, and a servant to attend to her."

"You would?" Piety could not conceal her surprise. "Forgive me, your ladyship, but why?"

"To be interviewed, that's why. On behalf of my late husband, may God rest his sainted soul. He was a life scholar, devoted tirelessly to the plight of African slaves in the American colonies. For years, he studied the slaving ships, the auctions, the plantations, the inhumanity of the whole beastly business. It was his life's work, really, outside of the duties of his title and estate, of course. Alas, he never had the opportunity to meet an actual American Negro. Not once. How absolutely thrilled he would be that you, Miss Baker, are standing right here in his library.

"You will be without a lady's maid, of course," she said to Piety. "But surely this dear woman deserves a holiday after what she's endured in service to you, being dragged across an ocean and God knows what else. I employ an abundance of maids. You may take one of mine until you hire your own."

For several long, heavy moments, no one said a word; then Piety cleared her throat and asked to speak with Tiny alone. Hands clasped, the two shuffled outside the library and shut the door behind them.

"You should do this," Piety whispered immediately.

"What? Now I know you've gone crazy, Missy Pie! I won't leave you."

"The house is unfit, and you know it. You said so yourself. You called it a death trap, among a million other names."

"It *is* a death trap! But it won't get any safer with me staying over here, while you go back alone! What would your father say? I swear, this journey just gets more wrong-headed by the day."

"No, don't you see, Tiny? This," she said, peeking back through the door at the marchioness, "may be the only thing that has gone precisely right. We need this woman to like us. To support us. To *lie for us* if Idelle turns up."

Tiny looked away.

"She likes you," continued Piety. "She's a little batty, perhaps overbearing. But she seems respectful to you, and she has promised you far more comforts than I can provide for quite some time."

"What about your hair?" Tiny asked. "I won't have you taking up with another maid."

"If my hair needs tending, I will march across the street, and you shall tend it. There will never be anyone to look after me but you, and you know it. You also know I am wholly self-sufficient. You were never meant to serve as my maid when we reached England anyway. You were meant to be my chaperone." She shrugged. "I suppose I hadn't thought it through."

"And who is going to protect you from Sir High-and-Mighty, the sour gentleman who can't be bothered to help you, but who won't stop staring at you?"

"Who? The earl? You sound worse than the marchioness. The last thing I need is protection from him. He'd do better to show me a little more generosity and less restraint. Besides, Miss Breedlowe will be with me."

"It is mighty nice here," Tiny said, looking around. "Warm. Dry. But where will you sleep until that house gets fixed?"

"I will sleep in the new house. I don't mind the dust—truly! I've come too far and invested too much not to get in there and make it my own from the ground up."

"You'll send for me if you need me? Even if it's the middle of the night?"

Piety grabbed her up and hugged her. "Even in the middle of the night."

CHAPTER FIVE

You wanted this, thought Jocelyn Breedlowe the next morning as she stepped heavily onto the marchioness's front stoop.

You wanted newness. You wanted purpose.

You wanted if not precisely this, then something akin to this.

Her thoughts were punctuated by the *whack* of Lady Frinfrock's front door slamming behind her. She squared her shoulders, embarking upon a slow and steady march to the four-story townhome mansion across the street. In each hand, she clutched a carpet bag that contained every material possession she owned.

Not an hour before, Miss Baker, the American girl's African maid, had settled into the marchioness's house.

Marissa, the housemaid on loan from Lady Frinfrock had dashed to the American's house at first light.

Everyone who was meant to come or go had done so, except Jocelyn, who could put it off no longer. It was true, she had no great wish to remain in the employ of the marchioness, but still. Her heart beat triple-time, her legs felt wobbly, and she was perspiring. She was afraid.

Chaperoning a young woman? She hadn't the slightest idea how to serve as a proper chaperone. And this wasn't just any young miss. Miss Grey was, for all practical purposes, a grown woman.

Piety Grey did not require an internal review of what she did or did not want. She didn't lose her voice in front of callous Lady Frinfrock or imposing Lord Falcondale. Her purpose seemed as much a part of her existence as her own two feet, which, in turn, had played their part by striding into the marchioness's library to admit every manner of bizarre circumstance without flinching.

And now, Jocelyn thought, *her preference and purpose is me.* There could be no mistaking it. When Lady Frinfrock had presented the opportunity, Miss Grey had all but begged her, however silently, to accept.

Jocelyn would now live in the rubble of a once grand house and watch it be made grand again. She was to… Well, it was impossible to say, really, but considering all that had happened, she knew it would be…

Precisely what I've wanted.

"Ah, here she is!" said Miss Grey, swinging the front door wide and heaving the grimy contents of a mop bucket onto the stoop. "Look out. Mind the water."

"How do you do, Miss Grey?" Jocelyn managed to greet Piety, while dancing to keep her hem dry. "I do believe it is my appointed time to join your, well, to join you."

"How ready we are." Piety nodded and handed the bucket to Marissa, who was hovering behind her. "Has Tiny settled in with the marchioness? I thought it best to see her over first thing. She is not comfortable in this house, and truly, at her age, I can hardly ask her to endure these early days of recon-struction. What an unexpected gift it was that the marchio-ness has taken her in. If she had not, I dare say I would have had to find other lodging for the old dear." She eyed Jocelyn. "But you are not afraid, are you, Miss Breedlowe? You have the look of someone with pioneering spirit."

"I am at your service, miss," said Jocelyn quietly, wonder-ing what sort of woman provided for her maid's comfort, but not her own. She moved again to avoid the wet, and Miss Grey wiped her hands on a crisp, white apron before gestur-ing her inside.

The front hall of the American's house could best be described as the scene of a great disaster. Tattered wall cover-ings drooped to the floor in ribbons; cracked plaster pocked the walls and speckled the floor. The marble itself was dulled with grime and tracked with mud. A stale, mildewed odor hung in the air, and odds and ends of broken furniture leaned in doorways or at a hasty angles against the walls. The ceiling sagged yellow and gray.

Wishing to appear helpful—or "pioneering," as Miss Grey had suggested—Jocelyn asked, "Are you…Might I…? That is, shall I, er, mop?"

"Oh, mop, sweep, drag, pile rubbish in heaps," Piety said enthusiastically, shoving a table out of the nearest doorway. "So far, we have limited supplies to see the job done properly, but I could not wait another moment to, at the very least, cut a swathe through the worst of the mess. Marissa has been quite alarmed by my enthusiasm, I daresay."

No doubt, Jocelyn thought, nodding to the maid. Marissa, formerly the marchioness's youngest, laziest housemaid, had been plucked from Lady Frinfrock's staff as an afterthought. Miss Grey had refused a stand-in for her own maid, but then she saw Marissa and changed her mind. The marchioness was delighted to be rid of the girl.

"We've actually made real progress on the ground floor, Marissa and I," continued Miss Grey. "And now, on to the next! My goal is to clear a path through every room before the carpenters arrive and the real work begins."

Piety took a deep breath. "Now am I dreaming, or did anyone else see my ill-tempered neighbor, Lord Falcondale, bolt off down the street on a stallion not five minutes ago?"

Jocelyn, caught off guard by the prospect of ascending the conspicuously *absent* stairwell in the rotunda, missed Piety's meaning and said, "I believe I did see him, miss." If nothing else, she could be helpful with details such as this.

"Ah-ha! I knew I was not mistaken." Miss Grey let her mop handle fall and walked into the first small sitting room off the main hall. The drapes were drawn tightly, shrouding the room in cool, murky dark. Miss Grey circumvented furniture and trunks and grabbed a fistful of curtain and began to drag. Bright morning light spilled across the dusty floor. "What a box seat the marchioness's parlor window provides," she said. "Certainly, she got an eyeful when I knocked on the earl's front door."

"Would that I could save you the bother of having to deal with Lord Falcondale ever again," said Jocelyn. "He was not what I would describe as cordial." The room was sunny now, and Jocelyn tried not to stare at a mildew, gray water stain on an adjacent wall.

"Hmmm," mused Miss Grey, "likely he would say the same thing about me. For better or for worse, he will have to shoulder the bulk of our uncordial intrusiveness for some time. I understand his reticence—really, I do—but unless he is being pursued by a pack of lunatic relatives bent on destroying his life, then my situation supersedes his. He is too unwilling to compromise."

"Compromise, did you say?" asked Jocelyn. She felt the first unsettling lurch of confusion. "Miss Grey?"

"Please," Piety said, yanking the curtains wider still, "call me Piety."

"All right, if you insist, *Piety*, but about the earl?"

"Of course I insist!" The drapes hit a snag and Piety Grey frowned. She found the curtain pull and jerked the string in short, frustrated yanks. "What is your given name, Miss Breedlowe?"

You wanted this, thought Jocelyn. Never once had an employer referred to her by her given name.

"I...ah. 'Tis Jocelyn, miss. I'm called Jocelyn."

"How pretty! *Jocelyn*. Do you mind?"

"If it pleases you."

Behind them, Marissa coughed. "Should we leave the curtains, miss?" She wrinkled her nose at the heavy, unmoving folds. The cobweb-covered drapes danced and jerked under Miss Grey's ministrations but refused to budge. Dust puffed forth with every yank.

"Oh, I nearly have it," Miss Grey said, pulling the cord with all her might. To Jocelyn, she added, "And of course it pleases me. *Jocelyn*."

She jerked again, and the entire rig—rod and rings and copious, heavy folds of dust-embedded curtains—popped from the wall and crashed to the floor. Miss Grey yelped and dove, barely escaping the falling mass. Jocelyn scuttled backward and Marissa disappeared from the room.

"Well, that's one way to do it!" Piety laughed, flapping a thick layer of dust from her skirts. "At least now we can see what we're doing. Let's have a look."

She bustled to the far wall, and Jocelyn noticed for the first time the line of shiny black trunks stacked in the far corner.

"As I was saying," Miss Grey went on, "Falcondale has only just left. But! I didn't see his manservant, Joseph, accompany him. These are ideal conditions, although who can say how much time we have.

"Marissa?" she called loudly. "Ah, there you are. Begin with the trunks on the end. Do not let the curtains alarm you. They are on the floor now; the danger has passed. We must make haste. Luckily, I have labeled each case according to its contents. If the men who unloaded my carriage followed my directive, they should be stacked in alphabetical order."

"The men who unloaded your carriage probably could not read," said Jocelyn softly, intimidated by the younger woman's confidence and enthusiasm. She could barely keep up. What, she wondered, had she meant by "not much time?"

"For the moment," said Piety, "we should require little more than old cloth to clean, buckets, soap, whatever hand tools have been left behind, brooms, and the mop. Look in the trunks for any of these. Marissa has already sent water up by the pulley in the kitchen. But take care as you gather; let us bring nothing too heavy, because we only have our three sets of hands."

"Miss Grey, er, Piety." Jocelyn attempted to keep up. "Forgive me, but what was it that you said about the earl? And *to the top of what*, exactly? I must admit to some confusion."

Piety piled a bulging stack of cotton cloth in Jocelyn's arms, nearly obscuring her face. "Oh, but you *didn't hear?*" Piety Grey asked, picking up her own burden of supplies and leading the way.

Jocelyn followed, given little choice but to trail behind Marissa. Piety led them out of the room, down the hall, and through the kitchens to the garden. It was only when Piety nudged the kitchen door open with her knee and broached the terrace that Jocelyn finally stopped.

"Miss Grey?" she said to her rapidly progressing back. "Miss Grey?" And finally: "*Piety!*"

The younger woman stopped, exhaled heavily, turned around.

"Forgive me," said Jocelyn with a shaky breath, "but *where* are we going?"

Piety sighed. "Try, dear Jocelyn, to keep an open mind." She shot her a hopeful glance.

Jocelyn blinked. She felt suddenly as if her entire professional life—in fact her very survival—hinged on this alleged *open mind*. When she spoke, the words came out very slowly. "Forgive me, but about what am I meant to have an open mind?"

"Well, about the stairs, of course."

"*What* about the stairs?"

"Impassable."

"Oh." Jocelyn said this only because she felt compelled to say *something*.

"The seller promised us that the damage had been remedied by the presence of scaffolding. But when we arrived, we found the scaffolding to be tenuous at best. 'Tenuous' is a very generous description, in fact.

"To that end," she went on meaningfully, "I'm endeavoring to strike a deal with Lord Falcondale next door. There is a second-floor passage that connects our two houses, you see. If I could just come and go from the upper floors of my house by way of the *earl's* stairwell, then my problem would be solved. It will be essential for making repairs before the new stairs are in."

"You're *what?*" Jocelyn strained to see her behind the armful of cloth.

"Well, originally," Piety said, "Tiny and I were meant to *lease* the earl's empty house and live next door, but then..." She trailed off.

"But then?" Jocelyn prompted.

Piety turned to Marissa and asked her to fetch another broom from the house. When the girl drifted away, she took a deep breath and explained the lot: the *previous* earl, now dead, the cancelled lease and usurped accommodations.

"And you cannot simply wait on the upper floors?" Jocelyn asked, feeling her own bright, new beginning slip away. She gripped the stack of rags so tightly, her fingers burned. "You could wait until your own stairs have been repaired." The alternative was an impossible, *impassable* solution. Surely she could see that.

Piety shook her head. "No," she said. She set down her basket and bucket. "No, I cannot."

"But why not?"

Piety ambled a slow circle around her supplies, rubbing two fingers back and forth across her brow.

Finally, she said, "My mother? These vile men, her stepsons? They could turn up here, in Henrietta Place, any day.

They can and, mind you, they *will*. And when they come, sooner rather than later, I must look established. Settled. I must look entirely immovable. I need to be in and out of every level of this house immediately, but not just me, carpenters, painters, delivery men with furniture, too."

"Your mother will come here?" asked Jocelyn. "I hadn't realized..."

"I have no doubt that they will chase me here. When they discover my precise location and rally their combined conniving spirit, they will come. It could be...Really, I suppose, it could be anytime, depending on how soon they managed to sail from New York behind me. That's the entire reason for my haste. It must look as if—nay, it must *be* that—all the money is spent, sunk irrevocably into this house. The fortune must look no longer available, even to me, save as a property that I now occupy."

Jocelyn blinked, tabling for a moment the topic of a joint passage shared with a bachelor earl. "But what will your mother do if she arrives to discover the money has *not* been spent?"

"If the money is not tied up, one way or the other, my mother will seize it for sure."

"But how? If the money is yours? If the house is yours?"

"She would haul me back to America and force me to marry one of her horrid stepsons. There is no *man* in this equation, don't you see? My father left his clear intentions in the will, but ultimately, I have very few rights. If my mother looks hard enough, she will discover a way to requisition the money."

"And you feel sure," Jocelyn asked, "that your mother does not have your best interest at heart? To settle you in a marriage that keeps you close to her care, perhaps, despite your distaste for the prospective groom?"

"Of this I am very sure." Piety sighed, toeing the weeds of the garden with her boot. "My mother doesn't want me. All she wants is the money. American dollars. Ready currency for ready spending. She's struck a deal with the Limpetts. If one of them manages to marry me, she and the husband will divide my money. They'll want nothing tied up in property, of course, and certainly not a property gutted by carpenters." She looked up and smiled a sad, tired smile.

Piety shook her head, gathering up her pail and basket. "I gave her my own house, you know. My father willed our New York house entirely to me. It is a lovely home filled with beautiful things, as she well knows. It took her less than a week to install the stocking king and his reptilian spawn throughout—and then to make designs on me. That is when I decided to come here. To select a new home for myself, as far away—and as difficult to wrench away—as possible. I gave myself three months in which to get my affairs in order and then stole away in the middle of the night."

She jostled the provisions, seeking a better grip. "So there you have it." She glanced up. "Please believe me when I say that I cannot, *will not*, wait."

Jocelyn nodded. It was a terrible tale; impossible, very sad. A greedy mother; an undesired match—or matches—so much money and a young woman's freedom at stake. Still, the plan she described? It could not be.

Marissa ambled up with a second broom and tipped the handle in Jocelyn's direction. Jocelyn strained around her rags to receive it and leaned in toward Piety. "Assuming you can convince the earl, himself, about this, er, *passage*," she whispered, "what will his family say? His friends? The marchioness believes he has released the staff, but surely not everyone has been let go. The gossip of only one chambermaid could cause a scandal from which you might not recover."

"Oh, the earl lives here alone," Piety said, apparently not caring if the maid overheard. "That's been the one lucky piece. And so far, the only staff I've discerned is a lone serving boy, very loyal. If the old earl had to die—may God rest his soul—then he has been replaced by the best-possible relation for my situation. A reclusive bachelor with no family or friends. He may be a little inflexible, but aren't we all? Before we've been made to see?"

Piety resumed her march across the garden. "Shall we?"

Jocelyn watched her go, watched Marissa follow—clearly the maid was wholly on her side—and watched her own new, exciting future disappear, too. Words formed in her throat to call after them, but no sound would come.

"But if the earl is not here?" Jocelyn managed to ask when they reached Falcondale's kitchen door.

"Oh, he's gone; you said so yourself, and thank goodness for that. But we shall call upon his boy, Joseph. Marissa? Have you met Lord Falcondale's manservant, Joseph?"

Jocelyn looked at Marissa, realization dawning. Her service as a maid was slow and begrudging, but she was pretty and young, with powder-blonde hair and blue eyes that now swept down in a coy flutter. Thin, too; lithe rather than underfed. It was a delicate sort of beauty, likely to inspire thoughts of rescue and heroics in certain young men.

Piety knocked on the earl's kitchen door with one hand and shoved Marissa to the forefront with the other. They heard footsteps. The latch was thrown. A young man, no more than fifteen, stared at the collected women in the garden.

"Hello, Joseph!" said Piety.

"'Ullo, miss?" The boy sounded uncertain.

"I'm so sorry to disturb, but would you believe there are matters of utmost importance to which I desperately need to attend upstairs? In my house? I was wondering if you could be so kind as to grant us entry. It's just the three of us, and we hoped to slip through the shared passage."

He studied them with wide, worried eyes and then looked over his shoulder and back again. He stammered, "Lord Falcondale said that—"

"Have you met my new maid, Marissa?" Piety asked, nudging the girl forward.

With an alacrity Jocelyn had never seen Marissa apply to housework, the girl instantly affected the look of near collapse, struggling under the weight of the basket of food and pail of soap that she had carried effortlessly across two gardens just moments before.

Joseph lunged to relieve her of the basket.

"Thank you," Marissa said, her voice husky.

Hesitating only a moment more, the boy unburdened Marissa of the pail and moved out of the way, allowing the three of them to pass.

Heart pounding, hands tightly gripping her stack of cloth, Jocelyn followed Piety, who followed the girl. Her shoulders trembled and her feet felt light, but, God help her, Jocelyn was unable to turn back.

Piety walked straight to a staircase, chattering to Joseph. At her side, Marissa drifted along with an expression of endurance and longing.

If nothing else, at least the earl's house seemed vacant, Jocelyn thought. But she cringed at the passing of each open door, half expecting a butler or housekeeper or a countess to pop out.

The top of the stair was just as deserted as the bottom, and the boy led the way down the landing, around a corner, and into an empty room with a small door at the far end.

The "passage." It was an elfin channel that extended no more than five feet through unfinished masonry and exposed brick into the dusty interior of a bedroom beyond. Judging by the size and Piety's comments about her plans for the room, this was the master bedchamber. It was to be *Piety's* bedroom.

His house connects to her bedroom?

Jocelyn winced, finding it suddenly difficult to breathe.

Piety appeared unfazed and ducked through. Marissa relieved Joseph of her provisions with a bashful smile and followed. Jocelyn had no choice but to stoop and cross, wobbling in the cramped, uneven space with her arms full of fabric and the extra broom. When they reached the other side, Joseph could be seen standing, bewildered and empty-handed, in the previous room.

"Thank you so much, Joseph," Piety called back at the boy. "We shouldn't bother you again until late in the day. When the house is, shall we say, *quiet*, we will have you slip us out again, all right? If I require anything at all, I shall send Marissa."

Jocelyn heard him croak something just as Piety whipped the door shut tight.

"Well," Piety said, dusting off. "That was an unpleasant bit of dishonesty, but I dare say it was worth it. Now, let us do our best to pull the shutters off of these windows and open them up to the world. Let us get a look at this place!"

CHAPTER SIX

T revor needed a woman.

Not a beautiful woman. Or a docile woman. Or even a young woman—although, he was willing to pay more for healthy, limber, and happy in her work.

Cleverness? Also not a concern. Indeed, it was better that she not be particularly bright. His new neighbor was clever. Quick. Diverting. And look where that got him: riding off to spend money that he did not have for the affections of a woman he did not know. It was a sordid business in which he rarely engaged and was loath to participate even now. And why? Well, the only reason he could fathom was that it had been far too long since he'd known the body-calming and brain-settling clarity of release. He needed a woman.

He'd been in England for what? Three weeks. He knew few people in London—none of them women—and he wished to know even fewer. In Greece, there had been women. Women of a certain age, a certain attitude, a certain situation.

But even with the Grecian women, it had been a while. Things had been complicated—his mother's death, the earldom, and the inheritance. By the time he'd reconciled himself to losing a mother and gaining a title, he'd sailed for England.

Where he knew no women.

Until Miss Piety Grey had popped through his wall. Smelling good, looking even better, and provoking him.

And the last thing Trevor needed was to be provoked.

After passing a disturbingly sleepless night thrashing around in his bed, he reasoned that he could either spend the rest of the day agonizing about the loveliness of Miss Grey, the proximity of Miss Grey, or the unconventional familiarity and boundary-averse nature of Miss Grey.

Or he could locate an available courtesan and rut himself into clear-headed, focused, satisfaction.

"Trevor, thank God," called a panting voice behind him, breaking his revelry, "I've been searching for you for an hour."

"Go away, Joseph," Trevor said, clipping up the steps of Madame Joie's discreet bordello on the edge of St. James.

"Can't. I've done something awful."

Trevor stopped short of knocking on Madame Joie's door and turned to the boy, trying to decipher the guilt that hung heavily on his face. "What awful thing?"

Joseph fidgeted, saying nothing.

Trevor tried again. "Is the house on fire?"

"No."

"Did you use my name or credit to purchase something of which, or hire someone of whom, I will not approve? And by this I mean did you purchase anything or hire anyone at all?"

"No, Trev, it's nothing like that."

"My God, Joseph." He groaned as he descended the steps, but he motioned the boy into the alley. "You look like you've swallowed a goat. What is it?"

"It's Miss Grey."

Trevor's eyes narrowed. "What about Miss Grey?"

"She's back."

"Back *where*?"

"She…She came to the garden door," he began.

"Tell me that you did not admit her."

"She was so strong."

"She is a young woman, Joseph. A female. And you are nearly as large as I am."

"Not strong in body, strong in words," insisted the boy.

"Of course." Trevor sighed deeply. "What did she do with her *strong* words? Talk you into doing this awful thing, whatever it may be?"

"She had a girl with her."

"Her African maid," Trevor guessed.

"No, she had the woman from across the street. And another girl. Blonde-haired. Blue eyes. They had so many things to carry."

Trevor pivoted, took half a step, and spun back. "So, she waited until I left the house unprotected and then appealed to you?" It took effort to keep his voice low. "Armed with the neighbor's nursemaid and an overburdened blonde girl?" He shook his head. "Oh, Joseph, you *did not*!"

Out in the street, two passing gentlemen peered into the alley. Trevor grabbed the boy by the elbow and tugged him out of earshot.

"She said she deserved to be let in," Joseph explained. "She went on and on. She is like a lightning storm, my lord. Honest to God, I could not stop her."

"But of course you could stop her." Trevor hissed out a long breath. "She is not a storm—although I appreciate your poetry— she's a girl, as I've already said, and she barely weighs nine stone." He released the boy and dropped his head back, speaking to the sky. "I cannot believe you admitted her, Joseph, I cannot."

"I knew you would be cross, but I came anyway."

"How brave you are. No fear of me but powerless in the face of Miss Piety Grey." He hovered for a second, weighing his options. And then, without another word to the boy, he made for the horses.

The ride home took ten minutes—ample time to determine what he would say. *Get out*, sprang repeatedly to mind, but no, that would never be sufficient.

"She only wished to stay the afternoon," Joseph said when they cleared Cavendish Square and cantered into Henrietta Place. "She said she would not make the slightest bother. She only wishes to be released in the evening, when the house is quiet."

"What the devil does that mean?" Trevor left his horse bridled in the mews and stormed inside.

"When you're away?" ventured Joseph.

"Precisely. *When I am away*. I don't care how quiet the house is when she comes and goes, Joseph; she's asked you to deceive me!" He charged up the stairs.

"I'm sorry, Trev." The boy managed to choke the words out, ducking his head. He had the foresight to look completely defeated, and Trevor groaned. Of course it was not the boy's fault. The woman was impossible. Aggressive. Unrelenting. And far too beautiful for her own good.

When they reached the music room, the doorknob to the illustrious shared door was rattling.

Trevor glowered at Joseph.

They heard a shuffling. Footsteps. The feminine sound of someone clearing her throat.

Then it came: three firm knocks.

Trevor nodded, pointing at the boy. "Of course. I've come here to evict her, yet she demands an audience with me?"

"Lord Falcondale?" Piety's muffled voice came from beyond the door. "I can hear you shouting, so I know you are there. If you please, would you mind opening the door?"

Trevor stared at the knob. "I want you out, Miss Grey!" He frowned at the door.

"I cannot get out if you do not open the door."

"You would not be *in* if you had not bullied your way past my man the very moment I left the house unguarded."

"There was no bullying," she corrected. "If you will only let me pass, I can explain."

Trevor swore under his breath and scowled at Joseph. He strode to the door.

"Lord Falcondale?" she called, relentlessly cheerful.

"A lightning storm, my lord," whispered Joseph behind him.

Trevor growled, whipping off his hat and coat and chucking them in his direction. "Get out, Joseph."

"Should I bring refreshment?" the boy offered.

"*Get out!*" Trevor repeated the order, and then sighing heavily, he reached out and flipped the lock. The door swung.

"Ah!" she said, popping through from the other side. "There we are. That's better."

Her hair, Trevor was irritated to see, was down. No pins. No band. No hat. Silky light-brown waves framed her face. Some fell heavily forward over her neck and shoulders, more fell down her back. A particularly unruly lock dangled in her face. Her cheek was smeared with dirt, and she looked moist. With sweat.

She was perspiring.

She had rolled up the sleeves on her veil-weight blouse, and several buttons were loose, revealing damp, creamy skin from her chin to…to much lower.

Dear God. She was not wearing shoes.

Trevor narrowed his eyes, trying not to linger over any of it—the wild hair or bare feet or any of the sweaty bits in between. He failed miserably and looked again, endeavoring to be quick about it—sweeping his gaze up and down the length of her body. Only when he'd seen it all three times, did he manage the restraint to focus on her face.

No surprise, she was smiling back at him sweetly. Smiling like an attendant at a wedding—a happy cousin, perhaps, enlisted to distribute refreshment. Smiling as if she'd just won top prize at the parish vegetable match.

Not at all, he thought, as if she were defying all social convention, repeatedly breaking into his home, and driving him mad with lust.

"I couldn't help but overhear—"

"What are you doing here?" His voice was flat.

"I'm sorry," she began, "but by *here* do you mean in the second floor of my house?" She gestured to the room. "Or here paying you a call?"

"You are not paying me a call, Miss Grey. You are breaking into my home like a criminal. And I mean *both*."

"Hardly breaking in. I knocked, and you admitted me."

"I was referring to your *breaking in* while I was out."

"Because the reason I've knocked and have been admitted *here*," she continued, ignoring him, "in your empty room, is to intervene. On behalf of Joseph. Please, my lord." She looked at him sweetly. "This is not his fault."

"At least we agree on that." His words were clipped. "Dare we risk some accord on whose fault, exactly, it might be?"

"Of course we dare," she said. "The fault lies with no one. Because no offense has been committed."

He pivoted away, shaking his head, and fell into an agitated line of pacing. Every moment or so, he stole a look at her. She smiled. It was then that it hit him—a moment of clarity—although he had no idea how he managed it. His current frame of mind was an agitated clash of anger and lust.

Why not, he thought, simply *concede*? Remove himself from the whole bloody cock-up and allow her to do as she pleased? Would it really be so bad? Could it ever be as bad as this?

He stopped pacing and spun, turning to face her. "Where are your shoes, Miss Grey?" he asked. He began a slow and steady march in her direction.

"My shoes are not relevant," she said, straightening her back. Her smile dissolved, just a touch. She appeared uncertain. "I...I paid to live in your house, my lord, but have—"

"Stop talking," he interrupted. "I have good news for you, Miss Grey, very good news indeed. You will absolutely want to hear it." He continued to advance. She stumbled back.

"You have *convinced* me," he said. "The passage is yours. The stairs. The kitchen door. Please, summon Joseph whenever you require entrance or aid, just as you did today. I will instruct him to attend you."

He took another step. She was forced to back up or be bumped by his chest. She reached behind her, feeling for the wall.

"Mine?" The word was followed by a raspy breath.

It was the shortest sentence she'd ever uttered in his presence. In the absence of words, he advanced until he found himself looming over her. He was so close, he could see the individual strands of gold that made up the curl that hung in her face. So close, he could see that curl flutter, ever so slightly, each time she breathed in and out. His hands twitched to reach out, to tug gently, to see how long it would extend, and then watch it bounce back.

He heard himself say, "It is not the lease arrangement you made with my uncle, but it is clearly something you are willing to lie, cheat, and steal to claim. I haven't the time or energy to fight you on it, so I concede. Take it. Use it. Leave me alone. I think, perhaps, it's the fastest way to allow both of us to get what we need."

She cleared her throat and looked up at him. "How unexpectedly magnanimous you have become." Her voice was lower. She spoke, rather than proclaimed. "How glad I am. And now I will match your generosity and respond in kind." She shook her head, tossing the errant curl back.

He raised one eyebrow.

"I will only require the use of this passage for the span of one week. After that, my own stairs will be complete."

"What?"

"Yes, that's right. I've just learned, my central stairwell will be ready in far less time than I imagined."

There was six inches between them, and he closed it. She hit the wall behind her with a bump.

"What idiot promised you completed stairs in a week?" He propped a hand over her head.

"My lead carpenter," she assured him, staring at his cravat. "I wrote him as soon as we made town. He was kind enough to dispatch a return note this morning. He assured me that new, passable stairs will be installed first thing—in a week, he said, more or less." She began to inch to the side.

He widened his stance, blocking her with his boot. "One week? Is that so? And what kind of stairs are these? Assembled in one week?"

"Oh, they're quite grand really. They will rise up from the center of the rotunda with a gentle curve that ends at a landing. The landing goes right and left and hangs above the room. Like the current stairwell, the balcony is rotted, too, but I've been assured all of it can be fixed, good as new."

"Do the stairs, I wonder, rise up from the floor—a solid ramp with walls beneath the steps, supporting them—or does the stairwell appear to float upward, extending from the wall into open space? Supported by beams?"

Piety nodded enthusiastically. "They do appear to float! The rotted stairs are quite dilapidated, but I can tell that, at one time, they were stunning. I wish for exactly the same effect when we restore them. My carpenter, as I've said, has assured me he can deliver."

"Deliver?" repeated Trevor. "Yes. Within a week or even two? Not likely—not at all, in fact."

Her eyes widened. She scrunched her small, perfect nose. "Oh, and you profess to know?" She arched a brow in challenge.

Her upturned face, the wrinkled nose, the sharp dare in her eyes—it was nearly too much. He growled and shoved off the wall, spinning away. Before he could stop himself, he said, "I do, in fact, profess as much."

She laughed. "Call me a provincial American, my lord, but it would never occur to me that a nobleman might know the first thing about building a stairwell."

"You're not provincial, Miss Grey, merely ignorant about my life."

She opened her mouth to speak, but he cut her off. "The earldom may be suffering a handful of financial missteps at the moment, and perhaps the title was never meant to come to me, but the truth is that my grandfather was earl, and I was educated to Oxford." He turned to face her. "Where I studied architecture."

She blinked at him and then nodded. "I did not mean to imply that you were not a scholar, my lord. Only that you were not a carpenter. Believe me, if I'd known you were capable, I would have offered you *sixty* pounds to repair my stairs yourself, rather than bothering either of us with the passage."

"I don't want to build your bloody stairs, Miss Piety Grey," he said firmly. "I don't want anything to do with you or your doomed home restoration at all." He strode back across the room, herding her into the wall, and planted his hands on either side of her shoulders. He nearly did it then—nearly descended on her mouth and kissed her until neither of them could breathe. Her face was inches from his. He only needed dip down to taste her.

"Why can they not build the stairs in a week or two?" she whispered.

He snatched his gaze from her mouth and stared at the wall beneath his hands. "They cannot build the stairs," he said authoritatively, "as anyone with even a cursory understanding of construction would know, because a grand staircase like you described—curved, floating, as you said, above the room—requires *cantilevering*. Each step must extend deep, deep into the wall beside it, so that it may support the weight of use, so that it won't collapse when you walk on it."

"But there are pillars," she said.

He drew breath to sigh, long and frustrated. "The pillars are not nearly enough. They are more ornamental than functional. Only when the steps are anchored in the wall, will the structure be safe. And the wall itself, mind you, must be secure and strong and entirely free of weakness or decay. To do the job properly, plaster must be removed, and the structural integrity of the wall must be assured. Then the wall must be rebuilt around the long treads. It's complicated, and that doesn't even begin to address the curved banisters, which must be steamed and bent in a workshop by a specially trained craftsman across town and transported to the job by carriage.

"Time," he continued. "Miss Grey, all of this takes time. Much more than two weeks. Perhaps they can stack together some basic tread-and-stringer construction for current use, but not your grand staircase. Do you see?"

He looked down at her, satisfied that, at last, he'd articulated something that might resonate with her.

"But I need it built now," she said relentlessly. "Right away. Every room, upstairs and down, must be a flurry of activity. I cannot be seen sleeping in the kitchens. I need bedrooms, washrooms, long walls lined with wardrobes for my dresses. I need progress. I need to *live* in this house." She leaned back against the wall and slid downward.

To sit.

On his floor.

He blinked, watching her descend. Past his chest. Past his bloody groin. Between his knees. She sat down on his floor, her bare feet and ankles sticking out from beneath her skirt like sweets from a pouch.

Fantastic, he thought, turning to the windows. As if wild-haired, unbuttoned, shoeless, stocking-less, and damp with sweat were not enough.

"Stand up," he said harshly, "if you please."

"I beg your pardon?"

"I am asking you to *stand up*."

"Yes, of course," she began, collecting her skirts. "How callous of me to sit on the floor, but you have no furniture, and—"

Growling, he reached down, yanked her up, and snatched her to his chest.

Without another word, he lowered his mouth to hers.

It was a hard kiss, full-on and open-mouthed. It had everything to do with proving a firm point and frightening her, and *nothing* to do with tenderness.

In the beginning.

He hadn't expected her to melt into him. He hadn't expected her to grab the sides of his vest in fistfuls. To hold on. To fall closer.

He hadn't expected her to kiss him back.

Almost immediately, he slowed—not to wind it down, but to prolong it. Kissing her was like taking a hasty bite of something he hadn't expected to find quite so delicious. Something warm and sweet and too sumptuous to be gobbled up in passing, without giving it its due. Without *savoring*.

Before he realized the motion, he'd locked his arm around her waist, sealing her against him. With his other hand, he touched her hair—finally, her hair. He lightly brushed the tips of the curls and then he buried his hand in the shiny, disheveled mass of it, reveling in the softness.

They remained locked in an embrace far longer than he knew. Long enough for his hands to leave her waist and hair and roam her shoulders, exploring the hollows of her neck, and then downward over her arms, her back, her small, curved waist.

Long enough to know he wanted much, much more.

But then she was moving, tugging backward, pulling away.

He was loath to let her go—loath to even use his brain to think—but he reared back and stepped away. Two steps. Another.

The retreat made him angry; angry like a thirsty man robbed of water after one sip. Everything about the embrace suddenly seemed wildly insufficient.

He wanted to snatch her back, to toss her over his shoulder.

He wanted her to want him in the same way.

"That," he said, breathing heavily, "is the result of your behavior today. In case you were not aware."

She stilled, and he advanced on her. "You cannot scuttle around, half dressed, your hair unkempt, entering my home alone, inciting me, *tempting* me. Do I make myself clear, Miss Grey? Because, God help me, I cannot promise that this is the last of it.

"If this be the result of your second-only jaunt through my music room," he continued, "what will happen next? I've given you free rein, but I still live here; I'll still eat in the kitchens and sleep down the hall. With this liberty comes responsibility," he said, feeling like a self-righteous prig yet unable to stop. "It...it...it starts with wearing shoes and goes up from there."

CHAPTER SEVEN

Well how do you like that?

Piety dropped her hand from her mouth. She blinked several times, willing the room to swing back into focus. She stumbled forward two steps. Her back was to him, thank God. He could not see…

See what?

She was endeavoring to control her breathing and steady her nerves, but it was not as if she was about to dissolve into tears. She felt no compulsion to slap him or to shake her fists in the air to rail at him, *Lord Falcondale, how dare you!*

The truth was, she knew exactly why he had kissed her. She'd goaded him, tempted him. *She* all but dared him.

Why have I even come? She wondered, glancing around. *Again?*

It had been his first question—an entirely legitimate one—and her excuse had been meaningless blather. She was here because she was curious. About him. Curious about his volatility. About his bitterness. About his refusal to cooperate. And yet, there was something more. Something in his eyes, perhaps. Desire? Yes, yes. She'd spotted that right away. Piety could fill a thimble with what she knew about men, but she could identify a hungry gaze when she saw one.

No, it wasn't that. Well, it wasn't *only* that. There was also deeper yearning, a sort of last-ditch hope. He was suspicious to her, but was it an optimistic sort of suspicion? Did such a thing exist?

She couldn't put her finger on it, really; there were so many unanswered questions. Perhaps *that's* why she was here. Curiosity. If only it were strong enough a term.

The more he spoke—telling her she could use the passage, explaining the bit about the stairs, warning her about propriety, scowling at her with more longing than menace—the more intriguing he became.

And he *argued* with her. As if she were a worthy and threatening adversary, he fought back. Naturally, she was tempted to argue more. He spoke to her as if she held as many cards as he did. As if she mattered.

She was, after all, a human female, with girlish weaknesses, just like any other twenty-five-year-old, unattached young woman. Unattached by choice, she reminded herself, because, unlike most—*ahem*—spinsters, she actually believed in distinguishing between one fabulously wealthy man and the next. How ironic, then, that the one man she distinguished to be intriguing happened to be not particularly wealthy nor possess any of the qualities she'd always sworn mattered. No generosity of spirit. No lively conversation. He wasn't even pleasant.

Well done, Piety, she chided herself. *You've managed to find yourself intrigued by the one man who can actually make your life more difficult than it already is.*

And, finally, most ridiculous of all, the man was stirring. The towering height, the broad shoulders. He wore only a vest and a crisp white shirt—not even a new shirt, *not even a nice shirt*—perfectly fitted, unadorned, unassuming, yet entirely appropriate for a gentleman. Not flashy. Not vain. Just…right.

And he never smiled. Even when she beamed at him. He simply looked back at her. Looked at her as if he dare look away, he might miss something important.

Sometimes, he even looked tempted to smile.

Tempted. By her.

She took a deep breath. Could there be a worse time to succumb to girlish whimsy? To notice crisp white shirts and the alleged desire to smile? Her timing had always been wretched, but honestly, of all the moments to finally experience a proper kiss. A real kiss. She gritted her teeth, remembering her first kiss that was not really a kiss at all, when her stepbrother Eli had first cornered her, restrained her with icicle fingers, and suffocated her with his slug of a tongue and shiny, wet lips.

But this…*this*…

Piety suddenly felt compelled to say, "I hope you are aware that I am not afraid of you."

"Well, then, that makes one of us." He crossed to the window and stared out into the street.

"In fact," she said, watching him, "I should like to learn the story of your life."

"Ha!" He laughed bitterly. "If you aren't afraid now, you will be."

"Oh, but I think you *want* to tell me about yourself."

He scanned her body again, up and then down. "There is something that I want with regard to you, Miss Grey, but it is not to tell you the history of my life."

"Then why did you tell me about your education? At Oxford? And your knowledge of what it would take to refurbish my stairs? You must have known I would pounce on that sort of information, considering my need for that very skill."

"I know no such thing. Every word out of your mouth is more outrageous than the next, and I am in complete and utter shock every time you open it." He stared at her. "I only told you about my years at Oxford because you've been trying to bribe me with money—money that I can only guess you assume that I need. I may be selling this house and leaving England, but it would be a mistake to regard me as destitute." He cleared his throat and returned his gaze to the street.

Piety's stomach flipped, surprising her. It mattered to him. What she thought.

"I could hardly think of an earl as destitute, my lord," she said. "On the contrary, I assumed the specifics of carpentry would be beneath you. I was mistaken, and it made me curious. Why do you know so much about cantilevers and curved banisters and removing all the plaster, as you said?"

He said nothing at first, and she turned to study him.

"Sod it," he said. "The bit about the stairs is common knowledge." He backed away from the window, roaming the room.

"But it is not common practice," she said, watching him, "for an heir to an earldom to build his own stairs. To build his own anything."

"Oh, mine sounds like practiced knowledge, does it?" He glanced at her. "I haven't built stairs so much as restored them, shored them up. Similar to what your workmen will do first. Most of the boarding houses in Athens were—*are*—in horrible disrepair."

"Athens?"

He shook his head.

Oh, you have no idea, she thought and waited patiently for him to elaborate.

He paced a moment more and then stopped and planted his hands on his hips. He tugged on his collar. He ran his fingers through his floppy hair. He appeared rumpled.

Dear Lord. She wanted to touch him.

Thankfully, before she could reach for him, he spoke.

"My late mother," he said, "became ill some fifteen years ago. She had always suffered from wheezing—a difficulty breathing—her entire life. She was frail and weak. I have come to realize that this is why my father fancied her. Her fragility made him feel strong. Unfortunately, it did not make him feel motivated to seek out proper care.

"I moved to Athens for her. Hauled her there, sick bed and all, and set up house. The warm sea air was meant to be good for her. I was scarcely out of Oxford then. France was at war, Italy was expensive, and I had studied modern Greek in school. Certainly the ancient ruins above Athens appealed to me. It seemed like a good idea at the time."

He'd wound his way back to the window and propped his hip onto the sill.

"Did the climate in Greece help your mother's condition?"

"It's difficult to say. She grew worse in other ways." He squinted at her. "I've said too much already. I can't believe we're talking like this. I can't believe that you're *still here.*"

Piety chuckled. "I'm on my way out, I promise. But you cannot stop now. I've never met anyone who's lived in Greece before. Before I go, won't you finish?"

"There's nothing more to tell."

"What work did you do in Greece? Or did your family support you."

Now it was his turn to laugh. "There was no support from my family. This, I assure you."

"So you worked as an architect?" she guessed.

"No, I worked as a lackey."

"But what is that?"

"Our neighbor had a son who was employed by the wealthy landlord of every house on the street—a man who owned half of Athens. This neighbor saw me making repairs to our house and introduced me to the next in command in the landlord's hierarchy of thugs. They valued my work, and I was hired to recommend repairs for the landlord's vast array of properties."

"You built stairways!" Piety was mesmerized. He might as well have told her that he mined for diamonds.

He rolled his eyes. "Yes, I built stairs. And doorways. And privies, and put support beams in cellars."

"But that's not a 'lackey,' that's a builder."

"Yes, well, I did a little bit of everything, working quickly and cheaply. I taught the landlord's other laborers modern technique. Within a year, I found myself rising in this wealthy Athenian's property empire. Soon the man himself wanted to meet me."

"And he loved you on sight?" she guessed again.

"And he loved the *idea* of me," he corrected. "He had come from nothing and was obsessed with rank and aristocratic lineage. He had enough money to buy whatever he wanted and a ruthless reputation to match; however, he could not buy social standing or respect. When he learned of my Oxford education and saw my manners, which I'm sure you have noticed are deplorable by English standards, he was dazzled."

"You dazzled him?"

"I was as shocked as you are, believe me. I cannot remember the last person I managed to impress, nor wanted to impress, but I suppose it didn't take much with this man, because he instantly promoted me from carpenter to consigliore."

"This must mean *lackey*."

"Yes. That is what it means. I became his right-hand man. His primary counselor, advisor, and—in my case—begrudging confidant."

"A promotion."

Trevor shook his head. "You would see it that way. In a word, *no*. It was not a promotion. It was…" He paused. "It was a way of life that I will not discuss with you now. Or ever, if there's any justice in the world."

She nodded slowly. She wanted to know more, could barely restrain herself from imploring him, but instead she said, "This is exactly what I worried would happen."

"It is unfortunate that I distress you, but if you insist upon engaging me, you should know my true nature and my—to put it very mildly—colorful past. If for nothing more than this, I'm glad that I've gone on as I have. Perhaps now, you'll see."

"Oh, it's not your true nature that gives me distress, my lord." She sighed and stepped closer to him.

He took a step back.

"I am distressed because now I must tell you my story."

His eyes narrowed, and she smiled.

"Did you hear anything I just said?" he asked.

She didn't answer, and he turned away. "I cannot worry about anyone else's story but my own. I cannot care, Piety, do you see? I *don't* wish to know. The only thing I wish is to throw you over my shoulder and carry you to my bedroom." He turned back. "And make love to you until you're too delirious to bother me ever again, and I can think with a level head!"

He spun away again. "There," he said, with a low growl. "I've said it. You push too far."

"Just to be clear," she said, rolling the words over in her mind, "the love making is meant to render *me* delirious but *you* able to think? Well. That makes no sense."

"Get out," he said, pivoting to grab her by the elbow and drag her to the passage. "Joseph will usher you down when you've finished." He shoved her through the small doorway. "After that, arrange with him when you want to come or go. I will take pains to be out of the bloody house."

"I won't inconvenience you unnecessarily," Piety said.

"Far too late for that, Miss Grey! Far too late for that!" And he slammed the door behind her.

CHAPTER EIGHT

Jocelyn was alarmed to learn that the most efficient way to clear the upper floors of debris and castoffs was to hurl it, timber and all, over the balcony ledge to the marble floor of the rotunda below. As cleaning strategies went, it was teeth-rattlingly loud but satisfying. Even Marissa, who embraced Piety's unconventional behavior far more readily than Jocelyn, hesitated before she grabbed up the nearest board and let it fly. Within minutes, all three women were laughing as they hurled first the shutters, then the drapes, over the edge.

It was physical work—exhausting but also, oddly, exhilarating—and they worked for the rest of the day. When darkness fell, Piety declared it well past time to make their way back downstairs to sleep for the night. She need only call Joseph, she said, so they could be admitted to the earl's house and descend by way of his stairs.

The earl. Jocelyn's head pounded at the very thought of him. And of Piety. Alone. Together. In his deserted music room. While she had been four bedrooms away, airing mattresses. She had discovered their interlude only after it happened, and she was still piecing together exactly where they had, collectively, gone so wrong.

Not a chaperone one full day and already a failure.

Jocelyn had come upon her stumbling through the passage from Falcondale's music room, with cheeks flushed and hair and dress more disheveled than when they'd last seen her, which was saying quite a lot, but making no excuses.

About her reasons for being next door, Piety had been carefully unspecific. She'd given a vague excuse about an extemporaneous meeting with the earl—something to do with hearing him berate Joseph through her bedroom wall and wishing to defend the boy. As explanations went, it did not sound fabricated, merely incomplete. It was the first topic on which Piety was nearly entirely mute.

When Jocelyn pressed, Piety had drifted over to the landing, dropped to her hands and knees and busied herself with pulling a stuck rug from the floorboards, one stringy strip at a time. There she had remained, strangely quiet, humming and avoiding everyone's gaze, for nearly an hour. When they grew hungry, they had convened to share food from the basket. Here, she was her usual chatty, helpful self, but she said nothing about the earl.

Finally, when they were nearly ready to call Joseph, Piety sent Marissa on an errand in the attic, and Jocelyn managed to approach her alone.

"So you are sure it will be the boy, Joseph, who will release us this evening and not the earl?" Jocelyn kept her eyes on her broom.

Piety was rummaging through a hallway cupboard. "'Twill be Joseph, I believe," she said, not pausing.

"I see." Jocelyn searched for the next, least-incriminating question. "So the boy has not been punished for admitting us?"

"No," Piety answered vaguely. "The earl was not cross, at least not with Joseph."

This was not near enough, and they both knew it. Jocelyn added, "But the earl is not too cross with you, I hope?"

Piety reached deeper into the cupboard and did not answer.

Jocelyn tried again. "Or, perhaps, Lord Falcondale has had a change of heart? Did he give you permission to use the passage?"

No answer.

Jocelyn pressed on. "Piety, has he agreed?"

Finally, Piety nodded her head. "He has, in fact," she said, and then she all but disappeared inside the cupboard, rifling and cleaning and…hiding.

Jocelyn hesitated a moment more, drifting closer. "I have wished, since I learned of your exchange, that you had summoned me," she said to Piety's back. "I am happy to help with the mattresses or whatever work is at hand, but my first business is your companionship. Please think nothing of finding me in these instances. I am more open than the marchioness to practicality, as you call it, but I will have my limits. I, too, must insist upon basic rights and wron—er, situations that may not be so right." She craned around, trying to see Piety's face. "Among them, you cannot meet this man alone; you simply cannot."

Piety nodded but said nothing, so Jocelyn waited. And waited.

Finally, punitively, speaking to a dusty comb she'd pulled from the cupboard, Piety said, "He...He is a complicated man—the earl. I am struggling with my temptation to leave him and his house entirely alone. To forget the option of using his stairway and the passage, even though he's now said he'll allow it. It's merely that I am not complicated, but my dilemma is." She nodded to herself and reversed from the cupboard, ambling across the landing to the master suite.

Jocelyn followed behind, weighing her words carefully. "Your situation *is* complicated. Perhaps if the earl learns of your circumstances, in the proper setting, of course, with the proper companionship, with your solicitors present, perhaps then there is a chance that he could be swayed. *This* would be allowed. It would be odd, but if properly overseen, it would be allowed."

Piety nodded grimly and looked at the floor.

"Right," said Jocelyn. "Well, then, what did you discuss when you were alone with him?" It was as direct a question as she had yet posed. Piety answered with a silent shrug, her eyes still downward.

Frustrated, Jocelyn tried another approach. "You appeared flustered. I hope there were no unpleasantries."

"Not unpleasant to me," Piety finally said. "We spoke of the passage. You know. Chatter. He is angry with me. I am trying to be reasonable." She crossed to the focal point of the room, an alcove seat, ringed with tall, boarded windows. Deftly climbing, she stood on the window seat and began testing the boards for give.

Without looking over her shoulder, Piety said, "His eyes convey a deep, sort of loneliness, don't you think?"

Jocelyn blinked and stepped closer. "I beg your pardon?"

"The earl," Piety explained, "Falcondale. He has lonely eyes."

"*Oh, no.*" Jocelyn sighed and drifted to the window seat, collapsing on the lumpy cushion.

"What?" Piety took a deep breath and pulled harder on the shutter. "I only mention it because it's something I observed, and it is at odds with the way he behaves. Perhaps you've noticed it, too."

"No, Piety, I have not. I'll tell you what I've noticed about his eyes—"

"Because," Piety continued, wresting the first board free and sailing it behind her with a *whoosh*, "he makes such an effort to not welcome people, but his eyes betray him. They are so lonely. What he needs is *more* people in his life, not fewer."

"What I've noticed about his eyes," Jocelyn said, "is that he stares at you like a wolf stares at sheep."

"Does he truly?"

"Piety!" She moaned, easing back against the shutter behind her. "This is a dangerous thing, not a desirable one. What am I to do? You're making me think that it's necessary to be with you every second."

"Don't be silly. I am a sensible girl, Jocelyn, truly. I merely find myself in a…in a senseless situation. Tiny and my father raised me properly. It's merely—" She pulled a second board from the next window. "I asked about his eyes, because I wondered if I was the only one who noticed. It's not like me. And, I've only just met him. And when he does not cooperate, he undermines my repairs."

"Piety, you've only just met me and look how much you have revealed. Your familiarity is part of your charm, but I worry about unleashing this charm on the so-called lonely-eyed bachelor next door. At least until we have working locks on all the doors and a proper place to dress and wash."

"Yes! Hear, hear!" she agreed. "My thoughts exactly. Locks, and furniture, and drapes, and stairs most of all. Oh, my kingdom for a staircase!"

Jocelyn nodded, trying to share Piety's optimism and carefree spirit, but too much had been left unsaid.

"Piety?" She kneeled beside her on the floor to help collect the cast-off shutters. "As happy as I am that you agreed to include me in this exciting business with your house, I was hired as your chaperone. And, you should know that I am neither trained in, nor, I think, predisposed toward, this sort of work. I know practically nothing about chaperoning."

They stood, each holding a pile of debris. Piety tried to interject, but Jocelyn shook her head and continued as they carried the rubble from the room. "I have had no exposure to the social whirl of high society and even less experience with young women of your age and station. Although I am grateful and, it should be said, *willing* to try, I would be remiss if I did not reveal to you how terribly afraid I am that I will be a disappointment at best and a failure at worst—both to you and the marchioness."

They reached the landing and heaved the dusty boards over the banister. When the ensuing crash died away, she continued speaking. "I have only the very vaguest notion of how to protect your reputation and absolutely no idea at all how to engender any sort of successful match with a suitable husband."

"Engender a successful match?" Piety laughed, clapping the dust from her hands.

"But, of course," Jocelyn said. "This is the primary task of a chaperone. To assess the current season's stable of eligible bachelors and to guide and gild her charge into capturing the affections of the most suitable one."

Piety cocked her head. "Did you say, *guide and gild?*"

"Perhaps a better phrase would have been to guide and *goad?*"

Piety let out a burst of laughter. "Believe me, Jocelyn Breedlowe, the last thing I require is to be guided, goaded, or gilded." She turned her back to the bannister and leaned, crossing her arms over her chest. "No, the *very* last thing I need in life is a bachelor, eligible or otherwise. So, if you're worried about dressing me up and launching me at some knight gallant, then stop. I have come to England to escape marriage, not to launch myself into one."

"But I am not even sure I can keep you properly situated in this neighborhood or in London society," said Jocelyn. "I've scarcely been in your service for six hours, and already I've allowed you to slip away and meet in private with a bachelor neighbor. I know you are accustomed to a very independent way of life, but in England, this sort of fraternization is strictly forbidden. The marchioness has assigned me here for a reason, perhaps an entirely selfish reason, but here I am. You must allow me to endeavor, at the very least, to do you a small amount of good."

"Of course, Jocelyn. I shall try, really, I shall. As to the other work, I hope you'll tell me if you do not wish to take part in the heavy lifting and deep cleaning of this house. I have a way of asking far too much of people, as I'm sure you've noticed."

"It's not that, Piety," said Jocelyn. "Truly, it is not. I am invigorated by the idea of this old house, and I pride myself on helpfulness, regardless of my position. Let us, at least endeavor to work together. To make a go of the sort of relationship that may suit the both of us. That is all I ask."

"Absolutely," Piety said, returning to the window-seat alcove, which glowed dimly with the setting sun. Grinning and holding out her arms, she spun in a slow circle in the soft light. "Just look at this room at sunset! Will it not be simply perfect? Oh, I cannot wait to begin work!"

Indeed, thought Jocelyn. *Work. Weeks and weeks of work.* She looked around. The room was, quite literally, coated with dust, swimming in moths, and pocked with eroding plaster. The windows were yellowed with neglect—two of them cracked—and the window-seat cushions coughed what looked like ash on contact. Could its current condition really be promise enough for a young woman of Miss Grey's station? Any lady of quality or means ever known to Jocelyn would have covered her face with a handkerchief and fled at the first sign of dank disorder.

But then again, perhaps Piety Grey was not the lady of quality and means that she portrayed herself to be; perhaps Lady Frinfrock's suspicions had been correct. It seemed nearly mutinous to consider it, but what did they really know about her? She was confident. Well spoken. She dressed exquisitely, and her manners were, if not always employed, then available to her when she felt a situation warranted them. She claimed to have bought the house, to have plans to employ workers and a staff, yet she thought nothing of pulling lumber off of windows with her own hands.

Considering this, Jocelyn watched Piety float around the room, smiling eagerly, poking her head in every nook, and running her hand along the dusty shelves. She seemed genuinely undisturbed by the chaotic state.

Curiosity got the better of Jocelyn. "Piety? Is this room as grand as your accommodation in New York City? In the house you deeded to your mother?"

"Well, it is certainly dirtier." She looked around. "And home to more vermin. And leaks."

"But this room pleases you? It is up to your previous standards?"

"Oh yes, very much. My previous standards amounted to a pin box at the top of five flights of stairs. It was lovely, but hardly spacious. Or convenient. My mother insisted that I remain in the nursery for years and years—far longer than is custom. Finally, when I was oh, about eleven or twelve, my father put his foot down and insisted I have my own suite of rooms elsewhere in the house. My mother responded with this ridiculous theory that I might appear overindulged—spoiled—if I had a lavish room on the family floor. So when I left the nursery, she installed me into a tiny guest room near the attic."

"Oh."

"That was where I grew up. And where I grew to understand that nothing I could do would please my mother. Not by living in the room she wished, not by living anywhere at all."

Jocelyn looked away, allowing her a private moment with such a sad memory. She thought of her own mama, sweet and generous to the end, begging Jocelyn to leave her sickbed, to find a husband while she was still young, rather than stay in Derbyshire to serve as nursemaid. Even as she lay dying, her mother's only thought had been of Jocelyn's future.

Across the room, Piety had begun to pull the faded cushions from the window seat and beat them with the broom. Clouds of dust rose from each strike, and Jocelyn moved to pry open a window.

"My heart aches for you, Piety," Jocelyn said. "That your mother is so, well, that your mother is as you say. Nothing can be done to salvage your relationship?"

"For that, dear Jocelyn, I have given up trying. Our rapport deteriorated rapidly after my father died, and I had to free myself from, well, from her. My first step was to move as far away as possible. My second step was to spend my money as quickly as possible. An investment in property, I'm told, will be more difficult for her to eventually wrestle away. Especially a property as difficult to re-sell as this one. I bought a house no one wanted. No one that is, but me."

She looked around again, holding her broom like a sword. "This house," she said, "and an ocean between us. It should be a very good start, don't you think? And now I shall have whichever bedroom I wish."

CHAPTER NINE

After an uncomfortable night spent on dusty, threadbare couches in a chilly parlor, Piety convened Jocelyn and Marissa in the drawing room to sort out their plan for the day. Coldness permeated the very brick and wood of the walls, their bleakest morning in the dilapidated house. It took longer than usual for Piety to stoke up her optimism and brightness, not unlike the smoky, struggling fire in the grate.

"I will call upon my London solicitor and banker before luncheon, if possible," Piety assured Jocelyn and Marissa over bitter coffee and yesterday's cake. "We will need far more money than what I brought from New York, not to mention a significant line of credit at a number of shops. Also, this business with the earl must be addressed by my solicitor. Joseph saw us out last night with no trouble, so perhaps Falcondale *has* relented about the passage, but I might as well get the terms in writing." She glanced to Jocelyn, hoping to reassure her.

"Next, we require a more reliable way to take our meals," she said, ticking off tasks on her fingers. "The kitchens are in no shape to yet bring in a cook, but that does not mean we cannot have fresh produce, cheese, and bread delivered each morning. Marissa, may I put you in charge of setting this up with runners from a market?" Marissa's eyes grew large, but she stood tall and nodded, clearly encouraged by the new responsibility.

"Finally," Piety said, taking up a large map of London she'd located in her luggage, "I shall begin to call on furniture-makers and other craftsmen to outfit this house. First and foremost, we require proper beds, we won't slee—"

"*Hallo?*" A deep voice resonated through the house. Heavy footsteps followed, echoing through the first floor.

Piety stilled. It was too soon for her mother to have located her, but the possibility was never far from her mind. She cocked her head to listen.

The footsteps grew nearer, and the voice called again. A man's voice, low and jolly.

"The carpenters?" Piety allowed the map to fall to the floor. She scurried from the room, patting her hair and smoothing the dress she'd slept in all night.

"You are expecting the carpenters today?" Jocelyn followed, with Marissa trailing behind.

"If we're lucky! The man I've hired to restore the house came very highly recommended, but, of course, I've never met him. I've sent word. He knows I wish to begin right away."

She cupped her hands around mouth and called, "Who's there?" She winked at Jocelyn.

"Spencer Burr!" came the booming reply. "Carpenter!"

"But it is him!" Piety said happily, hurrying down the hall to the rotunda. Jocelyn and Marissa scrambled to keep up.

"This way, Mr. Burr!" Piety called. She paused beside the derelict stairwell. "Do mind the rubble!"

The sound of the footsteps grew closer, and they craned their heads, watching for the figure of a man to match the voice. They were not disappointed. His bald head came first, poking through the opposite doorway like a battering ram on a tree-trunk neck. "You've left the door unlocked, miss," he said, grinning, "I hope you don't mind."

They took a collective step back. The precariousness of their circumstance—three women alone, making camp in a barely secure house—felt truly risky for the first time.

"Not at all," Piety said, more carefully now. Behind her, Jocelyn made a strangled noise. "Please, do come in. I am here with my staff."

He shouldered in, broad shoulders and a barrel chest filling the rounded doorway. When he stood to full height, he dwarfed the arch.

"Is this the home of Mistress Piety Grey, recently relocated from America?"

"Yes, it is." Piety laughed. "How glad I am to receive you, sir. I am Piety Grey." She wound her way through the littered rotunda and extended her hand.

"We meet at last!" the man said, "I am your carpenter, Miss Grey. Spencer Burr, at your service."

"How do you do, Mr. Burr," she said, some of her confidence returning. "What luck to meet you on my third day in town. I have been so grateful to receive your letters."

"Likewise, miss. We have been waiting expectantly for your arrival these many weeks. We'd begun to think you'd never arrive. My, but aren't you a young little thing."

"I am young, Mr. Burr, but I am rich."

"Are you now?" Spencer Burr chortled, punting a chicken pillow out of his way. "Well, we received the first bank notes, just as you promised, so I have no reason to doubt it."

"The job is substantial," Piety replied, looking around, "of that you can be sure. The stairs, certainly, are a total loss. Far worse than I predicted in my letters. Indeed, all the damage I described is trifling compared to the reality we now face. We'll have to prioritize and set down a schedule."

The large man nodded and began to walk a slow circle around the rotunda, studying the walls and ceiling. "Stairs lost, I should say." He stopped in front of a gaping hole where the main stair once rose.

Piety explained what she could remember of her conversation with the earl about the stairs, while Mr. Burr paced and nodded, extracting a piece of graphite from his pocket to scribble notes directly on the wall.

"Who can say," Piety went on, "perhaps the servants' stair in the kitchen will be easier to restore first."

"Only one way to determine," he said. "Let's have a look."

They looked for more than two hours. Piety walked through every room with Mr. Burr: the rustic kitchens; the damp, moldy cellar; and her favorite space, a jewel-shaped solarium with foggy glass on the edge of the garden. They discussed her expectations and his predictions for budget and schedule and feasibility for each. The stairs, he conceded, would, in fact, *not* be replaced in a week. On this, the earl had been correct. A trained architect would be required, he said, in order to direct their proper restoration.

There were other concerns: damage or decay that had not been accurately described, improper ventilation, and mice. So many mice.

Mr. Burr was thorough—in some instances, painfully so—but he was also resourceful. He provided Piety with the direction of possible architects she might hire for this or that reconstruction, including the oppressive stairs. He knew artisans who could rework the mosaic tiles in the solarium, and a man with little trained dogs who could come and help ferret out all the mice. When he had a working list of supplies and craftsmen needed, Mr. Burr, himself, took his leave, although a small crew remained to begin demolition.

Piety was grateful for the immediate progress—*any* progress—but the noise of construction grated more than she expected, and she found herself drifting. The house had a lovely garden terrace, and she wandered outside, squinting into the spring sunshine.

Oh, gracious, the growing list of needs, she thought, embarking on an overgrown garden path. The expense would be considerable. The repairs would take months, if not a full year.

Before she could stop herself, she glanced at Falcondale's house over her garden wall. She wondered if he would agree with Mr. Burr's assessments.

She came upon a stone bench and stared at it, too preoccupied to sit. She glanced again at his house.

He wouldn't care enough to agree, she thought. This work did not affect him beyond the imposition of the passage. And anyway, she dare not ask him. He was a distraction, and she could not afford to lose focus. She's wasted enough time thinking of their kiss. She'd lost sleep, wedged against the lumpy back of the velvet couch, reliving it. Even during her critical tour with Mr. Burr, her mind had drifted to it.

If she *must* obsess over it, perhaps she could force herself to feel badly about it. Penance, et cetera. In honor of Jocelyn, she tried to conjure up piteous feelings of guilt. Her chaperone had been entirely correct to remind her of the risks of such behavior. Piety knew all of the things that decent young ladies were meant to do and not to do, and kissing bachelor neighbors in deserted music rooms was not among them. If Jocelyn, or Tiny or, God forbid, the marchioness knew, her legitimacy as a well-meaning resident of this street in particular—and upstanding young lady in general—would be shot. She was independent, but she was not reckless, usually.

Piety's only excuse was how very *necessary* the entire interlude had seemed at the time. It had been as essential, somehow, as restoring the house or staying ahead of her mother. If she had anything to feel guilty about, it was that her priorities had become scrambled.

At the very least, the earl's kiss had been a singular, once-and-only kind of thing. She was intrigued by him and drawn to him, and kissing him had been one of the most thrilling experiences of her...well, in a very long time. But she was no fool. And Falcondale could not have been more clear. He disliked her. He would avoid her. He did not care about her house or her arrival to his street. Likely, they would never cross paths again. He intended to leave England forever, and any day. The thought of this, which drifted in and out of her mind with far too great a regularity, left her with an unexplained stew of indignation and frustration somewhere in her chest. It felt like being slowly submerged in water again and again. And that was the very last thing she needed. She had enough emotional flotsam and jetsam in her life to slowly drown. She needn't add more.

No, she thought, forcing herself back to the house, she would not kiss him again. If possible, she would not think of him again. Eventually she would have the time and energy to meet a man and perhaps even fall in love. And when that happened, it would not be with someone who would surely break her heart. The one thing her mother had taught her: How miserable it felt to love someone who could not love her in return.

CHAPTER TEN

24 May 1809

Dear Lord Falcondale,

I hope you'll forgive the intrusion of this written request, but circumstances have forced my hand. I had to, at the very least, try.

I am, as you predicted, in sore need of a trained architect. I have endeavored to hire the work from a firm in Eastcastle Street, but the recommended experts seem disinclined to take me on. Something about the lack of a proper "referral," although my suspicion is, they are opposed to working for a woman. So be it.

Our main problem is the stairs, another of your predictions. The carpenters were able to quickly erect rudimentary stairs in the servants' stairwell, and lucky for us. We have been able to come and go without intruding upon you.

Despite the progress, the main staircase is somewhat of a conundrum to my carpenters. Naturally, this as-yet-untouched heap is the only route wide enough to convey large furnishings up and down.

You spoke so knowledgably about the construction when we were last together, I wonder if you'd be willing to have a look? First and foremost, I want the workers making every concession toward safety and strength, but also I'd like the finished stairs to be a showpiece installment in my home. I have taken the liberty of attaching a handful of crude sketches made by my chief carpenter, Mr. S. Burr, and I have made notes about our questions (as he explained them to me).

Certainly if you are disinclined to help, then you may discard them without another thought. But, I approach you humbly, hat in hand. Your desire that we have no further contact could not have been made more clear last week, and how prudent you are. It is only in my hour of great need that I reach out. I am aware of your busy schedule and desire to be left alone, though I fully intend to compensate you for your time and effort spent.

If you are able to assist, I can be available to receive you anytime. Use the passage or my front door—however you feel most inclined.

Sincerely,
Miss Piety Grey

Chapter Eleven

Lady Frinfrock, flanked by Tiny and two footmen, rapped on Piety's front door immediately after luncheon on the first day of the second week of reconstruction. By this time, the ground floor, formerly dusty and cavernous, now appeared ransacked and torn to bits.

At least it looks like progress, Piety hoped as she ushered the marchioness inside. "I cannot guarantee your safety, my lady," she said. "You can barely turn round without encountering workmen or debris."

She had to shout to be heard over the deafening noise of construction. The high dome of the rotunda ceiling multiplied the cacophonous din of hammers and saws, tripling their original sound.

"I am not startled by the sights and sounds of honest work, Miss Grey," the marchioness said over her shoulder. She plodded down the hall with her cane. "Bernard and Julius are here to assist me should something unwieldy lay in my path. Oh, Miss Baker! Do mind the scaffolding!" She cautioned Tiny behind her.

Piety bit her lip and looked at Jocelyn. "You were right to cease our sleeping in the parlor and to arrange a real bedroom in the library," she whispered. "This will please Tiny."

"It's the very first thing her ladyship will ask," Jocelyn whispered back. She stared down the hall after her. "I cannot believe she's come. She rarely leaves the house, except for church."

"This house is an abomination." Lady Frinfrock's voice came from the rotunda. "Wherever do you sleep amid all the ruinous pit?"

Piety and Jocelyn hurried down the hall after her, spouting assurances, pointing out the still-standing features of the house, and giving her a tour of the library-turned-sleeping quarters. For whatever reason, the carpenters regarded the marchioness with an effusive deference, nearly genuflecting when she entered the room. It didn't hurt. Throughout it all, Tiny walked silently beside Lady Frinfrock, her arms tightly folded across her chest, shaking her head.

Jocelyn, bless her, discerned Piety's need to speak privately with Tiny, and she offered to give the marchioness a tour of the house's long-ignored solarium. Lady Frinfrock lit up like the sun at the mention of horticulture, and she scuttled to the hexagon-shaped glass room at the rear of the house.

"Do you think she will shut me down?" Piety asked Tiny as they watched the marchioness and Jocelyn go.

"The one who's shutting you down," said Tiny, drifting toward the kitchens, "is me. Missy Pie, this place is in worse shape than it was when we pried open the door that very first time. You can't think of living here in all of this filth. Bugs and rot and moldy curtains. I just saw a rat."

Piety took a deep breath. "It must get worse before it gets better."

"And it's crawling with men! You and Miss Breedlowe are over here *by yourselves!*" She ducked through the arched doorway to the kitchens and looked around.

"The men are merely workers," Piety said. "They are here to make repairs for us, not dance with us. By December, you and I will fill this room with all the smells and flavors of Christmas. Until then, well, Rome wasn't built in a day, was it? And, in the meantime, you have... Well, how is it, exactly? With the marchioness?"

The small woman shrugged and made her way to the window seat. "She is mighty nice. Very respectful. I'm not used to having so many people wait on me. Or such a big bed."

"Are you with her all day?"

"Only when it suits me. She wants to talk about a whole mess of things that I haven't talked about since God knows when. When I was a girl. My parents. My brothers. It isn't all bad."

"But it's not too much, Tiny?" Piety whispered, looking closely at her face. "Too personal or intrusive to discuss such things? You know we needn't do it simply because she bade us. I want you to be comfortable during the renovation, but I do not want your privacy to suffer. I do not want you to suffer at all."

Tiny rubbed her eyes. "No. I—I don't mind. It feels good to talk about it. Especially with someone I don't even know. To remember. The marchioness hangs on every word I say." She dropped her hands from her face and raised her chin.

Piety grinned. "Well, I suspect you are the first person ever to have that effect on her. And good for you both."

They laughed, and Piety swooped her up into a big hug, bending down to press her cheek against Tiny's. She closed her eyes and sighed. "It's going to be all right, Tiny. Everything is going to be all right. You'll see."

They embraced a moment more, and then, from the rotunda, they heard Jocelyn call. "Miss Grey?"

"We're here!" answered Piety, giving Tiny a peck on the cheek. "Would her ladyship like to see—"

Before she could finish, Lady Frinfrock pushed her way into the kitchen with Jocelyn scrambling to keep up. The marchioness's footman stumbled behind them, their arms full of dirty clay pots.

"Her ladyship would like to advise you on the revival of your solarium," Jocelyn said.

"I have no doubt that the solarium will be the very last room you look after," began the marchioness, "and what a shame. That solarium is the only redeeming quality of this house."

Piety smiled. "It was the glass solarium that convinced me to buy the house, my lady. From the moment the estate agent described it, I was enchanted. I hope to restore it as soon as the essential areas are underway."

"Yes, well, whether you will regard it as a novelty or truly nurture it remains to be seen." She waved her cane in Piety's direction. "In meantime, I am taking these pots in order that seedlings and bedding plants can take root in my own greenhouse while we are still under threat of a morning frost."

She bustled toward the door, without waiting for Piety's consent. "You will see these again, restored and full of life, when I have witnessed the careful restoration of the solarium and evidence of your proficiency with—and dedication to—delicate plant life."

You're taking my pots? Piety wanted to ask, but she said, "However can I thank you, my lady? How generous you are."

"You can thank me by staying inside this house and not admitting another soul from the street until it's been remade into a decent dwelling, fit for decent people." She scowled up and down the hallway as if it were the chief offender and then settled her gaze on Jocelyn. "Miss Breedlowe, as much as you annoy me, I cannot ask a fellow Englishwoman to endure this appalling level of decrepitude."

Piety gasped, but the marchioness ignored her, plodding back to the rotunda and motioning for the burdened footmen to follow. "I will hire some other unlucky soul to chaperone Miss Grey—a stalwart Bavarian, perhaps—and you may come home with Tiny and myself."

Jocelyn took a step after her. "If it pleases you, my lady," she said, raising her voice over the sound of the marchioness's cane, "I am not at all inconvenienced by the conditions here with Miss Grey. If you do not mind, I should like to stay."

The marchioness's steady plod ceased. She pivoted slowly.

Jocelyn continued undaunted. "I...I think I can do Miss Grey some good. For the benefit of the street. That is unless you require my attention and care."

The marchioness squinted at her. "I believe I have made it perfectly clear that *your care* is the very last thing I need." She studied the younger woman, leaning on her cane. "Very well," she finally said. "You may stay if you think you can bear it. But Tiny and I shall return every day or so. I wish to see real progress amid the chaos and the highest possible regard for propriety. This is not the American frontier, Miss Grey. England has long been the most civilized power in the modern world. If you intend to live among us, you must learn to behave as if a roof above your head and four standing walls are not merely a preference." Shaking her head, she resumed her progress toward the front door.

"Yes, my lady," Piety said, smiling after her. She grabbed Jocelyn's hand and the two women shared a look. Leaning in, she said lowly, "Thank you, Jocelyn. Well spoken!"

Jocelyn let out a shaky sigh and nodded. "Go," she whispered. "She'll expect to be seen to the door."

They linked arms and followed, lagging two rooms behind and whispering, until they heard the marchioness gasp. "And who in God's name are you, sir?"

"*Ah.*" A new voice, a man's voice, hedged. "No one of any consequence," the voice said. "Who are you?"

Falcondale.

Piety froze for half a beat and then yanked Jocelyn in the direction of the front door.

The next voice was Joseph's. "'Tis the earl, madam," the boy said, "Lord Falcondale."

"That'll do, Joseph," she heard Falcondale say. "Many apologies. I've merely come to return a note to Miss Grey. If you would be so kind to give it to her? Terribly sorry to intrude. I'll just be on—"

"Are you mad?" interrupted the marchioness. "Do I resemble the butler to you?"

Piety sprinted the last two yards, slowing only at the last corner.

She saw him first, a head taller than the women in the vestibule and the footmen with their dirty pots. Her breath caught. It had been one week.

The area of her stomach tried to flip-flop places with the area of her heart.

But everyone was hovering now, waiting, hanging on the anticipation of who would speak next and what he or she might say. Piety forced nonchalance.

"Lord Falcondale," she said, stepping up to the circle. "What a pleasure."

The heads in the circle made a collective turn. She could but smile. "If you please, I'd like to introduce you to our most esteemed neighbor, her ladyship, the Marchioness Frinfrock."

He stared at Piety, and then back at the old woman, and then back to Piety.

Please, she willed him. *Be affable.*

After a long moment, he mumbled the expected words. "Pleased to meet you, my lady."

"Your flower boxes are a disgrace to your house and to this street," the marchioness said.

Falcondale took of his hat and tapped it against his hand. "How good of you to notice."

"Ha!" The marchioness laughed without humor. "Dismiss me if it pleases you, but I have been the steward of this street since before you were born—both of you." She swung her cane at Falcondale. "You sir, what business do you have with the American girl?"

Careful…careful.

He opened his mouth and then closed it. He looked over the old woman's head, locking eyes with Piety. Her stomach swapped spaces again with her heart.

"Miss Grey has approached me," he said, not taking his eyes off Piety, "to assist with a handful of repairs in her new home. I've come with a neighborly reply."

The marchioness studied him. "Approached you, has she?"

"Yes." The word was clipped. He looked away from Piety to stare at the old woman. "By letter."

"How attentive of you to reply *in person*."

"Oh, yes, that's my middle name," he said, "*attentive*."

Piety leaned to Jocelyn. "There is a potential here, I think, for the two of them to be friends."

"Is this true?" Jocelyn whispered back. "Have you written to the earl?"

Piety wrinkled her nose.

"A lady," Jocelyn reminded softly, "would never pass letters between herself and a man to whom she has not been introduced."

Piety could not contain a burst of laughter. "Oh, we have been introduced."

Lady Frinfrock whirled around. "You find this diverting, Miss Grey?"

Piety coughed and gestured down the hall. "Lord Falcondale. Won't you come in? We've been giving Tiny and Lady Frinfrock a tour of the progress."

She glanced at him briefly and then away. It was not easy. She *wanted* to see him. She wanted the crowded entryway to disappear, so he was all she could see.

"No, I'm afraid not," he said. "I've intruded. I came only to give you these." He shoved a wrinkled stack of notes in her direction.

"The drawing of our stairs," Piety whispered, thumbing through.

Lady Frinfrock and Tiny leaned in, peering over her elbow.

She looked at him. He'd answered her request. In spades. There were pages and pages.

The earl cleared his throat. "Just some general direction. You should continue your search for an architect to do the job properly. This will only get you started."

Piety studied the parchment in her hand, taking in the straight, even lines of his handwriting. He'd put copious comments to Mr. Burr's drawings and added several pages of his own beautifully rendered sketches. They were sweeping and dimensional—works of art unto themselves—she had to remind herself that they were simply sketches. Practical, and technical, and exactly what she had asked him to do.

In no way were they a statement on his interest, or his affection, or evidence that he had passed the last seven days ruminating on her the way she had of him.

Even so, she had the thought: *I should tell him. About my mother. The Limpetts.*

He deserved to know why she had been so demanding from the start.

Not here, not now, but somewhere else. And soon. She felt a rush of anticipation. Twenty minutes, perhaps a half hour. Nothing more. To explain her repeated requests for his help.

For now, all she could do was look up and say, "Thank you. Again."

"'Tis nothing," he said, shoving his hat on his head and motioning to Joseph.

"But surely you cannot advise on a stairwell that you have not seen," said Lady Frinfrock, shuffling out of the way. "Unless, of course, you have been given a private tour before us?" She raised her eyebrows.

Piety glanced at Jocelyn. At least they were innocent of this. "No, the earl has not yet seen the stairs. Can we trouble you to see it, my lord?"

He hesitated, hovering on the threshold, and Lady Frinfrock turned back inside and began a slow march on the rotunda, her cane thumping regally. "Spare us, the theatrics, please, Falcondale. You cannot feign shyness now. Have a proper look. You've come this far."

Piety watched him, clutching his notes to her chest.

Tiny followed the marchioness, and Jocelyn and the footmen with their pots fell in behind. They trundled down the hall. Falcondale nodded to Joseph, and the boy slipped out the door and into the street.

They were alone in the vestibule. Her stomach and heart swung again.

"I'm sorry for the, er, committee," she told him. "This has proved to be a highly collaborative street."

"Ah, is that it? I knew there was some overriding reason. I make a rule never to collaborate. As I'm sure you noticed."

The notes in her hand betrayed this, and she stared at them again. "I've been compelled to accept help from every quarter," she said, "but the neighbors are to blame. The reason is…" She took a deep breath and leaned back, checking the proximity of the others.

"*Careful*," he said lowly, a whisper, leaning in. He gave a barely perceptible shake of his head.

She nodded and bit her lip, fighting the urge to bury her face in his neck. He was so close.

He emitted an endurance sigh and stared at her as if he wanted the same thing. Piety held her breath.

Ultimately, he pulled away. "There are stairs, Miss Grey?" he asked pointedly, swiping his hat off of his head. "Pray, lead the way."

Chapter Twelve

"Tell me again, Joseph," demanded Trevor two hours later, "why we called on her? Explain it to me. Please."

The boy stood at the basin in the kitchen, washing crockery. Trevor paced behind him, glaring at the floor.

"Because she wrote to you?" the boy suggested.

"Logical guess. She says jump, and I say *how high?*"

"I meant, it was polite to give some answer," the boy said.

"Logic again. But since when am I polite?"

"Oh, I believe Miss Grey can make even a brute like you seem refined."

"Refined, are we? Known her all of two weeks, and already, she's able to *refine?* What of her own refinement? Hmmm? To invite me to her home, to—"

An insistent knock interrupted his rant.

Trevor froze, staring at the kitchen door. She'd come. He knew it. Perhaps he'd gone mad, because he bloody well *felt* it.

"Joseph." The word was a warning. "Leave it. We're not at home."

The boy shot him an exasperated look, drying his hands. "You came home straight away and drew up more plans. You might as well give them to her." He crossed to the door.

"I was going to post the bloody scribbling."

Joseph opened the door.

"Ah, Joseph!" The accent was unmistakably American. "Thank you."

A basket emerged, heaped with pastries, thrust through the door by leather-gloved hands. Then there was the rest of her, bustling through the doorway with a whirl of her cloak that billowed behind her like a flag.

"Marissa bought too many fig tarts," she said, "and neither Jocelyn nor I can tolerate them. She cannot eat them all herself before they turn. Please take them for your tea."

"Leave my manservant out of this, if you will, Miss Grey," Trevor said, watching Joseph accept the basket with enthusiasm. "He can scarcely be trusted around you. When you hold out your maid and her figs, like a carrot on a stick, I have no authority whatsoever."

She ignored him and unfastened her cloak, popping one button at a time. "Aren't you a suspicious one? I merely offered the boy a pastry." The cloak came off in a deft, theatrical whirl and she draped it on a hook near the door.

Her gown was blue: icy and light and soft. It put him in the mind of a birthday gift. If he meant to unwrap her, he thought, where would he begin? At her neck, where tiny buttons marched from a small collar, downward over the curve of her breast? Along her back, where more buttons dotted the arc of her spine? Or at the hem, swaying gently when she walked?

He swallowed hard, allowing himself to speculate, if only for a moment. He had not been able to look at her—not really—when he'd called to her house today. He had not seen her for a week. Now he could not look away.

Her hair was twisted into an elaborate, caramel-colored knot. Wisps and curls escaped here and there, creating a halo around her face. He remembered the feel of that hair, unbound and heavy. His fingers twitched.

Without warning, she looked up from her cloak, and he blinked. He was never quite prepared for the brightness of her smile. He licked his lips. Only Joseph's polite cough reminded him that he stood, mutely taking it all in, devouring the sight of her.

"Where is your committee, Miss Grey?" He forced his eyes to his timepiece.

She laughed. "There was quite a crowd when you called. The marchioness does not forewarn us when she calls."

"Ah, well you two have that in common."

"I'm here to apologize for what a production it became. If only you'd turned up thirty minutes before, or after."

"Better yet, not at all."

"Oh, no, do not say that. We were in sore need of your drawings." She took three steps toward him. She was close now, close enough to smell. "In fact, we could use more of the same, if you can spare the time." She raised her eyebrows switching to a smile that was tentative and almost shy. She drifted closer. "The stairs are—"

"Why me, Miss Grey?"

Her head shot up at his interruption, and she studied him. It occurred to him that it might be taken as a philosophical question and not a challenge, as it was meant to be. He added, "I can't help but wonder: what if I had not had the misfortune of being your neighbor? What if you'd moved next door to some other poor sod who couldn't be counted on for passages and advice about design?"

Her smile fell, and she turned away. He saw her cast around uncomfortably, studying the floor, and Joseph beside the basin, and the door with its tiny portal window. She began to remove her gloves.

Oh, no, there is no need to remove the gloves. He watched the leather roll back to reveal delicate wrists and fingers.

"Jocelyn—that is, Miss Breedlowe—is on an errand," she said, "but she will be back soon. I am not hiding from her, mind you, just being strategic about when I come and go. Still, I should hate to be seen."

Then why come at all? This he actually said. "Then why come, Miss Grey?"

She nodded to herself but didn't answer, looking around again. Her gaze lit on the worn kitchen table in front of the fire and the abandoned chess game near the grate.

She looked up and smiled. "Chess?" she asked. "Who plays?"

Joseph was suddenly at her side, tugging her toward the board. "We both do, miss," the boy said. "His lordship taught me, and now I beat him quite regularly. We've a game going, even now."

"Oh, how grand." She chuckled and looked to Trevor with something akin to…was it sadness?

"Would you mind if I watched?" she asked. "Just a play or two? I haven't played since my father died. Chess was our special game, the two of us. But Tiny does not play."

"Yes, I do mind," said Trevor in the same moment Joseph said, "Please, miss, play my side." He nearly skidded into the fire in his scramble to lead her to his chair. "Against the earl. I don't mind at all. It would be a thrill to watch someone else hand him his hat."

"Oh, no I couldn't," she began.

"I would be honored, miss, please." The boy all but pushed her, forcibly, into the chair.

She laughed in earnest then, the sadness in her eyes nearly gone, but then she gasped and said, "Oh, Joseph! Had you seen this?" She moved the king's pawn to take one of Falcondale's knights. "I'm sorry, was it your turn?"

"It was, actually," said Trevor, leaning forward. "Although that move is well beyond Joseph's level of skill." Staring at the board a moment, he moved his queen's knight to defend his castle.

"Expected," Miss Grey said and countered his move.

Trevor couldn't remember exactly when they settled into the chairs, but he found himself comfortably seated by the fifth or sixth move. They went back and forth in silence for a few moments, and he grew increasingly impressed with the speed and alacrity of her play. Her strategy was complicated and unexpected.

"Your father taught you well, Miss Grey," he said.

"He loved chess, and he taught me to love it, too." She smiled. "How could I not, when it allowed me to spend so much time with him?" She made another move and called out *check*, removing his queen from the board.

"It enraged my mother," she continued, "who felt it was a man's game, not to be played by ladies. She was jealous of the time we spent together."

"My father taught me, as well," Trevor said, not knowing what to do with the information about her mother. "One of his few useful contributions to my upbringing."

"That reminds me," she chuckled. "I should buy a chessboard for the house before my mother arrives. Something lavish and difficult to move. Ivory and ebony pieces and perhaps a marble table. She will hate it."

"Your mother will come here? To London?" Trevor paused, his hand hovering over the board.

"She will. Undoubtedly."

"When? Not before your house is restored, I hope."

"I hope so, too." She looked up at him, honesty plain on her face. "But this is the reason for my great rush—for bullying you about the passage and now about the stairs. The more complete the renovations, the more difficult it will be for her to force me to leave."

"To leave for where?"

"To go back home, to New York. To be married."

Trevor leaned back in his chair and stared at her.

"Oh," he finally said. "I see. You've fled to London to escape an undesirable match. Hardly an original motive, but a far more elaborate strategy than I've ever before known. You bought an entire house, for God's sake. Halfway around the globe."

"Elaborate traps call for elaborate escapes."

They played again. Two moves for him, one for her. They did not take their eyes off the board. When he couldn't stand it a moment more, he asked, "Who is the fellow?"

"*Fellows*," she corrected. "There are five of them."

"Your mother wishes for you to marry *five* men?"

"I am to pick among the five sons of her new husband, my stepbrothers. There is one who seems particularly, er, aggressive, but I believe my mother thinks any of the brothers would do."

He scowled at her. "That's hitting close to home, isn't it? Marrying a stepbrother? Is this legally binding in America?"

"It is legally binding anywhere. They are not blood relations, merely the offspring of my mother's new husband."

"I take it none of the five appeals to you?"

She put down the pawn she was holding and looked up at him. "Oh, Falcondale," she said, "you do not wish to know."

That's the God's honest truth, he thought, but he had to fight the urge to ask.

He checked the board. She'd nearly beaten him, trapped him with a slick bit of strategy that she'd obviously employed before. He considered his move and made it. "How long will Miss Breedlowe be away?"

Her hand stilled above the board, and she looked up.

That came out wrongly.

He amended his words. "I am not angling to detain you. It's merely—"

"By no means," said Piety. "I have dallied too long. With some difficulty, I am settling into a routine of accountability—to a chaperone. I am accustomed to more freedom. However, Miss Breedlowe has sacrificed a lot to take me on, and I do not wish to take advantage. She and Marissa had planned a trip to the market for four o'clock, so I bade them go and took the opportunity to come here alone." She looked at the floor beside the chessboard. "We must know what's to be done with the stairs."

Trevor nodded and shoved out of his chair. "Yes, the stairs. I came home after your tour and drew up more specific designs, you might as well know. Now that I've seen the space. Still, measurements are required. Your man Mr. Burr can begin taking those and call on me with questions. In the meantime, it is imperative that you hire an actual working architect to direct the project."

"You've done more?" She stood. Her eyes shone with surprise and gratitude, like he'd just told her he managed to save a sick friend.

The tight coil within his chest unspooled again. He hadn't realized how anxious he had been to please her. He coughed and shoved to his feet, scrambling for a new topic. "You're beating me in chess. My brain is gruel. It has been since meeting your Lady Frinfrock."

She smiled again, the most genuine he'd seen in a day of smiles from Piety Grey. He looked away. It occurred to him that Joseph was gone. Conspicuously gone.

"The drawings are in my library." He took a step away from her, although it felt wrong, like stepping from an umbrella into the rain.

"After you," she said.

Trevor nodded and went, leading her from the kitchen, up the stairs to his library, checking every room as he went for his mutinous serving boy.

He went to his desk and rolled the drawings, tying them with a string. "I should have given this to you when you walked through the door," he said. He held out the parchment.

She reached for it.

He didn't let go.

"What's wrong with them? These stepbrothers? Why are they not fit to marry?"

Piety released her end. "Primarily?" she asked softly. "I do not love them—not any of them. I do not even *like* any of them. To a man, they are repugnant, really. And unhappy. And cruel."

"Ah," he said. "Of course. To whom, Miss Grey? To whom are they repugnant and unhappy and cruel? To you? In what way? Won't they bend to your iron will?" He heard himself growing louder, more demanding. He dropped the rolled parchment to his desk.

"My only will for them is to stay far away, but they are relentless. They work very hard to, er, make an impression on me. By the time I left New York, preening for me had become their sole, dogged occupation."

"What?" he heard himself ask. "Flowers, sonnets, nights at the theatre? Too much of the same? A woman of your means and appearance must see that all the time."

Piety shook her head. "On the contrary, my mother did not allow me to receive gentlemen for courtship until only recently. My dowry was—*is*—substantial, and she was not prepared to part with the money. But since the Limpetts..."

She trailed off then, and he waited. He would not allow himself to ask the question, but he could wait.

When she continued, her voice was gruff. "With my father gone, there is so much *more* money. This should afford me the possibility of real freedom. And it brought me here to England." She gestured broadly to the room. "But my mother cannot bear it, and so she has devised another way to control me. And the money.

"And *no*, the brothers have not courted me with flowers or poetry," she went on. "It's been mostly boasting and lordly behavior. Long, painful dinners around my mother's table while they drone on or tease."

"Perhaps they are young." The words were out before he could stop them. "Boys more than men."

She shook her head. "They are not young; they are ungracious. Two of them are shrewdly judgmental of nearly everyone, from the servants to their own petty friends. They gloat in the face of anyone less fortunate.

"Four of them aspire to nothing greater than prestige in New York's social whirl, propelled along by liquor and gambling and nightly excess, whatever it may be. They openly brag about their exploits and gloat about their lack of curiosity or outside interests or charity or, God forbid, enterprise. They have empty managerial positions in their father's stocking mill, but they ignore the company, even though it is rumored to be in deep debt."

He laughed. "Stocking mill?"

"Yes, the man my mother remarried is Owen Limpett. The stocking king of New York. The boys—Eli, Emmett, Ennis, Everett, and Eddie—"

"You cannot be serious." Trevor rubbed his jaw.

She nodded. "The next bit is silly, even superficial, I suppose, but all of them have abhorrent hygiene. Their complexions run from ruddy and shiny to pale and ashy. They smell of last night's bender; they have flaky hair, soft hands, watery eyes…Should I go on?"

Trevor couldn't speak. He wandered around the desk and propped his hip on the corner, crossing his arms over his chest.

"I tried to abide them, truly I did." She raised a hand to her cheek and closed her eyes for a moment. "Eventually, after repeated embarrassing outbursts and insults to friends, abuse to servants, rudeness to total strangers, I came to understand that theirs is a kind of inherent meanness. They seem to revel in it. They cannot be helped. Or abided. Not by me, anyway."

Trevor dropped his head and rubbed his eyes. He hadn't wanted to know. He could not care about this woman, her circumstances, her shiny-faced suitors, or their cruelty to housemaids. He had his own bloody problems.

Still, he found himself unable to turn away. He looked up, willing her to go on.

"They've struck a deal, my mother and the five of them. Whomever succeeds in making me his bride will control half of my fortune. The other half of the money will go to Idelle."

"Idelle is your mother, I presume? You don't refer to her as 'mother?'"

"Not often," she said sadly.

"But she does not have money of her own? And these brothers, are they not heirs to the, er, stocking coffers, however indebted?"

Piety shrugged. "My father left enough money for my mother's comforts, which are extravagant. I added to that by transferring even more to her accounts. I sold much of our property and gave all of those earnings to her as well. But it wasn't enough. She knows there is more—much more— and that I have it. The mere knowledge of this drives her. She wants the money *and* the power. She is…I believe her own childhood was troubled. She is not a happy woman.

"As to the Limpetts, I cannot say. She found ready allies in them. She was misled about the wealth of her new husband—their father—and all of them appear to be desperate for funds." She shrugged. "Is this why they agreed so readily to her scheme to marry me? This is a mystery, because truly they don't even like me. But this has been our guess. Tiny's and mine."

She took a deep breath and shook her head, clearly reaching for calm. "Regardless of their individual regard for me, which seems to range from salacious to envy to disdain, each of them leaped at the chance to make a deal with the devil, er, my mother." She looked away for a moment, and he realized she was fighting back tears. *Oh, God, now she would cry?*

Before he realized it, he had shoved off the desk and moved closer to her. He pulled a handkerchief from his pocket.

"I'm sorry," she said, swiping a finger beneath each eye. "I never intended to burden you with such excruciating detail. You needn't pity me, my lord. I have so much more than most people in the world. I'm...I'm a very lucky girl.

"And this is not my style." She chuckled through tears. "I am not above demanding, wheedling, or wearing someone down. But please know that I generally do not vie for sympathy."

The urge to reach out and touch her was nearly overwhelming. He fought it, occupying his hands with the handkerchief, thrusting it to her. She smiled and took it, pressing it gently to her lips.

Trevor shut his eyes and turned away. He would not reach for her. He would not care about her situation, or her future, or even her stairs—not anymore.

He cast around the room and caught sight of the drawings. He snatched them up and thrust them at her. "I intended to send Joseph with these," he said gruffly.

She took the parchment and held it to her chest. "You asked earlier about why I came?"

"Oh, I think I have some idea now."

"Not why I came to England. Why I am here. In your home. Now."

"Oh, yes," he said, his heartbeat accelerating, "that."

"I came because I enjoy you, my lord."

"You don't." A whisper.

The room around them felt suddenly small.

"Last week," she said, "in your, er, music room, I enjoyed myself. Spending time with you was diverting. Lord knows I could use a diversion."

He had no response to this, and they stared at one another. The only sound was the ticking clock. He felt himself drift toward her.

"You amuse and interest me, my lord." She spoke softly. "It is inconvenient, I know. But I cannot seem to help it. I cannot seem to stay away."

Now, he stepped up, his eyes not leaving hers.

A half-step more.

He was upon her. He towered, looking down. She did not move.

Without breaking her gaze, he nudged against her, pressing her to the wing-back chair in the center of the room. She allowed it, falling softly against the leather and turning up her face. Her eyes were closed.

It was enough.

He ignited, swooping down to kiss her.

CHAPTER THIRTEEN

Piety wrapped her arms around Lord Falcondale's broad shoulders and held on. The parchment fell from her hands, slid down his back, and rolled to the floor.

It was an instantaneous kiss. No playful nibbling, no closed-mouth prelude. He took her in his arms, and their lips collided.

They tumbled against the chair, tumbled *into* the chair—she didn't know and didn't care. In her mind she floated, she flew. She had the fleeting thought: *relax, slow, savor.* But his nearness only made her want to pull him closer, to kiss him more fiercely. She wanted to *devour* him.

He kissed her deeply—not punishingly like before, but hard and sure and focused. He left her lips only to scrape the stubble of his emerging beard across her cheek, her ear, to breathe in the scent of her hair, and trail back.

"This is madness." His tried to catch his breath between kisses. "Piety, please."

"Yes," she agreed. *Madness.*

"Please." He growled again, but he did not release her. He deepened the kiss, nudging his boot between her feet and his knee between her legs, lifting gently against the chair. She gasped at the intimate closeness, shocked and excited, barely able to keep up with the cascade of new sensations. She hooked one foot around the back of his boot. He groaned.

"Piety," he said lowly, "this cannot happen again."

"Too late, I'm afraid."

He raised his knee, hoisting her higher still, and she gasped again, blinking at the contact of his thigh.

"It's the last thing we both need."

"Why does it feel like the only thing?"

He groaned again, and Piety dropped her head back, allowing him access to her neck. She opened her eyes, only half seeing the dim library around her. Her breathing came in quick, desperate pants. He kissed his way back to her mouth, sinking his fingers into her hair, working the pins free.

"Trevor? Where'd you put the…Oh!" Joseph's voice sliced through their revelry, and they froze.

Piety squeezed her eyes shut. Falcondale dropped his face beside hers, shielding her.

"Out, Joseph, now," he said to the floor.

Piety heard a strangled yelp and rapidly retreating footsteps.

Falcondale held her against him a long, still moment. The only sound was their labored breath. Finally, he raised up, pulling her gently from the arm of the chair.

When she could stand upright without swaying, he stepped away.

"I apologize," he said. "Joseph has failed to keep us decent, and then he failed to allow us to…well, he failed us."

He retrieved the drawings from the floor and handed them to her.

She hesitated for a moment, hoping he would say something more.

He stared back in silence.

She took the rolled parchment, nodded mutely, and forced herself to put one shaky foot in front of the other. She walked unsteadily to the door.

I need more time, she thought, looking up and down the hallway.

Everything she wished to take slowly was glossed over: discovering Falcondale, gaining some trust with the marchioness, *not* lying to Jocelyn.

And everything she wanted to hurry along—the construction on her house—was taking forever.

Time. It was the one thing she could not buy.

"Piety, wait," called Falcondale from somewhere behind her.

"I'm going," she said, and she moved at a pace just shy of a sprint down the hall, down the main stairs, down to the kitchen. When she reached the back door, she tossed the drawings on the counter beside her gloves and snatched her cloak off the peg.

"Piety?" Falcondale came down the kitchen stairs. She turned away.

"You're cross," he said. "I've ruined your hair."

She raised an idle hand to her hair, pulling at the pins, releasing the scrambled knot down her back.

"This was Joseph's fault." His eyes were on her hands in her hair. "If he had not left us, then I would not have reached for you."

"You are astute at assigning blame," she said.

"Oh, I can assign blame. You want me to say the words? Fine, I'll say it: it's my fault. Look, Piety—*Miss Grey*—there is no denying that I am attracted to you."

"You know that you may call me Piety."

"I may call you 'Miss Grey,' as I should have done in every instance."

"Fine. I am Miss Grey."

"I don't think I have to tell you that you are a beautiful woman."

"Oh, no, please, may you never tell me that."

"You have a captivating smile and a body that would tempt any man. And I'm not able to resist you. It's a weakness—my response to you."

"You're not weak, my lord," she said, walking to the door. "You are lonely."

"You would see it that way. Wait," he called, and he reached for the knob at the same moment, covering her hand with his own. "We cannot carry on like this."

She did not remove her hand. She drew a breath and turned her face to him. His lips were mere inches from her own, and she heard him swear before he dipped down to kiss her again.

Here was the soft kiss they hadn't time for before. Slow. Lips closed. Nibbling and teasing. In seconds, it grew deeper, and she fell back against the door. He closed in over her and grabbed her up. For a long moment, she kissed him back. The tentative shyness from their previous embraces replaced by intuitive rhythm and an achingly familiar sort of possession. They belonged to each other. They suited. Together, they were better. *This* would good. *They would be so good.*

When his mouth left her lips to trail kisses down her neck, she turned her head and burrowed into his shoulder. She smelled the cotton of his shirt and his skin beneath. She nuzzled her cheek against his neck, reveling in the roughness of the stubble on his jaw. She pulled him closer, fusing them, but she ceased the kisses. She simply held him.

It took a moment for him to catch up, to stop kissing and hold her in return; but oh, when he did—the embrace was like coming home.

When had she last been held like this? When had she *ever* been held like this?

He lifted his head from her hair. "Marissa is in your back garden." His voice was hoarse.

"What? How do you know?"

"I can see her out the window."

Piety nodded and began to pull away. "They have returned. I must go."

"She's in your garden with my manservant."

"With Joseph? You're joking. Really?" Piety shoved off the door and turned around, trying to peek out the portal window. "Lift me up," she said. "I want to see."

"Piety, you test the limits of my self-control," he said.

"Oh, you don't even like me," she said. "Come on. Let's have a look."

"Right. I don't even like you," he repeated. Then he wrapped his hands around her waist and lifted her until she had a clear view. She tried not to focus on the ease with which he held her aloft, or his hard body, warm against her back. He kept his head turned away from her neck, though she could hear him breathing.

"I should go," she said, kicking a little. "If Marissa is back, so is Miss Breedlowe."

"I'll come with you."

"With me to my house? Oh, no. This is my subterfuge, not yours. Isn't that your battle cry? Let each take care of his own?"

"If your chaperone decides I've compromised you, which God knows I have, then it does concern me—intimately so. Let us go and explain it away together. And then let us put a stop to this. Once and for all." He took her shoulders gently and turned her to face him. For a moment, she thought he would kiss her again, and she held her breath.

"Piety," he said gravely, "I am resigned to never marry."

"What?" Piety nearly shouted, jumping back a step. "Who has begun to discuss *marriage*? I am not looking to marry, my lord. Indeed, I fled New York to *avoid* marriage."

"Proper neighbors do not carry on as you and I have done, Piety. Don't be coy. This can lead to one of two arrangements. I assume you are opposed to an affair."

She stared at him. "You assume correctly,"

"The other option is marriage." He shrugged. "And so allow me to repeat, I am resigned to never marry. Not now. Not in five years. Not when I'm old and facing a bitter, painful death entirely alone, cared for by strangers, and without an heir to this earldom."

"Well, all right. Good for you." She snatched up her gloves. Marriage? When had she insinuated even the slightest notion of *marriage*? Frustration replaced the languid pleasure slogging through her veins.

She could not look at him, but he droned on behind her, "Marriage would require, among other things, for me to fall in love—or at least to fall into some sort of happy rapport. Knowing what you know of my sour rapport with nearly everyone, particularly you, this comes as no great shock, I'm sure."

"Shocked is only a fraction of what I am feeling right now," she said.

"As I'm sure you know, there is more than one way to the altar." He raised his eyebrows. "Happens all the time. Marriage *without* the happy rapport. A reckless chap, forced by scandal, into an unwilling union. This, too, mind you, will never happen. *Not* to me. I'd like to avoid scandal if I can, but if scandal finds me, please be sure that I will laugh in the face of the gossipmongers and go about my merry way without ever looking back."

Piety nodded and hugged her cloak tightly around her. "I understand," she said solemnly, smoothing her hair. "You feel prematurely trapped into a phantom betrothal, which has been masterminded by me. Every unspeakable thing that has happened between us has been my fault or Joseph's. And I must cease pressing my shackle-minded devices onto your blameless—"

"On the contrary," he interrupted. "You are an unexpected weakness for whom I was wholly unprepared. It is me. I am the problem. And I am vowing to you that I will stay away. Beginning now."

Outwardly, Piety showed no reaction. She nodded and ran two fingers over her brow. She reached for the doorknob. Inside, however, she felt very still. And heavy. Like a stone had settled into the pit of her stomach, and it was sinking her to the bottom of a deep, dark pond.

She stared into the planks on the door, willing herself to be pragmatic, to keep her eye on the ultimate goal, which was finishing the house and staving off her mother. Never had it been the plan to become involved with a sad, difficult neighbor with strong arms and a confounding loneliness.

"Can you endeavor to do the same?" he asked quietly. "Let us stay out of our libraries and music rooms and lives."

"Yes, yes," she said, working to sound as if she did not care. In truth, she cared too much. She could see that now. He outlined his wholesale rejection of her so neatly, and then he not-so-neatly implied that she had scheming designs on his bachelorhood. She endured betrayal and blame at the same time.

"Oh, wait," he called. "Don't forget these." He held out the new drawings.

She chuckled miserably. "Oh yes. These. How could I forget? I seem determined to sabotage my own project, don't I? Now who's to blame?" She turned to go, but then she stopped. "But what if we have questions? What if I need more advice?"

"Then you may apply to a hired architect, as I have repeatedly said."

"Impossible. I've tried everyone in town and been turned away."

"Try again. Offer more coin."

She blew out an exasperated breath. "Or, I could simply hire you." Perhaps he could not withstand their mutual attraction, but she would be happy to demonstrate detached ambivalence if the situation called for it, and if it also got her the new stairs at the same bloody time.

"Piety," he began.

She held up a hand to stop him. Frustration surged. "Right." She forced her voice to sound light. "Very well. Thank you for this beginning, I suppose. And for the chess."

"Let us hope that my design is better than my chess."

Then Piety had a thought. Not a prudent thought. Not a sensible thought. Not a thought that did anything to extricate herself from the already painful and awkward situation. But it was an arresting, irresistible thought, just the same. A thought that just might speed along the construction of her stairs.

And it would mean...

Well, perhaps it would mean that their final farewell needn't be so bitter. It would mean they could ease out of this entanglement, rather than snap in two like the breaking of a bone.

"What would you say," she asked, clearing her throat, "if I knew a way to test your design work against your chess?"

He narrowed his eyes.

"Is there any way," she continued, "that you would consider a wager?"

"No."

"Hear me out."

"No."

"A friendly wager. A game of chess between you and me."

He moaned. "Did you not hear me, Miss Grey? I cannot be alone with you again."

"Not a private game. Something more sporting and gay. With my chaperone, Miss Breedlowe, in attendance. And Joseph. Anyone who wishes to come. At teatime perhaps. Whenever it's convenient, really."

"And what, might I ask, am I meant to wager?"

"What do you think? The further advisement and consultation on building my stairs. If I win," she continued, "then I will cease my frustrating struggle to hire someone elsewhere town—and instead *you* will oversee it. *You* will be my architect. And if you win, then I will *leave you alone.*"

"You will leave me alone regardless," he said harshly. "You cannot tell me that I haven't shocked you with my behavior—warned you, in more ways than one, of the result if you do not stay away."

"You flatter yourself, my lord." She managed to eke out the words. "I am not shocked, I am *inspired*. To defeat you in chess will mean seeing my renovations advance at a much faster pace. By the time my mother arrives, the sweeping stairwell will be through."

He laughed. "How confident you are. *When* you defeat me?"

She smiled and gave a shrug, already feeling better.

"Fine, Miss Grey," he said, whipping the door open wide. "I accept your wager. Just know my terms. When *I* win, there will be no more talk of the stairs or the passage, of me helping you or giving you my advice. You and I will be finished entirely. We will not write, we will not call, we will be separate at all times."

"Separate," she repeated, breezing out the door.

"And Miss Breedlowe must always be present."

"Miss Breedlowe will be thrilled to hear it." She smiled without looking back. "Good evening, my lord. I will be in touch about the game."

"Of this I have no doubt."

CHAPTER FOURTEEN

The first chess match ended in a draw.

They played for two afternoons, their gaming mood alternating between tense concentration and jovial ribbing, while their assembled audience took tea and watched.

On the first day, only Joseph, Marissa, and Miss Breedlowe convened. Because it was teatime, they brought a basket from the market, a kettle of tea, and a clattering stack of cups. Because it was Falcondale, he offered only his drafty drawing room, one chessboard, two stools, and a rickety side chair next to a dark grate, presumably for Miss Breedlowe. He remained silent while Piety buzzed through the house, scavenging proper chairs from other rooms, and Joseph laid a fire.

The following day, Lady Frinfrock, trailed by Tiny, rapped on his door and demanded to know what in God's name was going on. A carpenter, the marchioness said, had answered their daily call to survey the progress in Piety's house and informed them that the ladies could be found next door, playing chess. Curiosity and suspicion rerouted them to Falcondale's stoop, where the marchioness invited herself inside and took Joseph's seat beside Falcondale.

Prudently, no one explained the real stakes of the game to the marchioness, allowing the verbal banter and biting rivalry to suggest that victory for the winner would be a prize in and of itself.

For her first day in attendance, the marchioness cautiously nibbled the produce from the market and accepted a cup of tepid tea. But by the next day, she directed her staff to convey several tiered trays of cake, pastry, and sandwiches and a shiny silver tea trolley across the street. They set up in Falcondale's drawing room, and Piety poured for everyone, chatting easily about how civilized it all was and how lucky she had been to fall in with neighbors as pleasant as those of Henrietta Place.

They played for exactly one hour each afternoon while the spectators watched, whispering among themselves about the alacrity of play. Because Piety was careful not remain longer than an hour, the rematch dragged on for the better part of a week. When five o'clock struck each day, she would ask everyone to note the location of pieces on the board to vouch for the next day's commencement. After that, while Falcondale glared in silence, Piety would push back from the board, smile sweetly, and thank the earl for hosting. Invariably, he would scowl back, studying her, his eyes half-lidded and heavy with something she could not name.

Piety would be lying if she said she did not enjoy it. Lady Frinfrock was disagreeable and rude, but the earl had no qualms about laughing at her outrageousness, and she didn't seem to mind. Tiny was there every day, and it was gratifying to see her treated so well, like an honored guest for the first time in her life. And Miss Breedlowe was happy, because she felt as if she were doing her job. Even Lady Frinfrock ventured a handful of half-compliments about how the two of them were getting on.

And Falcondale...

Falcondale was like a daily indulgence that she allowed herself, if only in small doses. Although he was everything an indulgence was not—not charming, not flattering, not sweet, not gallant or even chatty. But when he did speak, he was bitingly funny, his chess playing was top notch, and he listened intently to everything she said. He pretended to ignore the idle chatter among the ladies and focus on the board, but she could see him cock his head, sometimes asking questions about life in New York, the slave trade in America, or what it was like to traverse the Atlantic on a ship.

And he watched her.

She took care with her appearance every day, but for the chess, she spent extra time. It was impossible to hide the effort from Jocelyn, so she asked for her help. And when Piety swept into his drawing room each afternoon in a favorite dress and her cheeks freshly pinched, his narrow-eyed reaction caused her stomach to flip.

Yet, she reminded herself that all of it—the attentiveness, however gruff; the watchfulness, however covert—meant nothing. She knew when the games finally came to a fair end, there would be no further reason for them to pass the time together. Counsel about the stairwell or no, she knew he had meant what he said when he'd asked her to retreat from his life forever.

But in the meantime, two of their games had ended a draw, and the third game had stretched over two afternoons, with the possibility of a fourth. And the house was coming along nicely, slowly but nicely. She and Jocelyn had begun to interview applicants for a real housekeeping staff. Even Lady Frinfrock had stray compliments for her progress. She had allowed herself to think that she might actually pull the whole thing off, that she might successfully move herself and her fortune to London, set up house, and live out her days safely and happily with new friends and a fresh start, free from her mother and the possibility of an oppressive marriage.

And then Eddie Limpett turned up.

He arrived at the end of the second week of chess—a Friday, rainy and gray. To say his arrival took everyone by surprise was like saying that her new home was *dusty*. She had never expected any of them to find her so soon, and Piety had but five-minute's advance warning to compose herself and prepare her defenses. Even those frantic moments were a stroke of unexpected luck—owed entirely to Mr. Spencer Burr, who interrupted their afternoon chess with a pounding on Falcondale's garden door.

"It's the garden door, Joseph," Falcondale said, staring at the chessboard. "Send them away."

"The boy will be run ragged, Falcondale," scolded Lady Frinfrock, watching Joseph jog from the room. "I cannot believe you've sacked the previous earl's entire staff and laid the work of fifteen servants at the feet of one boy. Is he to be butler, valet, footman, cook, and serving boy all in one? It's unchristian, Falcondale. Positively abusive."

"You've forgotten groom." The earl muttered the words under his breath. "He also is my groom. Ah, but here he is. It's a wonder he can still stand. Who was it, Joe, and what did they want?"

"Not what," he began, stammering a little, "*who.*"

There was a heavy silence, and the boy looked at Piety.

She froze. *Oh, God, no.* An icicle of dread dripped down her spine.

"It was the carpenter Mr. Burr. He came through the back gate. He says Miss Grey has a guest."

No. Not yet. Please.

"There's a man at her front door now," Joseph continued. "Mr. Burr said Miss Grey might wish to know before she receives him. Time to plan and all that."

Lady Frinfrock snorted. "Plan? Plan for what? My God, who is it, President Madison?"

"Name's *Limpett*," Joseph recited. "Mr. Edward Limpett. Claims to be one of Miss Grey's stepbrothers."

Of all of them, Piety thought, *at least it's Eddie.*

Piety floated up from her chair, her eyes not leaving Jocelyn's face. "He's sure?" Piety asked. "Mr. Burr is certain? It is Edward Limpett?"

"Oh, yes, Miss Grey," said the boy. "Mr. Burr said the gentleman is demanding to see you right away."

"*Oh, no,*" Piety said, shaking her head. Skirting the table, she spoke in a rush. "Tell Mr. Burr to *not* admit him. Above all. Not one foot inside the house. He must not see the condition. Tell him I'll come out. No." She snapped her fingers in frustration. "It's raining. Tell him…Well, I…I cannot say. I never expected to see them so soon." She looked frantically around the room, thinking. "Tell him…tell him…"

"*Tell him,*" intoned the marchioness, rising, "that you are taking tea as the guest of your neighbor, and that if he wishes to see you, he may call upon you here. Clearly, you are not at home to receive him. If what you say is true about these men, there is absolutely no need to jump simply because one of them turns up and croaks the word *toad*. Go, Joseph, tell the carpenter to convey this message and come right back."

They watched the boy dart out.

"Bring him here?" repeated Piety. "I couldn't possibly impose on the earl. And his house doesn't look much better than mine."

"It bloody well does," Falcondale said. Piety had been avoiding his gaze since the interruption, but now she hazarded a glance. He looked bored, she thought, and she let out a breath. At least he wasn't incensed. Or frantic, like she had become. At least he wasn't tossing them all out.

"Your house is a disgrace, and you know it," said the marchioness. "But we can hardly trail across the street in the rain to my parlor without looking ridiculous."

Joseph ran back into the room. "He's telling him."

"Good," the marchioness retorted. "Now, go out the back door, run through the alley, and cross at the end of the block to reach my house. Tell my footman Bernard to apprehend Miss Grey's guest in the street and escort the man to Falcondale's door. Instruct Bernard to walk him to the stoop and show him inside." She scowled at the earl. "Considering there is no butler, we shall leave the door ajar and allow them to breeze through without ceremony. Bernard is a professional, and he will behave as if it is nothing out of the ordinary. Go, now! Tell him exactly as I've said."

"Yes, my lady," said Joseph, darting out.

With wide, worried eyes, Piety watched him go. She looked at Jocelyn, not knowing what else to do. Her friend nodded, trying to reassure her.

She looked at Tiny.

"You better eat something," Tiny said. "It'll make things worse if you pass out."

"No, no, I couldn't possibly." She began to pace.

"No pacing, Miss Grey, if you *please*," implored Lady Frinfrock. "Compose yourself. Whatever the man has to say will be made no better by a rattled demeanor. Pray, do not let your anxiousness show. Better yet, rid yourself of anxiety altogether." She looked toward the earl. "Falcondale, your uncle typically convened formal guests in a small receiving room to the left of the front hall. Have you emptied it as well?"

"We sold everything," he said.

"Typical rash shortsightedness." She tsked and then she addressed the room. "Everyone! Take a chair and let us convey this pitiful smattering of furnishing to the receiving room. It is smaller and will look more fully appointed if we greet him there. Marissa, you return for the tea service. And perk up! This is a call from a bothersome relative; it is not an inquisition. He is the interloper here, not us."

Paralyzed with uncertainty, everyone stared.

"*Move!*" She glared at them all. They scurried to do her bidding.

The plan made sense in theory, Piety thought, dashing to the chessboard, grabbing up the pieces. She did not look at Falcondale across the board, although she could feel him watching her. He pushed out of his chair.

"I hope you'll remember where those go," he said. "I had nearly beaten you."

She stopped and looked up at him. "I'm so sorry, my lord," she whispered. "Truly."

His expression remained placid, even sleepy. He grabbed the fireplace poker and propped it on his shoulder.

She smiled weakly. "I never meant to involve you in this."

"That makes two of us." He scooped up four fresh logs stacked beside the fire and nodded to the door behind them. "Tell us, what can we expect from Mr. Edward Limpett, Stocking Heir? Besides scrutiny of my woefully insufficient receiving room. Will he bind you at the hands and feet and haul you away in a wheelbarrow?"

She chuckled. "Not this one. He is the little one."

The marchioness began barking orders again, and they each fell into place by her command. By the time Joseph popped through the door, scrambling to find them in a different room, they were seated serenely around a new fire, the marchioness lecturing them about calm reserve and the burden of explanation being on the guest, not the host.

"They are coming," the boy said gasping for breath. "I have opened the door."

"Pathetic protocol," mumbled the marchioness. "But he is American, perhaps he will not realize. You do the best with what you have." She looked at Piety. "Miss Grey, I trust you have reclaimed your composure and your confidence. You may do the honors. Falcondale, I'm convinced, would not know how to greet a guest in his own home if his life depended on it."

"I am prisoner of this ordeal," he said, resuming his slouch in the chair behind the chessboard. "Above all, I hope that can be acknowledged. Anything I do beyond tossing the lot of you out on your ears—the *Limpett brother first*—is more than should be expected of me."

"Do not speak too soon," Lady Frinfrock said, adjusting her skirts. "You may just have to do it. Ah, but here they are."

From the direction of the front hall, they heard a distinctive shuffling—Eddie traveled nowhere without copious effort—and Piety squinted her eyes shut, drawing three quick, shaky breaths.

Composed, she thought. *Just as the marchioness instructed. Confident.*

Beneath the table, she felt a rustling, and she looked down. It was Falcondale, tapping her skirt with his boot. Her gaze flew to his face, and she saw him roll his eyes. *I don't care about this*, he seemed to say, *and neither should you.*

She smiled, feeling calmer. The pressure on her leg was warm and steadying. She relaxed, just an iota. Just enough.

Behind them, the marchioness's servant, Bernard, stepped into room.

"Mr. Edward Limpett," the footman intoned, "of New York City. Here to see Miss Grey."

Just as the marchioness had commanded, Bernard's introduction sounded both imposing and proper, as if it were perfectly natural to show a strange man into a strange house from the rainy sidewalk. Piety drew a deep breath and smiled brilliantly. "Thank you, Bernard," she said. "Eddie. What a surprise."

The top of Eddie Limpett's balding head barely reached Piety's ear, and all of his other features followed suit: stumpy legs, short arms, and tiny hands. For whatever reason, likely wishful thinking, his clothes were cut for a larger man, and the resulting poor fit made him look like a marionette dressed in a puppet's slouchy suit. His demeanor, typically some mix of sour and suspicious, was invariably made worse by the fact that he always seemed to have too much to carry.

In spite of this, not to mention the dozen other unpalatable qualities he shared with his four brothers, Piety considered him to the most harmless of the Limpetts, primarily because he was so clearly not interested in her, at least not in a romantic sense. Who or what interested Eddie, she couldn't guess, but he had made it very clear that the sight of her held absolutely no appeal. In her darkest moments, when Piety imagined herself unable to escape her mother's plan, she resigned to marry Eddie. Out of all of them, he would be the least likely to make intimate demands on her.

He plodded into the room and squinted, searching every face before settling on Piety.

"The surprise is mine," he finally said, looking at her from head to toe, "considering I discovered a tradesman answering the door of that house your father's lawyers have told us you now own. His English was so garbled I could barely make out what he said. Sent me on a merry chase." He gave his bulky rain-soaked satchel a shake. "He claimed to be in charge of the *work?*" He gave Piety a suspicious look. "I dare not ask what you've done, Piety. I dare not ask." He began wrestling with his half-collapsed umbrella as it dripped down his leg.

"May Bernard take your things?" Piety asked, wincing at his wet, awkward struggle. "I'm still in the process of hiring a staff, but the carpenters are frequently at the front door to receive deliveries."

"Hiring a staff?" he repeated, untangling himself from the satchel strap. "Tiny is sitting right there, for God's sake. You would not believe the beastly service I've been shown since sailing from New York. Can't even get a decent glass of sherry at dinner. Tiny, I'll have whatever is hot. Coffee, I hope? Lots of sugar, no cream. Oh, but if it's gone cold, don't bother until you brew a fresh pot."

"Tiny is on holiday," said Piety, taking up a cup and saucer from the tea trolley. "The journey across the Atlantic was difficult for her, and she is not working as staff at the moment. But I will be happy to pour you a cup of tea. You'll find the coffee you're accustomed to in New York is positively bitter compared to English tea."

"Servants do not take holidays." He grinned at the room. "*Tiny* will be happy to fetch it. How often has your mother told you not to lower yourself to do the work of the maid? It breeds laziness."

"Eddie, please." Piety shoved a cup of tea at him. "If you'd like refreshment, help yourself, but no one is impressed by your rhetoric about staff."

"Help myself, you say?" Eddie said under his breath, leaning over the tea trolley. "Look who is behaving like mistress of the manor. I was led to believe this was not even your house." He took up a plate and began delicately piling it with food. "I swear, Piety, when we finally got your father's lawyer to tell us where you had run off to, our imaginations went wild. He assured us you'd bought a house—ha! As if this was a desirable thing! We could only guess what sort of *accommodation* you'd take a shine to in London, England." He chuckled.

"It's a house, as you saw. Very much like this, actually, only I'm having a few repairs made before I'm ready to receive guests. I wish you would have written that you were coming. Is Mother with you?

"I sailed first," he said, chewing. "Your mother needed time to pack. She was set to sail a week or so after me with the others. Eli and Ennis, you won't be shocked to know, are particularly angry that they've been made to come all of this way."

"A week or so?" she parroted his words, watching him look around for a place to sit. Unable to locate a free chair, he remained standing in the center of the room.

"They are due in England in seven days?"

"Or so." He grinned a rat's grin, happy in the cheese tray.

"I...I wish I had known of your timing. The lawyer sent no word."

"Oh, his legal practice has come to an untimely end, I'm afraid."

Her head shot up. "Mr. Merek was one of Papa's oldest friends, Edward. What did you do?"

"No," said Eddie loudly, spitting cake. "What did you do? An unmarried young woman may not relocate herself to another country and buy up a house; I don't care how rich her father was or who his friends may be."

Piety felt the blood drain from her face, but she remembered the marchioness's warning. Composure. Confidence. It was Eddie who looked foolish. She would not be bated by his theatrics. "It's regretful that I didn't know about your journey," she said calmly. "The house, as I've said, isn't ready to comfortably host guests."

"Oh, Piety, spare me the carrying on, as if you are cock of the walk." Eddie laughed. "The house will be easier to sell if you haven't rebuilt it to your own foolish, impractical specifications." He took a big bite of pastry, losing a dollop of jam filling to the rug, and then looked around the room. The assembled group stared at him mutely, open incredulity clear on their faces. He took another bite and stared back.

CHAPTER FIFTEEN

Trevor didn't know whether he wanted to laugh or hit something.

No. That wasn't true. He knew exactly what he wanted to do, but prudence demanded he remain silently in his chair, that he slouch lazily, exude boredom, and affect an air of superiority.

It was not without effort.

The superiority came naturally, perhaps, but his typical practiced detachment grew more elusive with each criticism this buffoon cast upon Piety like a long-suffering life tutor.

Piety said, "These, Edward, are my neighbors. Not that it concerns you, but I have been received most generously by the residents of this street, Henrietta Place. Her ladyship, the Marchioness Frinfrock." She gestured to the marchioness.

Limpett nodded his head. "Your majesty," he said with his mouth full.

The marchioness scowled at him, her eyes narrow slits.

Trevor hadn't expected the man's animosity toward Piety to be quite so palpable. He hadn't expected him to be so abjectly rude. He was swollen with misplaced arrogance and, from the looks of it, with cake. Piety had said they were awful, but when had she ever spoken of anyone or anything without hyperbole? Colorful exuberance was part of her script.

He had expected them to be undesirable matches, but he never expected them to be, well, *unthinkable*.

The truth was, he'd never expected to come face to face with any of the so-called Limpett brothers at all.

"Lord Trevor Rheese, Earl of Falcondale," Piety continued, backing up to indicate Trevor. "He is the host of our afternoon tea. This is his home."

Trevor felt absolutely no obligation to stand, so he did not. He nodded—curtly—and made a show of studying the little man. Under his scrutiny, Limpett had the decency to slow down his chewing and nod in return.

Trevor looked at Piety, who cringed as she watched her stepbrother endeavor to balance his plate and cup while he ate. Her smile, which had dazzled him almost to stupefaction all week, was gone now; her brow was creased with lines, and Trevor's disgust at Limpett burned into something stonier. She wasn't quaking in fear exactly, but her spirit had been dampened. She was anxious and shaky. He'd never seen her like this—not when she was recovering from his near tackle, not when surrounded by burly carpenters, or stroking the pride of their bully of a neighboring marchioness.

Yet, here she was, blushed and blotchy, jittery and distracted because of Edward Limpett?

"And finally, my chaperone, Miss Jocelyn Breedlowe," continued Piety.

"How do you do?" said Miss Breedlowe.

"Chaperone?" Limpett asked, his paw frozen over his plate. "Since when do you require chaperoning?"

"I am an unattached lady of marriageable age, Eddie. It's not an outrageous notion."

"But you are betrothed."

"I am not betrothed."

"You're nearly betrothed."

"To whom? To whom am I nearly betrothed?"

"To me or one of the others."

"How can one be nearly engaged to five different men? It's ridiculous, and you know it. I am not betrothed, so please do not repeat it. I've introduced you to a room full of people, Edward," Piety continued, "can you not, at the very least, say hello or acknowledge that you are a guest in a nobleman's home?"

"Which one goes with the house?"

Which one, my arse. Trevor stood.

"The house is mine," he said flatly. "The cake you're eating, the china on which you're eating it, the rug onto which you're dripping—all mine."

It wasn't entirely true, but he was making a bloody point.

"As host, it is only fair that I inform you that you're about thirty seconds and a mouthful of cake from taking your leave, Mr. Limpett. Kindly state your business with Miss Grey and be on your way. We were previously occupied before you turned up."

The little man had the decency to shuffle back a few steps. "This is English hospitality?" He looked at Piety. "I was told to expect this."

"Inhospitable, are they?" challenged Piety, snatching his plate. "I've made introductions, while you've done little more than issue orders and eat. You are a guest in this country, and in this house, and if you cannot be counted upon for manners exceeding this, I will surpass Lord Falcondale's request and toss you out myself."

"Fine. Allow me to resign to your *property*—whatever it is."

"No," she answered, her patience straining, "as I've said, my house is not yet ready to receive guests. Besides, a bachelor dare not visit me at home without making arrangements in advance. My chaperone would never allow it."

"Oh, please, Piety, we are family. I am your stepbrother."

"You've only just suggested that we were betrothed!"

"Another reason to admit me!"

"The lady has said no, Limpett," said Trevor. He moved to Piety's side, crossing his arms over his chest.

"I see," said Eddie, looking around. "Perhaps you could recommend a suite of rooms for hire. Or a coaching inn."

"I am afraid I cannot," Piety said. "You're a grown man. You've sailed halfway around the world, surely you are self-sufficient enough to locate a place to lodge."

"Perhaps you can put on a brave face and address me in your papa's-princess voice, but you know better than to take that tone with your mother." Limpett nodded, agreeing with himself. "Or with Eli. Or Ennis. It goes without saying, but mind you don't forget. Am I right, Tiny?" He turned to the maid. "Am I right?"

Piety sighed. "I'd not look for conspirators here, Eddie. And you may tell your family, when they arrive, that I will not, I'm afraid, be able to offer any of them lodging in my new home for quite some time. Not until the repairs are complete. So, if they are, indeed, traveling to England, due to arrive here in the near future, then they, too, shall need to find suitable lodging elsewhere."

"We'll see about that," he said, taking up his satchel. "At least I've located you. You're alive, and as insolent as ever."

"Yes," she replied, "I am still alive. I do hope that everyone from New York realizes that, should some unexpected *accident* befall me, the fortune goes entirely to my mother. Tell me that you and your brothers comprehend this fact. She will not share a penny if she is willed my money outright. Not a penny. You're only being included because she believes she needs you."

"And you're only flitting around the drawing room of a strange Englishman's house, showing off your *endowments* in your expensive frocks and fripperies because she has not yet found you and brought you to heel." He looked her up and down.

"That is enough, sir," Trevor said icily, shouldering around her to stand between them. "Allow me show you to the door."

"Don't trouble yourself. I knew to expect nothing but insolence and rudeness from Piety. I'm not surprised it extends to her so-called new friends. But take heart!" He waggled his finger at her. "Your mother will not be as easily tossed aside. Do not entertain the notion that she'll accept anything less than the best room in that rattletrap excuse for a house you've bought." He scowled at the tea trolley. "And far better refreshments." He scuttled over to Bernard to collect his sagging umbrella and wilted hat.

"Good day to you," he said to the room. "How decent you have all been to take in our Piety. She is a handful, I know. But not to worry, we'll be taking her back to New York, where she belongs, soon enough."

And then he shuffled out, dragging his umbrella behind him.

Silence filled the room, swallowing Eddie Limpett's departing footsteps.

They never heard the front door close; he must have limped outside without making the bother. In the street, the rain had slowed, softening the patter on the window to a barely perceptible tap. The only remaining sounds were the clock ticking in the next room and the marchioness's sawed breathing.

The earl backed up a step and looked around. The women watched him expectantly, but he said nothing. Joseph loped to the front door and could be heard pushing it shut. Bernard produced a whisk broom from his belt and began to sweep the man's tiny boot prints from the rug. In vacant silence, they watched him work.

Joseph returned from the door and crossed to the window, yanking the drapes together. "He's walking back and forth on the sidewalk," he said.

Piety floated to her chair and collapsed.

Finally, Jocelyn asked, "Does he always behave like this? Are they *all* like this?"

Tiny cleared her throat. "Always like this and worse, if you can believe it," she said. "Mr. Eddie is the stupid one. Rude and stupid. The others are smarter and meaner."

"Tiny, it's all right." Piety sighed and stole a look at Falcondale. He hadn't moved from the middle of the room, and now he eyed the door. He wanted out, and she couldn't blame him.

"I take it chess is finished for the day?" he said, not looking at her.

Piety stared at her knees. "This has been a horrible intrusion. Please accept my apology."

The marchioness scoffed. "He feels no intrusion, he feels ashamed. Difficult to play lord of the manor when half the manor has gone to the auction block. *Your china*, indeed!"

"Wrong on both accounts. I'm neither intruded upon nor ashamed. The exchange with Limpett is not your fault, Miss Grey. It is obvious that it was unavoidable. If anyone should apologize, let it be me. As her ladyship has, with great frequency, pointed out, I aspire to little more than ungraciousness of spirit and meagerness of home and hearth. I think we can all agree that my involvement in today's exchange only made things worse."

"See? You *are* ashamed," the marchioness said.

"The only player in today's drama to whom I would attach the word *shame* is Edward Limpett," he said. "What I feel is…" He looked around.

Oh, God, thought Piety. *Just say it.*

Disgust. Revulsion.

Pity.

Tears filled her eyes, and she turned away. Her own loss of composure was the one thing, perhaps, but that could make this day worse. She was not a damsel in distress in need of rescue. And he was certainly no knight in shining armor. To pretend otherwise would make a mockery of her and an ass of him.

Falcondale strode to the drapes and yanked them open.

"He's gone," he said, changing the topic. "You won't be bothered if you remain here the rest of the afternoon to avoid him. Stay as long as you like. Finish your refreshment. You'll have to excuse me, however. I have an engagement."

"Coward!" The marchioness wiggled from her chair. "Before he arrived, you went on and on about memorizing the chessboard in order to resume play!"

"Never let it be said that you suffer from poor hearing, my lady," he said. "You'll have to forgive me. I can no longer be detained."

He strode to the door but then paused, staring at the jamb. "Miss Grey?" he called. "I concede the game. You win. You may collect the spoils of your victory as you see fit. Arrange it with Joseph when you are ready."

Concede the game?

Piety stood. "It's not as bad as all that," she said.

"To me," he said, "it appeared very bad, indeed. I am disinclined to become involved, as you well know. But, in the very least, I can concede the wager."

She opened her mouth to thank him, but he was gone—whipping out the door without a backward glance. Joseph trotted glumly behind him.

"Well!" The marchioness scowled at the empty door. "He is as useless a champion as ever there was. Everything will obviously fall to me, and it's just as well, I suppose, considering who and what we face."

Still dazed by Falcondale's concession, Piety looked at the marchioness. "I beg your pardon, my lady? What shall fall to you?"

The marchioness did not answer. She issued orders to the room. "Bernard! Have Mrs. McGee send word to the staff at Garnettgate immediately. Prepare the house and kitchens and take on extra help. Expect our imminent arrival by next Friday at the latest. Myself and three guests, our personal attendants, and with a group of six or more arriving shortly after. Everything is to be to my exact specifications for a *royal* visit, Bernard. Be very clear. I will follow up with Mrs. McGee in the afternoon. But she must send a rider immediately, so tell her now. Go.

"Miss Breedlowe," she said next. "Your role is now doubly important. Miss Grey and you shall accompany me to the dressmakers first thing in the morning. That beige relic of yours is hardly the color of unspoken superiority.

"And Miss Grey?" she said finally turning to Piety. "Head up! This is no time to lose heart. You marched into my library and looked me in the eye without a moment's hesitation. Do not insult me by cowering before this peasant, with boorish manners and misplaced arrogance and a brain the size of an apple seed. Your new home is not yet ready. So be it. You and Miss Breedlowe will travel with Tiny and myself to my country estate, Garnettgate. In Berkshire. Splendid property. Beautiful this time of year.

"When the *Americans* arrive, instruct your bear of a carpenter to refuse them entrance at all costs, and inform them that, if they wish to see you, they may call as my guests to Garnettgate. Let them see how far poor manners and ingrate breeding will get them in a proper English manor."

Piety gasped, disbelieving. "Guests at your estate? But, my lady."

"You have little choice, Miss Grey, and you know it. It's all settled. Let them bully you in my presence. I'd like to see them try."

CHAPTER SIXTEEN

Trevor received Piety's final summons the day before she left for Berkshire. It was another note, passed through Joseph, and the mere sight of it—a telltale pink envelope clutched in the boy's sweaty palm—set his traitorous heart on an unsteadying, triple-time pace. With an unsteady hand, he ripped open the letter.

My Lord Falcondale,

By now, you may have heard that the marchioness, in a gesture of untold generosity, has invited me to be her guest at Garnettgate, her Berkshire estate.

Once relocated, I may more comfortably wait out the worst of my home repairs and enjoy a more suitable venue to receive my mother and her party. For better or worse, Lady Frinfrock has promised an enviable family reunion, with all the pomp and circumstance necessary to impress.

But I digress. Although we have not spoken, I have seen you in and around the stairwell working with Mr. Burr. I shall never be able to thank you enough for this loan of time and expertise. They tell me you are the finest architect with whom they have ever worked.

I hope you have time to continue to guide them while I am away. I have taken your participation for granted, I'm afraid and have been lazy about securing another architect to take over when you can no longer advise. If you find yourself unable to finish the job, would you recommend a local architect who might take over? Perhaps if the task of hiring this person comes from you, we should not have quite so much trouble.

I depart for Berkshire tomorrow, a happy detail for you, I'm sure. Before I go, I should like to know your most current predictions for the house, for my budget—including some compensation for you—and whether or not you will be able to see the job through before you set sail. In keeping with your request that—above all—we no longer speak, I look forward to a response by your hand or word from Joseph.

Sincerely yours,
Piety Grey

P.S. I should add here that I plan to be in my solarium at three o'clock this afternoon in order to make some notes for the workmen. If it suits your schedule (and if you can possibly bear it), perhaps we could meet in person to pin down these remaining details in a less formal and more expeditious manner. Only, mind you, if you prefer. —P.G.

Trevor raced through the letter, loosening his suffocating cravat while he read. When he'd finished, he crumpled the letter into a wad and tossed it on his desk. He yanked off his cravat.

He'd suspected for days that such a missive would come; he simply had not known when. For all the anticipation it caused, not to mention the heart-pounding, mouth-drying anxiety he'd experienced when he finally received the bloody thing, he half expected it to incinerate on his blotter while he stared at it.

But, no. It simply sat there, as the laws of nature and sanity demanded, giving off a potently familiar aroma, all but glowing pink.

Sighing, he snatched it back up and flattened it, re-reading every line, lingering on the, *I look forward to a response by your hand*…

Ah yes, he thought. *Let us write back and forth like devoted cousins, separated by miles but not memories.*

No, no, and no.

He let the letter fall on his blotter once more and rose to look out the library window. The green of their adjoining gardens glowed in the morning sun and the glass of her solarium glistened in blinding reflection.

He rubbed the back of his neck, considering.

She wanted to see him.

"Joseph!" He bellowed for his manservant as he scooped the cravat from his desk. "Shave!"

It was hot in the garden at three o'clock, but Trevor dared not remove his jacket. Nor his hat. He was formally dressed and impeccably so—a detail that meant he'd expended ten-times more effort on this meeting than he'd cared to. But he was endeavoring to appear businesslike. Cool. Self-possessed. Handsome? Hardly. Although when Joseph held out his best jacket, he hadn't argued. He'd drawn the line at gloves. It was one thing to appear formal, quite another to stand in the boiling sun of one's own garden, dressed for the bloody opera.

The fact that he he'd made the effort to dress up at all was true irony. He'd been the embodiment of cool-handed self-possession his entire life, regardless of the clothes he put on his back. Everyone knew him to be serious, prepared, businesslike—whether the business had been caring for his mother or trailing behind the flamboyantly dressed Janos Straka—he was a no-costume-required sort of fellow.

Only now, when faced with the green-eyed, quick-tongued, curve-enhanced perfection of Miss Piety Grey, had he been reduced to dressing the part and pacing anxiously on his overgrown garden path, sweating, and vowing to himself that he *would not touch her.*

The door to her foggy solarium rattled open at five past three, and she emerged alone, smiling when she saw him. She stole a look around both her garden and his and then motioned him inside the glass room.

Although he considered himself to be well acquainted with practically every structure found in Western design, from library to larder, he could honestly say he had never been inside a proper solarium. His mother had kept—and subsequently ignored—a small greenhouse when he was a boy, but this was something else entirely. The most striking feature was a great mosaic of tiny tiles in blues, grays, and white that had been laid in an intricate pattern spanning the length of the floor. At the walls, the mosaic climbed upward, extending the design until it met towering glass windows incased in age-greened copper panes. The windows, age-fogged and stained with condensation, still managed to filter sun into the room, casting it in warm and bright light.

All around the room, iron counters girded various areas with no specific order, housing dirty gardening tools, pots, and rusty watering cans. In the center of it all sat the room's showpiece: a large, raised fountain mosaicked in the same cool colors, now long dry and caked with mossy residue. The side of the fountain was high and flat, creating a seat from which to watch the water, or a ledge, perhaps, for potted plants.

"Now do you see why I bought the house?" she asked, watching him study the room.

"I will never see why you bought the house, but you will have a brilliant sanctuary when it is restored."

She nodded and nosed around. He allowed himself to stare at her, knowing it would likely be the last time. She'd worn a teal-colored dress that seemed to meld into the blue-green shadows of the room. Her hair fell in soft waves down her back. He thought he would travel the world and never see a woman as beautiful as she looked right now.

"You decided to meet me," she said, suddenly looking up. Her voice echoed in the room, and she continued in a lower strain. "I wasn't sure…"

"I may be slow to learn," he said, matching her tone, "but eventually I do catch on. To oppose you is futile."

She laughed. "I never meant to bully you." Trevor could not resist smiling along. He snatched the hat from his head and cast around for the least dirt-strewn surface.

"Let me be honest," she corrected herself. "I did mean to bully you. But I never intended for you to realize you were being bullied."

"So that's your game, is it? Smile so sweetly and ask so nicely; your victim never realizes he's being bent to your will? Why not put that impossible will of yours to use," he said solemnly, "on your mother?"

She made a dismissive sound and looked at the glass panels of the domed ceiling. "Yes." She laughed bitterly, shaking her head in a silent *no.*

"What? She's impervious to your infamous sugar-coated determination? This, I cannot believe. No one is that tough. You brought me to heel, after all, and I don't do anything that I don't have to do, not anymore."

She shook her head again.

"Look," he continued, tossing his hat on a countertop. "Joseph has said that you've tied yourself in knots about her arrival. If the money is yours, Piety, stand your ground and don't give it a second thought. She is merely one woman. If your father left the money to you, she cannot force you to do anything you do not wish. And certainly not marry someone against your will. Not you, of all people."

"So you say," she said, nodding her head.

"That's the weakest acquiescence I believe I have ever heard. And it's nothing like you. Come now."

She chuckled sadly. "Let's just say that the strength of my will becomes *a disadvantage* when faced with Idelle."

He cocked his eyebrow at her, unconvinced.

"She can be very cruel," she continued, looking down. "I find myself in a very small, very demurring place when she—"

"I was cruel. Did that stop you? I've bullied an army of Greeks thugs with more success than I ever caused you to even slow your step."

"You were never cruel. You were testy. Irritable. Blustery. But never cruel."

"You make me sound like an old woman. No wonder the Greeks let me go. No wonder you succeeded."

"I succeeded because what I wanted was not particularly precious to you. You had the ability to help me, and you did. But the thing that Idelle wants so badly is a great fortune. A great fortune and control—of me—which is nearly as important. She has wanted to control me from the very moment I endeavored to assert my own will. And now that she has discovered her new husband is not nearly as rich as she thought? My fortune will be essential to her. I cannot smile my way out of this one."

"Or kiss your way," he said, stealing a look. Their gazes locked and combusted. He turned away.

"I never kissed you," she said to his back. "That was entirely you. *Now* you behave like an old woman. Ha! As if I was trying to take advantage of your innocent sensibilities. If it had any effect at all, the—" She stopped and began again. "Our intimacy only undermined the urgency of the help I have needed from you."

He turned back to her. "It didn't hurt."

"Well, that's not what I intended. Now you're embarrassing me."

"But surely you know that this is why I've stayed away," he said, giving her a hard look. "*Tell me* that you know this. It has nearly killed me not to see you, but the road on which we so recklessly traveled would only lead to trouble for you. For us both. I stayed away to save us both a world of bother. Or worse."

Her voice was raw. "Then I suppose I should thank you."

"No, you should not." He sighed before striding to the ledge of the fountain and taking a seat, careless of the dust and grime. "I've made a shambles of this entire situation. From the beginning. We both know it. Miss Breedlowe knows it. Likely the marchioness could expound on the topic if asked. I should have finished what I began or, since we both know that was never going to happen, I should have never begun it in the first place. There is no suitable excuse. You are a beautiful girl, clever and bright and happy, and you test the outer limits of my self-control. But I cannot—"

"Stop," she said, breathless, and placed two fingers across his mouth. "Please stop. Do not say it again. I know. You've made yourself very clear. You do not want to *connect*. I understand."

He grew quiet, just as she bade, but not because there was nothing left to say. The pads of her fingertips struck him mute, soft and cool on his face. He looked into the deep green of her eyes—eyes somehow greener, smokier, more alive in the cool, gray solarium. He had sworn that he would not touch her but he had not counted on her touching him. And, dear God, not on the mouth.

"Piety?" He covered her wrist with his hand.

She tried to pull away. Slowly, she began to shake her head.

He tugged and she dropped, instead, into his lap.

"Please," he whispered against her ear. "I must find a way to say good-bye. This will be the end. I will be gone when you return from Berkshire, and I'll never bother you again. But you cannot leave without one more...without..."

She was pitifully easy to convince, turning her face and finding his lips, answering him with a light kiss, so sweet, so soft, with lips closed, eyes closed, hands tentatively on his shoulders.

He returned it with a ferociousness triggered by their agonizing separation. He devoured her, opening, licking, tasting. He slid his legs in front of him, lowering her position on his lap.

She giggled, holding on as he shifted her, and he laughed too. But then the laughter faded, the smile, the world. He ravaged her mouth, filling his hands with her silken hair, making a shambles of the soft, full waves. Reluctantly he left it, feeling his way downward. Desperate hands, possessive hands.

She leaned in, meeting him kiss for kiss. She made quick work of his jacket, unbuttoning it and sliding beneath to knead the muscles of his back. He sighed and released her with one hand so he could rip the jacket entirely away, hurling it over the pike of the fountain.

"Piety." He spoke against her mouth. "I have..." He broke off and kissed her. "I have wanted this since the chess." More kissing. "You tortured me every day for a bloody week. Every day. You did it on purpose." His voice sounded heavy and coarse.

She sighed, twisting closer. "I was merely playing chess."

"You were punishing me, and I deserved it."

He trailed kisses down her neck, sucking, wishing he hadn't shaved, wishing he could rub the rough stubble of his beard against her skin and leave a chafe. *Mine*, he thought. *Entirely mine.*

"Promise me," he said, his voice raspy, "that you will not let them touch you." He kissed her again, harder. "Limpett. The others. *Promise me.*"

He returned to her mouth for a quick kiss and then buried his face in her hair, kissing the soft, curl-wisped skin behind her ear. "You are stronger than that." He breathed in the scent of her. "You needn't be handled." He kissed her again. "Not one finger." He returned to her mouth, kissing, tasting, allowing his mind to float away on the warm, languid pleasure of it.

"What did you just say?"

"So beautiful." He left her mouth and trailed kisses to her chin, neck, throat. The sleeve of her gown enclosed her shoulder with a snug little cap, but only barely. The slightest nudge and it would fall away.

Piety spoke again. "Did you just tell me to *defend myself* against Edward Limpett? Against the brothers?"

She dropped her hands from around his middle and grabbed the shoulder of her gown. In an angry movement, she yanked it up.

"Tell me," she continued, her voice rising still, "that you did not just say, *you will not let them touch you. Tell me.*"

Did not just say? He grabbed the edge of the fountain, trying to focus.

"Excuse me," she said sharply and rolled to the side. She left him.

Trevor dropped his head in his hands and swore. "I'm sorry."

It was the truth. He was sorry. He ran his hand roughly through his hair and then shoved up. How in God's name were they discussing this again?

"*Do not* apologize again," she said from behind him. "I hate it. You're not even sorry for the correct thing. It's clear that you don't even know why I've stopped."

"Of course I do! You've stopped because it needed stopping. Because it was—*we were*—getting out of hand. Because I'm a blackguard, and you've taken it as your life's work to torture me. Because we were ripping at each other's clothes against the grime of a *ruined fountain!*" He laughed without humor. "No, Piety, I don't know why, but how lucky for us both that you did."

"It was nothing about the kiss," she said.

"The kiss was inexcusable."

"The kiss was lovely, but hardly your best work. I preferred our first kiss. In the music room. The afternoon you were trying to scare me."

"*Trying* to scare you, was I?" He rounded on her. "My best work? I'll show you my best work!" She had not moved from the ledge of the fountain and he dropped to one knee in front of her. Reaching up, he cupped her face and pulled her in for a hard kiss. He was bullying her, trying to make her feel vulnerable and cautious.

He failed at first touch, now as then. How did she manage to diffuse his anger into heat the instant his lips met hers?

He moaned, and surged up, sitting beside her on the fountain again and gathering her into his arms. She fell against him, and for one precious instant, kissed him in return. The easy familiarity with which they joined lips was another layer of delight; their kisses had a rhythm distinctly their own. She indulged in it a moment more and then let out a whimper. She pulled back, closing off. Her expression became remote, her posture distant. Her eyes were very sad, indeed.

He swore again and pushed himself away from the fountain. He stalked away.

Piety's most urgent point was not that she had stopped the kiss, but why.

"Did you, or did you not," she demanded, "just say: 'Promise me, *Piety*, that you won't let them touch you. Not one finger.' Is that what you said?"

"I had only just told you to stand up to your mother," Falcondale said defensively. "What I said about the Limpetts is more of the same. You should stand up to all of them."

"Forgive me if I interpreted the bit about my mother as encouragement," she replied, rising off the bench. "A cry for confidence. But to have you wheeze on about protecting myself from these men?"

"Mind yourself, Piety. I did not wheeze."

"You have no idea of the threat these men pose; furthermore, you don't want to know. You want me but not enough to do anything about them. So please. Do not try to go it halfway. It's not enough." She looked down at her wrinkled dress and gave her bodice a yank. There would be no hiding this interlude from Jocelyn; they'd managed to tear the muslin. She pulled and patted, keeping her hands busy, trying to maintain composure, while he stood there. Saying nothing. Watching her.

Promise me, he had pleaded. She shook her head. It was enough to make her ill. Physically ill.

"I warned you against the Limpetts," he said through clenched jaw, "because I do not wish you unpleasantness. Surely you must know that. I want you to be happy."

"Fine. Wish me well. Tell me to be happy. Kiss me to distraction, even. But *do not* suggest that you care if another man touches me." She glared at him, and he had the decency to look miserable.

"I understand." He gave curt nod. "To kiss you suggests that we—"

"Forget the kiss. It was never about the kiss. It was your words! Don't you see, Trevor?" She closed the space between them and rose up, inches from his face. "You wish for me to fend off the Limpett brothers? I will do it. I was *always* going to do it, even before I met you. But you have made no claim to me. Whatever happens with the Limpetts lives or dies by my own wits and will. I'm not going to keep myself from them as a favor to you."

"Not a favor to me. Do it for yourself!"

"But that's not what you said."

"I've explained to you why I cannot be your savior in this, Piety."

"I don't want you to be a savior. But don't profess to care what the Limpetts do to me while you're running the other direction. Do not acknowledge that I am in a rough spot and then flippantly bid me good luck sorting it all out!"

"Running the other way, am I? I have had *no* solitude for the last fifteen years. No diversions. No interests. No rest, for God's sake. From the moment I finished university, I was bridled by necessity, by obligation, and yes, by love. My mother was helpless, or at least helpless in her own mind. To her way of thinking, it was me or total despair and certain death. So there I remained—at her bedside, or hovering over her in the privy, or in the kitchens, walking her up and down the street.

Dutifully, painfully—and yes, after a while—resentfully. I cleaned soiled linens. I brushed the jam from her hair. I read the same bleeding romantic drivel to her again and again. I relocated to another country on the vain hope that she could simply draw breath."

He turned away, and Piety watched him walk the distance of the solarium and then turn back, pacing toward her. He looked at everything and nothing; his expression was trapped misery.

She said, "I did not know the extent to which you cared for your mother."

He stopped beside a tall, ceramic urn and grabbed the top of it. He looked inside. He rested his forehead against it, staring at the floor. "It wasn't her fault."

"You did not suggest that it was her fault."

"The next bit? The next bit was entirely my fault." He left the urn and turned to the foggy glass wall of the solarium, speaking to the garden beyond. "In the name of money and boredom, I allowed myself to be drafted into the service of a man who would kill us both if I made one false move. I was a party to violence, blackmail, threats. I managed enough gold on his behalf to support a flotilla of vices, many of which I watched destroy the lives around me."

"The landlord?"

He scoffed. "Landlord? Slumlord is more accurate. And it was my duty to resolve his cock-ups and keep the lot of us from execution by the Sultan.

"Summons in the middle of the night: *What do we do with the bodies, Tryphon?* Summons on Sunday: *Parents run off and their children have nowhere to go; what do we do with*

them, Tryphon? Summons every hour of the day: *Broken privy,
broken floorboards, broken stairs*—yes, it is more common than
you think! Not to mention, a hornet's nest of underworld
thugs to keep from strangling each other. It was nothing short
of a juggling act in the end. I managed Straka's empire from
the kitchen table of our villa so I could be near my mother.
When Straka's errands called me out, Joseph or our maid sat
with her. Between her demands and Straka's needs, I worked,
quite literally, around the clock. I slept when I could.

"This is but a small picture of my former life, Piety," he
said lowly, turning to face her. "A small picture. When my
mother finally died, I stayed on with this man, Janos Straka,
because I could not devise a reason for him to let me go. I had
no ambition toward the earldom, but thank God it fell to me.
The title impressed Straka enough to release me from his service. Freedom, just like that. Finally. It ignited a selfishness
in me, a detachment from all humanity that you may never
understand. And I clung to it. I am clinging to it now.

"I don't want a wife to support. I don't want children to
look after. I don't even really want any well-meaning friends.
I am entirely finished with the life-draining work of feeling
charitably toward anyone else.

"I cannot—I will not—obligate myself. Not even to you."
He took a step toward her. "Regardless of how beautiful you are.
Or charming. Or clever. Or how proficient at chess. Regardless
of how much I want to toss you over my shoulder and haul you
to my bed until the middle of next week." He looked away. "Or
how heartbreaking your situation. I simply cannot."

She stared at him, tears filling her eyes. The bitterness
of his pain and frustration was palpable in the solarium, a

chilling cloud, covering the sunlight. Add to that her own frustration. The futility of her argument. Even now, he did not comprehend why she was angry. He hadn't understood a word of what she had endeavored to say.

Slowly, she turned away.

He was the first to speak again. "Perhaps I should have explained my attitude weeks ago, before it came to this: rattling the walls of your lovely solarium with my resentment. But my detachment was meant to go both ways. I wanted no part of anyone else's problems or burdens; in return I vowed to keep my own problems to myself. I never wished to trouble you with the sordid details of my *lost youth*, as it were."

"You mistake me for someone who runs from the pain of others. I am happy to share your burdens. I *wanted* to hear."

"But I am not happy to share yours. As has been made painfully apparent today."

"Then let us simply say good-bye." She quickly swiped away her tears. "At last, what you've wanted. I have much larger problems ahead." She held out her hand to shake, just as she'd done the first time they met.

He smiled at her hand and took it. With his other hand, he topped his first, holding her hand with both of his own. "You should know that I've decided to leave the country, even without selling the house," he said, solemnly. "I'll be gone— sailing to Ottoman Syria—by the time you return from Berkshire."

She hadn't thought her heart could sink any lower, but it did, dropping from her aching chest to the pit of her leaden stomach. She nodded and tried to retract her hand. "Good for you. More of what you wanted."

He squeezed her hand and then replaced it, gently, to her side. "I've hired a house agent to take over the advertisement and sale of the house, but I've told him that you and your men should have the freedom to work on or around the premises. I will do as you've bade and hire another architect for you. He can take over my work on the stairs."

"Thank you."

Neither made a move to leave, but Piety gestured to his hat on the counter and his coat on the fountain pike. His footsteps echoed in the glass room and the area of her chest that formerly contained her heart.

Horrible, she thought as she watched him. The entire afternoon had been horribly contentious. And blameful. And sad. And now to part ways like combatants?

"My lord," she called after him.

"Please call me Trevor," he said. "I loved—" He stopped and shook his head, starting again. "It was nice when you said it, and what could it possibly matter now?"

"Trevor." She tried his name. "I want you to know that I've loved every single thing about England since I arrived. Even you. Thank you for…well, thank you." She left it at that.

He didn't answer—merely bowed formally and backed away. When he got to the door he raised a hand to wave but did not look back.

Like a fool, she waved in return, a gesture he would never see.

CHAPTER SEVENTEEN

Berkshire was a storybook setting come to life. Green hills with gently rounded crests bordered wide, fertile valleys, cut by swiftly moving streams, as clear as glass. Tidy stone walls marched across the horizon, hemming in fat sheep. Swathes of wildflowers fringed the roadside, the hillock, the mossy stream bank.

It caught Piety by surprise—this quiet, pastoral beauty—partly because her companions seemed wholly unmoved by it, and partly because she never expected to love any place more than she loved London. But the orderly bustle and stately gray-and-gold architecture of town was nothing compared to the serene, green dominion of the country.

When the marchioness's carriage lurched to a stop in the circular gravel drive of Garnettgate's magnificent manor house and the doors were pulled wide by nervous staff, the sight of rolling green parkland nearly took Piety's breath away.

The very broadness of it captivated in the same moment it dazed. It was no more than a field, really, a pasture—but so vast a field. Up and down it went, like the surface of a churning sea. The green was endless and occurred in every shade, from the paleness of a caterpillar's belly to the deep emerald of a pine bough.

"Stunning," Piety whispered, drifting toward the hedge that separated the garden from the rising landscape.

"The paddock?" Jocelyn asked, passing with two hand-held traveling cases.

Piety nodded, not taking her eyes off the landscape.

"Not half bad, I suppose." Jocelyn laughed. "I shouldn't jest. No proper Englishwoman would diminish the beauty of the Berkshire green. It warms me that you are impressed." She stepped beside Piety and breathed deeply. "Does it remind you of home?"

"Not at all. America is beautiful, certainly, but the landscape and vegetation is very untamed. Savage in comparison. This looks peaceful. Was it cultivated to sprawl in such an orderly rectangle, or is this the hand of God?"

"The land was cleared centuries ago, I'm sure, for crops and livestock."

Piety nodded. "I've never seen so much green."

They both laughed, and Jocelyn tucked her hand around Piety's waist, "What a sweet girl you are. England would be glad to have a flower such as you to liven up our greenness. Ah, but here is the marchioness. She will expect a fuss about the house and certainly the gardens. Let us not forget to carry on."

"The house is lovely, too, of course," Piety said, looking at the stark façade of the imposing building. "I cannot believe she owns all of this and yet she rarely visits. London is delightful, but this rivals even the loveliest park or mansion in town."

As country homes went, Jocelyn informed Piety, the manor itself was not overly large. But to Piety, the Palladian-style house was every inch as solid and austere as a gothic castle. Piety's childhood holidays had been spent at the family's estate in Rhode Island. The Summer House, as they called it, was known up and down the East Coast for its towers and turrets. It made an impression, certainly, but remembering it, Piety thought how grandiose and almost garish it seemed compared to stately, stoic Garnettgate.

"How lovely your home is, my lady," Piety told the marchioness, trailing behind her to the front door. "Like a storybook castle."

A footman raced to beat them to the door but failed.

The marchioness harrumphed. "With useless storybook servants." She waited impatiently for the darting footman. "Did a groom not ride ahead to alert them of our arrival? And here I stand, knocking on my own front door like a peddler!"

She squinted at Piety. "Never you worry. I'll have the lot of them whipped into line by the time the Americans arrive. Livery. A proper receiving line along the carriage drive. Standards flying. It is nuisance to reach the country, but I've stayed away too long, and now look at the state of things. I do hope Miss Baker is up to the task of advising me as we set things to rights."

"It already appears perfect to me," said Piety.

"Yes, but you live in a slum, so how could you possibly... Ah, here we are!" she said, as the door creaked open to a herd of wide-eyed, scrambling servants.

By early afternoon, they had settled into comfortable rooms, and Piety indulged in her first warm bath since she'd sailed from New York. The marchioness housed Jocelyn in a small guest room adjacent to Piety's, a true generosity, considering there were ample rooms for staff.

Tiny was given a large suite of rooms near the marchioness, and the two older women were immediately swept up in the business of haranguing the staff, ferreting out oversights in the housekeeping, and revising the proposed menus.

It was Piety's plan to explore the courtyard and gardens, and she urged Jocelyn to rest. While she walked, she composed letters in her head, which she would never send. Things she would never say aloud. All of it to Falcondale, a man she would never see again. When had she become such a fool?

It is lovely here in Berkshire, she would write.

We made it safely, if not comfortably, in her ladyship's dim, airless carriage, but the chamber I've been given is large and bright.

The Garnettgate kitchen garden produces all its own vegetables.

There are rabbits outside my window and fish in the fountain.

The village is charming. The crofters are welcoming.

Tiny has been put in charge of the menus.

Miss Breedlowe is teaching me the names of native birds.

We are keeping warm, even in the drafty house.

I miss you.

And wasn't that the silliest sentiment of all?

Miss him? Of course she missed him. She had allowed herself to fall in love with him, what else was there to do? If she hadn't realized her love over their daily chess, or when he evicted Eddie, or in the solarium...well, certainly she knew it now. It seemed as if missing him had always been a part of loving him. Even when they were together, he held himself apart.

And now, a lifetime of missing him stretched ahead of her. This trip to Berkshire was only the beginning of day-to-day diversions that they would never share.

CHAPTER EIGHTEEN

Trevor had every intention of handing over Piety's stairwell to the new man and walking away.

He'd found an architect quickly enough: an eager young man, fresh out of school, who seemed hard working and bright. Better still, he was available to begin work immediately, which meant Trevor could wash his hands of stairwells and passages and the all-consuming force that was Piety Grey.

And yet...

Day after day, he found himself drifting from his own library to Piety's now-vacant house. Sometimes, he went in search of Joseph. Piety had left her housemaid, Marissa, behind to receive deliveries. Judging from the amount of time Joseph had gone missing, she was receiving the boy as well.

Sometimes, Trevor found himself seeking out Mr. Burr and his crew to share their midday meal.

Other times, regrettable times that he could not explain, some memory of her would compel him to amble across their two gardens and simply *stand* in the house she had inhabited for her short but disruptive tenure in the street, to be among her possessions and her half-completed repairs and the trail of tiny footsteps she'd left in the sawdust.

Two days after she'd gone, he noticed a lathe among the tools on Mr. Burr's cart, and he'd bade Joseph to drag it into the garden. There it remained, tempting him, for another day and night. At the end of the first week, he found himself seated at the thing, his foot on the pedal, tinkering with designs for the balusters on her stairs. He worked hours shaving sculptural shapes into sticks of wood. The finished form, realized after hours of work, was elegant but unique, progressive, like Piety herself. She would like it, he'd thought—one of a thousand thoughts he had of her on any given day.

When he'd shown the baluster to Spencer Burr, the carpenter assured him that his crew could replicate his design, but Trevor persisted, returning to the lathe again and again to fashion the balusters himself. Considering the curve and height, Piety's stairwell would require dozens of them, and he put off his own work to craft another, and another, and another.

Just three more, he'd say, taking up the next stick of wood. *It's the least you can bloody do.*

And so he was at the lathe when Piety's mother and stepbrothers arrived in London and descended on her house. He heard them before he saw them: a jumble of footsteps and indistinguishable grumbling wafting through the open window. He paused. The voices grew closer, then angrier—loud enough to be heard over the pedal of the lathe.

Trevor silently laid the baluster in his hand on the ground.

"I asked for water," said a man's sharp voice.

Trevor stared at the kitchen window, trying to place the voice.

The reply was fearful. "Yes, sir." This voice, Trevor knew; it came from Joseph's sweetheart, the maid Marissa. "But this is what I brought you 'tis water, sir."

"English water tastes like swill," said the man. "Take it away."

Next, he heard the clatter of a brass tankard hitting the stone floor. Marissa gasped and cried out. He heard scrambling and cruel laughter. Marissa cried again.

Trevor swung his leg over the lathe.

There was more tussling, and then Marissa screamed.

Shoving up, Trevor crept, low and silent, to the kitchen door.

He saw the man first. He was big and fat, finely dressed—too fine, certainly, for the middle of the day—with lace cuffs and a suffocating cravat. His back was to Trevor, blocking his actions, but Marissa's skinny arm thrashed into view. The man had her pinned against the counter.

Trevor swore and took up an iron-nosed sledgehammer propped by the steps. He stepped through the door. Before he could sneak up behind them Joseph burst in, coming off the bottom step of the servants' stair like a shot.

The boy hurled himself and collided with the man's shoulder. The man let out an *oof* and thudded back. Joseph darted in front of Marissa and sunk into position, ready to fight.

"Joseph, wait," Trevor said, wanting to interrogate the man before Joseph beat him to a pulp. They both turned, but the man saw Trevor's hammer, saw he was outnumbered, and he used the distraction to swing at Joseph. Trevor winced, but Joseph reacted just in time, dodging right. The punch missed his chin and glanced his neck below his ear. Joseph growled and pounced.

"Joseph, I said hold!" Trevor shouted, but Joseph fought on, catching the man's arm and forcing it in a twist behind his back.

"Leave him, Joe," Trevor said. "See to the girl."

Reluctantly, the boy complied, releasing the man with a shove. Marissa flew at Joseph, and he gathered her up. Trevor jerked his head to the garden, and the boy hustled her outside.

When they were gone, Trevor turned on the man panting in the center of the kitchen. "Who are you and what is your business in this house?"

"I could ask the same thing of you." The man eyed him up and down, rubbing his shoulder.

The accent hit him. *Piety's family.* Trevor took a step closer, trying to recall her description of this family and square it with the swollen, sweating man before him.

Before either of them could speak, a clatter of footsteps could be heard descending the servants' stairs. Four more men filed in, followed by a middle-aged woman and Spencer Burr.

"We heard shouts," the woman said, her eyes darting wildly around the kitchen. She glared at Marissa's attacker. "Have you found her?"

The fat American was silent.

She nodded to Trevor. "Who is this man?"

"Who, indeed," Trevor said coldly, settling the sledgehammer on the stone countertop with a loud *plunk*, "Trevor Rheese, Earl of Falcondale. I own the home next door and employ the servants who were attacked by this man."

"His boy attacked *me!*" countered the fat brother.

"Silence, Ennis!" The woman stared at Trevor.

It was Piety's mother—really there could be no doubt. The resemblance was unmistakable, although she was brittle in every way that Piety was soft. And Piety's face was warm and approachable, beautiful in a sunny way, while her mother's beauty was cool and preserved. Her hair was much darker; she dyed it, he'd wager. The shiny blackness was a stark contrast to her tight, pale face. She scowled, he thought, as much as Piety smiled.

"May I impose upon you to restate your name, sir," she said, "as well as your business in this house?"

"This is the neighbor I was telling you about, madam," said a short brother, the one Trevor remembered as having interrupted their chess.

"Ah," said the woman, "so here is the English lord who has taken such a hospitable interest in our Piety." With cautious movements, she extended a hand.

Trevor made a barely perceptible nod over her fingers, not taking his eyes from her face.

"Edward has told us that the two of you are...*familiar*," she said. "I did not realize you'd been given leave to walk into her very kitchen unannounced."

"I could say the same of you."

The woman studied him. "I am Piety Grey's mother, Mrs. Idelle Grey-Limpett, and these are my stepsons. We've traveled from America to reconvene with Piety."

"Hmmm. More's the pity. She appears to be out."

"Do you know where she is?"

Trevor considered this. He played dumb and looked to Spencer Burr, leaning against the rear wall. "Where is she, Mr. Burr? Surely you've been told."

"Aye, my lord," said Burr, "Miss Grey left a letter; Marissa gave it to this lot straight away. I've told them myself she's traveled to Berkshire."

"That's right," Trevor said, "Berkshire. I believe she was to be a guest at the country estate of another neighbor, the Marchioness Frinfrock."

"How informed you are, Lord Falcondale." Idelle turned to the brothers and flicked her wrist. "Let me see the letter again."

Still another brother stepped forward. "Now, Mother," he said soothingly, "let us not trouble the earl with our misplaced sister. Not after he's suffered an attack on his servant." He smiled a peddler's smile. "My apologies, my lord. My brothers are barbarians—a sad circumstance, the consequences of which I have explained to them, repeatedly, but to no avail. I hope you'll allow me to offer to pay for any medical attention the boy may require. I'm Eli Limpett, by the way." He handed Piety's letter to her mother.

Trevor nodded. This brother was less over-done than the others, more guarded; his eyes were, well, if not clever, then sharp.

"Save the medicine for your associate," Trevor said. "Joseph is a skilled fighter. My concern was for the intent."

"Intent." Piety's mother laughed, looking up from her letter. "Then you really will have to forgive us, my lord. My stepsons are not accustomed to the docile ways of the English. Regrettably, we Americans rely on muscle and might to forge our way, as we always have."

"Let us not provoke the earl." Eli Limpett chuckled. "Remember we owe him our most sincere gratitude."

"You owe me nothing," Trevor said.

"But we've heard all about Piety's new neighbors and the great pains they have taken to look after her. She requires a lot of care, I'm afraid."

"Based on what I know of Miss Grey, she is largely self-sufficient."

"Ha! We can barely let her out of our sight."

"What my stepson means," said Piety's mother, shoving the letter at the nearest brother, "is that we've been worried sick since she set out. And then to learn she's sailed all the way to England on her own? We came after her as fast as we could. Of course, we had absolutely no idea what to expect. How could we *dream* that she'd sunk her inheritance into this decrepit pile of a house? And then to undertake the restoration alone? Surely you can imagine our worry and shock." She paused, studying him.

Trevor stared silently back.

She tried again, "Her recklessness knows no bounds. I would be remiss if I did not mention that she seems to have grown quite familiar with you, my lord."

"Take heart, madam," Trevor said, "I barely know your daughter."

"So you say," replied Mrs. Limpett. "Regardless, Eli and I intend to take Piety firmly in hand. I've a mind to put her on a return ship for New York before the end of this week.

"My God, what could she be thinking?" she continued, placing a weary hand to her brow. "To lead us all the way to London only to learn we must continue into the wilds of *Berkshire*?"

Eli Limpett smiled at Trevor. "What provincial colonials you must think us, Lord Falcondale. Misplacing our dear Piety. But you needn't worry. Things are now well in hand."

Trevor blinked at that statement and turned away.

This is not your problem, he told himself, breathing hard, opening and closing a fist. *Not. Your. Problem.* He stared at the worn divots in the stone countertop, thinking it again and again.

Eli Limpett continued, sounding inspired. "She isn't a bad girl, really. She simply needs to learn some deference and obedience. God only knows what her father was thinking by encouraging such independence. He did me no favor in spoiling her."

"Did *you* no favor?" Trevor asked.

"Oh, yes. Did she not tell you? We are betrothed—or nearly so. I have but to enact a formal proposal to her to make it official. It's a detail I intend to solve just as soon as I catch up to her, the wily minx. After that, wifely obedience should commence. Breaking her won't be easy," he said, looking at him conspiratorially, "but very much worth my time, I'm sure."

"*Get out.*" The words were out of Trevor's mouth before he could stop them.

"I beg your pardon," Eli said, and Trevor saw a flash of violence in his eyes.

Oh, I dare you, mate, he thought, but he said, "Beg all you like. But if you do not wish to speak with the constable about the attack on my manservant and the maid, then I suggest you take your leave. Now."

"I'll have you know, sir—" began Piety's mother, but Trevor cut her off.

"You have two minutes," he said in deadly calm. He took up the sledgehammer from the counter and propped it on his shoulder.

It had been some time since he'd fought five men at once, but by no means would it be the first time. He'd need Joseph, and he shouted for him to send Marissa away, but then

Spencer Burr—all six-and-a-half feet and twenty stone of him—shoved off the wall.

"Right," the carpenter said. "The earl has said good-bye. Out you go, gentlemen, madam."

"Ah, good man. If you would be so kind, Mr. Burr."

"Pleasure, m'lord." The carpenter clamped one bear-paw hand on Mrs. Limpett's waist and the other on her elbow. "You'll remember the way you came in, madam. Sirs." He swept the woman to the stairs.

The men grumbled, and Mrs. Limpett could be heard saying, "Surely *that man* cannot mean to remain inside, if we cann—" before Mr. Burr hustled her up the steps.

Eli Limpett lingered, casting an assessing look around the kitchen and garden beyond. He glanced at Trevor, looking between the hammer and his face and back again.

Trevor raised his eyebrows.

Finally, the man nodded curtly and disappeared after his brothers.

When the stairs were empty and the floorboards above him silent, Trevor walked to the window and looked out. Marissa and Joseph were nose-to-nose on a stone bench.

He turned and looked at the empty kitchen.

He looked down at the hammer, his hands tight around the handle.

This is not your problem, he repeated in his head. As soon as the words were conjured, they dissolved.

Instead, he thought of Piety. Optimistic, determined. He thought of the courage it had taken for her to leave New York, to come here, to lie in wait for them and then to hunker down and fight.

They are no match for her spirit, he thought. *Buffoons. Pompous and vain and stupid with greed.*

Still, they would descend on Berkshire with no other goal than to bully her and bleed her.

What had Eli Limpett said?

Breaking her won't be easy...

Trevor's hand burned, and he looked at the hammer. He tried to release it, but his hands would not let go.

"My lord?" Spencer Burr thudded down the stairs. "They've gone, and I've locked the door behind them. We'll take care to keep it bolted in future."

Trevor nodded. "Good man, Spencer. It's not your fault, of course. They are..." He exhaled an angry breath. "Unconscionable." He held out the hammer. "I believe this is yours."

"Nearly went to good use, did it?" Spencer chuckled, taking it up.

Trevor let out another tired breath and looked at the ceiling. In his mind's eye, he saw the Americans making their way to Piety.

Before he could stop himself, he asked, "Do you think they'll really go to Berkshire?"

Spencer looked thoughtful and shrugged. "Aye, my lord. I reckon they will."

Trevor nodded and walked in a slow circle. He stopped and looked at the carpenter. "I predict the same. Miss Grey left you the direction of the marchioness's estate, I presume?"

"Aye, my lord."

"Fetch it, will you? I feel the sudden need to visit the bloody country."

CHAPTER NINETEEN

The woman on Garnettgate's front stoop wasted no time with pleasantries. "Is this the home of one Frances Stroud, Marchioness Frinfrock?"

Jocelyn happened to be passing through the entryway, and the question froze her in place. The accent. Loud and foreign and demanding. It was unmistakable.

Oh, God. They've come.

Cradling her needlework to her chest, Jocelyn ducked behind a giant urn and listened. The butler Godfrey, whose great size alone would prevent him from ever being a truly discreet servant, did not help matters by blocking her view.

"The house is Garnettgate, madam," he told the woman. "Home of Marchioness Frinfrock. Who should I tell the marchioness is inquiring?"

"My identity has no bearing on you or your mistress," said the woman. "I am merely in search of a young woman who, I'm told, is in residence here. A guest—Miss Piety Grey?" Godfrey tried to answer, but she spoke over him. "If we have the correct house, please tell her to convene, with all of her belongings and her Negro maid, in the front drive. Immediately."

The normally unflappable Godfrey was nonplussed. "Beg your pardon?"

"Retrieve Miss Piety Grey, sir. *Now*."

Jocelyn winced, hesitated, and then, in a burst of courage, stepped forward, lightly clearing her throat. "Excuse me, Godfrey."

The large butler was slow to move, and she was forced to shoulder her way to the door, affording the woman on the stoop ample time to study her. Her gaze whipped across Jocelyn's hair, her dress, her face, and the needlework in her arms like a cold wind.

"Forgive me," Jocelyn began, "I could not help but overhear your inquiry. I should tell you that the young lady you seek, Miss Piety Grey, is indeed in residence here at Garnettgate. At the moment, she is in the garden, looking after the roses in company of the marchioness. Please, may I invite you inside while I inform them of your arrival?"

"As I told this one, that won't be necessary," the woman said. Her resemblance to Piety was uncanny. She looked like Piety, if Piety had starved herself for a week and aged fifty years.

Jocelyn sighed. "I beg your pardon, madam. May I be so bold as to presume that you are Miss Grey's family? Are you Mrs. Limpett?"

The woman squinted at her. After a long, assessing moment, she said, "I am Mrs. Grey-Limpett. Who, may I ask, are you?"

Jocelyn smiled. "I am Jocelyn Breedlowe, Miss Grey's chaperone." She nodded her head to the woman. "How do you do?"

"Chaperone!" said Mrs. Limpett. "Why in God's name would she require a chaperone?" Then she shook her head. "It makes no difference. I am her mother. Not only do I supersede your authority here, my very presence makes whatever services you may provide unnecessary. Now, if you please. I've come a very great distance to collect my daughter."

Jocelyn blinked at her. Did she really intend to extract Piety without introducing herself? Without even coming inside?

Before she could reply, the door to the hired carriage in the drive snapped open and a man emerged. He made nimble progress in their direction, despite his excessive clothing: a long coat for the warm day, billowy cuffs, a bright cravat with copious folds. While he came, he stared. Sharp, critical eyes darting in every direction.

"How do you do," he said, coming upon them. He smiled, but it did not reach his eyes. They were hard, his eyes—cold and flat and missing nothing. A shark's eyes, she thought, too small for his broad, shiny face.

Oh, Piety. Jocelyn ached for her friend. She had spoken of the brothers from time to time, describing how each was intolerable in his own awful way. From what Jocelyn could discern, the one she feared the most—the most threatening and the cruelest—had been a middle brother called Eli. Could this be him? Eli Limpett? Two feet away?

"How do you do." She bobbed her head again.

"Our mother is not being rude, I hope?"

Mrs. Limpett rolled her eyes. "We needn't play their silly games, Eli."

It was *him*.

"By no means." Jocelyn forced a smiled. "I was just inviting Mrs. Limpett and, indeed, your entire party, sir, inside. The marchioness is in the garden this morning, but it won't take a moment to announce your arrival."

"Excellent," said the man in the same moment Mrs. Limpett said, "Unnecessary."

"And you are?" the man asked, sweeping Jocelyn's body with his shark's eye.

"She's no one!" Mrs. Limpett exclaimed. "A servant. Claiming to be Piety's chaperone."

"Oh, excellent," said the man, flashing another disingenuous smile. "I'm relieved to know she's been looked after in our absence. I'm learning the hard way that she cannot be left alone, even a moment."

He affected a quick bow. "Eli Limpett," he informed her. "Soon-to-be fiancé of dear Miss Grey. You have met her mother, Mrs. Idelle Grey-Limpett. And my brothers are in the carriage. I hope you meant what you said about all of us. Meeting a"—he affected an air of breathlessness— "*marchioness*? You wouldn't believe the journey we've had."

Jocelyn led them all inside: the mother; the shark-eyed one; a fat one; a bald one; a tall one; and Edward, the smallest brother who had turned up in London the week before.

Jocelyn led them to the blue room, the only space beside the ballroom or the dining room that could comfortably contain a party so large. It was uncommonly cold in the blue room. At the moment, all the rugs had been removed to be aired on the line. Their collective footfalls on the bare marble raised quiet a clatter. She bade Godfrey to stoke the fires and convey refreshment. When they were settled, she bowed and first walked—then ran—for the garden.

Piety, she was frustrated to find, was covered in mud. Apparently the marchioness had taken issue with the way the gardener had cleared the weeds among the ivy. After several failed rounds of shouted instruction, Piety had shoved the beleaguered man aside and dropped to do it herself.

"So it begins," said the marchioness when she heard. She raised her parasol for a shaded view of the house. "Very good. But you cannot receive them like this, Miss Grey. Take the rear stairs and change and wash. Do you prefer Tiny to assist or Miss Breedlowe?"

"We'd do well to keep Tiny hidden for the duration," Piety said. "They are hateful to her. Truly awful."

"I am not afraid," said Tiny from beneath her parasol.

"Yes, but it unnerves me to hear the way they speak to you. Mother knows this, and she does it on purpose."

"You will not be unnerved by this or any other manipulation they play," said the marchioness. "You will be confident. You will be at ease. You will be self-possessed—just as we discussed. But you must not be"—she scowled at her—"caked in filth. Take yourself inside to change. I will receive them in the… Where did you put them, Miss Breedlowe?"

"They are waiting in the blue room."

"Douglas?" Lady Frinfrock turned to the gardener. "What is the time?"

"Half-past ten, my lady."

"Excellent. We will convene luncheon at twelve o'clock noon. Miss Breedlowe, inform Godfrey and the kitchen. Miss Baker, what do you wish? Will you see them with me or wait until the meal?"

"I'd just as soon help Miss Piety."

"As you will, then. Come along, Miss Breedlowe. Let us tame the beasts."

Jocelyn was the last to trail behind them into the blue room, and she was relieved to see that Godfrey had rallied since the encounter on the stoop.

"Her ladyship, the Marchioness Frinfrock," he announced, his spine pitchfork-straight, his eyes alert, fixed on the far wall.

Jocelyn fought the urge to seek out the most shadowy, far-flung chair, drifting instead to a fairly visible spot on a nearby settee. The Americans paid her absolutely no mind. The Americans huddled in small groups, two or three of them together, whispering. Only Eli stood apart, watching, taking in every detail of the marchioness's large, marble drawing room with fast, slitted eyes.

Once settled in a chair, Lady Frinfrock's expression was pleasant but unreadable as she examined each of the brothers. She studied Eli last, flicking him with a dismissive gaze before turning her attention to Mrs. Limpett. The American woman stared back, making no move to dip into a curtsy or even nod. None of them bobbed their heads—an absolutely glaring rudeness, and Piety would be mortified, Jocelyn thought, if she'd known. Behind them, the ebony grandfather clock marked the quiet with a slow and steady tick. No one spoke. Jocelyn twisted her hands into a tight, sweaty snarl. When she could endure the silent scrutiny no more, she wobbled to stand. "Your ladyship, may I introduce—"

"Formal introductions won't be necessary, Miss Breedlowe." The marchioness gestured for her to return to her seat. "Clearly, the Limpetts intend this to be a cursory, casual sort of visit, as no one has made a move even to say how-do-you-do."

One of the brothers snickered, and Eli Limpett spoke over him.

"Forgive our ignorance of proper custom, your ladyship," he said, bowing deeply. "We were unsure of whether it was appropriate to address you first or to wait."

The marchioness stared at him. "Save your restraint for the prince. Who are you, and why have you come?"

"Forgive me, again," he said, repeating his bow. "I am Eli Limpett, of New York City. In America."

"I am aware of the location of New York City, Mr. Limpett. Why are you in my drawing room?"

"We came here by invitation, actually," he said. He snapped his fingers over his shoulder, and the small brother, Edward, trudged forward and placed a folded missive in his hand. "Our dear stepsister, Miss Piety Grey is residing here with you, I believe. Your excellence."

"Let us not be coy. Miss Grey has led us to expect your arrival. It should be said, however, that her expectations put us more in the mind of a happy reunion, considering the length of time you have been apart and the great distance you have traveled—"

"Piety said *that?*" Edward Limpett cut off the marchioness's comment.

The marchioness ignored him. "Rather than a water stop for your livestock and the collection of Miss Grey's effects in the road." She stood.

"Of course, we are anxious to reunite with Piety," Eli Limpett said, "but we're hardly here to 'collect her effects.' " He laughed. "You make it sound as if she is, well, as if she were no longer among us."

"On the contrary, sir," said the marchioness, plodding toward him with her cane. "She is very much among us. And, as a living, breathing, young woman of consequence, she alone will decide where she goes, when she departs, and what she takes when she goes. I am perfectly happy to host you, all of you, as guests of Miss Grey. However"—she eyed all of them—"the invitation will be revoked immediately if your group cannot be counted upon for, at the very least, the most basic vestiges of decorum and civility. That includes, but is not limited to, employing some courtesy to myself and my staff."

"And what of Piety?" demanded little Edward.

"What of Miss Grey?" the marchioness replied coolly. "Her manners are impeccable. How impressed I have been from her first day I made her acquaintance. It begs the question, where was she trained?"

Mrs. Grey-Limpett stepped forward, chuckling. "You have been fooled, my lady. I see now the problem, and how silly of me. My daughter has misled you. Good manners weigh very meekly against her greater crimes. Namely, flight from home and country without as much as a good-bye, plunging us into heartbreak and worry. Me—*her own mother*—piecing together the details of where she had gone and why. The purchase of property and God knows what else without a trusted male advisor looking after her. What impact may manners have when compared to this?"

"Mrs. Limpett, I assume?" asked the marchioness.

The American woman smiled and nodded. Still, no introductions. Jocelyn fought another urge to bob from her seat.

"As her host, Mrs. Limpett," continued the marchioness, "I find myself less concerned about where Mrs. Grey travels or whom she alerts before she goes. Was she properly comported when she arrived in my street? Does she treat others as she, herself, wishes to be treated? These are the behaviors that have bearing on my small corner of the world. In this, you'll understand, I do not see myself as having been made a fool. Whatever foolishness you may or may not have earned as her mother is your business entirely."

The American woman's expression went a little off. "How very right you are. My business, indeed. Yet how may I conduct it if you hold my daughter hostage? Restraining us here, subjecting us to open judgment, while she is nowhere to be seen?"

Angrily, she looking at Eli. "Is this what you intended? To be at her mercy? I cannot see my own daughter without being scolded for manners!"

"*Mother.*" Eli's warning look encompassed them all.

"On the contrary," said the marchioness. "You are not at my mercy. By all means, tell me to go to the devil and take your leave from this house at once. However, I did make a promise to Miss Grey, and I intend to stand by it. It is at *her* mercy you find yourselves."

"But we haven't even been allowed to see her!"

"She was informed of your arrival at the same time as I. She comes and goes as she likes. I have no say as to who she sees and when."

"Then where is she?" demanded the American.

"I have no idea. I am her friend, not her keeper."

"She lives with you, but you do not know where she is?"

"She's your daughter, and you do not know?"

"*I am here*, Mother." Piety's voice rose softly from across the room. "I am sorry to have kept you waiting."

Every eye flew to the doorway where Piety, flanked by Tiny, stood solemnly.

She looked more lovely, Jocelyn thought, than ever she had seen her. Her hair was swept up and off of her shoulders in a loose knot. The effect matured her, but she showed no age. Her dress was a sunny, yellow color, pretty without being precious.

For a very long moment, no one spoke. Jocelyn rose from the settee, too nervous to sit. Eli blinked several times and then strode in her direction. Mrs. Limpett-Grey cut him off.

"*Piety*," she said eagerly, floating to the doorway with her arms outstretched. "You have scared the life out of us, my girl. The very life."

Their embrace was awkward, almost painful. Either they rarely hugged or Mrs. Grey-Limpett's stiffness precluded genuine affection.

"Forgive my lateness," Piety said. "I was not presentable after a morning in the garden. I only needed time to change. I see you have met dear Lady Frinfrock in the interim. And Miss Breedlowe. I hope you have been *gracious*."

Stepping around her mother, she walked toward the marchioness. Her words were strong, but she appeared to be a little unsure of the route between door and center of the room. Jocelyn willed her to remain strong.

"Have you been properly introduced to everyone, my lady?" Piety asked.

"I have been introduced to no one," said Lady Frinfrock.

"As I've said at least a dozen times," said Mrs. Limpett, trailing after her daughter, "introductions won't be necessary. Now that you have finally graced us with your presence, we will not linger."

"What a pity," said Piety. "No time to rest? Even for one night?"

"Oh, Piety, *do stop*." The woman laughed. "You cannot be serious. We've come all the way from America to collect you. You cannot believe we'd bide our time in the English countryside longer than necessary. Not when we have the house in London to sell."

"I don't intend to sell the London house, Mother. Nor do I intend to return to London. Not for some time. If you wish to see me, I am enjoying Berkshire at the moment. Feel free to accept the marchioness's kind offer to stay near me here at Garnettgate as her guest. However, as her guest, you must be cordial. Beginning with proper introductions, at the very least."

"I will not be cordial," said Idelle. "And I will not take orders from you, you ungrateful child. I am your mother. You are but a twenty-five-year-old girl, unmarried, running wild across the ocean and bleeding dry the Grey estate with absolutely no supervision. I regret that we're having to mete this out in front of your exalted new friends, but what choice do I have?

"Now," she said, "march upstairs and pack. Ah! And there is Tiny. I have a list for you, girl, you can count on it."

"No."

It was the loudest thing Piety had yet said.

"I beg your pardon," said Mrs. Limpett, spinning around.

"I said, *no*. I will not go upstairs. I will not pack. Furthermore, I will not leave. And do not address Tiny unless it is to say hello. She is on holiday."

Mrs. Limpett made a noise of shrill frustration, "Oh, good God!" She threw up her hands. "Eli! Do something."

Eli cleared his throat and stepped forward. "Might we have a moment alone with Miss Grey?"

"That is up to Miss Grey," said the marchioness.

"No," Piety said again, louder still. "Speaking in private will not be necessary."

"Come now, Piety." Eli spoke to her as if she were a petulant child. "You're behaving as if you're scared to be alone with us."

"I am scared to be alone with you, Eli, and you are fully aware why."

"Now you're being outrageous simply for dramatic effect, Piety," Mrs. Limpett said. "You've done enough damage without heaping slander on Eli. For God's sakes, he is your fiancé."

"Eli is not my fiancé, Mother, and pray, do not say that again."

"All right, stop!" said Eli Limpett, his voice much harder than before. "Idelle," he called, "brothers. Let us do as dear Piety bids. We are irritable from our travels, and the marchioness offers a generous repast. There is no reason for our reunion with Piety to be so contentious. Piety is, obviously, not yet ready to take her leave. Let us indulge her a few hours more. As guests in this lovely estate, I know we'll all find quiet moments and private places to *reunite*. I cannot think why Piety would wish to air her family's conflicts in full view of her new friend, the marchioness, a woman who clearly thinks so highly of the girl's comportment. But then again, we are merely guests. And what good ones we intend to be." He flashed his false, toothy smile around the room.

He continued, "Pray, my lady, where should I tell our coachman to stable the livestock, and is there a place that we might wash?"

Lady Frinfrock stared at him, considering. "Very well," she finally said. "Godfrey will show you to rooms and instruct your grooms on baggage and the carriage. Luncheon convenes at twelve o'clock noon. Please plan to join us in the dining room."

"Splendid." He bowed again. "Thank you so much for your hospitality." He shot Mrs. Limpett a shrewd look.

"Yes," said the American woman flatly. "Your kindness is an unexpected delight."

Godfrey, bless him, appeared in the next instant, making further conversation unnecessary. "This way, if you will, madam, sirs," he said, and they filed out behind him, some scowling at Piety, some whispering.

Eli and Mrs. Limpett stared straight ahead.

Chapter Twenty

"You were right all along, my girl, and how brilliant I am to have seen it," the marchioness said, taking a sip of lemonade. "You may relax now, to be sure. Enjoy the histrionics. I intend to, certainly."

The marchioness sat on a high stool, cool drink in hand, while Piety stood beside her in the red parlor outside the dining room. Tiny and Jocelyn whispered in the corner.

"We've merely made them angrier," Piety said, shaking her head. She set her goblet, still full, on the sideboard and looked again to the main stair. Vacant. How very like them to convene for luncheon late, another arrogant rudeness. Piety nodded to herself. "How I wish I wasn't right about this, my lady; but believe me, this is the quiet before the storm."

They'd gone upstairs an hour ago, all six of them, while Piety had smiled blankly, her trembling hands clutched behind her back. Godfrey had installed them in guest rooms on the third floor, and it was there that they remained—quiet, making no special requests—until well after the appointed time for luncheon.

"They have used this time to conspire," Piety said.

"They've been huddled around a book of table manners, if they know what is good for them," said the marchioness, chewing on a sprig of mint from her glass. "They may conspire all they wish, but you've told them what you intend, and they have stayed, haven't they?" She chuckled. "What a sight it was!

"To be honest," the marchioness continued, "I wasn't entirely sure of your claim to this alleged fortune, myself. I was willing to help you regardless, mind you, but I half expected them to turn up with a court order that demanded you hand over the money and the house and all of it. God knows what kind of legal trip-trap they might have summoned. But what did they reveal? Nothing! Entirely empty-handed, with bad attitudes and even worse manners. And to stay after they embarrassed themselves and you behaved so stoically? It tells me but one thing. You hold all the cards, girl, just as you have been saying from the start. 'Tis brilliant. Brilliantly played and precisely what they deserve, the presumptive wretches. I insist you cease sulking this instant."

"I'm not sulking, my lady. I'm bolstering."

"Please! You look like a red fox with his ear to the ground, listening for the hooves of the hunt. How plainly I see it. And sloshing lemonade on my carpets to boot! What you need is to calm and settle yourself. Put some muscle into those pronouncements. They cannot force you; if they could, they would have already done it."

"You do not know them."

"They do not know *you!*"

Collected footsteps rang on the stairs, and Piety looked up.

They descended the stairwell in a flock. Eli and Idelle first, clutching hands, their expressions innocuously pleasant. The other brothers fanned out behind them in an arrow pattern, piranha in a school. Everyone wore a change of clothes—more feathers and fringe, copious cuffs and collars, jewelry. Ridiculous Ennis carried a new cane. They'd obviously come to a collective decision about their disposition. The greedy eyes and cunning smiles on each face were one and the same. They appeared pleased. Engaged. Eager. Like naughty children trying so hard to be well behaved the night before Christmas.

Piety took a deep breath and snatched up her drink to keep her hands busy. She had endured a lifetime of her mother's insults and intimidations, but the threat of Eli's aggression was new and frightening. He had been easily managed until he realized how steadfast she was in her rejection. In the weeks before she left New York, he had grown bolder, more aggressive. He discovered new ways to come upon her when she was alone. Once he had tried to restrain her, to kiss her and touch her.

She began plotting her move to London that very night.

And now, here he was. And, Piety had only her resolve for freedom to sustain her. She reminded herself to stand up straight, to raise her chin. She forced a smile. "Hello, Mother," she said, bowing slightly.

"Daughter," said Idelle coolly.

Eli bowed, too. "We should like," he paused for effect, "to begin again."

He smiled at everyone: the marchioness, Jocelyn, even Tiny. He stopped short of smiling at Piety, likely because she recoiled visibly when he did.

"We failed miserably with introductions before," he went on. "An unconscionable breech. And we are hoping, Piety"—he shot her a look—"that you would do the honors?"

No, thought Piety, even as she nodded to the floor. What choice did she have?

"Your ladyship," she said wearily, "may I present my mother, Mrs. Idelle Grey-Limpett of New York City." Idelle dipped into a slow and deep bow. "And you'll remember meeting her stepson, Mr. Edward Limpett."

Edward stepped forward and bowed.

"And Mr. Ennis Limpett, another stepson." *He spits when he talks.*

Fat Ennis marched forward with his new cane and affected a deep bow.

"And still another brother, Mr. Everett Limpett." *Whose hands are always sweaty and whose hair is speckled with tiny white flecks.*

Reed-thin and perennially stooped, Everett spidered forth.

"Also, Mr. Emmett Limpett." *Who smells funny and will assault one of the maids before we eat.*

Shiny headed, with pants nearly to his armpits, Emmett stepped forward and bowed.

"And finally, Mr. Eli Limpett." *Who scares me to death.*

The memory of their last encounter came flashing back—hands and mouth and sour breath. She shivered but did not allow herself to step back.

The marchioness watched the procession with detached interest, nodding slightly.

"How do you do, my lady?" They all mumbled pleasantries compliantly, shuffling to various areas of the small space.

"Your home is lovely, marchioness," said Ennis, gesturing broadly at the walls of what was easily the smallest and least-grand room of the estate.

"Thank you, Mr. Limpett. I trust you found your rooms adequate?"

There was a resounding affirmative response, and Eli added, "It is obvious why my fiancée enjoys your hospitality."

"I have asked you not to imply that we are betrothed, Eli," said Piety.

"Miss Grey wishes to be properly wooed," interjected Emmett, chuckling. "Women do have their ways."

"I do not wish to be wooed. I wish to be left alone."

"But, sweetling, it is you who has insisted that we stay." Eli's words oozed with forced charm.

"You may stay if it pleases you, but do so knowing that your presence here has no bearing on me."

"No bearing?" said Idelle. "We've just chased you halfway across the globe. We are here *because of* you, darling. To *see you*. We miss you, dearest."

Piety nodded. "I am well aware of what you miss."

"Ah, but here is Godfrey." The marchioness eased from her stool. "I hope our American guests convene with an appetite. Garnettgate boasts a talented and generous cook, and English cuisine is not for those with paltry constitutions." She glanced at Piety's wispy mother.

They entered the dining room on a chorus of professed starvation, followed by exaggerated praise about the appointments of the dining room: the china, the chandelier, the linens, the soup already in bowls at everyone's seat. Only the place cards distracted them. Seating had been prearranged by Piety and the marchioness, but the Limpetts embarked on a nearly instantaneous petition to rearrange them. Lady Frinfrock ignored them.

Piety was seated to the right of the marchioness, with Jocelyn beside her. Tiny sat on the other side of the marchioness. Tiny was seated next to Edward, who was obviously affronted by the arrangement, but he was powerless to do anything about it. Idelle sat beside Jocelyn. The other brothers fell into line down the table, with Eli, thankfully, the farthest away.

When the marchioness picked up her spoon to test the soup, everyone gingerly followed, murmuring their delight at the taste, texture, color; someone even praised the temperature of the dish. Piety rolled her eyes. It was if they hadn't been fed in weeks.

After two bites, Idelle, cleared her throat and said pleasantly, "I hope you'll allow me to continue to explain our rudeness—mine especially, your ladyship—when we arrived."

"No explanation is necessary, Mrs. Limpett," said the marchioness. "Please enjoy the soup."

"Oh, but I insist," Idelle said.

Piety jabbed at a fleck of thyme floating in her bowl. She had seen her mother embody artifice in so many forms; she assumed that no new subterfuge could surprise her. But sweet, imploring amends? This was as unexpected as it was suspect.

Adding a note of pout to her voice, Idelle continued, "I think I speak for all of us when I say we arrived here under the assumption that Piety would be cross with us."

"Cross?" Piety asked.

"But of course, dear," continued Idelle, bereaved. "What else were we to think? You left New York with no warning. Under the cover of darkness. Without as much as a good-bye. When we finally, *thankfully* discovered that you had sailed abroad, what else were we to assume? We asked ourselves again and again: What on earth could drive you to behave so irresponsibly?" She patted her neck and chest, reaching for composure. "The most obvious conclusion was that you left in an angry rage. Too furious with us to even say good-bye."

Idelle turned to the marchioness. "Do you have a daughter, Lady Frinfrock?"

Piety shut her eyes. *So it begins.*

"My husband and I were not blessed with children," said Lady Frinfrock, enjoying a hank of bread.

"Oh, my lady!" Idelle attempted to sound sympathetic. "What a cruel trick of nature. How sorry I am."

"Your sorrow is misplaced, Mrs. Limpett. It did not trouble us. Our lives were very full with our own happy companionship and other interests. I am an avid naturalist, as you'll see if you have the opportunity to tour my gardens, and the late marquis was a noted historian of some merit."

"Yes, but now he is gone. And you are here alone, with no devoted children to look after you. As you advance in years, my lady, who will see to your health and care?"

"If you must know, Mrs. Limpett," the marchioness said, resting her spoon and motioning a footman to remove her bowl. "I am entirely self-sufficient and in near perfect health. And, should I need anything, Miss Breedlowe here has also served as my paid companion."

Oh, no, thought Piety, pushing her uneaten soup away. *No, no, no.*

"Miss Breedlowe?" Eli repeated the name, confusion in his voice. "Forgive me, marchioness, but I was under the impression that Miss Breedlowe served as Piety's chaperone."

"She does," the marchioness said simply.

The footmen descended on everyone's soup, replacing it with quail and vegetables. Eli sneered at the imposition of the servant in his way. "So which is she? Her ladyship's companion or Piety's chaperone? Surely she cannot do both. Not with any real effectiveness."

The marchioness eyed him shrewdly but said nothing. Piety looked at the fowl on her plate and felt ill.

Beside her, Jocelyn cleared her throat slightly and said, "I was hired—originally—to serve the marchioness. But when it quickly became obvious that her ladyship is wholly independent and requires no outside care—"

"I beg your pardon," Eli cut in. "Who was it that 'originally hired' you, Miss Breedlowe?"

Piety tossed her napkin over her plate. "What difference does it make, Eli? Do you require the services of a paid companion?"

"Don't be absurd." He smiled. "Her ladyship mentioned that she has no children to look after her, so it begs the question, who hired Miss Breedlowe to serve as her ladyship's companion?"

"My solicitors," said the marchioness, taking up her knife. "Miss Breedlowe was hired by my solicitors. But it quickly became obvious that we were a poor fit. Primarily due to lack of need."

"And so you exchanged her for Tiny." This deduction from fat Ennis, his mouth full.

"Now there's a worthy question," Idelle said. "I am beside myself with curiosity with regard to our Tiny Baker." She ticked a finger back and forth between Tiny and Lady Frinfrock. "How did Piety's lifelong maid wind up in the service of an English aristocrat? This surprises me, Tiny." Idelle inclined her head. "I thought your devotion to Piety was absolute."

The marchioness frowned. "I will not discuss Miss Baker's relationship to me, except to say that she is a guest in this house and at this table and is, in no way, in service. I also will not discuss my solicitors, my health, or my decision to forego the companionship of Miss Breedlowe. Miss Breedlowe transferred her employ to Miss Grey's household. Really, there's nothing more to be said on the topic."

Idelle scoffed. "Household? *What* household?" The new tone—her *real tone*—triggered a fresh knot of dread in Piety's throat, and she stared at her mother. It was early in the proceedings for her to lose her composure, but Piety knew that tone.

Idelle voraciously attacked the fowl on her plate with fork and knife. Never had she seen her mother eat more than three bites at any given meal, yet now she verily sawed her quail in two.

"You cannot mean *that* house?" Idelle continued, feigning surprise. "In London? Please, your ladyship. I would expect a woman of your wisdom and experience to embody a right-minded influence on my misguided daughter." She stabbed a piece of fowl and studied it. "Let us not encourage her to keep up the charade of *playing house* in that rattletrap calamity, which awaits only a strong gust of wind to topple into the street. I cannot hear it referred to as a household again, truly, I cannot." She gobbled the quail with a strangled expression.

Idelle swallowed and continued the rant. "Really, it's one thing for you to cause such trouble, but to involve an innocent old woman? Whose lawyers are obviously already concerned about the soundness of her faculties?"

Piety stared at her plate, fighting the irrational urge to crawl beneath the table. She forced herself to speak up. "Your assumptions are not only rude, they are incorrect."

"Oh, was that rude? Forgive me." She laughed gamely. "I wish to abide by the rules!"

Down the table, Eli cleared his throat. Idelle waved him off. "I am merely saying that Piety suffers from poor judgment and willful disobedience. It is restraint she should seek from her elders, not encouragement!"

"I do not suffer, Mother," said Piety. "In no way, do I suffer."

"Do not suffer? My girl! You've spent God knows how much money on a house that isn't fit to stable cattle. Not only did you buy it, but you moved yourself and a fortune in dresses and jewelry inside. Alone! Without so much as a mature advisor to look after you. I pray you: Do *I* sound like the maddened woman here?" Idelle looked frantically right and left.

Up and down the table, the Limpett brothers stabbed hunks of quail with their forks and shook their heads.

The marchioness finished eating and signaled for her place to be cleared.

Jocelyn stared into her lap.

Piety felt the color drain from her face, and she squeezed her hands together to contain the tremble. This had been a mistake. Her mother's insults typically ranged from unpleasant to disconcerting—but to endure this in the presence of her friends? To have her friends be insulted as well? The result was excruciating.

Idelle's voice rose. "Surely *I* am not the only one who thinks Piety's behavior is entirely unacceptable, bordering on scandalous? Surely *I* am not the only one who finds her entirely out of hand? Who feels she's put herself and her reputation at risk?"

Piety dropped both hands on the table with a thump. "My house is not that bad."

"'Tis that bad, and worse. If one brick were knocked loose, the entire structure would crumble. And it's crawling with workmen!"

"The men are there to make repairs. And I am not alone with them. I am appropriately chaperoned all of the time."

"By the nursemaid of your elderly neighbor? I hope you won't take this as an insult Miss…?" Idelle cocked her head toward Jocelyn beside her. "Forgive me, remind me of your name?"

"Jocelyn Breedlowe."

"Right, *Miss* Breedlowe. Can we presume, considering your dual professions of caregiver and chaperone, that you have no husband or children? That you, too, are an unmarried woman? If so, you hardly qualify as a suitable chaperone."

"Must you offend everyone at the table, Mother?"

"What offense? I am telling her that she is still free to marry. It is a good thing."

"Is Miss Breedlowe not married?" This from Emmett, ever in search of his next conquest.

"Well," said Idelle, pushing away her plate of triple-cut food. "All I can say is that Eli has been mortified at the indecency of it."

"I do not care what Eli thinks," said Piety.

Idelle gasped. "What's this? What way is this to regard the fair opinion of your, if I do say so myself, *indulgent* fiancé?"

"He is not my fiancé," Piety said.

"Well, he will be in short order!" said Idelle. "After this stunt, I hope you realize that you'll no longer be allowed the freedom of unattached idleness. I won't stand for you putting off this wedding for one season longer! You must be made to listen to reason. If not by me, then by a husband with your best interest at heart!

"Your ladyship, please." Idelle appealed to the marchioness. "Clearly my daughter respects you. You must help her to see that a twenty-five-year-old young lady cannot flee her home and country and carry on abroad without some consequence. A safe, respectable marriage is the natural course for an unattached girl of her age and means, especially one so given to the scandalous combination of peculiarity and strong will."

"Mining my experience and wisdom, are you?" said the marchioness. "I'd say Miss Grey is of an appropriate age to marry. But whether she is forced to marry her own stepbrother seems a separate issue from whether she should marry at all."

"But he is the only one to have her!" Idelle laughed bitterly. "Do you think respectable men from decent families would even consider her after she's fled our shores without a backward glance and purchased ill-advised property in another country? Entirely on her own? Decent men find her alarming! And difficult. They always have. But now? After this? There isn't a man in New York who would consider her troth. Yet Eli…" She paused to point down the table.

Unable to resist, Piety stole a look at him. He sat back in his chair, humbly blotting his mouth with his napkin.

"Eli shall!" Idelle practically sang the words, as if his mere willingness were a precious gift. "So besotted is he, that he is willing to overlook her recklessness, her impetuousness, her departure from decency. And yet, she has the cheek to sit here and insult him? Forgive me this outburst, my lady, but it's unconscionable. Simply unconscionable!"

"As I explained to you before I left New York, Mother, Eli and I do not suit," Piety said so quietly that she was barely heard over her mother's muffled sniffing.

"Piety," Eli said, "do not say that."

"I will say it," she replied, her voice loud for the first time. "I do not like you, Eli. Furthermore, you do not like me! Is it not reckless for two people who do not enjoy each other's company—and that is putting it very mildly—to marry each other?"

"Your affection will grow, darling," said Idelle, nearly instantly recovered. "Marriage is not all roses and butterflies. A good match has so very little to do with romantic love, whatever that may be. Even you know this. The real happy ending is *security*."

"I have my own security."

"Oh, you mean the money? Good God, Piety, do not be crass. How dare you speak of such things at the table and in the presence of strangers."

The marchioness laughed—a loud cackling that drew everyone's attention. "Forgive me. I have heard that irony is lost on Americans, but we English do enjoy it so."

"I will raise it," said Piety, her voice growing louder still. Every head swiveled back to Piety. "You have stopped at no embarrassment in your discussion of me. Why should I not simply voice the real reason that you've come?"

"Fine," Idelle said, folding her napkin and tossing it over her plate. "You wish to discuss this? Here and now? Fine. You believe, simply because you are in possession of this fortune, that it alone will keep you safe from gossip? From slander? From exile? You think your nursemaid-chaperone will keep you respectable, even though you live alone in a giant, unfit house, with no man to look after you?

"A whore!" she said, the real venom of her voice filling the room. "That's what you'll be. Received nowhere. Tradesmen, shopkeepers, dressmakers—they will only do business with you for so long, considering the reputation you'll earn. You may have allies now, an old woman who befriends Negro maids and her former nurse, but it won't be long until the stigma of your impropriety will taint their reputation as well. Is that what you want?"

"I don't believe you," said Piety. This wasn't entirely true; she did worry about her reputation, her ability to survive as an unattached young woman, but she was determined to call her mother's bluff.

"*Piety*," Eli said, as if speaking to a child.

"Well I don't!" It was a lie. "My experience in England has been nothing like you describe. I am received everywhere. People are lovely! The house needs a few repairs, but by no means is it unlivable. On the contrary, it will be a very fine house. Very fine, indeed!" She scooted back in her chair, and a footman leaped forward to remove it. She stood.

"Look," said Eli, "if it's so important to you, then you and I shall live here for a time. In London. In this house of yours."

Piety looked at him, saw the calculation in his eyes, heard the succinct way he forced out the words. Her stomach constricted in fear, but she said, "*No.* You shall not live with me in London for a time. You will never live with me, Eli.

"Look," she continued, gesturing up and down the table. "Shall I simply give you the money? If I sign over Papa's fortune to the lot of you, would you leave me alone? Leave all of us entirely alone?"

"Would you do that?" asked Edward, who was shushed almost immediately by Idelle.

"It's not about the money," Idelle insisted. "I want to see you married. I want you under the control of someone responsible and trusted in our own circle, *immediately*. Before you embarrass yourself—before you embarrass all of us—beyond repair."

"Papa left me the resources to live beyond your control."

"Your father is dead, Piety." Her tone was final. "He cannot indulge you any longer. Now you must live by society's rules, and mine. Perhaps you think you're paving the way to bohemian freedom with this stunt, but believe me, every defiance, every harebrained scheme that you pull, edges me a little closer to proving that you are entirely incompetent to be responsible for the fortune that has been bestowed upon you. I shall enjoy this holiday to England, truly I will, but there are only so many hurdles over which I am willing to leap before I put an end to it all!"

It was the closest she had come to actually threatening that Piety was not fit to manage her own affairs. It was Piety's greatest fear laid bare, and it nearly silenced her, but the mention of her father had the opposite effect. She had to work to smother a shriek of rage in her throat. Idelle hadn't regarded him in life, except to needle him with relentless complaints or excise more money, why regard him in death?

"If you'll not have Eli," Idelle said, gesturing at each stepson in turn, "then pick one of the others."

"Madam!" Eli was instantly incensed. He slammed his fist on the table, rattling the plates and nearly toppling the centerpiece. Jocelyn lunged for it, while Piety shut her eyes against the escalating ridiculousness of the scene. At the head of the table, Lady Frinfrock merely chuckled. No, not a chuckle, she truly, heartily laughed: a snicker that grew to a full-chested guffaw, eventually cresting in hoots and sputters. Shaking her head, she wiped tears of mirth from the corner of her eye.

"I'm sorry," Idelle said, scowling at her, "I did not realize our family's pain was quite so diverting."

The marchioness tried to respond but failed, holding out a hand while she struggled for composure. "Forgive me," she finally said, still sputtering. "I cannot remember when I have been so entertained over luncheon. I regret that it is at the expense of my dear friend, Miss Grey, and how nobly she has borne it, but truly! You were doing so well, Mrs. Limpett. I was nearly convinced you actually cared about the girl's well-being."

"I *do* care. I care for her future."

"But not my happiness," said Piety.

"You have squandered your claim to happiness with foolish behavior."

"What of the house?" Piety demanded. "What if the house makes me happy?"

"The house is a fantasy that has run its course, Piety." Idelle raised her chin. "It's over—a house of cards, is what it is."

"You are mistaken," Piety said, steel in her voice. "It is a house of brick and mortar, timber and tile. Marble and glass. It is a beautiful home, and I'd like to see you try to take it away from me."

"Did you not hear me?" Eli growled and shoved out of his chair. "You may keep the house. We shall live there, together."

"Oh, Eli, stop talking! Stop!" Piety was suddenly less afraid. "You have absolutely no say. No one here has any say but me." She turned on her mother. "How much? How much of the estate would motivate you to leave here, to cease pretending you care about my future? How much?"

"This is not a solution," Idelle said. "The only solution is for you to marry one of the Limpetts. And I demand that you stop this childish fit before you turn all of them from you for good."

"If only turning them were possible!"

"Fine!" Idelle was shouting now. "Continue on! Continue on until there is no man left on God's earth to have you. Is that what your father wanted? For you to be alone? Childless? Banished for your indecent life?"

Her proclamation sliced through the air, rattling the crystal beads of the chandelier and trembling the water in the goblets. Piety rolled her eyes and drew breath to refute it—same song, second verse—but then Godfrey stepped lightly into the room, clearing his throat. His very presence seemed to embody the distraction they all required, and they turned and watched him stoop and whisper something in the marchioness's ear.

"You're joking," Lady Frinfrock said, setting down her goblet.

The butler shook his head and whispered again.

Lady Frinfrock shoved back from the table. Before a footman could scramble to pull out her chair, a sound from outside the door broke the awkward silence of the room.

It was a cough. Someone clearing his throat. Piety looked around. She knew that cough.

Falcondale.

Before she could react, he poked his head around the door jamb. It was him. Rumpled, covered in dust from the road. He looked casual, and passive, and mouth-wateringly handsome.

"*Right. I…*" he began, looking around the room.

Piety's heart leaped at the sight of him—a surge of gratefulness and joy so sweet that she wanted to laugh. She blinked. She grabbed hold of the back of her chair. She did all the ridiculous, useless, inane things that ridiculous, useless girls do when they unexpectedly find themselves staring at the man that they absolutely did not expect to see. The very man that they regrettably, painfully, unfortunately were so very gratified to see.

"Many apologies for the interruption, my lady," Falcondale said, still halfway out of the room. "No time to send word. I hope you don't mind the intrusion." He glanced quickly to Piety and then away.

"Your man bade me wait in the drawing room, but I smelled…Is that quail?" He raised his eyebrows at the heaping spread on the sideboard. "If it wouldn't be too much trouble," he said, "I rode through lunch."

Chapter Twenty-One

Trevor was not offered quail.

He was not introduced.

He was not bade warm welcome.

No servant offered to take his mud-caked coat or filthy hat.

In fact, the marchioness ordered him immediately from the dining room. Trevor consented, but only after he shared a long, gratifying look with Piety, who stood behind her chair, head high, cheeks bright with color. He trailed behind the marchioness's great bear of a butler, exasperated and hungry, asking himself for the thousandth time why he'd come.

You knew there would be an inquisition, he told himself, ducking into the same small, airless receiving room in which the butler had tried to contain him when he arrived.

You knew there would be suspicion. Deliberation. Ceremony.

You knew there would be a need for a complicated testimony.

You knew there would be no lunch.

He looked around the small golden room and wondered if a tray of quail could be conveyed herein. How much trouble could it be?

Far too much, obviously, as the marchioness bustled into the room behind him. "What business could you possibly have in Berkshire, Falcondale?" she asked.

"I cannot say entirely," he said, exhaling tiredly. It was the truth.

"You will not say?" The marchioness arched one brow. "Or you do not know?"

Both, he thought, turning his back to her. He strode to the window. His sole plan, if he had one at all, had been to ride in on a gust of derring-do. Surprise and impress them all so very much, that they became too distracted to hold him to any sort of accountable dialogue about, well, about what business he had in Berkshire.

To him, it was perfectly obvious. Surely it was just as obvious to the old bat, but, of course, she wanted to make him say it. Why, in God's name, could not the very act of turning up, unannounced, at the country estate of a neighbor he didn't really even know, be enough? He had business enough back in London, travel on which to embark, and a house to sell. Berkshire was, in no way, part of his plan—of any plan. Coming here was easily the most demonstrative thing he'd ever done. Were words really necessary?

He sighed and ran a frustrated hand through his hair.

Lady Frinfrock studied him with assessing, half-lidded eyes. "Would it be useful for me to summon Miss Grey?" she asked.

"Ah..." He hedged, wondering if that would make things better or worse.

Lust-crazed idiot, he chided himself. As if seeing her, even for a moment, was not the entire reason for his ill-advised flight from town.

"It's a start." He managed to choke the words out. "Would you... Would that be possible?"

"Anything is possible, my lord. You are here, aren't you? Although for what reason, I still do not know. If you are to do any good whatsoever, I suggest you locate your tongue."

She rang for Godfrey and gave him orders to summon Piety. Trevor paced while they waited, and the marchioness watched him, making an open study of his face, his travel clothes, and his fidgety progress around the room. He felt like an insect, but he let her look. Her stare was preferable to her interrogation.

He wondered again about the proceedings in the dining room. He had not known what to expect when he arrived, but he would tell them to all go to the devil and dare them try to insult Piety in his presence if so inclined. But the situation did not seem to lend itself, particularly, to his immediate interference. She appeared to be standing her own, and he would not want to overplay his hand the moment he walked in. The American brothers, he noticed, appeared just as smug and opportunist as they had in London; their regard for Piety seemed to simmer somewhere between stare or scowl. It would be an extreme pleasure to hand them their hats, he thought, when the time came. He glanced at Lady Frinfrock. She wished to know why he was here. Well, he could hardly tell her that.

Suddenly, the doorknob rattled, and something in his chest gave a hitch. He turned and trained his eyes on the door, unable to hide his eagerness.

It was Piety, slipping into the room with less bustle and breathlessness than ever he had seen. Her eyes sought his and then lowered. She dipped into a bow. "My lord," she said quietly.

Trevor blinked. He had dreamed of her nearly every night since she left, but his dreams did nothing to prepare him for the flesh-and-blood sight of her. She was as soft and beautiful as always, and yet, her expression was closed. There was no telltale smile. He had never seen her quite so resigned. He didn't like it.

But they were waiting for some greeting. He forced himself to bow in her direction. "Miss Grey," he said.

The marchioness pointed to a chair. "Miss Grey, please sit. I will not lose my lunch because of your forced pleasantries, the pair of you. How obvious it is that you are more than casually acquainted. Let us not forget that I watched you make eyes at each other over the chessboard for more than a week. You may sit, too, Falcondale, before you wear a path in the rug."

"If you'll permit it," said Trevor, "I'd rather stand, my lady." He remained by the window, his eyes fixed on Piety.

Her dress was new; something he'd never seen before. Yellow. Fluttery. It would make a hundred women appear sallow or ill, or, at the very least, silly. On her, it was fresh and light and it would put him in a better mood, he knew, if he were not so damned anxious about her reception of him. Even now, she looked at him for only a moment before she fixed her gaze resolutely at her knees. If he could not see her smile, he reasoned, at least her dress was an echo of her former cheerfulness. It was rationalization, he thought, and a bloody weak one at that. And now it would appear he would be forced to speak, because she would not.

"Look," he began, shoving his hands into his pockets, "you wish to know why I've come. I had the misfortune of meeting Miss Grey's relatives earlier in the week. They arrived in Henrietta Place, made improper advances on her maid, and got into a row with my boy Joseph. I was compelled to evict them from the premises."

Piety's gaze shot up. "Marissa?"

"The servants have recovered, I assume," said the marchioness.

Trevor waved the topic away. "You have to be quite a fighter to get the best of Joseph. And the girl is fine, as well. However, to say that I was not impressed with their behavior is an understatement. How accurate you have been, Miss Grey. They are an abomination. You were right to come here. And, your generosity to Miss Grey is remarkable, my lady. Garnettgate is a gem, by the way."

"Nearly forgotten the loveliness of your home country, had you, Falcondale? I have no doubt that your own country estate in Staffordshire could be made twice as lovely."

He looked away. "Indeed."

"So, what are we meant to take from your revelations, my lord?" asked the marchioness. "You've come all this way to tell us Miss Grey's family is repugnant? If so, you're a month late. Miss Grey and Miss Baker have been saying as much since they arrived in London."

"I came to be another hand on deck, so to speak," he said, and from the corner of his eye, he saw Piety's head rise.

"Another hand," said the marchioness. "Aha. How lucky for us. Let me guess. You will design an ancient Greek structure in which to corral the ghastly Americans? Something with fluted columns? A great many steps?"

"Clever, my lady," he said. Unable to keep the distance between himself and Piety, he ambled behind her. He could just smell the sweet notes of her perfume, see the curls that escaped her chignon. "If everyone in England was like you," he said, "I may never have left."

"Better that you did," she said. "Few people can tolerate either of us. But returning to the topic of your so-called 'handiness.' What can you possibly contribute to the situation?"

Trevor stared at her. "You mean specifically?"

The marchioness narrowed her eyes. "Miss Grey is comporting herself quite admirably. Her mother has no dearth of insults, painful ones, too, invoking the name of her dead father, calling her names. The whole lot of them are tenacious as wolfhounds, and they work well together in a pack. Intimidating— even to this one. Look at her." She nodded toward Piety.

Trevor looked. He'd ridden for two days with thought of little else.

The marchioness sighed. "They may eventually wear us all down. Additional help could not hurt."

"I have no doubt Miss Grey could put them firmly in place." He found himself unprepared to go on. Perhaps he had not thought this through. He could not predict that the marchioness would make him put such a fine point on the reason that he'd come. How could he? He had not wanted to acknowledge what it meant to be here himself.

Beside him, Piety stared at her hands. He wondered if she was curious about it. Did she wish him away? Whatever she wanted, whatever she felt, *why not bloody look up and say it?*

Bollocks, he thought, circumventing her chair and standing in front of her. I'll *say it.*

"I thought perhaps Miss Grey might find it useful if someone else, another man, pressed his suit," he said in a rush. "To...to...scare the Americans away."

The room was silent after this admission, and he paced a line to the window and back. "There," he continued. "I've said it. This is why I am in Berkshire." He looked back at Piety. She stared at her hands. No reaction whatsoever. Not even a glance.

"If Miss Grey is amenable to it, of course. Her attachment to another respectable man might ground her to England, show that she has opportunities."

"And *you,*" asked the marchioness, "are to be this respectable Englishman, I presume?"

"I'm hardly a member of the court, but I am a bloody earl, or so they tell me."

"So all of this is to say that you have turned up here to *court* Miss Grey?"

He held out a hand. "Wait. Let me be clear. I have come here to *pretend* to court Miss Grey."

"That is ridiculous." She thumped her cane. "That won't even get you lunch, Falcondale."

"You couldn't know this, madam," he said, exasperated, "but I have been very clear with Miss Grey from the start, as she has been with me. There was no other protocol than honesty on this score when a beautiful and spirited young woman moves next door to a bachelor of my situation. We were both unattached, as it were, and we got on quite well. I saw fit to be very clear. I have absolutely no wish to marry. Anyone.

I intimated this to Miss Grey almost immediately upon her arrival. It made everything simpler."

"What a lucky girl." The marchioness harrumphed.

"Considering this, it would be unfair to court Miss Grey in earnest. Furthermore, as I understand it, Miss Grey has similarly low aspirations toward matrimony.

"However," he pressed on, "there is no reason the Americans need know this. For all they shall see, I will be wholly devoted to her, earnestly trying to woo her. I will be besotted."

Piety's head slowly rose from her lap. She blinked at him. He stared back, locking eyes.

"I understand what the Americans are meant to think." The marchioness sighed. "What I do not understand is what *you* think. Why? Why on earth would you bother to enact such a subterfuge?"

Because I've gone mad.

Because I could not seem not to do it.

Because I would not have them touch her.

Because it would mean a few more days.

"I want to help," was all he said.

"Because you care so very much about Miss Grey? The girl you will never consent to marry?"

"No," he said, but then he reversed to, "Yes." He shoved a hand through his hair. "It's not...Let us just say I would do it, because I can. And why not?"

He looked at them. They looked back.

"Shall I say it?" he asked.

"I don't know," said Lady Frinfrock. "Shall you? I have no idea what you're talking about. You've scarcely made sense in the half hour you've been in my company."

"Right," he said with steady calm. "Do I care what happens to Miss Grey? Yes. Yes, I suppose *that* is the reason that I would help her. If you must know it."

"You mean *pretend* to help her," the marchioness corrected. She looked at Piety. "Miss Grey? What say you? The earl suggests that some measure of this may be comprehendible to you."

Nervously, his mouth dry, Trevor watched Piety. Before she spoke, she began to nod, and he felt himself draw breath.

Next, in a small, foreign voice, she said, "Yes, my lady. I do understand. The earl wishes to pretend to court me so that the Limpetts will be dissuaded. The courtship is meant to be a sham. He maintains his bachelorhood, and I proceed with my motivating priority, which was to escape a marriage, not find it."

She smiled sadly at Trevor. It felt like a punch in the gut. He welcomed it. At least she had not sent him away.

"Although Lord Falcondale and I would never suit in a romantic sense, we were friends, and I know this gesture comes with deep personal sacrifice. It's very generous, really."

"My house in London has not yet sold," he explained, watching her. "My plan was to eventually sail for Syria, but I have latitude with the departure. There is idle time while I await a buyer. I might as well spend it here as elsewhere." He waited for her to affirm this, trying to see some trace of the unrelenting Piety he knew.

Her silence continued, and he felt himself flounder—a rare feeling, indeed, and he turned away. She knew what he offered. He'd blurted it out plainly enough.

Behind him, he heard her rise.

"I should like to accept his lordship's offer, my lady," she finally said. "If you do not take issue with it. It never hurts to have reinforcements. And I shan't be so agonized if they insult Falcondale. Not as I am when they insult you."

A surge of relief coursed through him, and he felt himself draw a ragged breath. Of all that he had not expected about his flight to Berkshire, Piety's strange, sad silence had been the most disturbing surprise. How foolish of him to assume she would be unchanged in the face of this onslaught from her family. How foolish of him to assume that her sunny, effusive regard for him was guaranteed.

Had he assumed this, he wondered? More like, he had not thought of it at all. Suddenly, it seemed he could think of little else.

"Do not fret on my behalf, girl." The marchioness scooted from her chair. "Although I do see how Falcondale would be convenient to insult. Very well. He may stay."

She was hobbling to the door, but she turned and lashed Trevor with a hard look. "I assume you do know how to properly court a young woman? Or *pretend* to court her, I should say?"

"Likely, I do not."

"Expected. I shall have to take you on, too." She opened the door. "Very well. I am sending Miss Breedlowe in straight away, with orders to be far more vigilant than she has obviously been. There is a familiarity between the two of you that is not borne of passing in the street like neighbors. I don't care what promises you've made to each other about an unattached future. I dare not ask what's been going on in that house of yours, Miss Grey, but it shall not go on here."

"Yes, my lady," said Trevor, while at the same time Piety muttered, "Of course, Lady Frinfrock."

"Very well. I shall return to the dining room and announce…" She turned. "Well, whatever should I tell them? They deserve no explanations, but if our goal is to make a show of the courtship, we might as well talk it up."

Piety nodded, and Trevor shrugged. The marchioness harrumphed. "I'll tell them that Falcondale was overcome with lovesickness after Miss Grey's departure and has ridden for Berkshire with the goal of winning her heart."

Piety chuckled, and he smiled, in spite of himself. He caught Piety's gaze and held it. The muscles in his chest clenched again. "That just about sums it up, I suppose," he said.

"You're playing with fire, the both of you. I hope you know it."

"It is better than playing with the Limpetts," Piety said. "There will be nothing to worry about, my lady. You'll see. A farce, simple as that. We are grown adults. We know the story and how it should go. Thank you for allowing the earl to be included. Thank you for everything."

The marchioness rolled her eyes and left them, slamming the door in her wake.

Trevor looked up.

Piety smiled at him, not her usual smile, but much closer to it. He took a halting step toward her, fighting the urge to reach down and snatch her up. She had accepted his help, but he didn't know how she truly felt about his presence here.

"You needn't worry about my illusions of grandeur," she said. "I wasn't lying when I assured the marchioness.

I understand this is a charade. And I thank you. It might actually do some good. My mother's primary strategy seems to be calling into question the shamefulness of my unattached state. It can only help to suggest I might actually wed. Someday. Not you, of course. But someone."

He nodded. It was hardly the invitation to jerk her into his arms, but he supposed he should appreciate the sentiment. She was being careful. One of them should be.

He took another step closer. "Do me this favor," he said. "Do not speak of the other man you may someday marry."

She narrowed her eyes and frowned. She hated his implication of possessiveness, but he could not seem to stop. Despite the frown, she was blushing now; she must have seen the heat in his eyes. He took another step. He was nearly to her. He was close enough to smell the familiar fragrance of her skin.

"Yes," she said. "No mention of future husbands. I remember now. You prefer to live within the moment of your delight and otherwise leave me to my own devices, whatever they may be. I'm proud of you, my lord. Really I am. What progressive thinking it must have required to move yourself from the moment of your"—she sized him up—"should I call it loneliness? To riding halfway 'cross the country."

She was baiting him, thank God. More like her former self. He was meant to volley back some retort—but his brain was mush. All he could do was *want*.

He reached out and grabbed her wrist.

"I believe I *will* call it loneliness," she continued, but she didn't pull away. "You felt lonely in London. And your solution for said loneliness was to ride here and pretend to court me. My eventual fate be damned."

"I...God, Piety. I can barely think," he whispered, tugging her up to him. She rolled from the chair and fell against his chest with a sigh. "When does it begin?"

"When does what begin?" she said to his shirt.

"The courtship." He released her wrist and slid his hands into hers, rubbing small circles in her palms with his thumbs.

"Well," she said softly, looking up, "Since it is only a charade, I suppose we may start whenever we like. You're the one who rode to Berkshire, overcome by lovesickness."

"*Now.*" He clutched her to him. "It starts now."

His mouth was on hers in the next instant, a kiss that required no preamble. She greeted him with the same fire, the timing and rhythm familiar now, perfect, as if they kissed every day.

"It's only for a week or so, Piety." He kissed her cheek, her ear, her hair, and back again to her mouth. "I cannot put off my departure for long. But maybe it will do some good? Damn, I don't know." He returned to her mouth, savoring the familiar taste of her. "I am a selfish bloody bastard, but I don't care. I—"

The door creaked open then, and Miss Breedlowe stepped inside. She gasped quietly and cleared her throat.

"The marchioness sent for me," she said, "and, I can see she was right. This? My lord? Miss Grey? This will never, ever do."

Chapter Twenty-Two

Jocelyn suggested an outdoor diversion—something that would give the Limpetts the time they needed to adjust to the rather sudden news that Piety would now entertain a suitor. The outdoors might also, Jocelyn suggested privately to Piety, allow the reunited couple to cool their not-so-faux-looking ardor.

Falcondale agreed immediately to a ride to Garnettgate's pond and back. This surprised Piety, as he'd just ridden two days from London, and she was in no way accustomed to his immediate consent.

And best not to become accustomed, she reminded herself, leaning into him as he led her outside on his arm. His agreeability, she chanted, was all for show. He did not really wish to be with her—well, he did not really wish to *stay* with her. It was a favor, nothing more.

As favors went, it was highly effective. The Limpetts were incensed at the notion of Falcondale in general and a ride in particular, even with Jocelyn in attendance. The five brothers and Piety's mother trailed them out of the house.

"If Piety is so desperate to posture over the English countryside," Ennis Limpett said, "then why do it with this fellow? Surely Lord Falcondale is already familiar with the charms of his own country. We, however, would love a tour, sister."

"You miss the point," Falcondale said. "It's not the countryside I wish to see; it is Miss Grey."

"Well," Idelle said, huffing out a breath, "this is quite a change of tune since we met you in London last week. Why, you indicated only a passing acquaintance with my daughter."

"Absence makes the heart grow fonder," Falcondale replied.

Piety looked back at their collective stunned reactions. How nice it was to have someone else engage them.

"If Piety insists on an outing," Eli said, stepping to the front of the pack, "then I insist upon joining the ride."

Some new confidence made Piety say, "You were not invited, Eli. And there aren't enough horses."

"We came by carriage, which was pulled by *four* horses," he said.

"Your team requires rest, you know this," said Piety. "Falcondale will borrow from Garnettgate's stables, but there are only so many fresh mounts. There's no need to abuse the livestock. Besides, you would dislike it immensely."

"You have no idea what I dislike," he said bitingly.

"If you must see the countryside, I can coordinate a group outing to the pond tomorrow. We could arrange a picnic."

"I don't want to picnic," he said petulantly. "I want to be with you."

"Yes, how very much you sound as if you *want to be with me*. You fool no one, Eli."

"How dare you accuse Eli of subterfuge when you have snapped your fingers and somehow materialized a suitor out of thin air," said Idelle.

Piety stopped walking. "Is it so hard to believe that a man would fancy me, Mother?"

"*Someone is lying*," said Mrs. Limpett, coming upon her. "Either Lord Falcondale misrepresented how familiar he was with you in London, or he is lying about his interest in you now. Or both."

The stables were behind them, and Falcondale and Jocelyn stepped up to speak to the grooms about three saddled mounts. Piety turned to her mother. "You look for falsehoods, madam, because of your own habit of bending the truth."

"I will *overlook* the fact that you've just called me a liar," said Idelle, "if you would but cease your childish games. We've journeyed a very long way to see to the serious business of getting you under control. We have no time for foolishness."

"No one asked you to come," Piety replied. "So pray, spare us the burden of your arduous journey to save me from myself. I do not require saving."

Idelle sucked in breath to retort, but Eli stepped in front of her. "How bold you have grown, Piety." She recognized his expression from the night he tried to restrain her. "I can see now why your new friends are so important to you. They encourage your innate defiance."

Piety swallowed hard but refused to shuffle back.

"Go," he went on, nodding to the stable. "Take your ride with Lord Falcondale. Certainly I would never expect to pursue a woman who wasn't the envy of other men. The earl fancies you, as well he should. You are a beautiful, spirited girl, and I understand his suit, however…sudden. That said, you should know that I expect the same attention to my own affections. I should like to escort you, too. Wherever you like. Show me this country with which you've become so enchanted. Surely you would not allow me to travel all this way to refuse me even one word in private. One audience."

"Surely I would," answered Piety, meeting his gaze. Her heart pounded louder than the stomping horses.

"I beg your pardon?" Eli said, shoving up to her, his chest puffed out.

Suddenly, Falcondale was at her side.

"No, I beg *yours*, sir." The earl took her elbow and tucked her close to his side. He began to work his hands into soft leather gloves. "Mind yourself, Limpett," he said casually, but with a faint note of threat. "There are few things more pathetic than a man playing at bully to a lady. Especially Miss Grey. Perhaps you haven't noticed; she is beyond intimidation." He opened and closed his fingers in the gloves and then took Piety by the hand, leading her to the hitching post.

"Pity about the horses," he called over his shoulder. "Sometimes there simply isn't enough to go around."

Ten minutes later, Piety and Trevor stood alone in the bend of a drystone wall, overlooking the green meadow that spilled downward to Garnettgate below. Behind them, the horses grazed and Miss Breedlowe sat at the base of a maple tree, reading a book.

Trevor sighed. "The Americans are horrible. But perhaps worse, they are persistent. Still, they are not impossible. Half the battle is standing firm in the face of their relentless rudeness."

"I don't want to talk about the Limpetts," Piety said.

He nodded and they stared into the sunny horizon together. After a moment, he said, "I would be remiss if I did not say this one more time: You realize that I must go, Piety. After this threat has passed. I still must go."

She had no wish to talk about his departure, either.

She glanced at him. "Of course," she said.

She plucked a flower from the wall, a frail daisy. It sprouted ambitiously from the dirt-caked grooves between the stones. She twirled it between her fingers, watching it dance, this way and that.

"We must both understand this inevitability," he continued. "You convinced the marchioness, but I'm not so sure. When it's over, will you be able to walk away? When I sail east, and your family leaves you in peace, will you be happy?"

"Will *you*?" She jabbed the flower in her hair.

"No. Yes. No. But this is my choice." He scrubbed a hand over his face. "I have said before that I am absolutely unfit to be anyone's husband. Yes, I will be happy—whatever that means—because it is exactly what I've always wanted."

"Well," she said, nodding again, "it's my choice, too. You may rest assured that, although I lack your wanderlust, my desire to remain unattached is just as strong. So you needn't worry."

It was a lie, but what choice did she have? He had never misled her about his intentions. He was here as a favor to her. And his willingness to grant favors was admittedly very slim. She would not take advantage. She would not trap him. If he needed her to tell him she could walk away unhurt, she would tell him. The hurt would be unavoidable, but what really mattered was her commitment to say good-bye when the time came.

"Trust me," she finally said, plucking the flower from her hair. "You needn't worry about me becoming attached and trying to wrestle you down the aisle." She tossed the daisy to the ground.

"You're sure?"

She laughed. "You're an arrogant one. Do you think I cannot resist you?"

"Hardly." And now he laughed. "On the contrary, you're a beautiful girl, Piety. Clever. Resourceful. Charming and kind-hearted. There are hundreds of gentlemen in London who would be deliriously happy to bask in your attentions. I have puzzled over your affection for me, of all men, from the beginning, but I'm too selfish to stay away. I'm here to support you, but you're managing beautifully on your own. You could stand up to them without me. You have never needed my help."

"Untrue. When we could not figure out about the stairs, I needed your help."

"Bollocks. I posed an irresistible challenge. I know you." He pointed at her. "Any solution so easy and uncomplicated as hiring your own man would seem premature and undercooked in your view. Admit it, you considered it cheating." He turned away and leaned his elbows on the wall. "It makes no sense, Piety. I'm selfish and rotten to the core. I have no idea why you tolerate me." He turned to stare down at her.

"Well, you take me seriously," she said, surprising them both. She'd never considered this in as many words, but it was true. He might as well know.

He stared a moment more and then looked away. "Another lie," he said to the pasture. "I've told you repeatedly that your new house is fantasy. I've been like a human stone around the neck of your ambition and your dreams. And I hate myself for it, Piety, because I know what it means to have your dream postponed."

"You *challenged* my dream, made me fight for it, but you never told me I could not have it. And you allowed me use of the passage. You designed my stairwell. You have been generous with my workmen."

He made a scoffing noise and shook his head.

"If you must know," she said nestling closer to him, "I like your hair." On a whim, she reached out and tousled her favorite lock, the heavy, deep auburn curl that fell across his brow. He lifted his head, his eyes suddenly hot, and he leaned into her hand, pulling it from his hair to his cheek, then to his mouth. He began gently kissing her palm.

"And I like your boots," she continued, tapping his tall, black Hessians with her toe. "I like the way you stride around and make horrible, sweeping generalities that, deep down, you hope are not true."

She took a deep breath. "And I love that you cared for your mother."

His kisses ceased. "What?"

"You could have easily foisted her off on a cheaply paid caregiver," she said. "But you didn't. You stayed. And that is to be commended."

"Do not deceive yourself, Piety," he said. "I resent those years with my mother. The only reason I did not foist her off on someone else is because there was no money to do it.

My family provided absolutely nothing beyond my education. I risked my life and sold my soul in service to Janos Straka in order to support us in Greece—and that is a threat I may never outrun. No, 'resentment,' is perhaps too mild a term for what I feel for my mother."

"Yet you did not cross her?"

He shook his head. "She was the weakest, most pathetic creature you can imagine, due to her own, self-reveling misery, perhaps, but she knew very few, if any, comforts in life. For whatever reason, my nearness brought her a small amount of cheer. So I stayed."

"And *that* is what I like."

He stared at her.

"Well, you did ask." She chuckled.

"My hair, my boots, and my mother. Forgive me if I am unconvinced."

"You're forgiven," she said, and she grabbed his hand. They walked along in silence for five minutes, then ten. They'd nearly made it to the line of trees at the edge of the field when Piety asked, "Was the work you did for this man in Athens, this Janos Straka, completely horrid? Did none of the work satisfy you in a way?"

He laughed bitterly. "Satisfy me? Let me see. It provided me with money, most of it stolen from someone else. There was copious liquor, should I wish to remain foxed at all hours of day and night, which I did not, as one needs to remain alert if one wishes to remain alive. There were also whores, should I wish to catch a pox or father an orphanage-full of bastard children—also not my ambition. And let's not forget the tenuous respect of the brood of ruthless underlings who would just as soon slit my throat and replace me as do what I say. Oh, but I did learn to fight, which has been useful. So I suppose there was that."

"And you're telling me that you never stirred some mercy into the mix? If you were in such a position of power, you could do good things, as well as bad. Help widows and orphans. Improve horrible living conditions. Look at me and tell me you never did these things."

"Oh, no, you don't," he said. "Do not romanticize it, Piety. It was a means to an end. I did it to provide comfort for my mother. After she died, I did it because I hadn't yet discovered a way *not* to do it."

He had not affirmed or denied her suggestion of mercy, but she did not press. After a moment, she said, "And then you became earl."

"Yes. And then I became earl."

"And you lorded over him?"

"God, no. *No one* lords over Janos Straka. He has a deep-seated fascination with nobility. He came from nothing and has amassed considerable wealth, but proper respect has always eluded him—primarily because he is a ruthless criminal. When he learned I had inherited an earldom, he was soundly impressed, I think. He simply let me go."

"Just like that?"

"As far as I know." He flashed a reckless smile that made her stomach flip. "He said he understood that I must return home to take my rightful place, et cetera, et cetera, and I did not bother to dissuade him. Joseph and I packed our meager belongings, and we fled.

"To start a new life."

"To start my life at all." He laughed. "No sick mother, no Greek thugs…"

Piety thought, *Only me and my complicated problems, instead*. This reality hung, unsaid, between them.

After a moment, she said, "You were unhappy with your lot, Trevor, but it is an honorable thing to make the best of a bad situation, as you did with your mother."

"Honor?" He stopped walking and released her hand. "Honor? She suffocated me, Piety. My family betrayed me. Friends were nowhere to be seen. *No one* gave aid. As an eight-year-old boy, I didn't understand it. As man, I accept it, but there is no honor."

Piety continued to walk, but she turned around, facing him. "Well, you could have walked away. A lesser man would have made some arrangement, however insufficient, and vanished. You were dealt a bad hand, Trevor, this I see. No boy should have to act as caregiver to his own parent and give up so much. And yours is a curious, intelligent mind; what a waste to lock it away from opportunity and prosperity. But you did what you had to."

"Ah, this is your own guilt talking."

"I beg your pardon?" It was her turn to stop.

"You think of your own indulged childhood, and mine sounds unlivable. I did not embark on this conversation to elicit your pity."

"I don't pity you, you impossible man, I'm trying to convey a compliment! And I harbor no guilty feelings about my childhood." She resumed walking, increasing her pace. "You wish for *my* life, Trevor? Would you like to trade my mother for yours? Do you know how many nights I have cried myself to sleep—*cried*—because I wanted so desperately for my mother to want me, to love me, to care about anything remotely connected to me? Why even have a mother if her only purpose is to torment you and wring personal gain from manipulating you? No amount of crying will answer that question or make the circumstances new. This I know. But have I sworn off all human connection because my mother hates me? No, I have not. Indeed, I look to other people—to you and Miss Breedlowe, and the marchioness, and Mr. Burr, and anyone else who is willing—to help me get through. And, in return, I will endeavor to help them. In any small way that I can. You'd be surprised how easy it is to help. How painless. Encouragement. A listening ear. Advice. A fresh point of view. And both parties are rewarded. Not burdened, as you insist. Not trapped. Simply better."

"All I meant to infer," he said, catching up, "was that, barring your mother, who is, obviously, deranged, people love you. They want to help you."

"Oh, and people run screaming when they see you?"

"They have. In the past. When I was a boy, they did."

"But some boys are beaten, Trevor. Abandoned. They know every manner of abuse and neglect. Your mother may have been needy and ill, but she obviously loved you. It's no small thing, knowing a mother's love."

"Try as I might, I cannot weep for you, Piety. How bad can it be, with a millionaire father you adored?"

She stopped walking and shrieked, a noise of frustration and anger. "I will not," she said gruffly, "stand here and trade childhood abuses with you, Trevor Rheese, *Lord Falcondale.*

Life is too short to debate which wounded soul had the worst life. I will not!"

"That's not what I'm trying to do. Damn it, Piety! Do you think I've ever told anyone this insufferable dribble but you?" He took her by the shoulders. "You cause me to reveal things I would ordinarily never say outside of my own head. Ever! *You* asked me about this, Piety."

"Yes, and acknowledge that it helps, Trevor. Talking as we are is how people discover each other. This is what happens when you allow someone into your life, to give them a glimpse of your fears and dreams. You speak. You reveal truths. *You share.* Be horrified if you must, but admit it: The burden is not so great, hearing about my life. Listening and understanding. And what have you received in return? You have unburdened your own mind of old hurts and anxieties. It's better. *It makes you feel better.* We both feel better."

"I do not feel bloody better," he said. "I feel awful, and look at you. You're three shades of red and wheezing, for God's sake! We're shouting at each other in a bloody field."

"Fine!" She threw up her hands and backed away.

"So be it!" He scowled back at her.

Silence descended between them; their panting was the only sound. They glowered at each other, shoulders tensed, fists clenched.

When they finally moved, it was as one.

She opened her arms, a questioning gesture; he reached for her. She allowed herself to be pulled, and he brought her to his chest.

"Even shaking with anger," he whispered, "why can I not resist you?"

He leaned down to gently kiss her lips. Once, twice, three times. He checked the location of Miss Breedlowe—a spec on the horizon, some distance away—and then he dipped for a fourth time, sinking deep into a kiss that went on and on.

"Our words," she said, coming up for air and pulling back, "are intimate and our bodies long for the same intimacies."

"My body longs for something," he said, capturing her mouth again, "but words are not it."

With little care and no finesse, they fell against the dry-stone wall, dislodging a hail of pebbles. He pressed against her, fusing their bodies, and she arched, straining for the same closeness.

Without breaking the kiss, he picked her up and plunked her down on the top of the wall.

"I simply want you to be willing to..." she tried to say, kissing every area of his face.

"*So willing,*" he agreed, slanting his head, trying to catch her mouth.

"Willing to reach out," she managed to say. "Friendships. In Syria. Wherever you go." After a foray down his neck and throat, she returned to his mouth. "There may be a woman there," she continued. "You may—you *should*—find some comfort with a special girl. You may find love. Simply consider it, Trevor. You think you want to be alone forever, but you deserve so much more. Someone deserves *you.*"

"I don't want anyone but you," he said, kissing her. "You are the beginning and the end for me. More than enough. You are far better than I deserve. No one could ever exceed you, ever, and I will take these memories with me to my grave." He dropped onto the wall beside her and pulled her into his lap, kissing her anew.

"Piety!"

She heard him calling her name, and she moaned.

"*Piety?*"

No. Wait. *Not* him.

"Piety Grey!"

Someone else. Calling her. Tinny and dim in the distance.

They both ignored it, allowing the kiss to rage on.

"Piety!" the voice said again. "*Lord Falcondale!*"

So loud. So ill-timed. *Just a moment more.*

"Your lordship! Piety, please!"

It was Trevor who finally pulled away. He swore and rested his head against her cheek, breathing hard. He held her so tightly, she could barely draw her own labored breath.

"It's Jocelyn," Piety whispered.

"So I collect," he said.

"She's only doing her job. I'm awful to her. Truly, I don't see why she puts up with me. I'm the worst-behaved girl ever to be chaperoned."

"I doubt that sincerely." He lifted her out of his lap and smoothed her dress back in place, glancing at the chaperone now fifteen yards away. "She is waiting patiently. She can see we are now, er, in possession of our faculties." He began to right his own clothes. He ran a hand through his rumpled hair. "But she won't insist that—"

"Take heart," Piety said tiredly. "Miss Breedlowe understands the circumstance. She will not be happy, and she will blame herself, but she knows this means nothing."

"Right," he said, nodding and rubbing the back of his neck. "I will...I will see to the horses." And then he strode away, nodding curtly to Jocelyn as he followed the wall back to where they had begun.

"Piety," said Jocelyn, rushing to her side. "You cannot be serious. This is how we're meant to carry on? What am I to do?"

Piety leaned back on the wall, too overwhelmed to even venture an apology. "Question of the hour, Jocelyn." She sighed and threw her head back to stare at the sky. "What, in God's name, are any of us to do?"

CHAPTER TWENTY-THREE

On the edge of Garnettgate's expansive gardens stood a stone chapel and family crypt, where the marquis, they were told, was interned. Although small and vacant of a regular vicar, the chapel could easily host a modest congregation for family weddings or christenings and had done so for centuries. Like every other corner of the property, the chapel and grounds were meticulously maintained to her ladyship's stern expectations.

To Piety, the church seemed like something out of a legend: vine-swathed and dotted with climbing roses, its cracked walls were a hodgepodge of sturdy stone. She'd seen it with Miss Breedlowe the week she arrived and loved it on sight but had yet to go inside.

A week after he arrived, Falcondale announced an errand. This was the same day Idelle and all the stepsons mounted a trip to the village. With everyone occupied, Piety found herself finally able, indeed eager, to explore the church.

Behind the heavy oak door, the chapel appeared even more charming and serene. There was no hint of staleness or gloom so frequent in ancient stone structures. Fresh flowers had been placed at the altar, and the candles were new. Piety lit a candle for her father, another two for Miss Breedlowe's parents, two more for Tiny's brothers, and one for the Marquis Frinfrock.

When the candles flickered in the chancel aisle, Piety slid into the second pew and studied the stained glass windows that formed a colorful mural along the side of the church. In browns and tans, purples and burgundy, the windows depicted the long, noble march of stoic crusaders, off to conquer the infidels. A beastly business, the crusades, but the stained glass was no-less a work of art, and she leaned back and sighed, enjoying the play of color and light.

How long, she wondered, had it been since she allowed herself to simply sit, and stare, and think. She'd been running for so long: from America to London, from London to Berkshire. Running from her mother into the arms of Falcondale who wanted to help her but not to have her. Or to love her.

Not that she required his long-term aid, she reminded herself.

Retain the fortune. Restore the house. Establish yourself as an independent woman, free to do as you please.

Then, and only then, would she begin to think about suitors or her future as someone's wife, if she so chose. Someone willing and open. Someone without agonized notions of being alone forever because it was less of a pain in the neck.

She shook her head and slid from the seat onto the kneeler at the base of the next pew.

My Father, who art in heaven, she began, feeling tears sting the corner of her eyes at the familiar cadence of Christ's model prayer. She continued, reciting it three times more, mindful of the simple meaning, breathing deeply, embracing the serenity, and feeling more at peace than she had in a long, long time.

It was at the close of the third recitation that she heard the first unfamiliar sound. A click. It was small and distant yet eerily out of place in the quiet church. She paused and looked up.

The click was followed by a scrape—wood on stone—at the rear of the chapel.

She turned and squinted into the chapel's shady vestibule.

The front door, she decided. It rattled open and then snapped shut. But admitting whom? Wary, she half rose. She heard footsteps and stepped into the aisle.

"Who's there?" she called.

"Please," replied a voice from the shadows. "Do not allow me to disturb."

It was a voice she knew well. Eli.

"Continue," he urged, still hidden.

His voice sounded mocking and bitter, terrifying—a voice that lurked in the shadows of her darkest dreams.

Her initial wariness crystalized into a sharp, cold fear. She froze in the aisle, still craning to see.

It was useless to pretend he'd merely happened upon her. He'd been trying to corner her all week. She'd deftly avoided him so far, and she had only ventured out alone because she believed he was in town with his brothers.

He's merely a man. She looked right and left, searching for another way out. There were no obvious side doors, only the heavy double doors at the front. She judged the distance between the concealed spot where he now stood and the doors. Eli was vengeful, ambitious, and he had taken rough, frightening liberties with her before, but he was not supernatural. He could only bully her if she allowed it. He'd found her alone and unaware, but this did not spell certain doom.

She looked again for another door.

Nothing.

She studied the windows.

Entirely sealed.

Eli remained hidden, but he called out, "It took some effort, but it looks as if I finally found you without the adoring attention of your assembled retinue. Please carry on with your prayers."

"I wish to be alone, Eli." She stepped back into the pew and edged to the far end. "Miss Breedlowe will join me shortly, however. Please excuse me until she comes."

"I, too, wish to be alone," he said.

By his certain design, everything he said made her more uneasy. It took work to make her voice steady and firm. "If you are with me, Eli, then you will not be alone," she said. "If you must be here, then I will go."

She could hear him moving into the nave, but she forced herself not to look. She would not show fear. She focused on her skirts, her prayer book, the loose candles that she'd left in the pew. She stacked her belongings neatly and moved to the next row.

"It's a rare moment, indeed," Eli continued, stepping closer, "to find you quiet and still. I could get used to it. Please. Return to your seat. Sit down. Kneel and pray. Prepare your heart for what I have to say."

"No, thank you," she said levelly. "I shall not sit. Nor shall I allow your crudeness or arrogance to ruin my time in church."

She spun out of the pew and began a confident march down the center aisle. He loomed in the arch of the nave, but she kept her eyes on the door behind him. He laughed, loudly, crudely, but she refused to look.

Even so, she caught his first lunge in her peripheral view.

It was just a blur of momentum and a guttural oath. He dove, and she darted sideways, trying to skitter away. He missed her shoulders but managed to clamp his hand on her elbow. She yanked her arm back, but he held.

"So jittery, sister." He chuckled cruelly, pinching her elbow painfully, locking her to him. "Why is that? No self-important earl on hand to embolden your insults and defiance?"

"Defiance?" she said, trying again to jerk free. "How can I defy you if you hold no authority over me? There is only disdain. You are not in charge. Stop playing games, and let me go."

"Games are over," he said. "We're straight business now. Come." He dragged her to the side of the church. "Let us have a word."

"I will not!" she said, struggling to get away. He held firm, half shoving her, half carrying her. When they reached the wall, he backed her against it. She tried to push free, but he captured her other hand, manacling her wrist.

"Where's *my* kiss, Piety?" He took a breath, his eyes mere slits. "I've seen the way the earl looks at you, and I'm no fool. God knows what you've given up to him—the least of which would be a kiss. Surely you have at least one or two left? For old time's sake?"

She refused to answer and turned her head—right, left, right again. He pressed closer, his face descending to catch her mouth. Twice he made contact, narrowly missing her lips and landing a slobbery lave on her chin and cheek. Her stomach lurched. She struggled to breathe.

"When will you learn, Piety? I enjoy it all the more when you fight."

His words propelled her, and she fought, ignoring his foul breath, the soft, patchy stubble of his beard, the slick sweat. She tried to scream.

"You think anyone can hear?" He laughed—a cruel, guttural sound—and raised one knee, forcing his thigh between her legs, lifting her. It upset her balance, and she fell against him.

He released one wrist to swat her on the behind. She grabbed his shoulder for support, teetering on his knee. His hand slid from bottom to ankle, fishing for her leg in the hem of her skirts. His fingernails were long, and he tore her stockings, digging violently to reach skin beneath the silk.

The new violation compounded her fear, but she fought harder, trying to keep her wits, keep her balance, keep her will. She would not submit.

When he'd shredded her stockings, his hand massaged up, awkwardly groping, tangling with garters and petticoats. He withdrew it and then plunged in again.

Now, she thought, and she jabbed her free hand to his right eye with a cry, driving down, thumb first, into the bulging, lust-clouded socket. He bellowed and reared back, wrenching them both from the wall.

He nearly dropped her and Piety bucked, kicking off of his leg. She had one solid foot on the ground. The other was tangled in her skirts, but she turned, pulled, and hopped in the direction of the door.

It wasn't enough. Eli recovered and sprang, flinging himself down the aisle and catching the hem of her skirt. One firm yank, and the wool tore, toppling her.

Next he had her ankle, and then he had all of her.

"You pride yourself on humiliating me!" He growled, throwing her against the end of a pew. She flashed him a look of pure defiance and tried to wiggle herself free. He let her go, allowing her to topple backward and scramble along the floor. She was level with his boots now, and she reversed her feet and kicked him. Hard. He nearly fell, groaning in pain.

"Bitch!" He reached down and slapped her square across the face. The room spun, but she kept her focus on the end of the row, struggling to stand as she scooted backward.

"How amusing." He mocked her attempts to flee. "You think you're getting away. About to make a run for it, are you? Here's some news, Piety. We're *finished* running. You. Me. My brothers. Your mother. We're all through! How long did you think you could make us dance to your little tune?" He lashed out and grabbed her chin, forcing her head up. "Skipping merrily around the world?" He rattled her chin, trying to wring an answer. "How long?"

"I'm not trying to make you do anything but leave me alone. All I've ever wanted was for you to go!"

"So you may pursue your life with the earl?" He growled again. "I hope you know he's never going to marry you. Never. You think I enjoy watching him stare at you, and laugh with you, and escort you on bloody walks through the goddamn countryside?"

"I don't care what you do or don't wish to see! You don't own me, Eli!"

"Yes, but has Lord High-and-Mighty *had* you? Has he, Piety?" He hauled back to slap her again, but she turned her face away. He used the force to shove her shoulder. She fell back again.

"The only reason we remain here and allow you to *carry on* with this man," he continued, "is so that he can fuck you well and sure enough to ruin you—ruin you beyond any question of a doubt. After that, marriage to me will be your only remaining option."

Forgetting the danger of his palm, Piety stared at him, disbelieving horror plain on her face. Could her mother possibly know of this plan? Consent to this plan? Surely this could not be her scheme, too. After everything else, this would not be the way Idelle would finally force her to heel.

Eli used her stunned moment to seize her. He grabbed her by both shoulders and drove her into the wall at the end of the pew.

She screamed. "Eli, please!"

He ignored her and ground his fat, wet lips against hers, holding her in place with a suffocating hand to her throat. It muzzled her. She could no longer scream, couldn't even whimper. Inside her head, rage rose to a deafening roar, even while she felt herself slip away.

But then, somewhere in the distance, a new sound. Desperate and urgent and feral.

A bellow—a roar—of rage.

"Release her!" the voice shouted. *"Get off!"*

The clear, angry words spiked over her blankness and startled her just enough. She surged upward to fight again, applying her last gush of strength to pull her head to the side and gasp for air.

"Limpett!" the voice continued, more clearly now. "I said, get off!"

Falcondale. He barreled down the aisle, growling, vaulting over pews, his outrage rattling the stained glass. When he reached them, he grabbed Eli by the shoulder and ripped him away in a yank, his fist connecting with Eli's nose in a sickening crunch.

Now free, Piety spun sideways, gasping and coughing, staggering down the wall. She saw Eli land on his hands and knees. Falcondale kicked him flat to the stone floor. Eli squirmed but did not rise.

"Are you all right?" Falcondale asked, turning his attention to her. He stared wildly at every part of her.

Crying, she ran into his arms. He kissed the top of her head—one quick, hard smack—and pushed her back. "Go outside," he said. "Wait for me."

Before she could object, he stalked away.

"You are a dead man, Limpett!" she heard him say. "If ever—*ever*—you touch her again, I will kill you where you stand. That is, if I do not kill you now."

Eli groaned and swore, cursing his name.

Trevor grabbed him by back of his collar and yanked him to his feet.

"Trevor, no!"

"Piety, I told you to go!"

"See if she minds you any better than she minds me." Eli's mouth twisted into a sneer. "Spoiled rotten, that one."

Falcondale snarled and swung, connecting with Eli's jaw and sending him reeling. Blood spewed across the chancel, staining the satin pennant on the pulpit.

He dropped again to the ground, and Falcondale was on him. He yanked him up by his lapels to hit him again...and again...and again...beating him with a wildness Piety had never seen.

"Leave him!" She scrambled up the aisle. "You know that he is not worth this!"

Trevor was angry enough to kill—skilled enough to do it, too—but to kill someone with his bare hands, even to avenge her, was not a burden she wanted on his head. Eli was defeated. It was enough.

Trevor grunted, going for Eli again, but she grabbed him by the elbow. He propped his hands to his knees and drew labored breaths. Eli, now a pathetic heap of a man, lay fetal on the floor.

"This is finished, and we're leaving," Piety said, trying to lead him away. "Trevor be reasonable. This is not you."

"This *is* me, Piety!" he said, pulling his arm free. "Now you see it. Any fantasy you have entertained about me—about how I passed my time in Greece—let it now be vanquished. Housing orphans and finding work for widows? Try beating people to a bloody pulp. And sometimes," he said, pouncing on Eli again, "they even deserved it."

Trevor yanked him up by his hair. "If ever you touch her again, nay, if ever you *look* at her again, I will finish what I have begun. Do you hear me?"

"Go to hell."

Falcondale released him, and he fell in a heap to the ground.

Piety screamed Trevor's name, stunned by the raw violence.

He pivoted and strode toward the door. For a second, she thought he would leave her there. He didn't look at her, didn't speak to her, but he snatched her hand as he walked by, dragging her behind him.

They were at the doors in the next moment, Trevor shoving them open with the heel of his hand. Barely breaking stride, he pulled her through the churchyard, past the gate, down the path, and up the side of a moss-covered knoll near the edge of the wood.

"Trevor, please," Piety said, struggling to keep up. He ignored her and blazed ahead. Only when they reached the shade of the trees did he drop her hand and stalk on alone.

Piety followed a few steps and then stared after him. "What is wrong with you?"

He slowed, stopped, and then spun to face her. "Are you able to walk?" he asked.

Able to walk? "Yes," she said, "I can walk. Did you think I floated from the church behind you?"

He scowled at her and looked at the sky. He flexed his shoulders, opening and closing his fists.

He began to pace.

She watched a moment, wondering how to proceed. "You're bleeding," she said.

He grunted.

She reached out and brushed a trickle of blood from the corner of his mouth. He ducked away.

"You're angry," she said.

"Anger does not begin to explain what I feel at this moment, Piety. Try rage. Or worse. What is worse than rage? Fury?" He glanced at her. "But not with you."

She nodded and looked back at the church. "If you're trying to frighten me with your violent display, you've failed."

"Let me make it clear that I do not regret what I've done. My only regret is that you prevented me from finishing it."

"I don't regret what you've done, either. I'm grateful. Any woman would be. But it's over, and now..." She stepped closer.

He looked away.

She stepped closer still. He sighed heavily. He seemed determined not to look at her.

"Trevor," she said simply, "will you not touch me?"

He was silent and still, like a stag in view of a huntsman. She wanted to howl with frustration. Could he not bear to look at her? Now, of all times?

"Trevor," she repeated, her voice taut. "I need you. You need me. We need each other. Look, and you will see."

"You need Miss Breedlowe." He glanced at her and then away. "The marchioness. Your friends should care for you. A doctor, too."

"No," she said. "I need *you*. You are behaving as if you are afraid to touch me. I will not break, Trevor. I think Eli made that very clear."

"Do not speak his name!" He took two steps back and bellowed—*shouted*—at the sky. Not a curse, not a discernable word. A howl of frustration and futility and rage. After that, while his voice still echoed in the trees, he lunged, and swept her off of her feet and into his arms. Carrying her, he stalked up the path to the house.

She was taken entirely off guard. One moment he was shouting at the heavens and the next, he carried her. She barely managed an outraged squeak. When she found her arms and legs, aching though they were, she kicked. She pummeled. She made every ineffectual effort to pull away. She wanted him to touch her, but not like this.

"Put me down," she said, squirming, "I've told you I can walk."

He ignored her and stared sternly ahead, plodding toward the manor house.

"Trevor," she repeated. "I said, put me down. Oh, why must you make everything more difficult than it needs to be?"

He shook his head and continued forward, refusing to even look at her. Piety shoved him once more and then sighed deeply, wincing at the pain in her ribs.

She gave up. The will to fight was gone. She could not take on his stubbornness, his black mood, and his strength to hold her. Most of all, she could not fight her own will to resist him. She lay her head on his shoulder.

It was hardly an embrace—more of a sturdy haul than anything else—but it was a closeness just the same. It felt familiar, warm, and safe. She snuggled deeper, turning into his shoulder and breathing in the smell of him: leather, sweat, and *him*. She looped her aching arms around his neck and held on tightly, drawing herself closer with each jostle and jut. If he noticed her shift, he gave no indication. He strode on, blazing up the path, across the green, and clipping up the steps to the rear terrace of Garnettgate.

When the sound of his footfalls turned from gravelly crunch to paved stone, Piety tentatively raised her head and peeked at the advancing house in the distance. The first thing she saw was mid-morning tea. The marchioness was there with Tiny and Jocelyn. Several servants stood sentry.

Oh, God, I cannot.

The thought of a spectacle in front of everyone, of having them see her sullied, helpless, discouraged, was mortification renewed. She returned her face to Falcondale's chest and whispered, "Please, Trevor, no. Can you take me in the side door? To my room?" She could not face them in this condition. She would rather die than frighten them or seem anything less than happy and in control.

"No, I cannot," he said. "The marchioness will fetch a doctor directly, but first she must know why. And I must speak to your mother."

CHAPTER TWENTY-FOUR

The marchioness spotted them before Trevor reached the terrace with Piety in his arms. "Falcondale! Must you now carry her? Is it not enough that the two of you pass every waking moment joined at the elbow, with hands clasped, mooning at each other wherever you go?" The marchioness paused in her tirade. "Good God, is that blood?"

Next came the screech of chairs and hurried footsteps. They had been taking some refreshment in the bright, crisp morning sun. Miss Breedlowe hurried toward them, concern etching her forehead. "Piety! What's happened? My lord, but she is wounded?"

They were upon them then, pawing and patting. In his arms, Piety refused to look up.

Through his haze of anger and fear, Trevor managed to bite out a working sentence. "Miss Grey requires the attention of a doctor."

The marchioness dispatched a footman to fetch the doctor, while Miss Breedlowe and Tiny tugged gently at her, trying to discover the source of her injuries. He did not put her down. It was possible, he thought angrily, that he would never put her down again.

Piety held to him, hiding her face, while her friends attended to her with wet napkins and gentle fingers. Someone loosened her shoes. Her face was burrowed so deeply in his chest, he worried the wool of his vest would chafe her skin. He leaned down, whispering endearments, promising he would take her inside as soon as he'd seen her mother. She whimpered.

"I require an audience with Mrs. Grey-Limpett," Trevor told Lady Frinfrock. "Immediately."

The marchioness studied them both. "Fetch the American," she told a footman. "She's just returned from the village."

"Also," continued Trevor, "Mr. Limpett can likely be found bleeding upon the floor of your chapel."

She looked in the direction of the chapel and then back to the earl. "Let him bleed," she said. "What's happened, Falcondale? Are her legs broken? Can you not put her down?"

Piety finally reared her head, and there was a collective gasp at the sight of her battered face. Trevor could barely look at the gathering bruises and cut lip without charging back up to the chapel to finish what he had begun. He would not insult her by looking away, but he closed his eyes and pressed a soft kiss to a rising welt on her forehead.

The marchioness was the first to speak. "Miss Breedlowe, I ask you, what manner of chaperoning is this? I'm beginning to think you are as unfit as the Americans claim. I thought you said the girl went alone to the chapel to pray."

"But that was her intention." Miss Breedlowe was nearly in tears. She gently smoothed the fabric of Piety's torn gown.

"I suppose you cannot be blamed," continued the marchioness, "but it must be said: The girl cannot be safely left alone, even for a moment. Bleeding and wounded and carried around like a battlefield casualty? What are the servants to think? Their gawking is epidemic as is. This house will be the talk of the county."

Behind them, the door to the terrace swung outward, admitting Mrs. Grey-Limpett to the sun. Piety ducked her head, hiding in Trevor's chest. There was silence. Miss Breedlowe and Tiny shuffled back.

"Am I to be made to guess?" Mrs. Limpett asked.

Trevor gritted his teeth, jostling Piety in his arms. "Try again, madam," he said.

"My, God, Piety, what have you done now? Will your theatrics never cease? Whatever is afoot, I can assure you that no one is amused."

Trevor made a growling sound low in his chest and then said, "Because you seem unable or unwilling to explore the circumstances for yourself, allow me to enlighten you. Your daughter has been beaten."

Idelle sighed. "Yes, yes, but you do not know her as I do. Mark my words, the sooner you cease fussing over her, the sooner we will hear some very far-fetched and unlikely reason. Will you not put her down, Falcondale? It is ridiculous to carry her."

"Ridiculous?" he asked, hoisting Piety higher. "Pray, let me show you ridiculous."

While the assembled women watched, he carried her damaged body to her mother. Piety whimpered and clung more tightly, but he whispered, "I'm so sorry, darling, but she forces my hand."

"No, please don't make me face her." She cried softly. "She will twist it. She will mock me."

"Please, Piety," he said quietly, kneeling beside a chair and settling her in it. "Their abuse persists because no one has ever brought them to heel. But that stops today. Now. You must show her. Let her see what you have endured." He brought her hands from around his neck. "This will be the sort of unflinching courage that demonstrates your strength, not weakness. I am here, but you can do this."

She resisted a moment more, but then he felt her release. She nodded against his shoulder. "Only for a moment," she said.

"Of course." He stood and stepped back. Piety, God love her, raised her chin and stared at her mother through her swollen eye.

Her friends tsked and cried out when they saw her face again; even her mother could not suppress her shock.

"Look, madam," Trevor said, "at the damage wrought by your stepson. The man you would have your daughter marry. Eli Limpett has done this."

"But that is impossible. You lie, sir. Eli prizes Piety above all! He loves her."

"It's no lie," Trevor said simply. "Either the liar is you, or you have been shamefully deceived. I came upon Miss Grey and Limpett in the Garnettgate chapel. I heard a commotion and ran inside. Limpett had her pinned against the side of the church with brute force. He struck her three times before I could reach them. The violence says nothing of the railing, the profanity, and the ungodly names he called her, issuing every manner of insult, not to mention what damage he may have done before I was within earshot."

Piety had ducked her head and turned away, and Trevor stepped forward and kneeled beside her chair once more, taking up her hands. Her mother had seen enough.

"What say you now, Mrs. Limpett?" he asked. "Do you see theatrics in this? Entertainment?"

"I say, fairness dictates that we hear Eli's side of the tale."

Trevor shook his head. "He may spout defenses until the Christ returns, but he may never approach Miss Grey again." The words were out before he fully considered them.

"The devil you say!" Mrs. Limpett shouted. "You have no authority to rule over my daughter's encounters!"

No, he thought, *but I will*. And in that moment, he made up his mind. There was no other way.

He jerked his head at Tiny, who, along with Miss Breedlowe, rushed to Piety's side.

"Perhaps not," he said, rising to advance on her mother, "but you might as well know, *everyone* might as well know. Beginning this moment, it is with *absolute authority* that I rule over Miss Grey and everything to do with her."

Idelle laughed. "You may carry her—bloody and doe-eyed—around the castle grounds, sir, putting on quite a show, but you are by no means her keeper."

He glanced at Piety. She had pushed her friends aside. Her face was filled with questions.

"No, madam," he said, taking a step backward, "not her keeper. But as soon as I can get a license, I will be her husband."

It was, quite possibly, the most inarticulate proposal ever uttered, and it was met by stunned silence.

He risked a glance at Piety. She'd sat up in the chair, her bloodied mouth open, one of her hands frozen, halfway to her face. He was just about to order Miss Breedlowe to settle her, when her eyes rolled back in her head, and she fainted.

"I refuse to speak of her future until she comes to," Trevor told Idelle Limpett fifteen minutes later in the marchioness's salon. "Do not ask again."

The woman gasped, but he ignored her, standing over Piety, watching her breathe in and out, telling himself again that marrying her was the only conceivable course of action. Telling himself that, if handled correctly, marrying her would mean the least amount of bother for both of them and the most effective means of getting rid of the Limpetts forever.

Obviously, the idea had come as quite a shock to Piety. But when she came to, she would see the practicality of it. She had to see. The alternative was no longer an option.

"Forgive me, my lady," Idelle Limpett asked the marchioness, "would you be so kind as to educate my colonial ignorance? Can marriage to the earl make my daughter a...a countess?"

Insatiable pit of nerve, he thought, glancing over his shoulder. "Do not begin polishing your coronet yet, madam, I am an earl, but my wealth is negligible. The previous earl drove the estate into debt, and I am only now digging it out. You may view me as a gentleman scholar and nothing more. Your daughter brings far more wealth to the union than me."

Mrs. Limpett gasped, her eyes grew large, and she clutched the arm of a chair. "So you admit it. You pursue my daughter merely to gain her fortune?"

"I admit to pursuing your daughter to protect her from you," he countered. "And because I enjoy her company. Other than that, I've said I do not wish to discuss it."

"You'll forgive me for pointing out that I find your entire, impromptu courtship to be wholly suspect. And now to hear about your financial situation?" She looked around, concerned. "I cannot believe no one has yet mentioned this."

"How ironic," he said. "Piety speaks of your financial circumstance all the time."

She narrowed her eyes. "Bear in mind, my lord, that you claimed to hardly know her in London, while now you are her devoted suitor. Now you carry her around, bloody and battered. You suffer some altercation with my stepson, who is your chief competitor for her interests."

"Speculate all you like," Trevor said, "but know this: the man hit your daughter in the face—repeatedly—and then nearly disgraced her against the wall of a church. He received exactly what he deserved. I don't care what you believe about my regard for Piety or our courtship, but please understand that I am deadly serious about what I saw and the action I chose to take—and will take again—if ever I detect the slightest provocation."

"My concern at the moment is for your seriousness to this engagement, my lord," Mrs. Limpett said. "Rage and bluster all you must about your own heroics, but I hope you understand that the *announcement* of an engagement will do very little, indeed, to put my mind at ease about Piety's future. Whatever you two have cooked up, a lot of ghoulish theatrics if you ask me—"

"You, madam, are heartless," Trevor said.

"Call me names if you wish," she continued, "but keep in mind that we will be *disinclined* to leave Piety unattended until we see a wedding in deed. *Not* the *promise* of a wedding."

"Why, pray, is it so hard to believe I would want your daughter?"

"Falcondale, please." The marchioness gestured toward Piety.

There was a rustling from the chaise lounge, and Trevor heard a weak voice ask, "Oh, God, please tell me I didn't swoon."

All heads turned to Piety. She tried to sit up, but Miss Breedlowe and her maid rushed to urge her back. Trevor held himself in check but only barely.

Seeing her, hearing her, *hurting* on behalf of the damage to her beautiful face, made his promise of marriage easier to accept. There was no other way. A wedding was imminent— but heartbreak need not be. Not if he stopped allowing himself to indulge in her affection. Not if he stopped *pretending* to pretend to be her lover. Now they could not be lovers at all.

He could not touch her. Ever again. Not in affection. Not to care for her wounds. Not to give or, God forbid, receive any sort of comfort. And certainly not in desire. It was the only way to navigate a marriage that they later planned to dissolve.

And they absolutely must dissolve the marriage in the near future. His regard for her compelled him to marry her now but only for a time.

"I'd require ten minutes of privacy to speak to Piety alone," he said to the women gathered around the chaise.

"Without a chaperone?" Mrs. Limpett asked incredulously, from her place beside the window.

"Leave us." Trevor jerked his head toward the door. "I've offered for her, and we will be married immediately. She's bleeding, for God's sake. What inappropriateness could I possibly conduct?"

The marchioness led the way. "So be it, Falcondale, but the doctor will be here within the hour." She shuffled to the door. "Do not dally. He cannot loiter here the entire afternoon. He'll get an eyeful simply waiting in the hall."

Stillness and quiet settled in their wake, and the hollow space made him nervous. Trevor hadn't realized how distracting the room had been until it was empty. He walked to the window, feeling suddenly choked. After a long moment, he ventured a look at Piety.

"I should have bade them bring tea," he said.

She endeavored to sit up, and it caused her to wince. "Stop," she said weakly.

"What?"

"The last thing that the two of us need is tea." She ceased struggling and looked at him. "What are you doing, Trevor?"

"What do you mean, what am I doing? I am thinking of your comfort. You should take something. Eat something."

"Not about the tea. What is this business of a proposal? *What are you doing?*"

He nodded and turned back to the window. "Do not vex yourself," he said to the pane.

"I'm already vexed, Trevor. Can you not see how *vexed* I am? This proposal—a marriage—is exactly what you said you did not want," she said. "Many times, I was told that you did not want this. And that doesn't even begin to address what I've said I wanted. We cannot get married, Trevor. Why would you say such a thing?"

"To begin, I had no choice," he said. "Even a self-involved blighter like myself would not leave you to be harassed by this pack of mongrels. It's one thing to hound you for money, Piety, quite another for one of them to assault your person."

"Yes, but now that he's done it, perhaps I can go to the authorities."

"What? And drag this out for weeks? I don't wish to expend another hour on the lot of them. My wish is for it to end—for your sake, as much as mine. If we rely on the constable or the magistrate to sort it out, God only knows how long it would take. And who would protect you in the interim? Not to mention that I've beaten the man nearly to death. Hopefully, justice would be served, but the only eye witnesses were the three of us. Let us not involve the law, Piety. Let us end this."

"Oh," she said. "I see. Your idea is to *say* that we're getting married. To *pretend* to be engaged." Idly, she fingered her blood-matted hair.

"Well, yes, in the beginning, that was my idea. However, your mother informed me in no uncertain terms that she would not leave until we are properly wed."

"She called our bluff."

"That is putting it very charitably."

"Well, *you* cannot mean for us to actually wed."

"Yes. I can," he said. "And I do. We shall wed, but we'll do it in name only."

"Oh, God." Piety moaned.

"Please," he said, pacing in front of her, "allow me to finish. It truly is the most practical and least complicated solution."

He paused to glance at her. She stared back at him as if he were mad. He resumed pacing. "Consider it: We get shackled, and rapidly so. I'll get a special license. We allow your family to witness the whole thing: ceremony, wedding breakfast, all of it. I theorize that, without the further promise of money, they will depart almost immediately after the nuptials. And after they go, I will, too. Just as I always planned. First, to London to provision and pack. Then I'll sail for Syria. For all practical purposes, I will be deserting you, my countess."

She looked miserable, but he could not dwell on her misery or even his own. Of course it would be difficult when he went, but at least she would be safe from her family, and he would be free.

He carried on. "After a time, depending on how long it takes you to invest your money or your family to lose interest, we will then have the marriage annulled."

"Annulled?" she repeated, dazed.

"Right. I will have deserted you, and we will have lived apart for the entire marriage. To be honest, we can even tell the courts the truth: that I married you in order to scare off your lunatic family. I don't care. We will not have consummated the union or ever lived as husband and wife, so it really should not be a problem."

"This is the least complicated course of action? *This?*"

"I caution you from thinking about it in specific terms, Piety. It is a broad solution. *Broadly*, it will work."

"Fine. *Broadly speaking*, what if it is more difficult to receive an annulment than you think?"

"The alternative is that we remain married, but live apart." He gave her a pointed look. "That's right," he continued,

"I live alone, in Syria. Egypt. Wherever. I have every intention of being a resident of the world. And you live however you like—in London or beyond. You have the protection of my name, but neither of us have the burden of a real union."

"Burden?" she asked in misery.

He refused to hear her distress. "The problem with this, of course, is that you may never marry someone else if you are married to me. I assume you will take lovers," he went on, looking away, "but you will have no children. Well, no legitimate children." He ventured a glance at her face. "It is a path that I expect that you would not want."

"Well, you expect correctly." She sat up. "I can think of few things worse than becoming the forgotten countess of a world wanderer. Entertaining lovers, and with no children of my own? I'd rather take my chances fending off Eli!"

"That is out of the question," he said, frustrated, running a hand through his hair. "We will marry. We will live apart. We will pursue an annulment and go our separate ways."

"We will," she added, "become embroiled in an elaborate lie and subsequent court proceedings, all because I have been cursed with impossible relatives and you had the misfortune of living next door."

This was true, of course. Piety had posed one challenge after the other since the moment she arrived. Funny how, looking back, he no longer regarded these challenges as unpleasant. They did not so much subvert his life as they felt like life itself. But that was Piety, wasn't it? She brought life to every situation—even construction. Even chess. It was the reason he'd proposed. He could not bear the thought of anyone or anything getting in the way of her sheer abundance of spirit. To protect her now did not waylay him, he thought, it only gave him purpose until he left. He dare not ruminate on this purpose, just like he dare not predict the pain of his ultimate departure. He bolstered himself only with the guarantee that he could, in fact, depart. When the time came. When he cared to. He would be free to go.

After a time, she said, "If we do this, I insist upon paying you. For your trouble. God knows it's a far better use of money than giving it to my mother or the Limpetts."

"You will not pay me," he said and moved to sit beside her. "If I *could* handle the responsibility of a wife or family, Piety, you would be exactly what I would want. When I am an old man, sick and dying, the memories of this time will sustain me. That is its own reward."

"Oh, Falcondale, only a fool would aspire to die alone, clinging to memories of, well, of anything to do with me or my convoluted situation. But who am I to argue? The way you explain it, and assuming you are really willing to do it, I think it might actually work."

The last word came out like a squeak, and she looked up at him and chuckled. He harrumphed. She started laughing. He laughed, too, using the force of his laughter to push his unidentified feelings, his questions about annulment, and his worry about lying at the altar from his head; instead he filled his thoughts with the sound of her mirth.

"So, Piety Grey," he said, endeavoring to sound businesslike. "Will you marry me? For a time?"

With a hand that should not have shaken and fingers that should not have fumbled, he pulled a velvet ring box from his coat and plopped it on the chaise beside her.

She gasped, scooping up the box. "How have you produced jewelry?"

"If I knew nothing else about this subterfuge, it was that no engagement would pass muster without proper gemstones. Your mother would otherwise never believe." Unable to bear his own eagerness, he shoved from the seat and returned to the window. He stuffed his hands into his pockets.

"But wherever did you get it?"

"Even before the altercation with Eli, I suspected this moment might come. So I wrote Joseph and bade him to locate my mother's ring. Just this morning, I met him to collect it. This is why I was away when you...when Limpett..." He trailed off, unable to relive Limpett's attack on Piety. What if he had not arrived when he did?

"You have saved me so many times over." She sighed. "Today with Eli. All week against my mother. Helping me with the house. And now this."

He turned around then. He could not resist the sight of her with the ring.

"It's a beautiful stone," she was saying to her hand. "I've never seen anything quite like it."

He nodded. "One of my few luxury possessions. The center stone is known as a yellow sapphire. My mother always complained that the amber color made her appear more sallow, as if that was possible. And she claimed it irritated the skin on her hand. But it looks glorious on you. As I knew it would. It's yours forever, now. I won't need it, certainly, after the annulment."

"Oh, let us not speak of the annulment, not yet," she said. "Let us enjoy this moment."

"Piety."

"Oh, no, you don't," she said lightly. "Do not ruin my counterfeit joy by lecturing me on the falseness of it all. I understand that it is only a means to an end. I will not trap you with sentimental, guilty lovesickness." She held her hand in the air and stared at the ring. "Simply, let me enjoy the twinkle."

Trevor allowed himself to enjoy her delight for only a moment, but then he returned to her. "Ah, Piety?"

She looked up from the ring.

"You know that if this engagement was *not* a charade—if we tried to be married in earnest—I would make your existence a living hell with my detachment and ultimately, my absence. You comprehend that, right?"

"Yes, Falcondale," she said dutifully, removing the ring and trying it on other fingers. "How awful you are, vanquishing evil stepbrothers, giving me jewelry, and kissing me senseless. I can barely stand to look at you."

"We cannot make this a joke." He sighed, rubbing the back of his neck. "And the kissing must stop. We may be affectionate only enough to convince everyone that the engagement and wedding are real. But your closeness, to put it very mildly, tests the outer limits of my self-control, and we're not merely talking about a week in the country now, are we? Married couples do not employ vigilant chaperones to keep them out of trouble. The annulment hinges on the 'in-name-only' nature of our marriage. Let us be practical about it." He sat at the end of the chaise.

"I am the soul of practicality," she told him, eyeing him over the top of the ring.

"Piety." He said her name as he leaned in. "This cannot be said enough. We must be in agreement. So that no one gets hurt. So that the scheme bloody well works."

"We agree," she whispered. But the way she looked at him was an open invitation, daring him to reach out and gather her up. He shoved his twitching hands into his pockets.

"I won't hold you back, Trevor," she said softly. "Letting you go is the very least I can do."

CHAPTER TWENTY-FIVE

Piety elected to host an evening wedding and dance like those she had attended in America, rather than the traditional English breakfast affair.

She envisioned a garden ceremony, mottled in late-afternoon sunlight, staged beneath Garnettgate's densely blooming rose trellis. There would be musicians on the terrace and a raised dais for the marchioness. Bedecked tables would offer an abundance of hearty food and drink. Someone would erect a Maypole. Happy guests would arrive in the late afternoon and celebrate until well after dark. Neighboring farmers, local gentry, shopkeepers from the village, elderly grandmamas and children of every age—she would invite them all.

The grand scheme, when fully realized, occupied two weeks of planning and then a mad scramble of provisioning, cooking, and decorating. Piety was grateful for the distraction. What else was she to do while Trevor's detachment slowly broke her heart and her mother filled the crevices with criticism and doubt?

"I feel like I'm on holiday, despite the wedding preparations," Jocelyn told Piety five days before the ceremony. They were in the village for another round of shopping and invitations. The villagers of Hare Hatch had thrilled to the notion of a posh wedding to which they all would be invited. Today a trail of eager children skipped happily behind them as they made their way from shop to shop.

The Limpett brothers had wisely removed themselves from Garnettgate after the attack, taking rooms at the inn in town. Only Idelle remained as a guest of the marchioness. The women felt confident the brothers would keep their distance, but they were ever mindful of their menacing presence when they were in the village. They did not wish to come upon them alone.

Piety made no comment, and Jocelyn tried again, "Will the earl not consider even five minutes alone with you, Piety? Or to ride to the village and back? I will feel horrible, taking a salary when there is no amorous couple to oversee."

"Don't be silly, Jocelyn. I would be lost without you."

"I am forever here, Piety, as I hope you know. But I am worried about this new rapport with him. The change is like night and day. Even in London, when the two of you competed at chess, Falcondale was friendly and forthcoming. He teased and goaded and flirted. But now…"

"Flirting is absolutely out, isn't it?" Piety said sadly. "The offer of marriage was such a departure for him, I think he has nothing left to give."

Jocelyn shook her head. "I understand the expectations have changed, but he cannot force detachment, not on you, of all people. It will hardly put the annulment in danger to speak to each other with some measure of warmth or familiarity. You are to be married, for goodness sakes."

They ducked into the grassy lane behind the shops on High Street to escape the children.

"I think he believes that anything we have to say, may be said over dinner," Piety said with a sigh, "while everyone listens in. He doesn't trust himself to be alone with me, I suppose. Or he doesn't trust me."

"Well, you cannot be expected to marry a man and not even know the date he intends to desert you for God knows where."

"Syria." Even the word sounded lonesome to Piety.

"Wherever that may be. The details of his travel would be fair game, and you can hardly ask *this* over dinner. The whole business of him *sailing away* is very vague, indeed. Unfair, certainly. It would not be crazy to think he could be persuaded to take you with him if he must go." She ventured a look at her friend.

"He's going." Piety reminded her—reminded them both. "Alone. This was the agreement from the start. No amount of private conversations or rides alone will change this. Nothing I do will change it." She sighed and switched her basket from right hand to left. It was an excruciating conversation. Piety put on a brave face; it wasn't Jocelyn's fault that the silence and distance from Trevor was slowly eating her alive.

"Whether he goes or does not go remains to be seen," said Jocelyn, shaking dust from her hem. "It's as if the pretend courtship was authentic, and the real engagement is pretend. Forcing himself to resist you? Please. I am a mediocre chaperone at best, but I can assure you that the man wants you desperately. Even Lady Frinfrock can see this. There is no hiding his desire. Even over dinner."

"It's complicated," Piety said simply. Jocelyn was kind to rally for her side, but it did no good to point out that Trevor wanted her. Yes, he wanted her; he simply wanted his freedom more. The reality of his priorities resounded in her head every day. Especially at dinner, when he bade her goodnight and walked away.

"Trust me, he has made it very clear that he is determined to follow the plan. We will annul the marriage at some point in the future. This cannot happen if we have—" She took a deep breath. "If we are intimate. And he sees no other way to avoid falling into bed with me than to keep as much distance as possible. He goes to great pains to ensure we never even touch, as you have obviously seen."

"Not even for a turn around the terrace before luncheon?"

Tears filled Piety's eyes. She shook her head.

They reached the end of the lane and looked right and left.

"Piety, I'm sorry," Jocelyn said softly. "I have distressed you." She extended a handkerchief, but Piety declined it. "Is it awful, to miss him so?"

Piety's voice broke. "It's as if he's already gone."

"You must know he suffers, too."

"Falcondale has a renewed sadness about him." She nodded. "I'll give him that. If I thought his eyes were lonely when we first met, now they are positively hollow. If I did not know better, I would think he harbored some regret—that he felt he had been *trapped* into rescuing me. But he insisted upon the wedding. I tried to change his mind. He wanted this. But he wants it on his terms. A marriage entirely 'in-name-only.' "

Jocelyn nodded grimly and peered around the corner at the tidy shops of High Street. The cheese-maker's was on the corner, and she gestured to it with her umbrella.

"I hope you don't think me too bold in asking this," Jocelyn began as they made their way down the street, "but what of the wedding night? Your mother will stand for nothing less than a traditional bridal suite. What of this forced detachment then?"

"Who can say? At the moment, I am following his lead. If I had to guess, I'd say his strategy is that the two of us will pass our wedding night playing chess. Or sleeping. On separate pieces of furniture."

"And *your* strategy?"

Piety's cheeks grew warm, and she tried to hide a smile and turn her head away.

The cheese shop was shuttered, and they peered through a slit in the window. "You treat him as if he might shatter, Piety," said Jocelyn, "while his behavior toward you is the real abuse. I don't mind saying that I find him to be ruder now—crueler, perhaps—than when he was in London, shouting at you about the house or the passage. At least then he regarded you, no?"

"How can we paint him rude or cruel when he is *marrying me* to save me from my own family?"

"Well, I refuse to consider you to be a burden. You are a victim."

"Not much better, I'm afraid, in his eyes. He has played the savior for far too long. If I am a victim, he is, too."

"Yes, poor Falcondale. Forced to take a young, beautiful, rich wife, who is obviously in love with him. What a pitiful lot. How will he ever survive?"

"It's not what he wants."

"If you ask me," said Jocelyn, spotting the shopkeeper through the window. She waved, and he rushed from the back to open the door. "That man has no idea what he wants."

Five days later, on the afternoon of his wedding, Trevor stood at his window and watched droves of expectantly dressed strangers flood Lady Frinfrock's garden: villagers, farmers, country squires. They assembled with what appeared to be their collected families and more than a few hounds, not to mention a battalion of servants he'd never seen before and a ten-piece band. A gypsy camp would have been less chaotic and certainly less public.

Why, he wondered, had he not been consulted about the guest list for this affair? Or the scope and scale? The amount of fuss? His inattention had been careless, and this was the result.

He thought he'd been doing them both a favor to detach. Why torture either of them by hovering, conspiring over the plans for a wedding that was, in all reality, a complete sham?

To prevent this, that is why.

"She does it on purpose, Joe," Trevor said, turning away from the window. The boy had ridden from London to attend the wedding, and Trevor was glad to have him.

"Does what, my lord?" Joseph held out his coat.

"Makes any given situation ten-times more complicated than it needs to be. She's invited half of Berkshire to this wedding, possibly just to spite me."

"Oh, it couldn't be that, my lord. She is very generous!"

"Generous to everyone but me. What of our quiet, discreet wedding? The wedding we will eventually swear to a judge was a horrible, hasty mistake? Now it is to be witnessed by a crowd of well-wishers, all desperate to make this the happiest day of our lives."

"Perhaps it will be the happiest day."

"It makes no difference how the day goes," he said, shouldering into his coat. "My only concern is that we successfully annul the thing later."

"Or," said the boy importantly, "you could not."

"Could not *what*?"

"Not annul the marriage. You could marry her and remain married forever. You could be a proper husband and wife."

"Joseph, do not start." He rolled his shoulders, fighting against the constraint of the formal coat.

"Have you thought of it?"

Irritation flared and he reeled around. "Of course I've thought of it. *It* has been the only thing *to* think except how much I desire her but, at the moment, cannot have her."

"You could have her if you made the marriage real."

"I am well aware of the myriad of ways I *might have her*, thank you very much. I am a roiling vessel of need when it comes to her. But being with Piety has never been the problem, Joseph—it's *staying with her* that scares me."

"Oh, she is not frightening, Trevor, not even a little."

Trevor sighed. "I am not afraid *of* her, I am afraid of my ability to provide for her.

"What if I resent her because I had plans—vivid, detailed, highly prized plans—and being a husband, even to her, interrupts them? What then? She *needs* me now, and I am here, but I cannot make the hasty decision to promise myself to her until-death-us-do-part. Not now. Not without the danger of looking over my shoulder and wallowing in regret. I've wanted freedom for far longer than I have wanted her.

"If I eventually regret the marriage, I would be a pathetic husband to her. No, worse than pathetic; I'd be bitter and callous and cruel. *This* is what I am afraid of. I respect her enough to protect her from that very likely eventuality." He stared at the boy, willing him to understand, willing *his own self* to fully conceive of a future where his restlessness might hurt her.

The boy stared back, slowly shaking his head.

"Fine," Trevor went on, turning away, "think of this: Think of Janos Straka, then. What of him? Straka let us leave Athens, but he could always change his mind. Every day that we linger in England, we are in danger of him turning up here, seeking to recover me. I have no choice but to stay ahead of him—very far ahead. Would it be fair to drag a new wife along?

"She's just bought a house, for God's sake, and she's building a new life. Who will be bitter then if I take her from this? She never asked to sail around the world; that is my dream." His voice was louder now, and he said the last words tapping his fist against his chest. He was angry—angrier than he should have been—and going over it again only made it worse. As if he had not thought about it, nearly without ceasing, every bloody day. As if it did not kill him to think of leaving her, despite his good intentions. As if his heart were not hardening a little more, one calloused layer at a time.

The wedding ceremony revealed itself to be just as over-wrought as the guest list, and every moment was a heartrending exercise in restraint.

Trevor restrained himself from getting lost in the forest-green eyes of a woman very much deluded about his value as a husband, even for a time. He restrained himself from becoming caught up in each vow. He restrained the smile that threatened when she beamed at him with her heart in her eyes.

All the while, Piety was openness and light; her eyes were bright with unshed tears, more dazzling than ever he had seen. Occasionally, she gazed adoringly at the glittering ring on her hand. Sometimes she nodded agreeably to the vicar, encouraging him; she also shared knowing glances with Miss Breedlowe, who stood to attend her. It was almost like watch-ing a play. A play with a lovely and talented lead who assumed the role, heart and soul, of a radiant, blissful bride, deeply in love.

Only, it did not seem as if she play-acted.

He had wondered how she would handle the vows, as he knew her to be a spiritual girl, and to take the oaths would, in many ways, be like making a false promise to God. Trevor himself could barely stomach it, but he saw no other way. He lied to protect her. Surely God would understand the neces-sity of the thing. He wasn't sure why she lied, beyond the obvious reason that it saved her from her family. But when the time came, despite the charade, she spoke the timeless words loud and clear.

Near the end, he was finally forced to look away. Inside his chest, he felt a swelling, a filling. The sensation would not diminish, no matter where he looked. It was warm and fortifying, and it seemed to permeate outward, causing his skin to redden and his eyes to mist. He hated it. He hated it and loved it.

Why, he marveled, swallowing hard, *must she insist on making it appear so genuine?*

Perhaps she was putting on the best show possible for her enthusiastic and grateful guests. Perhaps she wished to really convince her mother. Or maybe she simply wished to throw caution to the wind and, God help them, *pretend* that her feelings were real and their union really was heaven-blessed. It was impossible to tell, but Trevor could hardly make her enthusiasm look foolish by appearing flat and unaffected now. He saw no other course than to follow suit, at least in his own way.

Finally, after what seemed like an eternity of song and scripture and prayer-book recitation, he took her hands and held them firmly. He repeated the sacred words in a low, clear voice. It seemed like a sacrilege to overdo, to pretend he was giddy with young love when what he really felt was humbled and fiercely protective. He hadn't meant to be quite so solemn, but the words would come out no other way.

Finally, the vicar made the flamboyant call for a kiss. The man knew his audience and aimed to please. The congregation let out a cheer of encouragement and joy, clapping and whistling and waving their hats. Never had he been given such a clear directive. Trevor sighed and looked at Piety. She looked back, her smile a little wary, her eyes unsure.

What? he thought, allowing himself to smile back. *As if we could leave this bit out? After everything else?*

He grabbed her around the waist and pulled her to him. The audience let fly with hoots and whistles.

As if... he thought again, looking down at her startled, upturned face.

The undeniable truth was that he had been waiting—*burning*—to kiss any part of her, all of her, for days. And now he had no choice. Well, thank God for that. It was one thing to desire her and to fight it; it was quite another to stand two feet from her, hold her hands, look deeply into her eyes, and to hear her vow eternal love. To him. As if she meant it.

Of course he would kiss his bride. He should like to see someone try to stop him.

He leaned in, his lips the merest breath away from hers, and stared down, determined to do it, but not *overdo*. Behind him, the whistles in the crowd turn to cheers. She smiled fully then, her old smile, just for him, and he dropped a kiss onto that smile. One firm kiss, square on her lips. Oh, but that would never do, and he descended again for a second kiss, a third.

The fourth kiss felt more necessary somehow than the first, and he closed in again and slowed down, softening his mouth. He breathed in. His head swam with the smell of flowers and sunshine and her: the feel of her body beneath his hands; the close-up sight of her, head back, eyes closed, clinging to him; the taste of her on his tongue. He was lost: lost in the kiss and lost in her. The world slowed down, time shifted, the background of humanity melted away.

Mine. All mine. For today and a little bit longer. Mine.

He meant the kiss to be affectionate, thorough, and rewarding for them both. Also, in the spirit of their copious witnesses, he meant it to be a satisfying show. Piety played her part by drinking it in, kissing him back. When she sighed, ever so slightly, and followed his retreating mouth with her own, demanding one more taste, he nearly lost it. He departed "affectionate and rewarding," and veered into something more akin to "urgent and hot." The whole business went on thirty-seconds longer than prudent, but he didn't care. The cheers in the congregation turned to whoops, and Miss Breedlowe giggled. Beside them, the vicar cleared his throat.

Thankfully, Piety had the forbearance to eventually pull away and rest her forehead on his chin. He could feel her grinning at his throat. He kissed her on her forehead, too, getting a mouthful of hair and an eyeful of fresh flowers from her veil, but he didn't care. She was in his arms again, and it felt good. So very good.

The crowd roared, surprising him, because for a moment he had forgotten time and place. He blinked, grinned, and nodded to the masses. Nearly a hundred smiling faces cheered in return. Even the marchioness bobbed a hearty salute with her head.

Only the Limpetts had sour faces. They were all in attendance except Eli, sitting in the second row with various strangers who seemed to be—

Oh, God.

Trevor's body went taut and his breath caught. His fingers closed around Piety's arms so tightly, she gasped and looked up.

No.

He blinked and looked again, staring hard into the face of the man beside the Limpetts. There he sat, casual as you please, clapping along with villagers and the farmers and a hundred other strangers: Janos Straka, his former boss.

At his wedding.

All the way from bloody Greece, along with two of his most vicious retainers, also painfully familiar to Trevor.

It took work for Trevor to maintain his blissful expression and relaxed posture, but he forced himself to loosen his hold on Piety. He slid his fingers down her arm and took her by the hand.

He shook hands with the vicar.

He shook hands with Joseph, who was so surprised by the gesture that he missed the look of warning in his eyes.

He bowed over Miss Breedlowe's hand.

With playful affection, he gathered his wife more closely—tightly—to his side.

When he looked up again, the Greek slumlord and his henchmen were gone.

CHAPTER TWENTY-SIX

The wedding party spun against a backdrop of waning golden sun and twirled merrily into the night. Due to continued requests, the band left off playing classical pieces and veered almost entirely to a lively, modern-jig songbook. A fair number of guests embarked upon spirited singing.

When someone made a call for the bride and groom to give a song, the earl and countess agreed that it was time to express their thanks to Lady Frinfrock, to say good-bye to Tiny and Miss Breedlowe, and to retire for the night. They would have escaped cleanly, too, if Idelle had not cornered Piety alone near the row of torches that led to the house.

"Well done, daughter," Idelle said coolly.

"Thank you," Piety said softly. It had been her mother's first effort to speak to her that day, and it startled her. She hadn't thought that Idelle would seek her out.

"So you've married an earl."

"So I have."

"He's penniless, of course. And his regard for you seems to alternate between vulgar affection and cold remoteness, but you have not sought my counsel—you never have—so I leave you to your own result."

"He is a good man, Mother," Piety said.

Idelle snorted. "There is no such thing as a 'good man.' And even if there was, I would hardly characterize your illustrious Lord Falcondale as such. I looked at the belly of a snake for enough years to know scales when I see them."

Piety refused to allow the thinly veiled jab at her father to affect her. "I appreciate your concern," she said simply. "How long do you plan to remain in England?"

Idelle scoffed. "Aren't you an eager miss?"

Piety stared at her.

"We haven't decided," said her mother. "I wish to be certain you are *settled* in this new life you've designed." She watched Piety closely. "Your marriage intrigues me, Piety. How very discreet you've all been, you and this cast of players who supports you. But appearances can only be maintained for so long."

"There isn't always a villain behind every bush, Mother. Some circumstances simply fall together. No dark, secretive scheme; none at all."

"Yes," agreed Idelle. "Perhaps. But not this time."

Piety made a noise of frustration and threw her hands in the air. She'd spent years ignoring her mother—how much simpler it seemed to walk away—but she felt suddenly compelled to win a point. Just once. "Aren't you weary? Tired of following me around, finding new things to hector? Do our accusations about the Limpetts not disturb you? I'm sorry Papa did not leave the money to you, but I've offered to divide it equally, many times. You don't seem to want it unless it comes with a pound of my flesh. I will never marry Eli or any of the Limpetts. They are horrid, and it breaks my heart that you, of all people, have tried to force them upon me."

"Oh, do grow up, girl! Men can be managed. This month's awful suitor is next month's benign husband. If you had given me even *an ounce* of the respect that I deserve, I could have taught you a thing or two about how to procure what you need from a man, rather than running away from him. But you've always been so strong-headed. So independent."

"I had no choice but to make my own way! You wanted no part of me. Do not pretend that you did."

Idelle rolled her eyes, gesturing in short, angry chops. "How dare you cry neglect of me? Papa's little princess. All of his attention; his pride and joy. And now all of his money!" She pointed a long, thin finger. "I will take the money—all of it—when I earn what was duly mine, not when you toss it at my feet like alms to the poor."

"It was meant to be a draft from the bank," said Piety quietly. "I've 'tossed' nothing. How would you earn it? By *selling me* to Eli?"

"It was meant to be the union of two strong, well-placed families. We could rule New York!"

"Why would I wish to *rule* New York? All I want—all I've *ever* wanted—is to see new places and meet new people and to live in a happy home. A husband to love. Children!" Her voice broke, and she turned away.

And then she saw Falcondale. He stood behind her, taking in every word.

Oh, God.

Behind her, Idelle chuckled. "Ah, and here he is, the man himself. Do go on. How clear it is that his lordship wishes to hear more of this dream you hold for home and hearth."

Falcondale did not allow Piety to answer. "Indeed," he said. "But first, *my* dream. My dream is to never lay eyes on you, madam, ever again." He stepped into the path and held out a hand. "Come, darling. I couldn't find you, and it alarmed me. Let us ask Joseph to arrange for Mrs. Limpett's immediate departure."

Piety went to him, allowing him to sweep her into a tight, almost fierce, embrace. She melted into his strong, solid warmth, and he bent forward to drop a kiss on the top of her head. Piety's composure nearly dissolved.

"Look after her, your lordship," called Idelle. "If you can keep up with her, you'll earn every gold coin!"

Fresh rage erupted in Piety's chest, and she spun around. "It's not a matter of money, Mother!" she said. "It's a matter of love. If you'd loved Papa, he would have left the fortune to you. If you loved me, I would freely give it to you. What do you want? What do you *want*?"

"I want you to snap out of this fairy-tale world that you've built in your fluff-headed imagination! You always thought you deserved better than the rest of us. Well, look where it's gotten you."

"Yes!" Piety shouted, striding back. "I've married a fine man from a noble family. A man who loves me and wishes to share his life with me. I've bought a house that I adore in a city that enchants me. I have friends who look after me. My life—my real life, *not* a fairy tale—is only beginning!"

Idelle did not blink. "Is it?" She studied the man beside her.

Falcondale soured under her gaze. "Perhaps I was not clear. This celebration is over for you, madam." He stepped forward again to retrieve Piety, pulling her tightly into his arms. "I would have you go. *Now*. Please be aware that the countess and I intend to leave for London in the morning. Whether you are welcome here in Berkshire after we go, I cannot say, but you should be advised that neither you nor your family will be admitted to our home in Henrietta Place."

"And which home would that be? Piety's rattletrap construction or your empty shell of a foreclosed relic?"

"Make no mistake, madam," Falcondale said. "If I see even the feather of your bonnet, I will summon the authorities."

"And allege what? You do not own the streets of London."

Gently, he set Piety aside and stepped closer. "That I am the bloody Earl of Falcondale, and that myself and my lady wife are being harassed by a pack of maddened sock-factory workers from America. One of whom assaulted the countess and did his level best to bludgeon me." He lanced her with one, final pitying glare, took Piety's hand, and turned to go.

"Good-bye, Mother," Piety said over her shoulder, following along. "Please, please return home. I think it will be best for everyone."

Falcondale tugged Piety by the hand, nearly dragging her, shaking his head as they rounded first one rhododendron and then another on the dark path.

"Where in God's name does this lead? It's a wonder I found you at all. What were you doing, off in the shadows?"

"Slow down, Trevor. My shoes!" She stumbled, and he slowed, but only a little. "It's the path to the fountain. Regardless, I am not—"

She stopped herself; it wouldn't do to accuse. He'd been agreeable all day despite the obvious shock of the large audience and an extravagant celebration. More softly, she said, "I have been coming and going on my own for so long, I am not accustomed to accounting for my whereabouts. I was lecturing footmen about the torches. It never occurred to me that you would be alarmed."

"Yes, well, your mother is poison in human form." He sounded distracted. "I thought we agreed that you would keep out of her way."

"She sought me out."

They rounded a hedge and found themselves on the terrace, looking out over the party. Falcondale scanned the crowd. "If you were like me," he said, "you would purposefully avoid her. Avoid everyone. Run *from* people, rather than *to* them."

"May I never be like you," she whispered.

He looked down at her. "How right you are. May you never be like me."

She narrowed her eyes. After two weeks of silence, the last thing she wished to finally hear was him agreeing that he was a selfish lout.

"You…you are unnerved about what I said to my mother. When I described our marriage. I'm sorry."

Falcondale shook his head. "I'm not unnerved, Piety, merely disappointed. I wish I could be the man you require."

She smiled weakly at his back. "You have saved me from her; what more could I need?"

He paused. "I am sorry that I am not a fine man from a noble family, as you said. I—"

"Do not feel sorry for me, Trevor. Just because you are not sweeping me off to a world of domesticity and love does not mean that you are not rescuing me, just the same. And that is enough."

He nodded and looked away. His expression was new. Worry? Anxiety? Anguish? She could not read it. She ventured instead to console him. "Don't look so tortured, Falcondale. It makes *me* want to rescue *you*, and you've said that I cannot."

"Piety," he said, glossing over her last comment, "why did you invite so many people? Why is this wedding so large and elaborate? The guests are strangers who couldn't possibly wish to celebrate us."

It was the last thing she expected him to say, but she nodded and spoke to the ground. "Well, planning a large affair took my mind off of the fact that you had grown so incredibly remote."

When she looked up, he was staring down at her with an intensity that made her blink.

"I stayed away to protect us both. You know this. To protect our future."

"Not *our* future," she corrected with a bitter laugh. "*Your* future and *my* future. Our *separate* futures. But do not feel guilty. I know this was the agreement." She took a deep breath. "The large party is hardly your style, I know, but did you mind too terribly? Are you cross?"

"How did you decide on the guest list?"

Another unexpected question. She looked around, eyeing the guests dancing beyond the terrace gate. "Well, it was an open invitation, really. Everyone in the village. This is a fine home. Lady Frinfrock lays a colorful feast. People enjoy fancy dress, and music, and dancing. It is a rare and special night for them, even if they don't know you or me. It made me happy to invite them. And Lady Frinfrock, for all her bluster, is a generous landowner. She deserves to see their gratitude."

"But did you invite anyone specifically?" he asked, his face still tight. "Anyone by name? Were printed invitations sent by post?"

"In what time?" She laughed. "Everything happened in such a rush. No, Jocelyn and I rode around in the wagon and put out a personal invitation." She studied him, trying to determine what he wanted from this conversation. "You are disturbed by the Limpetts," she guessed. "I'm sorry, but it was easier not to fight them. Mother said everyone but Eli intended to come, and it took too much energy to change her mind. I knew they would be harmless at such a public event. But perhaps—"

"No, Piety it is fine," he interrupted her, exhaling heavily and shaking his head. "The Limpetts are inconsequential to me, as they should be to everyone." He took her hand. "Let's go."

The contact was so quick and purposeful—one minute they were talking, the next he was dragging her along—that Piety giggled. "But where are we going?"

"Excellent question." He glanced over his shoulder. "What were your plans for after?"

Her laughter stopped. "You mean to sleep?"

He nodded once. "Yes. To sleep. You cannot tell me that this is the one detail you failed to elaborately construct."

"Well," she began, feeling unaccustomed shyness, "I thought of my own chambers, because there is an adjoining room with a second bed. For the maid. I thought—"

"Perfect," he said, veering left at the terrace steps, clipping up. "I trust you have everything you need."

Piety stumbled. "We're not leaving now, are we? But we've not bid these people a proper goodnight. We haven't even paid our respects to the marchioness."

"Did you hear the hoots and hollers when we kissed, Piety? I'd say that slipping away into the night is no less than anyone expects. As for the marchioness, you may pay your respects in the morning. I want you safe behind a locked door. *Now*."

Piety was puzzling over this statement when Falcondale stopped short. She would have collided with him if he hadn't spun, reached out, and scooped her into his arms.

There was naught to do but gasp.

And hold tight.

He strode purposefully up the stairs, carrying her in his arms, down the landing and into her bed chamber. He locked the door behind them.

CHAPTER TWENTY-SEVEN

Falcondale deposited Piety in the center of her bedroom. "Which door leads to the maid's anteroom?"

Piety could only react. "There." She pointed across the room.

He nodded and strode to the small door, disappearing into the anteroom beyond.

He would sleep there, Piety knew, anywhere but in the bed with her. She had not expected him to stake it out immediately, but so be it. She had taken care to prepare the room with fresh linens, doing the work herself so as to not elicit talk among the maids. It was small, but he needn't be uncomfortable, merely separate.

You knew this, she told herself, fighting back tears. She had promised herself that she would not react, no matter how well the ceremony had gone. And yet—

There was a second door in the little room, which led to the servants' stairs. Now she heard it open and shut, and for a moment, she thought he'd let himself out and slipped away. It was only a matter of time. He'd made that very clear. But now the stairwell door clicked shut, the lock snapping into place. She heard footsteps.

"Are there any other ways in or out of your chambers besides these two doors and the windows?" he asked, returning to her.

Truly? she thought, studying him. *Doors and locks? This is to be our diversion?*

She shook her head. "It is a closed room. That is all. Are you...?" She tried again, watching him yank back draperies to inspect the windows. "If you're not displeased about the Limpetts, then what has you so unsettled? You're prowling like a caged beast."

"A caged beast would make quick work of the lock on these windows," he said absently, studying the pane. "Are they painted shut?"

"Planning a speedy escape?"

"Would that I could," he mumbled.

Likely, he hadn't meant for her to hear. She stared at her hands. The shimmering stones in her new ring flashed, mocking her. She bit her lip and closed her eyes.

"I don't mean to escape *you*, Piety," he said. "It's merely my desire for—" He stopped, and she looked up, raising her eyebrows. "Merely my desire."

"Well, you've identified two locked doors and four windows," she said. "It's doubtful you'll have to break through a wall to outrun your desire. I apologize that we have to pass this night in such close confines, but my mother would notice if we did not retire together. It would be odd to anyone, I'm afraid."

"Of course," he said, resignedly. A servant had left a tray of fruit, cheese, and bread. He came upon it and stopped, staring down at the food.

"Are you hungry?"

"There was no way around this, Piety," he told her. "You needn't feel responsible. You needn't feel anything at all but relief. The ordeal is almost over."

She nodded numbly. *The ordeal.*

He went on, "And I don't care what we do. To pass the time. What do you wish?"

She shrugged. Before the day began, before the crowded party and the emotional ceremony, before he'd carried her up the stairs and locked them in together, she had fantasized that they might indulge in a brief, celebratory embrace at the end of the night. Nothing overly passionate or committed, simply affectionate, a comfort. She envisioned them sitting side-by-side in the cushioned window seat, rehashing the party. She thought she might lay her head on his shoulder. They might laugh and revel in how they had outsmarted the Limpetts; how they had portrayed the crusty marchioness as a generous host.

Now the very thought seemed indulgent and wishful and naive. Any contact at all seemed entirely out of the question. God forbid she brush up against him in passing or bump feet beneath the table. His remoteness was as before, but there was a new nervousness, an anxiety. Was it so difficult to be alone with her? In his mind, had he already sailed away?

It was a deeper, lower rung of sadness, this. They would not even have this night. She tried to muster the energy and spirit to overcome, to cheerfully soldier on, but her reserve of stoic optimism was spent. She had given all she had to the wedding. He had gone along and not challenged the great fuss of it all. Beyond that? What more had he done than turn up?

It should have been enough.

"The groom is responsible for the wedding night, Falcondale," she told him. "Surely you have more in mind than inventorying the locks and doors." She bypassed the food and made for the drinks cart. She took up a diminutive crystal glass and decanter of sherry.

Behind her, he said, "We could play chess."

Ah, yes, chess. The old standby. There was a board set up across the room. The marchioness had had it sent up when Piety arrived.

She took a sip. "Yes."

The sherry went down bitter, burning her throat. It reminded her of the discomfort of her dress and veil; her pointy-toed shoes. There hadn't been time for a proper wedding dress, but she'd sent to London for her favorite evening gown—a shimmery, pale-pink silk that fell simply and whispered when she walked. Marissa packed it with care and sent it by messenger to Berkshire. Piety had felt festive and pretty in it, but now it suffocated.

A seamstress from the village had been commissioned to construct the veil, another success, but now the weight and biting pins that held it in place felt excruciating.

She rolled her neck and tugged on the long, heavy headpiece. Speaking to the drink in her glass, she said, "If you don't mind, I should like to change from my wedding frock."

She glanced at the silk negligee that Tiny had artfully arranged on a chair in the corner of the room—another gift from the marchioness. Lady Frinfrock had not acknowledged it, but it had shown up earlier in the week in a dove-gray box, sumptuously wrapped. When Piety questioned the maids, they said her ladyship had it sent from London. The gown inside was a confection of silk, lace, and a sprinkle of tiny ivory beads. So soft, so finely made. A sugary color of pale green with rich, ivory trim.

Falcondale, too, glanced at the nightgown and then quickly away. Naturally, he would hate it, disavowing the entire notion of nightgowns and soft silk and loveliness. It had been cheeky and presumptive of Tiny to lay it out, but Piety had seen her do it and could not bear to stop her.

A trickle of perspiration ran down Piety's back, and it occurred to her that perhaps she didn't care how he felt—not about the nightgown or anything else. Perhaps this was her room, and her gown, and her own hot, itchy skin beneath layers of pink satin that she'd worn for nine hours.

Across the room, Falcondale hedged. "Do you think changing would be…" His voice cracked, and he cleared his throat. "Do you think it's prudent to change? I'm quite comfortable. At the moment."

"I'm entirely *uncomfortable*," she said, "at the moment."

The veil was the biggest offender; it absolutely had to go. She could undo the pins and pluck out the flowers herself, and she did so right away. Flowers molted to the floor as she drifted to her dressing table, pulling and plucking. She piled all of it next to the mirror and bent at the waist, flipping her hair forward to shake it free. More vegetation fell to the floor, pins, too. She swayed her head back and forth, running her fingers through her hair. The freedom and looseness felt heavenly.

It felt so good, in fact, Piety realized then that the gown must follow. Immediately. If she couldn't indulge in the green negligee, she'd dig out a wool winter nightgown and heavy velvet robe. Either way, the pink satin could not be tolerated a moment more. She was just about to announce as much when she came back up and caught her husband's stare.

He *watched her.*

The suggestion of the robe caught in her throat.

Piety stared back, not blinking.

By some instinct, she shook her head again. Her hair bounced over her shoulders and fell beside her face. She gathered up one side, swept the curls high, let it fall.

Trevor's face tightened. He clenched his jaw.

She heard herself whisper, "I want free of this dress, and I have no maid. You'll have to unfasten me."

He blinked. "Piety, I *know* that is not prudent." His voice was hoarse.

She didn't answer. She went to him, not taking her eyes from his tortured face. She pivoted slowly, presenting him with the seam of tiny buttons running the length of her back.

Silently, she lifted her hair.

She heard him let out a long, slow breath. She heard him suck in. She heard him shuffle. She heard him loosen his cravat.

She waited.

"Trevor?" she whispered, looking back. "Please? I am suffocating. Unfasten me." The last word was a caress, barely audible.

"*Piety.*" His voice was low and rumbly.

She leaned into him, suddenly emboldened. It had not been honest to say she didn't care how they passed this night. She cared very much. This night was, quite literally, the only one they would have. She wanted to seize it, to devour it, to remember it in the lifetime that lay ahead. Until she saw his face, she had not been certain he wanted the same. But oh, the heat in his eyes. The hitch in his breath. He stared at her like a starving man.

"You are allowed to touch me, Trevor," she said softly. "You will not turn to stone."

He let out a strangled, bitter laugh. "Too late for that." But she felt him take up both sides of her gown at the shoulders and unbutton the first hook.

"There is no way around our closeness tonight; in the same way, there is no way around our separation when you go. Why not revel in tonight?"

"If we act on this impulse, we will be forced to lie to the court to be free. You've already lied at the altar today, isn't that enough?" She felt his hands shake as he unfastened another hook and another. The neckline of the gown began to sag. She let it fall.

"I did not lie today." Her voice was barely above a whisper.

His hands stilled against her back, and she heard him blow out a ragged breath.

"And I am not lying now. There's no manipulation here. I have no intention of confining you in this marriage after tonight, regardless of what happens. If you do not wish to lie to the court, then can we not *almost* consummate the marriage? Can we not *nearly* consummate it, but not entirely?"

He made a strained, scoffing sound and returned to the hooks, working faster now. "What you suggest is playing with fire."

"Ah, well, we've done that from the start, haven't we?" The dress was nearly open, barely hanging on. She felt him reach the final button and stop. His hands remained at her waist.

She looked over her shoulder. "The corset, as well? If you please."

He made a scoffing sound and backed away. He swore. She heard rustling, yanking. His coat went flying to the back of a nearby chair. His cravat followed.

He cleared his throat and returned to her, tugging the silk lacing of the corset. Quick, efficient movements. Urgent or detached? She couldn't tell. But, oh, the tingling relief of looseness at her ribs. Sweet freedom from the pinch and bind of the stays. Finally, she could breathe. One more tug, and the corset fell away and caught on her sagging bodice.

"Bloody hell, the tightness of this thing," Trevor said, reaching out to brush his hand against the fabric of her shift. She shivered, and he replaced his hand with two warm fingers, slowly tracing the notches of her spine, up and down, and up again.

Her shift was thin, the finest linen, soft and pliable. She could feel the rough pads of his finger through the cloth.

When he reached the top of her spine, he brushed her hair off of her shoulders. She felt his breath on her neck.

When his fingers went down again, he followed the scoop of her waist lower, lower to the swell of her bottom. She gasped, and she heard him chuckle, an arrogant, satisfied sound.

His fingers continued their exploration, fanning out. Kneading gently, he located the very spots where the corset had bitten into her skin. The flair of her waist. The tender skin beneath her arms, just a freckle from her breasts. Here, he rubbed. Small circles. Her body came alive, awakening for what felt like the very first time.

She sighed, and his touch became heavier. He lingered with each pass. Her skin seemed to pulse beneath his fingers, the sensation radiating. She sucked in breath and turned her head to the side, seeking his kiss. "Trevor," she said softly, begging him for more.

"Shh," he replied, his own breath shallow. He scraped his palms downward, learning every contour, while his fingertips feathered across her belly.

And now up again. His knuckles grazed the underside of her breasts.

Down again. Her shift was bunched at her waist; her open dress hung from her body.

Piety arched her back, and he seized her, his hands locking around her waist. He nudged closer. She could feel the heat of him from her neck to her heels.

"You are perfection, Piety," he whispered against her ear. "I don't deserve you. Not even for one night."

"Perhaps, but I do," she whispered back. "For memory's sake. One night to cherish forever. No one ever need know."

She heard him swallow hard. His hands made another slow, massaging perusal of her back, her belly, the rounded curve of her breasts. Piety made a gasping sound, and her legs began to give way. She stumbled. He steadied her.

"I...I don't understand why you would offer yourself to me like this."

She looked over her shoulder. "I don't understand why you would refuse."

He growled at that, gathering her tightly against his chest. She felt his arousal against her bottom, his broad chest against her bare shoulders. He bent beside her head, burying his face in her hair.

"I cannot resist you. I promised myself that I would leave this union having only given aid. I would not have you hate me. But I guarantee it, Piety, to carry on like this will plant the seed of something very near hate. Resentment..." He pressed his lips to her neck, not a kiss, simply a melding of his mouth to her skin.

"I love you, Trevor." She sagged against him. "There can be no hate."

How good it felt to finally say it. So good, she almost laughed. She wanted to laugh, to fly, to love him with her body like she loved him with her heart.

She leaned her head against his shoulder and raised her chin, offering her neck, her mouth. "You must have known that I love you. I will always love you, regardless."

He opened his mouth to answer her or to kiss her, but a knock sounded at the door.

Piety let out a small gasp, and Trevor looked up.

He reached for the sagging bodice of her dress and drew it to her, hooking it on her shoulders. He stood her upright and gently set her apart. She stumbled again, and he balanced her on her own two feet.

"Piety," he said in a firm voice, "go into the maid's anteroom. Do not come out until I call you."

"But I—"

"In this you may not argue. I am expecting Joseph. With a message. Likely, it's nothing more, but I need you to go. *Now*."

"Joseph?"

"Piety, *go!*" He set her away from him, shoving her gently in the direction of the door.

She went, holding her dress loosely around her. She reached the threshold but turned to hover, watching him. Instead of crossing to the door, Trevor edged up from the side, laying himself flat against the wall, listening, studying the knob.

All of this for Joseph?

A prickly sense of alarm burned the back of her neck, and she shuffled two steps back.

Beside the door, Trevor whispered the boy's name. There was some answer, and he cautiously unlocked the key and opened the door. Slowly, he edged out, his head alone. Whispering ensued. Trevor nodded, asked something, nodded again. He stood so rigid; his face was so grim. He spoke in harsh, clipped words. The entire exchange embodied dread.

Now he spared a glance back. He caught sight of her and made a face, slicing the air with a curt gesture. *Stay back.*

Piety skittered back, but she could still see him. There was more whispering, glances up and down the hall, a check to the clock on the mantle. She saw him nod once, twice, and then softly shut the door, clicking the lock firmly in place. He sighed heavily and leaned against the wood, scrunching his eyes shut.

She disappeared into the tiny room. After a moment, she called his name.

Silence.

She tried again, "Trevor, is anything the matter?" She kicked her shoes from her feet and hiked up her skirt to peel off her stockings.

"It's nothing," Trevor called back. She heard him prowling the room.

"May I come out?"

Another silence.

She went still and looked up.

The length of the quiet was deafening, and she felt the charged passion drain from the room. The reckless intimacy had slipped away. He was cautious and closed again.

Piety squeezed her eyes shut and bit back a yelp of frustration. She took three calming breaths. She looked down at her body, still tingling from his touch. The bodice of her dress sagged at her waist.

There was only one thing to do.

Working quickly, she finished tugging her stockings free and jerked the dress from her body. Next she shed her petticoats, leaving them in a frilly heap on the floor, and slipped from her shift. Her drawers were last, and she hesitated only a moment before shimmying them off.

"Trevor?" she called again. A bold, new power made her voice strong.

She shook back her hair and walked, naked, into the room.

"Piety, I'm not su—" He stared with an expression so hot, she felt the sizzle on her skin. He drank in the sight of her.

She went to him, and God love him, he met her more than halfway. They collided in the center of the room, and he snatched her to his chest. Only her name—a whisper, a wish—escaped his lips as he descended, kissing her.

Piety returned his ardor, kissing him back, grabbing handfuls of the cotton of his shirt.

"Why must you make yourself impossible for any reasonable man to resist?" He swept her into his arms, striding to the bed. He tossed her in the center and she laughed. Suddenly shy, she scrambled for the coverlet. She looked up, expecting to share in the laugh, but his expression had gone serious. He studied her with something akin to reverence and an unerring need. Her laughter faded away, and she sat back on her haunches. She let the coverlet fall.

Falcondale growled, pulling off his shirt in rough, staccato movements, never taking his eyes from hers.

She lifted her chin, welcoming his gaze and rose up. She kneed to the edge of the bed. He froze in the act of removing his shirt, stricken by the sight of her, and she laughed and reached for him, peeling the shirt back and tossing it to the floor.

When he was bare to the waist, he put his knee on the mattress and nudged her back, chasing his hands in hungry circles across her back. She landed against the pillows with a soft *thump*, and he followed her down, spreading himself on top of her.

It was new—laying beneath him—and the weight of him and the head-to-toe contact set off a new awakening. She reveled in the tickle of the hair on his chest against her breasts, the immovable, muscled hardness of his shoulders, the musky scent of his closeness. Her hands moved of their own accord, exploring every contour.

"Piety, there is a way." His breath quickened from kissing her. "A way to give you pleasure without sacrificing your virginity." He pulled away and stared down at her. "But if we lose control? I do not want to risk that."

She urged him on. "Risk it."

He laughed and ran a heavy hand over the dips and swells of her torso, setting off a trail of shivery sensation. When he reached her knee, he grabbed the tangled wad of the coverlet and tugged it down.

"This is so much better than chess," he said, rising up to stare at her body again. She laughed, and he pounced on her mouth, smothering the sound.

CHAPTER TWENTY-EIGHT

Making love to Piety on his wedding night was perhaps the first reckless, indulgent, truly *selfish* thing Trevor had allowed himself in fifteen long years of self-sacrifice and restraint.

Well, *almost* making love to his wife.

He reminded himself of this critical provision again and again as he devoured her body with his hands and kissed her until he could barely remember his name.

It will be enough, he told himself, trying to reason through the lust fogging his brain.

It would, in truth, be too much, considering he'd put the annulment in serious jeopardy merely by touching her. Their future rapport was destroyed for certain. She'd told him she loved him, for God's sake. And now this?

Why, he wondered, could he not stop? Was he such a slave to his desires? To her body? Was he rotten to the core? He wanted, needed, to mete this out—what was *wrong* with him—but at the moment, everything seemed so very right. His ability to reason, right from wrong, was rapidly vanishing.

Beneath him, she widened her legs, allowing their bodies to slide together—a timeless, perfect fit. They both sighed; it felt universally *right*. Piety laughed, making no effort to hide her delight. Naturally she would smile and exude happiness and light, even in bed.

Trevor tried to hold himself up and *away*, but she laughed again and hitched up her knees. He was given no choice but to surrender. A growl. Another kiss. He dropped against her. His only hope for holding back was the sobering memory of Janos Straka sitting among the guests at his wedding.

He'd charged Joseph with learning where Straka had gone and his general purpose; but the boy had returned empty-handed. It was careless to leave these questions unanswered—dangerous, really—but at the moment...

It would do.

If it allowed for *this*.

Not all *the way*, he somehow managed to remind himself, kissing the soft skin of her ear, reveling in the silky, fragrant veil of her hair. He would stop *just* short. And in the morning, he would leave her in the safety of Joseph's guard, while he, himself, located and dealt with Straka.

But tonight...

Trevor worked his way back to her mouth, scrambling to capture her hands in his own. If she didn't stop the sweet torture of her touch, he would not last. Naturally, she would not cooperate, and her hands skittered away. Trevor growled and went up on one elbow.

It was impossible not to stare. If he had to have a wife— and, considering her circumstances, he absolutely *did* have to have a wife—why not have the most perfect specimen of the female form?

He reached out, wanting to memorize her body: the perfect curve of her breast, the rise of her hip beyond the indention of her waist, the ticklish crease beneath her deliciously rounded bottom, the space behind her knee, the arch of her tiny foot.

She allowed it, murmuring and sighing, writhing beneath his touch, driving him to a new level of distraction with her enthusiastic response. He'd thought he would not undress any further—every article of clothing was another barrier against losing control—but now trousers seemed entirely out of the question. He would die if he weren't naked beside her. Just the briefest of moments. As she'd said: just one night.

When she realized his purpose, she sat up and watched him peel the trousers away with wide, curious eyes. It was a whole new level of seduction. Every delighted intake of breath, every bend of her head, every expression of pleasure only served to drive his need.

"May I touch?" she asked, already reaching for him.

Trevor chuckled and collapsed on the bed beside her, kicking the trousers free. "I want you," was all he could think to say, and Piety, God love her, considered that an affirmation. Lightly at first, so lightly he thought he would burst, she tickled and brushed and tested, but then he found her breast with his mouth, and she lost focus, throwing her head back and grabbing him.

"*Piety*, we mu—" He broke into a laugh because, with one grip, she had rendered him unable to even speak.

"Oh," she said. She arched against him. "I've only just…"

"There is more; there is better," he said. He skated his hand down her arm until he found her wrist and managed to pull her away. "You cannot touch me like this."

"But why?" She moaned with desire. "You are so touchable." She reached out again.

"Yes." He kissed her. "But I'll embarrass myself. Let us return to that, er, later." He gathered her beneath him. She sighed, squaring herself. He found her mouth, allowing himself to feast like never before. No chaperones, no hiding in the dusty music room. Simply his wife, moving beneath him, learning the rhythm, stoking his desire to unknown heat.

When he felt her begin to seek, to *need* as he needed, his thin rein on control snapped.

Instinct took over, rational thought vanished, and he rose, poised to finish it. Some primal reaction answered him, and she slid, centered, and opened. She softly called his name.

"Piety, no." He took a shuddering breath, the ebb and flow of reason washing back. He rolled to one side. "What are we doing? We cannot."

He wanted to weep, but instead he kissed her and rocked against her body, mimicking what he truly wanted. Each push was heaven, yet out of reach.

Moving expertly for someone so new, she rocked back, driving him rapidly to the edge. His fingertips fumbled against her skin and then stopped, entirely without use.

Never had he been like this. Never. She consumed him completely.

"Stop." He moaned as he rose over her. "Piety, please. We must *stop*. I can help you, without—I never meant to go this far."

"Oh, God, Trevor, it's so…it so…" she whispered, struggling to articulate. "I can feel it, and I don't know even what it is. Don't you want it?" she asked, her hands clinging around his neck.

"Yes, I bloody want it," he said. "I've wanted it since the first moment I saw you. But I'm trying to protect you."

"Love me, Trevor!" She wasn't above begging. "I'll stop if you make me yours."

"No."

"*Yes*. I don't care about the rest. Give this to us: this memory. Something to hold to when you've gone. We're married. How can it be wrong?"

"Piety, stop."

"I won't."

All at once, his resistance snapped.

She said it again: "I will not stop." And then, "Please!"

"Fine." The word came out in a hiss. He used his knee to knock her legs apart. "You want this?"

"Yes!" she said, pulling him down. "Please, my husband, please!"

Those words were his final undoing. With a shout of pleasure, he drove into her.

"Ouch!" She yelped, and he was reminded to slow down, to give her time. He gathered her up and kissed her, waiting for her body to accommodate him.

"It's like a knife," she said into his neck.

"I'm sorry, darling." He comforted her. "Deep breath. That's right." He dropped soft kisses across her cheeks and brow. It took all of his self-control not to move until she was ready, but the kisses helped, distracting them both. In a timeless interval, she began to move again, making the sounds of pleasure. He sighed and moved, too. She cried out again, and again he waited. It was an exquisite eternity.

Finally, she pulsed upward with her hips—once, twice, then a rapidly advancing rhythm. The motion set him on fire. He tried to go gently, God, how he tried, but he had waited so long to have her—indeed, he thought he never would—and now he could barely contain the pounding need. And she did so very little to help him. How quickly she had become accustomed to the timeless dance of making love.

Within seconds, he lost himself. He meant to go slow, but she began to sigh and gasp, coiling herself around him. He was incapable of doing little more than *feeling*, reverberating, inside and out, soul-deep.

By some miracle, considering his sloppy, selfish efforts, she peaked before him. It was the final, unbearable impetus. She gasped and cried out his name, and he finished it, letting out a near-animal sound of complete and blissful surrender. When he was spent, he collapsed on top of her, trying to catch his breath.

"Are you all right?" she asked after a moment, squirming beneath him.

He laughed. "Am I all right? I just ravished you in the most selfish way, and you are inquiring about *my* well-being?"

She was quiet a moment. "It's merely that I have never heard you be quite so enthusiastic. About anything."

"Well," he said thoughtfully, swallowing hard, "I have never felt so enthusiastic. About anything. Are you hurt?"

"Hurt? Ah, no. I am well."

He lifted himself up and stared at her, worried. "Well?"

"Perhaps a trifle better than well." She smiled at him. "Is it always like that?"

"I can honestly say that it has never actually been like that before." He rolled off her, gathering her against him. "But I believe we have the idea."

"Oh," she said. "Perhaps I am good at it."

"Darling," he said, kissing her hair, "as with everything else you undertake, you are indisputably good at it."

"Then we must try it again," she said matter-of-factly. "I love doing things at which I excel."

He rolled over, foisting her on top of him. "Why not give me a chance at aptitude this time, hmmm?"

She laughed, looking down, "But you were perfect!"

"I was entirely out of control, selfish, and boorish. But that is not typically the case."

She swatted him. "Do not speak of your other women."

"Please know that any other woman is but a faint, pale haze on the horizon of my memory when compared to you. I should like to have *you* howling at the moon and begging for more, instead of me."

"But I liked it when you begged." She toyed with his hair.

"I could tell. But it's only fair to let everyone have a turn, no?"

"Well..."

"Believe me," he said, rising up to capture her mouth again. "I will beg, too." She kissed him back. "I can scarcely contain my begging right now." He grabbed her bottom, pressing her against him. He felt a flicker of fresh desire and sighed in spite of himself.

She giggled. "Now you know how I felt, begging you all those weeks for help with my stairs."

"You did not beg." He growled and flipped her over. "At least not in this manner—and thank God for that."

CHAPTER TWENTY-NINE

The Earl and Countess Falcondale were awakened by an insistent rapping on the bedroom door, not ten minutes after seven o'clock. Piety was the first to hear it, and she sat up in bed, wondering who in God's name dared to disturb them on this of all mornings.

"I wish to examine the sheets," came a muffled proclamation from the hallway.

It was Idelle. Of course.

"She knows no shame." Piety glanced to Trevor. His eyes were still closed. He rolled to hide his face.

"Your mother is deranged," he mumbled into the pillow.

"We are asleep, Mother," said Piety. "Go away!"

"I will not go away!" came the shouted reply.

Falcondale swore and pushed himself up to the edge of the bed. He sat there for a moment, staring at the floor. Piety reached out to touch him, her flat palm in the center of his broad back. She could never, she thought, grow tired of touching him. How long would he allow it? He did not mind her touch—considering his enthusiasm the night before, she knew this was true—but his future did not adhere to likes or dislikes, only freedom.

Idelle knocked again, and he shrugged her hand away. His trousers and shirt were on the floor, and he turned his back and yanked them on. Piety watched, remembering the planes of his body that her hands had learned last night. He took care to not look at her, trudging to the door, whipping it open.

"You were asked to leave," he said.

"My lord." Idelle studied him carefully. "As the bride's mother, I have every right—"

"You have no rights whatsoever. Get out."

"Mind the linens are not laundered before I inspect them!" She called the instructions as the door slammed in her face.

"Part of me wants to simply show them to her," said Piety from the bed. She fingered a smudge on the sheets. "Maybe she would finally leave me alone."

Trevor shook his head. "That would be a death knell to the annulment. Parading around with sheets from our wedding night? No."

She watched him stalk around the room, clearly disinclined to return to bed as she'd vainly hoped. Disappointment settled in like a fog that choked out the sun. The sheets felt cold. The night was over. He was as before.

Before she could stop herself, she said, "Won't you come back to bed? We needn't rise simply because she disturbed us. No one will expect—"

"I have business to attend in Berkshire before we leave. It's quite urgent, actually. But hopefully it will be quickly resolved, and we can make haste for London." He walked to the middle of the room, hands on his hips. He looked around. "Boots? Where are my boots?"

The room had seemed warm when she awakened, but now she could scarcely contain her shivering. She pulled the sheets up to cover herself and watched him.

He found his boots beneath the bed and dropped to all fours to fish for them. His cuff links were on the cart with the food, his suspenders on the floor. Watching him dress, however hastily, was a new and intimate thing, and her heart broke a little more, thinking she would never again see him wrestle into his boots, give his coat a shake, or shrug it onto his shoulders.

If he disliked her watching him, he did not say. He stole glances at her every now and again. A quick look between buttons. Another when he struggled with his cravat. She raised her eyebrows and stared back, but he looked away.

Soon he was a disheveled, untucked version of himself the day before. His hair was curly and floppy, falling into his eyes. It took all of her strength not to go to him, to straighten his collar, to smooth the wool of his coat. To kiss him one last time.

"Where are you going?" she asked. "What is your business in Berkshire?"

"It's nothing to concern yourself with," he said.

Piety nodded to herself. Deflection. This was new. In the past, if he had not wanted to include her, he would say, *no*, but also why not.

Tears burned the backs of her eyes, and she squeezed them shut. She slid to the edge of the bed.

He saw, of course, and she heard him sigh. "*Piety.*"

She shook her head and padded to her dressing table, taking a seat and staring at her reflection in the mirror. She barely recognized the woman in the glass. Wild, disheveled hair. Whisker-bussed cheeks. Kiss-swollen mouth. Heartbreak, clear in her eyes.

She saw him watch her reflection in the mirror and then briskly walk to the door. He paused. "This just keeps getting worse and worse."

There was so much more to say, Trevor thought, volumes of things: apologies, considerations. But also was there *no time*. No time to entertain it; not to mention, no idea how to begin to mince through the emotional and logistical labyrinth of it all.

Instead, Trevor summoned Miss Breedlowe and bade her to remain with Piety every second. They were not to leave the house or garden, he told her, and they were not to speak to anyone but the marchioness, Tiny, Joseph, or Garnettgate's familiar staff.

In the meantime, he would locate Straka, discover his purpose, and concoct some way to dispatch him. Only then could he allow himself to contemplate the possibility of a wife.

He searched first for Joseph. Predictably, the boy could be found in the presence of food. Trevor found him in the kitchen, taking breakfast with the staff.

"Please tell me," Trevor whispered, leaning beside him at the long table, "that you've been up since dawn, searching for our uninvited guest."

The boy swallowed, grabbed a stack of toast, and trailed behind him to the stable.

"I have, actually," Joseph said. "I would have come for you, if I'd seen anything, Trev. But I didn't want to, ah, disturb you. With no news."

"What about the tavern in Ruscombe?" Trevor asked.

"Aye. And in Twyford. I checked everywhere. He's nowhere. Not a trace. I would think you dreamed it, if I hadn't seen him with my own eyes."

"But you did see him, no? I have not imagined this. Straka was *there*."

"Oh, yes," said Joseph, "he was there, big as you please, Iros and Demetrios with him. All dressed up like English gentlemen."

Trevor nodded, running a hand through his hair. "What in God's name could they want?" He began to pace. "Straka *allowed me to go*. Gave me his bloody blessing!" He stopped and stared at Joseph. "Was I fool to believe that it would be that simple?"

"Maybe he was here to wish you well? To celebrate your wedding?"

"Ha!" Trevor scoffed, looking around. "He detests weddings—hates the whole institution of marriage. It was one of the few things on which he and I were in total accord. Besides, the wedding's only been on for two weeks, and I've told no one. Without telling her why, I've asked Piety if she invited anyone by name. God knows I've prattled on about Straka enough that she could have misconstrued my affiliation to him and invited him as a surprise. But she said there were no posted invitations, and I believe her."

Trevor stropped pacing and studied the trees beyond the garden. "No, he's had me followed. Likely, he's kept tabs all this time. Damn!" He turned away and strode to the stable door. "Why have I lingered in England? It was foolish and reckless and indulgent to stay. "Instead I…" He thought of Piety. Piety laughing, Piety teasing, Piety listening or fighting or reaching for him. Piety vowing at their wedding to love him forever.

He sighed heavily. What a disaster.

"How is the countess?" asked Joseph, watching him.

"Fine. Thank you. I would say, 'None of your business,' but I need you to guard her now—immediately, as soon as we've finished here. She's been unprotected in her chamber for too long already. I will commence the search." He squinted down the long gravel drive to the road beyond. "Straka could be anywhere. He is just as likely to make camp and sleep in the woods as take rooms at an inn."

"Perhaps he's gone back to Athens," the boy said. "Maybe he wanted to see if you really were an earl. Now he's seen it, and he's gone."

"Yes," Trevor glanced at him, "or maybe he wants me dead. It's far more likely. You were too young to understand the subtleties of his regard for me, Joseph, although you have heard me complain often enough. I may have been a close confidant and valued advisor, but he would easily kill me, given half the reason. He's killed for less than half. I have seen him beat his own cousin to death for a petty slight to his manhood. How do you think he became ruler of his seedy domain? Ruthlessness, that's how. No," Trevor went on, "he *wants* something. And he won't leave for Athens or anywhere else unless it's got."

"Why did he disappear, then?" asked Joseph. "Why come to the wedding only to vanish?"

"Oh, but this is one of his favorite tricks, or don't you remember?" Trevor located his horse in the third stall. A groom dashed to assist, but he waved him away. "He loves nothing more than popping up, unexpected, making himself known, and then disappearing, leaving his quarry to wonder and worry and become full-blown panicked by the time he turns up again."

Trevor checked over his horse, stroked him, and led him into the sun. He worked quickly to saddle the animal, collecting his tack from pegs on the wall.

"Have you told Miss Piety? Er, Lady Piety?" asked Joseph. "About Straka? Does she know he's in Berkshire?"

"Absolutely not, and I won't." He glanced up. "And neither will you, do you hear? You will remain outside her door until she emerges, and then close by her side wherever she goes. If she questions you, tell her that I've assigned you to guard her against the Limpetts. That won't be too far off the mark, considering her mother's already snooping around."

"Yes, my lord," said Joseph, watching him mount.

"Joseph?" Trevor added, looking down. "Thank you. I know you would have rather enjoyed the party last night than prowl around, searching for a man who is an expert at not being found." The horse danced beneath him. Trevor whipped around to finish. "Assuming I can put things to right with Straka and set him on his way, you and I will most likely sail when we return to London. Prepare yourself. It will be a rushed thing, but considering this new intrusion, I see no other way."

"And Lady Piety? She will come with us?"

"I don't know, Joe. We shall see. That was never the arrangement."

The last thing Trevor saw before he allowed the horse to run was Joseph's emerging smile, spreading wide. He refused to allow himself to react to the cautious delight, clear on the boy's face.

CHAPTER THIRTY

Janos Straka and his two henchmen had taken rooms at the village church. With Trevor's new notoriety as Bridegroom Extraordinaire, it took less than an hour to discover this. The villagers fell over themselves to answer his casual inquiries.

Of course Joseph had not thought of the church, because it was the last place Janos Straka had ever been known to visit. But Straka had a fondness for bitter irony, especially when it made a fool of someone new, and what was more ironic than a criminal overlord taking refuge in a house of God?

Trevor rode to the parsonage and circled at a distance, confirming his hunch. A spirited black stallion was tied in the yard, much too tall and too high-tempered for Straka. A very likely sign. Straka insisted on the showiest mounts, the taller and more belligerent, the better. There were also two lesser animals, clearly for Iros and Demetrios, and a crude fire scorching a blackened hole in the middle of the vicar's formerly bright, lush garden.

Around this fire, they would have stayed up all hours, drinking and eating and laughing. If there were village women of a certain age, a certain ilk, all the better. Add gypsies from a nearby camp, and Trevor could recall the scene from hundreds of his resented yesterdays. It lacked only his bitter, former self, slouching drowsily in the shadows, willing the night to end so he could get some sleep or check on his mother.

But now that he'd found them, what was the best way to approach them?

If possible, Trevor wished *not* to involve the vicar. Whatever his future with Piety, she would likely remain friends with the marchioness, and she would be back to Hare Hatch at times throughout her life. His chief goal—beyond dispatching Straka—was keeping the stench of his lawlessness and violence far from her.

In the end, he chose the graveyard. It was on a hill, some distance from the church, bordered on one side by a stand of holly trees that blocked a corner from view. The whole place looked like a bucolic oil landscape, something framed in gold and hanging above a cozy fire. Shallow grass swayed with cornflowers and bluebells. Animals foraged. Birds sang.

Enter a middle-aged Greek slumlord with whom Trevor would barter for his life, and the joke would be complete.

He waited an hour for Straka to emerge. When he did, likely after seeing Trevor stalking the property and making him purposefully wait, the old man pushed open the door to the parsonage and staggered into the sunny churchyard. He was laughing, of course. Chuckling at first, rising to full-blown guffaws. It was his signature greeting, meant to signify either that he was glad to see you or soon you would die. Or both.

Trevor forced himself not to flinch. He refused to stray from his relaxed—nay, *bored*—slouch on the cemetery wall.

He moved only his head, cocking it to study the old man. By the time Iros and Demetrios had stumbled from the house, Straka was halfway up the hill, still chuckling.

He was a large man; tall, with a rotund belly, thick shoulders and hands. He was dressed in his native garb now, a deep purple kaftan with a yellow kalpak on his bald head. These did nothing to minimize his brawn—likely another calculated choice. When he reached the wall, he held his arms wide, an invitation to embrace, but Trevor refused even to stand. Instead, he raised his chin and said in smooth Greek, "What can I do for you, Janos?"

"But what is this greeting?" Straka said in a deep booming voice. "No embrace for your old boss? No welcome to your country? After all this time?"

"It's been three months, Straka," said Trevor, "and you are no longer my employer. You let me go, remember? My time in Athens has come and gone."

The old man studied him, running a hand over his salt-and-pepper beard. "Did I let you go, Tryphon?" he asked, feigning confusion. "Or did I let you *leave*?"

Trevor shrugged. "Either way, I am gone. I have a new life now."

"And a new wife!"

Trevor bristled at the mention of Piety, but he tamped it down. "Why are you here, Straka?"

"I have come to see you! How we have missed you at home. Things are not the same. The money, the Sultan; there are many problems. People are angry. There is trouble." He shrugged.

Casually, the old man took a knife from his belt and held it out, gauging the distance to a nearby tree. With a flick of the wrist, he threw the knife. Trevor heard it plant with a *thwack* in the trunk and hang there, thrumming from the force of the throw. He refused to look.

"What kind of trouble?"

Behind Straka, Iros and Demetrios were heaving and sawing their way to the top of the hill. Straka retrieved his knife and shouted for them to wait at a distance. The duo grimaced and turned around.

"Ah, but surely we won't discuss business *now*," said Straka. "Let us celebrate this reunion. Let us celebrate your marriage." He turned to the tree and hurled the knife again.

"You hate weddings, Straka. It's why you have countless mistresses. You hate reunions, too."

Straka shrugged and pulled the knife from the tree.

"Look," Trevor went on, "it's been nostalgic to see you, but please be aware that I am set to leave Berkshire this morning and return to London. After that, I will leave Britain altogether. If you have business with me—though what it might possibly be, I cannot guess, because you and I are no longer affiliated—please, let's have it. As I've said, I live a very different life now. I have my own commitments and obligations. You understand obligation, I know."

"Obligation," Straka said, studying the tip of his knife, "yes, I understand." His grin dropped into a hard line. "Very well, we will dispense with the niceties. You always were a miserable son of a bitch."

"Yes," Trevor said, "I'm no fun at all."

Straka let the knife fly a third time and crossed his arms above his heavy belly. "I need one favor, Tryphon. A final favor."

"What kind of *favor*?"

Straka's head shot up, and the rage in his eyes Trevor made his heart stop.

"Your word, not mine," Trevor said.

After a heavy moment, Straka said, "So it is. But you may term it however you like. Favor, errand, task. I don't care." He looked at Trevor. "I need money, Tryphon."

"Money? You're one of the richest men in Greece. You have more money than the Sultan."

"Yes, but the Serbian uprising? The independence? I gambled on the wrong side of the conflict, and I lost. A lot—too much. I did not count on the Sultan letting them go. The war has cost me."

Trevor thought about this, his mind filtering what he knew of the Serbians and their revolt against Ottoman rule some five years ago. He'd been conscripted to work for Straka about six months after the truce. The conflict had not seemed relevant to his duties for Straka. The old man never chose sides. He followed the money, *only* the money.

Not wanting to sound too interested, Trevor asked, "Cost you how?"

Straka swore and waved his thick arms dismissively, rattling off the details of an arrangement he'd made with the Sultan before the revolt. The Sultan had allowed Straka to lease-hold half the tenement slums in Belgrade, but the new Serbian government began to reclaim the property when the Serbs won their independence. Straka no longer had claim to their rents.

There was more. He'd been skimming money off the top, not giving the proper cut to the Sultan, and now the Serbs were extorting him for double-crossing the Sultan all those years. He owed money coming and going. His summation was accurate: there was trouble.

But it was not Trevor's trouble. He hadn't managed this corner of Straka's empire; he'd never even been to Serbia. And either way, Trevor didn't have any money to give him.

He shoved off the wall and shook his head. "I hear your dilemma, Janos, but you've come to the wrong man. I have no advice on your swindling Serbia or double-crossing the Sultan, and I've no money to give you at all. You've journeyed a long way, and I appreciate the confidence in me, but I cannot work for you again. My responsibilities to the earldom are too great."

"No money?" said Straka, seizing on the heart of the matter. "You wouldn't expect me to believe that an earl, a peer of the realm, a man to whom they say, *no, my lord*, and *yes, your lordship*, does not have money?"

"I cannot be responsible for what you believe, only what I know to be." Trevor told him about his wastrel uncle, the cost of settling the debt. "Old titles are expensive and time consuming. I cannot help you with Serbia; I've problems of my own."

"Fancy wedding for someone who claims he's penniless," said Straka, his voice light but potent. He retrieved his knife and threw it again. "Musicians. Dancing. Lavish feast. Imagine my surprise to arrive in London, searching for you, only to be told you were in the countryside, getting shackled. And then to follow that trail all the way to a castle—"

"Hardly a castle," interrupted Trevor, "the manor house belongs to a well-meaning neighbor of the woman I married. The wedding was her gift to the bride."

"Lot of trouble for a well-meaning neighbor."

"She has a grandmotherly affection for the bride."

"Information we gathered about *the bride* was she's as rich as Croesus."

With considerable effort, Trevor kept his expression neutral. "Well, your information is not true."

"When you lie to me," Straka said, wrenching the knife from the tree, "you only make things worse. For everyone."

And there's a thinly veiled threat, thought Trevor, his anger flaring. But he kept his tone lazy and bored. "The woman I married owns some property in London—a townhome next to mine. This is how we became acquainted. But her money has been sunk into the house and its repairs. Her parents were wealthy Americans, but her father is dead and her mother holds the key to the coffers now. That's why she fled to London; her mother was starving her out. They never got on. You know how it is."

"I know there must be money somewhere." Straka chuckled and sent the knife flying again. "Knew it soon as I clapped eyes on her pretty little face. Why, I could *smell* the money. Maybe you are in the poor house with your uncle's title, but I don't believe this is the case with your wife. Not for a second."

"You don't take my meaning, Janos." Trevor emphasized each word, hating the desperation in his tone. "If you must know, the woman that I married and I agreed to the wedding in order to keep her mother from marrying her off to someone else. The other man did not suit—he was violent and cruel—and she deserved better. You know how I feel about this sort of thing. 'Soft,' I believe was your frequent term for my sympathetic bent.

"We do not operate as an authentic married couple. We will not become 'a family.' We are not 'in love.' In truth, we barely know each other." It was only as the words left his mouth that he realized how much it hurt to say them. The first rule of lying—learned at Straka's knee—was to stay as close to the truth as possible. To say he did not know her? That she was not his family? It felt as far from the truth as possible.

"Our plan is to annul the whole thing next year," he went on, "when her mother is gone. Even our households will remain apart. I'm selling my London house to travel, and she is restoring hers to move in. Even if my"—he stopped himself from saying *wife*—"even if the woman I married was in possession of some great fortune, which she is *not*, I could not get to it, because this was not part of our arrangement. It's a union in name only."

"Looked very real to me. Why, I almost choked up, listening to you whisper your heartfelt vows."

"Believe what you wish, but I am telling you the truth," said Trevor, barely hanging on to calm.

"And what did you get, Tryphon? For pretending to marry her, as you say?"

"I know this is difficult for you to grasp, Janos, but I did it because it was the *right thing to do*. It's as simple as that. There was no direct benefit to me."

"Oh, I know what you got," Straka said knowingly, "paying it off on her back, is she, Tryph—"

"*We are not intimate*, and that's all I have to say on the matter. I will not discuss this woman with you. There was no payout. She has no money to pay, even if there was. And I have no money at all. You have come to the wrong man."

Straka stared at him a long moment, and Trevor raised his eyebrows, a challenge. He hoped it was enough of a show, even while his heart raced and he was covered in a cold sweat. It was a new response; the old man had not had this effect on him in the past. It was one of the reasons they had gotten on so well. Trevor had been impossible to bully. But there had never been anything at stake before, never anything to lose.

Janos laughed, the exact sound you did not want to hear when trying to stave off panic. "But of course I did not come here to take *your* money," he said. "Whether you have it or not." His laughter died away, and he shot Trevor a hard look. "I would not steal from my most loyal and trusted advisor."

Well, that's a lie, Trevor thought.

"But I do appreciate your long and elaborate protestations. An earl with no money? Ha! A wife who is really no wife at all?" He pushed the notion away with a bat of his hand. "But this is not what I want. *What I want* is someone else's money."

Right. Trevor swallowed hard. When the second option sounded better, it was always worse. Always. "Whose?"

"He is a young man, like you. And an English lord, also like you. A viscount." Straka shrugged. "I knew his father— *he* was the viscount then. He and his lady wife came to the Greek islands from time to time. A holiday tour. They had certain, shall we say *tastes* that could not be satisfied on *this* island."

"Get on with it, Straka."

"The old viscount is now dead; his wife, sick and old." He waved his hands dismissively. "Wastrels, both of them. Addicts. Available for diversions but absent when the markers came due. Perhaps your uncle was the same?"

"My uncle liked expensive things."

Straka went on, "Ultimately, the old viscount met a tragic end. Drowned in a river, or so I hear. He had no self-control; it was only a matter of time." He shrugged. "When he died, their son became the viscount. But he is a very different sort of man. Serious. Good with money—very good. And my spies tell me he is desperate to restore the family name and erase the reputation of his parents as hedonists." Straka smiled largely, gesturing with his fingers. "Did you hear that, Tryphon? *Desperate.* You know how I love a desperate man."

Oh, God, Trevor thought.

"Here is the favor I ask of you. Are you listening?"

Trevor looked at him blankly.

"I have *stories* I could tell about the former viscount, the dead father. Shocking stories. *Obscene* stories. The man indulged in predilections that fell well below what even I enjoy. These details, these stories, are succulent morsels that I am sure his son, the new viscount, would not wish to be known among high society or his lucrative business partners. They say he's building a shipping empire."

"Is that what they say?" Trevor's voice was strangled.

"Oh, yes. He's very rich, very rich indeed. And I am of a mind that he'll pay handsomely to have these stories disappear altogether. Here." He removed a sweaty stack of papers from his robe and held them out. "See for yourself."

"You want me to blackmail a wealthy English viscount? Oh, God, Straka." Trevor scrubbed a hand over his face. "Why involve me? Why not do it yourself?" Cautiously he accepted the documents.

"Do it myself? But why should I? You know the customs of the rich and well-heeled. You'll travel in the same circles as a viscount. *You are one of them.* I am from the outside. You might even know him. The man's name is Bryson Courtland, Viscount Rainsleigh."

"I do not. I've never heard of him in my life."

"Well, *discover him.*" Straka's menacing tone brooked no argument. He trudged to the tree and yanked his knife from the bark.

Trevor watched, saying nothing, as Straka veered to the wall beside him and propped his hip against the stones.

"I know you will not disappoint me," he said coolly. "I came to you, because you're the only man who's never failed me. Who *solved* problems. I could depend on you."

"Am I also the only man you knew in England?"

Straka laughed—a short, bitter bark—but then he sobered. "In my gratitude, I am willing to release you from future service to me—"

"What?" Trevor shoved off the wall.

The old man went on, "You were under the impression that this was already your situation but, please. When have I allowed an arrangement such as this? To let something so valuable simply *go*? But, it is true, you are *soft*." Straka chuckled. "And you have asked me boldly to move away from this life—my life. No threats. No lies.

"And so I have thought, all right. Perhaps I will honor this request because you were always so loyal and useful to me." He held up a fat, gold-ringed finger. "But, before you go. I will need this one, final favor. Get me the money from this desperate man."

Trevor closed his eyes, breathing deeply and dropped his head. He felt his throat closing and heard ringing in his ears. He saw his future, and Piety's future, and whatever hope he had for freedom and a happy bloody life floating away on the Berkshire breeze.

"You *understand?*" Straka asked.

"No." Trevor sighed, shuffling the papers he'd been handed.

"If you want to be released, you must do this, or my gratitude for your previous service will rapidly fade away."

"But Janos," Trevor said, frustration rising.

"*But nothing.*" Straka let out a hiss, low and final. "Make this happen or… Well, I don't have to elaborate on the result, if you deny me."

Trevor drew breath to challenge him, but Straka cut him off.

"Ah, ah, ah! And don't go telling me you are unmoved by my threats. Maybe you are, maybe you are not. But I know one person who will be, and that is your new lady wife. No, forgive me, your *fictional* lady wife." He chuckled. He raised his knife, balancing the handle in his palm. "If you cared enough to marry her, then you will care enough to do this thing for me. To ensure her *safekeeping.*"

Trevor stared, the anger pulsing with every heartbeat. He fought the urge to grab the knife and drive it home.

Straka laughed and pointed in the distance, at the gentle hillside beyond the cemetery wall. A rabbit hopped into to view, stopping in a puff of clover to feed. Straka smiled, delight clear on his ruddy face.

"Ah, look a moving target. My preference." He gripped his knife, leaned back, and hurled the blade at the rabbit in the grass, stabbing it in the neck, and killing it dead.

CHAPTER THIRTY-ONE

The moment Trevor was out of sight of the Greeks, he ran flat out, mounting his horse in one lunge, digging his heels into the stallion's flanks, and bolting down the hillside. He rode hard through the village and down the tree-lined drive to Garnettgate, not allowing the animal to rest until he clattered into the stable, flinging dust and rock.

Inside the house, he took the staircase three at a time, down the landing, and around the corner to the door of Piety's chamber.

Joseph waited dutifully outside, alert but sitting on the floor. The boy scrambled to his feet when he saw him.

"Wait here," Trevor said, knocking once before throwing open the door.

Piety was inside, thank God. Trevor allowed himself to draw his first conscious breath.

Logic had told him that she would, of course, be safely here, especially if Joseph was at his post, but he was flooded with relief. He'd needed to see her with his own eyes.

Miss Breedlowe attended her. They were bent over a pile of trunks, discussing a heap of garments on the bed. Her head popped up at the sound of the door, and she studied his face.

It took every ounce of self-control not to yank her against him and bury his face in her hair, to assure himself that she was safe, that she had not grown to resent him already.

Instead, he nodded curtly and said, "I'm sorry, Piety, but we must leave within the hour."

Her face fell. "Well, that's impossible. I won't even be dressed in an hour. Let alone packed."

"You must be, and you will be," he said. "I have new, pressing business in London that prevents me from lingering in Berkshire, even until afternoon. It's eleven o'clock. I give you to twelve thirty. Pack whatever you can in that time, and then send for the rest."

Piety raised her chin. "If *you* must go, then go. Miss Breedlowe and I will follow later today. Or tomorrow."

Trevor sucked in breath. Absolutely, that would not happen. "*No.* We go together and we go by twelve thirty. You are a married woman now, Piety—married to me—and you must do as I say.

"I will be too busy," he continued, looking away from her stunned expression, "to show my gratitude to the marchioness. May I count on you to make our farewells and thank her on my behalf?"

Piety stared at him a long moment, searching his face, clutching a stack of linens to her chest.

Do it, he willed in his head. *Do everything I say, exactly as I say it, so that I may keep you safe. Do not argue. For once. Acquiesce.*

He held his breath.

"Fine," she said at last, glancing regretfully at Miss Breedlowe. She waved him away. "It will be as you wish. *My lord.* Leave us, so I can meet your deadline." She turned away.

Trevor nodded and fought a second urge to go to her.

In the hall, he motioned for the Joseph to follow him into the shadows.

"Did you find him?" Joseph asked.

Trevor nodded. "He's asked me the bloody impossible."

"What does he want? Do we have to return to Athens?"

"No. He's cooked up a scheme that has me blackmailing a rich viscount."

"Blackmail." Joseph chewed his lip thoughtfully. "But what will we do?"

Trevor smiled, in spite of himself. Joseph was loyal to the end. "At the moment, I've got no plan. There's no appointed time to return to Straka with the money. He's said he will contact me. This means we're being followed. He's watching us—all of us. So, above all, starting now, Lady Piety may never be left unprotected. I'll not have Straka or his spies anywhere near her. We cannot leave her, even for a moment, do you understand?

"Added to that," he said in a rush, "I must be careful to not appear to be too involved with her or her daily routine. Not affectionate, especially. I've told him that I have no access to her money, because ours is a marriage of convenience. I've told him that we intend to live apart and eventually separate. Because of this, you and I will return to the empty house in Henrietta Place, and Piety will return to her renovations next door."

"But you will tell her *why* you must live apart. You'll tell her you cannot be seen too attached because of Straka?"

Trevor shook his head. "I will not. If she knew, I could not prevent her from paying Straka herself, with her own fortune." He looked at her closed door. "Because she would do it. God love her, she would do it in a second."

Joseph made a sound of frustration. "But maybe she should pay him, Trevor. I think she would rather part with the money than to go along, believing that you wish to live apart."

"We were always meant to live apart, Joseph. We are merely carrying out our plan. It was all decided before I agreed to marry her. *In name only.* This was the pact. She *knew* it would be this way."

Joseph shook his head, "But at the wedding? And then last night? I thought…"

Trevor growled in frustration. "There's no time to explore the wedding or last night or what anyone thought, don't you see? Our very lives are in danger. I must get rid of Straka before anything else can be addressed. I must rely on you to help keep Piety safe. To keep my dealings with Straka unknown to her and anyone else."

"Yes, yes, my lord—Trevor. Of course, you can rely on me."

Trevor took a deep breath and straightened, looking around. He nodded. "Very good. I must ready the horses, see to the carriage. You remain outside this door until she emerges, and then do not leave her side."

"Yes, my lord." He studied Trevor with a frustrated mix of disappointment and devotion.

Trevor walked him back to his position by the doorway and said, "I could not do this without you, Joseph."

"And I would never do it if you weren't forc—er, asking me. Not this way."

To that, there was no answer. Trevor looked once more at the door and strode away.

By Trevor's edict, they were on the road to London by half-past noon. The journey took two days, even at Trevor's punishing pace.

For the duration, Jocelyn sat beside Piety in the carriage, while he rode on horseback outside. It was a ridiculous arrangement, as ridiculous as it had been to leave Berkshire in a blind rush, especially in the spitting rain. But Piety dare not quibble.

How much wiser and less hurtful to do it *his* way, to ride in the rain rather than be tempted by each other. But, how could she pretend?

In fact, she thought again, *how can he?*

His resolve to push her away served only to magnify her broken heart. Not to mention, he was distracted and impatient and cagey.

He is only your husband for a time.

Jocelyn tried to cheer her, speculating about the changes to her house. Mr. Burr's last letter had assured her it was nearly complete, and she could reside comfortably in any room instead of making camp. Piety clung to this, but when they arrived, it was too dark to see beyond the open front door. Fumbling around in the dark was the last, proverbial straw, and Piety summoned Joseph to fetch Mr. Burr. She would have a tour, she told Jocelyn, even in the middle of the night. Trevor opposed this, naturally; he only spoke when he could be contrary, but Piety asked him what else they intended to do, alone together, in an empty house after dark.

Mr. Burr arrived presently with workmen and lanterns and candles and led them through every room. The restoration was stunning, even unfinished and lovelier than her wildest dreams. Piety clapped her hands together and raved at each new appointment, but in her heart, she merely followed along. All she saw, room after room, was herself alone without Trevor, closed in by four walls.

Trevor trailed behind them, saying little or nothing at all. Mr. Burr took care to point out the earl's many contributions, but he barely had the courtesy to nod.

"You know, we haven't seen the solarium," Piety told Trevor, thirty minutes in. "Lady Frinfrock will return within the week, and seeing it will be her first request."

"Consider the hour, Piety, please." Trevor checked his timepiece. "Why not allow Spencer to continue the tour in the proper light of day? When you detain him late into the night, you set back his duties for morning."

"Don't bother on our account, my lord," Spencer said jovially. "The solarium is not so far along, but they have begun to reset the tile in the mosaic. Quite lovely, that mosaic."

"I should *love* to see the mosaic, Mr. Burr," Piety said pointedly. She turned away.

Trevor grabbed her by the arm. "Piety?"

She stared at his hand on her arm and then back at him.

"I have to go out," he said.

"Out?" This was a surprise, indeed. As far as she knew, Trevor had never caroused the streets of London at night.

"It's this business I have," he said. "It cannot wait, even until morning. We left Berkshire at breakneck speed for a reason."

"I suppose I should count myself lucky that you spared precious minutes to take this tour."

"I would not leave you until I was satisfied with the security of the house," he said tiredly.

She considered this, studying him, willing him to say more. After a moment, she said, "Is something the matter, Trevor? What's happened? What *business?*"

He shook his head. "It's nothing with which to concern yourself. A loose end with my uncle's estate. Joseph will remain here to keep watch. Do not dissuade him or send him away, Piety. Please."

She studied him a moment longer. All day, she'd wondered about the weariness in his eyes. A different weariness than ever she had seen before. Was it desperation? Regret? She felt the first pangs of concern. It was not like him to be vague. Even when she did not like his words, he had always been explicitly honest. Now, he hedged, she was sure of it. The look in his eye, the evasiveness? This was something else. Was he afraid?

"When will you return?" she asked him.

"I don't know—late."

"Will you return to me here, or..."

"You will be asleep when I come in, but I won't disturb you when I..." He looked away and then back. "I will return to my uncle's house."

Piety blinked. And there it was. Hot tears stung her eyes.

Trevor opened his mouth to say something, but no words came.

"Very well," she said, nodding her head tersely and raising her chin. She would not try to persuade him.

"Piety, I..."

She waited half of a second more, willing him to confide in her. He hesitated, and she turned away. She felt him watch her as she disappeared around the corner and into the solarium beyond.

Trevor bolted from Henrietta Place on horseback. The tour had been interminable, but he couldn't leave Piety in an unfinished structure with bricks propped against doors instead of locks. It was difficult enough to leave her at all. She was heartbroken and confused, and it pained him, but his sole focus must become locating Viscount Rainsleigh, the bloody target of Straka's bloody blackmail plot, whomever he was.

The preliminaries for blackmail were simple, and God forgive him, Trevor knew them well. Devote several weeks to learning the target and setting up the meet; then designate a smaller window of time to close in and demand the money. Trevor had every intention of working *around* the crime instead of committing it, but a double-cross would take twice the work in half the time. Discovering Rainsleigh's location and routine, his known associates and his vices should have already begun.

The two gentleman's clubs in St. James were an obvious first stop. Trevor had never set foot inside Brooks's or White's, but his uncle had been a legacy member of both, and the dues were paid through year's end, thank God. These clubs teemed with well-heeled gentleman, all of whom should be drinking swiftly and talking freely by this hour of night. Trevor flipped a coin and started at White's.

"You mean *Viscount* Rainsleigh?" repeated an old baronet, an hour after he arrived. He'd chosen the old man for his flashy cuff links and big mouth. Trevor had allowed him to win at cards twice.

"That's right," Trevor said casually. "Happen to know the fellow?"

"The father or the son?"

"Father is dead, or so I'm told."

"Quite so," said the baronet, "drowned in a stream. He was a wastrel and a letch. Not fit for decent company. But the son's a different story." He stabbed a cheroot in his mouth. "Built a bloody shipyard in Blackwall. Made enough to dig the estate in Wiltshire out of hock."

"Quite unseemly for a gentleman to *work*," Trevor suggested, fishing.

"No life of leisure for that one. Got his nose in his ledger all the bloody time."

"Is he ever seen here—or across the street?"

The baronet laughed. "God no, I've never once seen him out. He does not socialize, as far as I know. Keeps himself away from spirits, gambling, turtledoves—no fun at all, really. He makes a point to be as righteous as his father was corrupt. 'Lord Immaculate,' they call him."

"Of course they do." Trevor sighed, and raised his glass. In his head, he cursed Janos Straka to hell and back.

His next stop was the river—the docks along Blackwall, where Rainsleigh was building his shipping empire. Trevor ambled from pub to pub, leaning against bars; lurking near boisterous, crowded tables; playing darts. Finally, a stumbling group of steelworkers fell into an argument over a serving wench, and Trevor stepped in. He bought a round of drinks for the men and tipped the girl enough to take the rest of the night off.

"Aye, we know Lord Rainsleigh," said a burly steelworker when Trevor settled in to share their ale. "Knew him before he was a fancy cock o' the walk, too. Worked right alongside him on the docks for years without even knowing he was waiting to become a lord. He lived in London then."

Trevor choked. "Does he not still reside in town?" It had not occurred to him that he might have to leave London to find this man.

The big man shrugged, but another said, "He came into a mansion in Mayfair when his father went on. But he sold it, straight away, and moved to the country. Wiltshire, maybe?"

A third man spoke up, "He was a hard worker, that one. Always up for a job. Course he owns half the river now."

The first man continued, "Aye. I'd look for work in his shop if he'd have me."

"Hmm," Trevor said thoughtfully, "has all the help he needs, does he?"

The men around the table laughed, and his informant's face turned pink. The big man narrowed his eyes as if deciding whether to take offense, but then he shrugged and threw back his drink. "Can't meet his bloody standards, guv'nor," he admitted, slamming his tankard down. "The viscount only takes the most skilled trades. Me? I work hard, but I've had no proper training."

"Is that right?" Trevor signaled for another round of drinks. "Sounds like a hard man."

"He's all right," finished the first man. "Builds a beauty of a ship. Treats his men fair. Doesn't suffer laziness or fools."

"That cuts us out!" said another man, and the table burst into more laughter. Trevor smiled weakly, barely able to fake it, and paid the tab.

By the time Trevor rode for home, he had a frustratingly clear picture of "Lord Immaculate." Hard working, fair, principled. The most difficult possible blackmail mark. He might as well have been a priest. He reached Henrietta Place bone tired and plagued with worry, but he would not rest until he checked on Piety. He entered his own house for the benefit of Straka's spies and then crept through Piety's rear garden.

"No trouble, then?" he asked Joseph when he found him. "Were you able to see a watch in the street?"

"No, but I can't guard her and prowl around." The boy looked around the kitchen and yawned. "You're back now; I'll make a loop."

Trevor shook his head. "No, get some sleep. I did a thorough round just now. Nothing's amiss. It's almost morning. The doors are locked. We will begin again tomorrow."

"Did you find the viscount?"

Trevor took a deep, weary breath and let it out, rehashing the facts he discovered over the course of the night.

When he finished, Joseph asked, "Be hard to blackmail him if he's not even in town."

"That's the God's-honest truth. But, you know, Joseph, I'm racking my brain for a way *not* to blackmail the bloody man. I can't commit a crime on Straka's behalf. Not here in England. Not against a viscount who's known as 'Lord Immaculate.' It was one thing to run schemes in Greece, where corruption is a way of life, but in England? There has to be some other way."

Joseph grinned. "I'm glad you won't do it."

"Well, I've said I will *try* not to do it. If the man is in London, I hope to set up a meeting under the auspices of investing in his ships. By the time he figures out I have no money and no interest in shipping, hopefully I will have learned something useful."

"Learned something useful about what?" said a sleep-rasped voice from the doorway.

Trevor craned around.

His wife stood at the base of the servants' stairs clad only in a thin night rail. Her hair was wild and loose. Her feet, bare. She squinted, sleep still in her eyes.

Trevor glanced at Joseph, dismissing him, and went to her, whipping off his coat to cover her shoulders.

"What are you doing awake at this hour?" he asked softly.

"Couldn't sleep." She snuggled into the coat. "Why are you here? Is anything the matter?"

"No, no, I am merely checking on Joseph."

They looked up, and the boy was gone.

"Do you want something from the kitchen?" he asked her. "Joseph had the kettle on."

She shook her head and turned to go.

"Piety, wait."

She paused on the stair.

"Let me walk you up. There are strewn nails and tools and loose timber. You mustn't walk around without shoes in the dark."

He clipped up the stairs beside her, and as they wound up the small staircase, his hand hovered at the small of her back. He intended to leave her in the hallway outside her chamber, but she fumbled with the knob. Her hand was lost in the sleeve of his jacket.

He toed the door with his boot, and she padded past him. Her loose hair grazed his face. The sweet scent of her—floral soap and clean cotton—wafted over him. He followed.

"In the bed you go," he heard himself say, taking his coat. He would merely see her safely beneath the covers.

She said nothing, crawling sleepily into the bed. Her gown was voluminous, and her feet were tangled, briefly, in the hem. He reached out to pull it free, and his thumb grazed her ankle.

She extended her leg.

He caught her foot in his hand.

She looked up. Of its own volition, his hand slid upward. With half-lidded eyes, he watched his fingers trace her trim ankle, bare leg, knee.

He stopped. He looked at her. She was propped back on her elbows, staring back. She blinked.

"Under the covers now," he whispered. His voice was a useless crackle of reverence and desire.

She went opposite the covers, sliding her other leg beside the first. She pointed her toes.

He stared at her feet. Small. Arched. Five tiny toes on each dainty foot.

He had never felt so stricken with the need to touch, to skate his hand down and outline one perfect arch with his finger and glide it back up again.

He forced himself to whisper. "I said *beneath* the covers, Piety."

The sheet was beneath her, and he used one hand to slide it free. With the other hand, he held her ankle.

Holding the sheet out, he stared at his fingers surrounding her foot.

She wiggled the toes of the other.

He dropped the sheet and seized that foot as well.

Piety let out a whimper, rubbing her feet together and dropping back against the pillow on a sigh.

Trevor increased the pressure, massaging the smooth, firm skin of her feet—then her ankles. His hands went higher with each pass. Up her legs and down. Now to her knees, and down. Now higher, above her knees. Her night rail was a twist across her thighs.

His breathing grew ragged. He felt the rapid thud of his own accelerated heartbeat. She arched back, pointing her toes in delight.

On the final pass, he slid his hands up the sides of her legs, over her hips and waist, up to her breasts and then, gathering the fabric of her night rail, he fleeced the thin garment over her head, leaving her naked before him.

He swallowed and stared down.

"One small, goodnight kiss?" she asked.

On a growl, Trevor flung the night rail away and fell into bed.

"I'm sorry, Piety," he said. "This is unfair, and wrong."

"If you say that again," she said, "I will bite you."

And then she bit him anyway, but ever so softly, just behind his ear. He moaned, and they worked very diligently to kiss goodnight, until the sun awakened the sky.

CHAPTER THIRTY-TWO

Piety was anxious to get a real look at the progress of her house in the clear light of day. Falcondale did not awaken when she left the bed, but when she returned from breakfast, he was gone.

It was a waste of time to be surprised. She would have been shocked to find him in her chamber or anywhere in the house. Their separate lives had begun.

Ha. Our separate lives have resumed.

Her only solace was that he had wanted her. Desperately. As desperately as she wanted him. If she thought he had not, if she thought he had been indulging her or simply going through the motions, she would not have consented. But the desire, so plain on his face, so tense through his body, had ignited her own need. And what was one more night? Soon he would be gone, and she'd have only the memories to keep her warm. Why not make as many as possible?

Now it was almost luncheon, and she had nearly unpacked. Only one trunk remained from her time in Berkshire. She bent over it, pulling out reticules and shoes, reminding herself to stay busy, to concentrate on the exciting work of her house rather than her husband's heart-wrenching stubbornness.

She picked her way down the landing, armed with the reticules, and nearly collided with Spencer Burr.

"Oh, Mr. Burr," she said, craning to see him over the bundle, "the molding in my bedroom is positively sculptural. I love it!"

"It was the earl's design, my lady. He constructed it from the st—"

Crack!

In the middle of his sentence, the wood of the landing on which they stood gave a jolt beneath their feet.

Piety staggered, and Mr. Burr let out a yelp. He lunged to the bannister and looked over the edge.

Piety opened her mouth to ask him what was amiss, but before she could speak, the wood jolted again. There was another crack. A groan.

She reached for the banister, dropping the bags without a thought. Mr. Burr reached out to steady her.

A new sound filled the rotunda. A splintering. Piety gripped the railing, looking wildly in the direction of the noise. An expanse of fresh plaster had buckled on the side of the stairwell below.

Mr. Burr shouted for her to get back, but there was no time. The floor trembled again. The plaster tore in two directions, now three. After a deafening pop, it began to drop off in chunks.

Piety screamed, and Mr. Burr reached for her.

It was the last thing she remembered before the stairwell crumbled, pulling the landing down with it, and they fell, fell, fell.

Jocelyn knew from the sound of the crash that something terrible had happened. The noise itself was alarming, but with it came a jolt that shook the house and a gush of stale air that blew the fine hair away from her face.

Jocelyn rose up and then froze, listening to the ringing silence. Marissa dropped the tablecloth she had been folding and bolted toward the door.

"Marissa, wait!" Jocelyn called, unsure of what awaited them in the next room. "Not that way," she said. "Go through the kitchens to the stables and fetch the new grooms—all of them. Then go to the marchioness's house and tell Bernard to send for the doctor."

The girl looked skeptical, more intent on saving her own skin, but Jocelyn refused to be ignored. "Marissa, go! Something awful has happened! Run as fast as you can!"

The girl nodded and fled.

Jocelyn ran toward the sound.

"Oh, God, no," she whispered, when she rounded the arched doorway and took in the disaster.

Lumber, beams, and plaster poked every-which-way in an angry, tangled heap, like a giant's overturned rubbish bin. Above, the balcony looked as if the same giant had taken a huge bite from the landing. Where walkway and balustrade once ran, now there was nothing—an expanse of raw, jagged boards and drooping rug. Dust and grit swirled in the air between the break and the pile.

Tentatively, Jocelyn took a step closer, eyeing the heap and the second floor, distrustful of more falling debris. Then she saw Piety. The bright fabric of her favorite yellow day dress was impossible to miss, even half-buried. Without thinking, Jocelyn waded into the rubble and began to pick her way to Piety, calling her name.

Are there others? she wondered frantically, ducking chunks of lumber that continued to drop from above. "Piety! I am coming!" Her voice was high and weak with fear.

She discovered Mr. Burr by nearly stepping on him. He was half-buried under wood and plaster, his body camouflaged by slate-colored dust.

"Mr. Burr!" she exclaimed, scrambling to make room. "Mr. Burr?" He made no response. She screamed into the silence of the house. "Help! Please, someone help!"

She heard no answer. *Please, Marissa, bring help.*

She looked back to the deathly stillness of Piety and Mr. Burr, trying to decide whom to go to first. Mr. Burr was closer—just a step way—so she stooped and began to dig, pulling first one board, then another. Her hands shook, and she coughed on the grit rising from the rubble. Tentative picking did nothing; either the wood would not budge or it disintegrated in her hand. She cried out in frustration. Now she dropped to her knees and put her back into it, choking back tears. This was more effective. A big heap toppled with her first significant pull. Just like that, Mr. Burr's legs were relieved of the larger of two boards.

She scrambled to his chest and listened. A heartbeat.

Thank you, God!

And a breath! He was alive and breathing. Another prayer of thanks.

Feeling more confident, she began to pick her way to Piety. Tears filled her eyes when she discovered that Piety, too, was breathing. But the yellow fabric on the sleeve of her gown was entirely soaked with blood. Again, Jocelyn dug, picking away at the plaster that had settled around her, careful not to upset her position.

When the debris was gone, she could see the source of the blood: a nail, bent and rusty, had rammed through Piety's arm. The pocked, gnarled point of it jutted out of her sleeve, aiming grimly toward the ceiling.

Jocelyn clapped her hand over her mouth and willed herself to think. The bleeding had to be stopped, but how? She looked around, trying to be resourceful and calm. *Solve it, solve it, solve it.*

She had just lifted her hem to rip a strip from her petticoats, when she heard footsteps. She cried out, staggering to stand.

It was Falcondale. He sprinted into the room with Joseph behind him, the look on his face one of sheer terror. "My God, what's happened?"

And then he saw Piety.

"No!" He darted toward the unsteady pile.

"Please, my lord!" called Jocelyn, holding out a hand. "She is alive, but we must have more help and perhaps even a doctor before we unsettle her. I have sent Marissa for the doctor, but until he arrives, I believe it is important to take the utmost care not to cause more damage."

"Who else is hurt?"

"Mr. Burr is there." She indicated his position with a tilt of her head. "There may be others. Careful, Falcondale; the debris is very unstable!"

For a moment, she thought he would ignore her. He looked as if he hadn't heard; his face was wild with worry. Joseph grabbed his arm from behind.

"Let me loose!" He growled, shrugging away, but he stopped at the base of the pile and looked up. "What in God's name happened?"

"Lady Piety was unpacking trunks on the second floor," Jocelyn said. "I do not know about Mr. Burr. I assume they were going about their business when the rotten section of the landing gave way."

Falcondale swore. "I told the architect that *all* of the old wood had to go. I should have seen to it myself! Will this heap hold my weight?"

"I cannot say. You must proceed carefully. One step at a time. Do not charge up."

With as much speed as careful steps would allow, Falcondale and Joseph waded into the rubble toward Piety. The earl redirected the boy to Mr. Burr.

When Falcondale saw Piety's trapped, bloody body, he dropped to his knees with a noise of pure agony.

"We must stop the bleeding," he said.

"Yes," agreed Jocelyn, "but the nail."

"I see it. Please, can you find something clean to stop the flow of blood?"

She nodded and tried to step backward, teetering. They heard voices.

It was the grooms. "Miss! Miss!" came men's cries from the main hall. They rounded the corner, continuing, "Oy! What's happened?"

Jocelyn waved them in, and Falcondale shot to his feet, informing them of the obvious. He dispatched one for more medical help and another to locate the remainder of Mr. Burr's crew. The other four were ordered to work in pairs to remove the pieces of wood and rubble from around Mr. Burr and the countess. Jocelyn hurried off for make-shift bandages, returning quickly with linen napkins that she and Marissa had just unpacked from a trunk.

Falcondale presided over the rescue efforts until the doctors came, working alongside the grooms, with a calm, clear authority, giving equal attention to Mr. Burr and his wife. Jocelyn was glad to defer to him. Her hands shook, and her nerves were shot. She helped where she could.

They pried Mr. Burr free and rolled him onto a wide board so that he was flat and stable.

Refusing help, Falcondale gently laid Piety on a second board and hovered over her, arranging her torn dress and smoothing the hair away from her face. When she was settled, he carefully examined her arm. "It's run clean through the flesh," he told Jocelyn, taking a moment to breathe deeply and wipe his eyes. "But it's somehow missed the bone."

Jocelyn nodded. Of all the ways to suffer a nail through the arm, this had to be the most preferable.

"We cannot properly stave off the bleeding with the nail in her arm. It must come out."

"Are you certain, my lord?"

Falcondale nodded grimly. "I saw every manner of injury during my time in Greece. The man for whom I worked retained a private surgeon, but he was not always around. You learn things. Common sense. This nail is filthy and precludes any pressure to the wound. It cannot stay in her arm."

Before she could ask him how she might help, he braced one hand on the board and quickly but steadily slid the nail from Piety's arm in one fluid motion. Jocelyn gasped. Piety cried out, although she was still unconscious and did not awaken. Tears, Jocelyn saw, streamed down the earl's cheeks as he bent near her ear and whispered as he stroked her face. Then he returned to her arm, examining the wound. He motioned to Jocelyn, and she moved in quickly with the linen, working beside him to stop the flow of blood that now coursed from the puncture.

Sometime after that—minutes? An hour?—the doctors arrived, rushing inside with Marissa and members of Lady Frinfrock's staff. On the earl's command, the two physicians split, each giving their full attention to one patient. One doctor was accompanied by an assistant, and Jocelyn insisted that the two men work together on Piety, while she offered to aid the doctor with Mr. Burr. His leg, the doctor determined, was badly broken, but he would survive. Holding him down while the doctor set the large man's leg took all her strength, plus the strength of three grooms. He came to with a loud, forceful string of profanity.

When he was stable and out of danger, she hurried back to Piety and the earl.

"The doctor," Falcondale told her, "believes the puncture wound may be the worst of what he can tell so far." He sat on the floor with Piety slumped half in his lap. "Of course any internal damage to the head and neck can only be assessed when she awakens."

"Of course," whispered Jocelyn, taking up one of Piety's limp hands. "She is cold. I will get blankets."

"Thank you, Miss Breedlowe. How is Mr. Burr?"

"He has broken his right leg, but he will survive. He has regained consciousness."

"I would speak to him," began the earl, "but I cannot leave her."

"Do not worry yourself. He is taking full responsibility and agonizing about the countess, but I will assure him."

"Thank you. I will speak to him presently." He looked down at his wife's peaceful face. "Piety's bed chamber is out of the question. In fact, no one should go upstairs until I have looked over the damage myself. When she is stable, I will move Piety to the master suite of my house."

Jocelyn nodded. "Of course, my lord."

"We must send a messenger to fetch Miss Baker from Berkshire. Piety will want to see her when she…" He trailed off.

"She will awaken when the shock to her body has passed, my lord. Please do not lose heart."

He looked up, squeezing his eyes shut, and Jocelyn saw tears leak from their corners.

She looked discreetly away and added, "She is a fighter—Piety Rheese."

"That she is," the earl agreed gruffly. "And thank God for that."

CHAPTER THIRTY-THREE

Piety regained consciousness in fits and starts. Whenever awake, Tiny and Jocelyn plied her with nourishment—broth, bread, sweets, water, wine, anything they could ladle down her throat—though she had no appetite. The last thing she wanted to do in her few, precious moments of lucidity was eat. Or speak, for that matter. Yet, just when her mouth was full, they invariably demanded she tell them how she felt.

She felt vague. Fuzzy. Hurt. Everything hurt, especially her arm.

When she slept, she dreamed. She dreamed of her father urging her to read to him, riding with her through the summer marshland surrounding their home in Rhode Island. And she dreamed of Falcondale. Laughing, kissing her, carrying her up the stairs after their wedding. In bed. Walking beside the wall on a hillside. Throwing pebbles in a pond. Other dreams were dark: Eli upon her, restraining her, slapping her; her mother laughing at her while she tried to run away.

Throughout it all, she was cold. Shivering, from icy toes to shuddering shoulders. In the moments before they shoved spoonfuls of food in her mouth, she begged for more blankets and a hotter fire.

After days, she woke up for all of thirty minutes—long enough to actually speak between bites of her force-fed meal.

"Where are we?" The frail hoarseness in her voice sounded strange to her own ears. She looked blinkingly around a sparse, dark room.

"'Tis the master chamber in Falcondale's home, my lady," Jocelyn said. "Will you take more bread?"

"No, please. Has he…Has the earl gone?"

"Gone?" asked Jocelyn.

"On his journey. To Syria?"

Her friend chuckled. "He's scarcely left your side since the accident. He will be disappointed that you've awakened when he had an errand in St. James. He's been a constant fixture here, I would say."

"Oh, God." Piety moaned. She tried to touch her hand to her forehead but recoiled at the pain in her arm.

"I would not worry so, my lady. I think your near-death experience may have caused him to see his own heart in a new light. He's been given quite a scare."

"All this from a nail? Why can't I get up?"

"Your bruising is substantial, but the doctors believe that your bones and muscles are intact. The trouble is with the puncture. An infection set in, and you are suffering from fever. Your body is fighting the infection."

"I feel a little better. Am I improving?"

"In time, my lady," said Jocelyn, but Piety saw her look away.

"So I am very sick, indeed."

"You are alive, Piety, and that is what matters now. You have regained consciousness with clear eyes and speech. You know us. This is progress, indeed. The infection in your arm is our next concern. One thing at a time."

Tiny leaned in next, plying her with water. "The doctor is coming again this afternoon. There is no use guessing how sick you are until he has his say. All you need to worry about is eating and sleeping."

"Why am I so cold?"

"'Tis the fever, my lady," said Jocelyn. "I will get a hot cloth for your face."

"How is Mr. Burr?" she asked, feeling her eyelids grow heavy.

"A broken leg. He will recover fully."

Piety wanted to ask more, but she could feel herself drifting back into oblivion.

Before she fell unconscious again, there was something of dire importance she wished to say. "Jocelyn?"

"I am here."

"I...I need to ask a colossal favor. It is difficult, and you will not like it, but it is essential to me."

"How serious this sounds," said Jocelyn, smiling.

Piety looked at the blankets covering her body. "I cannot stay here," she said resolutely. "In the earl's house. You've...You must help me to move."

"Move?" Tiny's expression was mutinous.

In the same moment, Jocelyn said, "Help you *what*?"

"To a rented hotel suite. To hired apartments. Perhaps to Lady Frinfrock's, if she will help me once more. I hate to impose, really I do, but I see no choice."

"But, Piety, why? You are staying awake long enough to make conversation, but this business with the puncture wound is very serious. I did not want to alarm you, but the doctor has suggested that the infection could cause you to lose your arm. We dare not unsettle you and set back your recovery. You have every comfort here with the earl. And it is your place to be with your husband. Please make no mistake, your condition is very fragile."

"Lose my arm?" she repeated. Her breathing was shallow and raspy. "If that is the case, then I am even more determined. I cannot bear to be a burden. Not to him, of all people."

"Burden? What burden? You have not heard or seen his devotion. You misjudge his attitude since the fall. He does not at all seem put out or burdened in the least. Indeed, attending to you seems to be his very life's work."

"Oh, God. What a nightmare. Do you not see? This is exactly the situation he endured with his mother! She was a convalescent, and he was forced, *duty-bound*, to care for her. I will not impose the same."

"Forgive me if I sound unsupportive or unhelpful, my lady, but I would go so far as to say that his lordship would be *angry* if you relocated—especially without his knowledge. He is very intent about your care. He has hired a staff: maids, footmen, a cook, and a kitchen girl. They make sure we have everything we need. But most of all, the earl himself has been so very vigilant. Hardly a moment has passed when he is not here with you—and of his own accord. We have said nothing. In fact, we have urged him to leave you to take his own rest. This brief departure today is rare. He has been very steadfast. Very steadfast, indeed."

Piety moaned again. "Worse, still." She rolled painfully to her side. "All he wanted was an uncomplicated life, with no one to look after but himself. And now I'm an invalid who may lose her arm. I will not be a burden to him. Will not—"

"You stop right there, Missy Pie," Tiny interrupted. "How can you be a burden when all you do is lay in the bed?"

Piety shook her head. "Everything you say only convinces me more. Who wishes for a wife confined to her bed? It was one thing for me to insist that we could make a go of this marriage when I was capable and energetic and able to solve problems and make our lives easier. But now? When I can scarcely stay awake from moment to the next? When I may *lose my arm*!"

"Come now." Jocelyn tried to sooth her. "The doctor has not—"

"We know enough to know that the danger is real. What in God's name would Falcondale do with a one-armed wife? Assuming I live long enough to have it taken from me. Jocelyn! Tiny! Please, you *must* relocate me."

"And say what to your husband?" asked Tiny. "What are we supposed to say after we steal you away from his own house? The man will be furious and come after us! When he does, for once, he'll be right."

"Miss Baker is correct, Piety. The earl could charge us with…with *abduction*."

"Please. *The earl* will recover, I assure you. As for me? There's no guarantee, is there? Knowing this, and knowing his history, I cannot stay."

They stared blankly at her, committing to nothing, and Piety tried to sit up in the bed. "Tell me I'm fabricating this worry," she said. "Convince me that I do not embody the precise, *helpless* condition that he has worked meticulously to avoid." She fell back on the pillows, drawing shallow, ragged breaths. "I am correct in this. You *know* I'm correct. I cannot stay."

Piety turned her head to the side, tears streaming down her cheeks. She would not be deterred. She would die before he saw her helpless and needy.

"The marchioness will understand," Piety said softly to the wall. "And she will help you move me. There is money enough for whatever you need. Please, Jocelyn, Tiny. If ever you cared for me, help me in this."

Jocelyn sounded miserable when she said, "I will try, my lady. I will try."

"I don't suppose this is any worse of an idea than your other wild schemes." Tiny grumbled and fussed with the bedclothes. "Still, I don't like it. I don't like it one bit, and I'll march you back up to this room myself if I see your fever rise one mark."

"Thank you," Piety whispered, and then she drifted into a dark and dreamless sleep.

Trevor walked into Piety's sick room four days later to the devastating discovery that his wife was gone.

The bedchamber was empty.

His bed—the bed which just hours before had contained his frail wife—was vacant. Not just empty, but made up with brisk precision. Piety's possessions were gone. Her trunk of clothes, the stack of blankets, her medicines and bandages, the vases and vases of fresh flowers were all gone. The room stood cold and empty, even the fire had been extinguished and the ash carried away. It looked just as it had before the accident.

His first thought, God help him, his first thought was that she was...that she had...

He stopped breathing. His heart ceased beating. He nearly lost his footing and dropped to one knee. Fear closed his throat.

It was inconceivable, what he thought, and thank God he was able to reason his way out of the ensuing panic. Someone would have alerted him if she had made a turn for the worse.

No, he thought. *Not that.*

"Joseph! Joseph!" He heaved up and staggered mindlessly around the room, stripping back bed linens and upsetting empty drawers, looking for any clue. He threw open the window and shouted her name into the quiet street. He lunged from closet to closet, yanking open doors. He was just about to race down the hall, to attack the rooms in which Miss Breedlowe and Miss Baker had been staying, when Joseph skidded up to him.

"I've seen, my lord," the boy said, waving his arms to make sure Trevor didn't step on him. "The house was too quiet when I returned from the market, and I raced up. The entire house is empty! There's nothing. I was about to come for you!"

"The market?" Trevor roared. "I would not have gone if I could not trust you to remain here to stand guard. How could you leave her?"

"They tricked me, Trevor! Miss Breedlowe asked me to run to the market to fetch an herb for Lady Piety's salve. It seemed urgent, and Iros was no longer watching the house because he left when you did, trailing you. I was only gone long enough to sprint to the market and back, but when I returned, she was gone. Everyone was gone."

Trevor shook his head, unable to hear excuses. He continued down the stairs at a fast clip. "Muster the staff. All the new maids. The grooms from the countess's stable. We'll hear a report from everyone."

"But what staff? What maids? Did you hear me, Trevor? They're all gone! Only Marissa remains, and she has returned to the employ of Lady Frinfrock. The house is vacant."

Trevor paused and looked at Joseph, confused. "Gone where? A house full of people and a woman clinging to life do not just disappear, Joseph. My God, I was only gone for an hour!" He'd only left because his meeting with the viscount had been today. If anything had happened to Piety while he was away on Straka's goddamned errand, he would kill the old man with his own two hands.

The thought of Straka struck Trevor with a new, more chilling layer of fear. "Straka would not abduct her." He said the thought out loud, trying to stave off his own panic. "The hassle of an injured woman would not seem worth it. Do you agree?" He stared at the boy. "Straka has shown no particular interest in her since the beginning. Iros and Demetrios watch only me."

"It wasn't Straka, Trevor." Joseph shook his head. No, I think..." Joseph faltered and cleared his throat. "I think she may have run away."

Trevor growled again and sprinted to the top step, grabbing Joseph's shoulder. "And why would you think that? She cannot even stand, let alone run."

"I don't know, but men could be hired to carry her. The marchioness and Miss Breedlowe do her bidding without question. I'm just suggesting—"

"What you suggest," said Trevor, shoving the boy back against the opposite wall, "is that you know more than you are letting on. I left you here to guard her. *Where* is she?"

"I don't know." A tear tumbled down Joseph's cheek, and he tried to block his face from Trevor's view. "I failed you, Trev, I'm sorry. I should have known the errand to the market was a trick."

Trevor made a sound of frustrated agony, overwhelmed with the terror knifing through his body. He lowered his face an inch from Joseph's. "I'm going to ask you one more time. If you know anything, anything at all about where she might be or how she left, tell me now. The truth. Think very hard about how you answer because I love you like a brother, Joseph, I honestly do, but by God, I'll turn you out into the street without a backward glance if you lie to me now."

"I know nothing more than I've told you," the boy said, looking him squarely in the eye. "Except we're wasting time. I know you're afraid, but let us work together to find someone who will give us clues. We should be looking for something she left behind."

Trevor gave him a hard, heavy look, and then released his shoulder and stepped back. Swearing, he spun around and raked a shaky hand through his hair. "Run away, you said? Why would she run away?"

Joseph shrugged. "Well…"

"Say it," Trevor ordered through gritted teeth.

"You know as well as I do that you were going to leave her, Trev. She loved you, and you were going to leave her so you could be *free*." His voice was thick with tears.

Trevor squeezed his eyes shut, forcing himself to acknowledge this truth. He'd known it even before the boy said it.

If he'd driven her to run in her fragile condition, he would never forgive himself.

Joseph could not look at him—an awkward hurt that he would not soon forget—but there was no time for recriminations. "If I've caused her to run," Trevor said lowly, "I'm sure Miss Breedlowe can be found at her side." He glanced at Joseph. "You have been right all along. I'm sorry I doubted you, Joe."

"I understand, my lord. We will find her. Shall we go to the marchioness?"

"No," he said, turning. "Bring me your ladylove. The maid. Marissa."

Marissa was thankfully easy to crack. Within fifteen seconds, she hid her face in her hands and shook her head mutely, seemingly too overset to even sob. Piety *was* running away. From him. His wife could scarcely sit up, but she wanted to free herself from him so badly, she'd devoted her few lucid moments to planning an elaborate escape.

When the interrogation was finished, Trevor was confident that the maid knew very little, indeed. How clever they were to keep Marissa in the dark, especially since they had not taken her with them to wherever they had gone. He could easily bully her into spilling her deepest secrets—if only she had secrets to tell.

He shoved his chair back and waved the maid away.

Dear God, he'd only left her side for an hour! The pressing need to locate the bloody viscount had hovered over his head like an ax. When the man said he would see him, Trevor had no choice but to go. It was the fastest meeting possible, and Trevor had come away with the same feeling he'd had from the start: He could not bring himself to blackmail this man. It would be a great dishonor, not to mention, he would never succeed. Rainsleigh was too powerful and too smart.

When the meeting was over, he had raced back to Henrietta Place, only to discover the women had been waiting days for just such a moment. According to Marissa, they'd stolen out of the house as soon as he'd gone and Joseph was dispatched to the market. Piety lay prone on stretcher while grooms conveyed her to a hired carriage.

The timing had been impeccable.

Trevor yearned to hit something. He yearned to pound the coachman and the grooms who consented to move a sick woman down stairs and into the damp morning fog merely because she waved a bag of coin. He wanted to rage at the new staff for slipping away for the same bloody reason. And the marchioness? She was the worst of all! What in God's name had she been thinking not to put a stop to such a reckless plan.

But mostly, he ached to hold his wife. To see for himself that she was safe, and well, *his*.

He had to find her. He *would* find her. Maybe she could no longer bear him. Maybe his self-involved remoteness or his cryptic distractedness became too much. Maybe she'd simply stopped caring. In any instance, he would not permit her give up. Her affection may have finally snapped, but the depth of *his* commitment was endless.

He had never been more prepared to convince her to give him a second, third, fourth, *hundredth* chance.

How many times had he failed her? Too many to count, but she could not give up on him now. Not when he had finally, stupidly, belatedly—but *comprehensively*—been jolted into acknowledging his deep and abiding love.

Not when he was more determined than ever to cast off Straka.

Not now.

Please Piety, he prayed in his head. *Not yet. Come back to me.*

He watched Joseph lead Marissa, quivery and mournful, from the room, his brain spinning for his next play, when the girl let fly a kernel of useful information.

Sniffling and mumbling as she leaned on Joseph, she said, "Even the marchioness does not know the location of her sick room. That is why Miss Breedlowe is to visit Lady Frinfrock every night. Her ladyship is anxious for reports on her progress. If they won't tell Lady Frinfrock where she is, why would the tell me?"

"*Wait*," Trevor ordered.

The maid froze, realizing what she'd said, and she collapsed into Joseph's arms, hiding her face. Joseph shot Trevor an irritated look and patted her gently. "Let me, Trev. You've terrorized her enough." Whispering, he asked, "When, muffin? When will Miss Breedlowe visit the marchioness?"

"Every night," the maid said into Joseph's shirt. "Every night at eight o'clock. But I'll be sacked if they find out I told you."

"No one will be sacked," the earl said, reaching for his hat, shoving it on his head. "How does she come?"

"I'm to meet Miss Breedlowe at the stable door and follow her inside the house so she may call upon the marchioness. If Lady Piety requires anything from the house, I'm to run and fetch it."

The earl studied her for a moment, rolling the new information around in his head. Finally, he nodded and turned away.

They chose to approach Miss Breedlowe after her next nightly meeting with the marchioness. If Lady Frinfrock learned that Trevor was on Piety's trail, she might move all of London to relocate Piety before Trevor had a chance to find her.

He and Joseph were prepared to crouch beside the stable door for hours, waiting for Miss Breedlowe's visit to end, but apparently the nightly reports were meant to be short and to the point. Miss Breedlowe stepped briskly out the back door, Marissa behind her, in just ten minutes' time. Willing himself to be calm and cordial, Trevor stepped out of the shadows to block her path.

"A word, if you will, Miss Breedlowe," he said.

Miss Breedlowe skittered back against a drain pipe, clutching her chest. "My lord! You startled me!"

Trevor made no move to calm her. "Tell me where she is."

She glanced at Marissa, acutely disappointed, and then back at the earl. She opened her mouth and then closed it. Shoving off of the drain pipe, she took a deep breath and smoothed her gloves over shaking hands. She flicked raindrops off her coat.

"It was only a matter of time," Trevor went on, watching her. "The marchioness and yourself—and especially, *my wife*—should be warned: I will be *tireless* in my search for her."

Miss Breedlowe nodded to the ground, clearly bolstering herself, and then met his gaze. "I cannot speak for Lady Frinfrock, my lord, but rest assured that your wife is aware of no such conviction." She took a step toward the gate.

He blocked her. "Meaning what?"

"I'm sorry, my lord. I want to help you, truly I do, but my duty is to the countess."

Trevor growled. "Then do your duty and allow me to provide for her. We can, I believe, both agree that her condition is fragile, and that she requires the attention of the most talented doctors and the most comfortable lodging. She requires care at all hours. How in God's name can she receive this if she is separated from her husband, out of her house, in a bloody *hired room*, somewhere across town?"

"I can assure you, my lord, that she is quite comfortable and receives only the best care."

"I must see her!" He banged an open palm against the wall. Miss Breedlowe jumped but stood firm.

Trevor swore under his breath and stared at his hand on the wall. Trying again, he said more softly, "Please. Miss Breedlowe—Jocelyn. I know my behavior up until this point has been selfish and deplorable and without constancy. But I cannot be shut out now of all times. She *cannot* welcome my help with that ridiculous passage or those vile Americans and then choose *now* to run. Please, Miss Breedlowe. You know that I only want…" He was at a loss for words.

"You only want *what* for her?" Miss Breedlowe cut in. "What, precisely, is your goal in finding her? Your behavior after the collapse can be viewed as nothing less than admirable—devoted, even—but is it out of order to suggest that any lasting sentiment in this vein would be very new, indeed? I will be the first to admit that I was against relocating her, as was the marchioness. But she insisted and her reasons were strongly held. Surely if you study your behavior of the last weeks, you will not be confused as to why."

"Because she finds me abhorrent," he said miserably. "I know why!"

"On the contrary. Because she finds you absent."

"But I am here! I am begging for access to my own wife!"

"Yes, you are here, and besides startling the wits out of me, your sense of urgency and insistence is very stirring, to be sure. But for how long are you here?" She took a deep breath and rubbed a gloved hand across her brow. She started again, "The countess has asked to be removed for very firmly held reasons, but, as her devoted friend, I have reasons of my own. I have agreed to be a party to her scheme because of these." She took another deep breath. "Piety cannot survive your attention today, my lord, and your abandonment next week. She cannot. Of this, Miss Baker and I are all very sure. It is the sole reason we have consented to assist her. The marchioness agrees."

"Lady Frinfrock knew about the annulment?"

"She would not help us any other way."

"I appreciate your concern," he said, "but I cannot be concerned about what any of you think. Piety herself must allow me to explain. *I have no intention of leaving her.*"

"I believe the countess's worry may be—and I betray her by revealing even this much—that your current urgency and insistence may grow to something more akin to irritation and resentment in the future."

"Irritation? Resentment?" he repeated. But then he understood. Cold, suffocating regret dawned and sunk in with dull, painful teeth. He grabbed the wall beside him for support.

"In her view, the unthinkable has happened," Miss Breedlowe said. "Exactly what you did not want. She will not be a burden to you, Lord Falcondale. She would rather die first. It was one thing for her to entertain your indecision when she was hale and hearty. But she now views herself as an invalid, and she cannot—*will not*—see you turn away from her in that state. She would rather disappear from your life."

"*No,*" Trevor said, pounding the wall again. "Oh, God, what have I done? I want her. I want her however she may be. I merely want her happy. And healthy! And safe! Not for my sake, for her own!"

Miss Breedlowe studied him for a moment, considering. Finally, she said, "You must tell her, my lord."

"How can I? I don't bloody know where she is!" Trevor spun away, hissing profanity and raking his hand through his hair. "I will locate her," he continued, adamant, "even if I have to tear this city apart. In the meantime, I am counting on you to ensure the utmost level of care. If her condition slips even one degree…" He let the threat fade away, daring not to bluster and bully. Not yet.

Instead, he seized on his very real desperation. "I can also add," he said, "that there are new dangers. An old associate of mine has turned up from Greece. He has made threatening remarks and put me out of my mind with fear for Piety's safety. My most recent distraction has been to deal with him. Not to desert Piety, to *protect* her."

Miss Breedlowe studied him, saying nothing.

Trevor breathed heavily, in and out. "Please, Miss Breedlowe. Please."

Finally, she said, "Everyone is determined that the countess continues to improve. But, as you know, her prognosis is vague, at best. The doctor's predictions, which you, yourself, heard many times, are unchanged. She may very well lose the infected arm. Have you thought, my lord, of your future with a wife so disabled? Have you thought beyond your current discomfort and worry at all?"

His only answer was to growl again.

"This is her concern. And this is why she forced our hand and saw herself removed from your home and your care to a situation more self-sufficient."

"Please," he implored again, "I must see her." His words were imbued with humility. "Please tell me where she is. I will not disappoint her. I love her. *However* she is, I love her."

Miss Breedlowe considered this. "She's in Knightsbridge, my lord," she finally said. She gave him the street and number. "Please do not tell her you heard it from me. And do not make me regret my decision."

"I won't. And Miss Breedlowe? I will come straight away, but she need not know that I am there until she is strong enough to hear what I have to say. I do not want to distress her. She's run for a reason. I don't want her to feel hunted. Will you help me?"

"I think it is wise, my lord, not to distress her. I cannot say how she will react when she sees you. There is a small parlor in the flat. We can conceal you there if you arrive when she is awake."

"Yes. Good. We're agreed."

"I would not say that, but I will try to accommodate you."

"I will be forever grateful."

She bobbed a quick curtsy and then turned to go. Joseph and Marissa skittered against the wall to make room.

Trevor followed her through the gate and into the mews— long enough to see her safely received by a waiting carriage. When she rolled away, he sprinted home.

CHAPTER THIRTY-FOUR

"You'll go to her straight away?" Joseph scrambled to keep up as Trevor darted across the street. The carriage containing Miss Breedlowe had just turned the corner at Cavendish Square and disappeared into the night.

"Yes," Trevor said immediately, "I'll go to her. Although—no. Yes." He stopped in the street and looked at the night sky. "I don't know."

"You're worried Straka is watching you?"

Trevor laughed bitterly. "Oh, I think I've given up on all pretense that our marriage is a sham. What a bloody cock-up. I've mangled this so badly. She's in danger if I don't go to her because they may have followed her. She's in danger if I do go because I will be followed for sure."

He ran his hand through his hair. "I don't wish to push her further away, but I must see her safety and wellness with my own eyes." He looked at Joseph. "If nothing else, we will ride to Knightsbridge and locate the bloody building. I'll wait in the lobby night and day and go to her when Miss Breedlowe will allow it. I have no doubt that I will be followed, but at least I will be there to stand over her."

"I'm so sorry I wasn't here when she fled, Trevor."

Trevor shook his head. "It's not your fault. She has tricked you before, and she will likely do it again." He looked away. "God willing. But now, hurry," he went on gruffly, pointing to the mews. "Saddle the horses. I will quickly pack a satchel. When we reach her, I won't come back until she is at my side even if I have to make camp in the alley."

"Falcondale?" A voice from the street broke their huddled conversation. Trevor whirled around.

Rainsleigh?

The viscount with whom he'd met earlier today, the man he'd been charged with blackmailing, stepped from a well-appointed carriage, parked in the shadows.

Trevor went immediately on alert. He assessed the man, looking to the lurking grooms positioned in intermittent dark spots on the lamp-lit sidewalk. It was far too late for a social call.

"Can I help you?" Trevor asked cautiously.

"Is this your home?" The viscount stared up at the shadowed façade.

Trevor hesitated only a second, weighing his words. "Yes. It is my house. But you'll have to forgive me. I cannot invite you inside. Something's just come up, and I need to—"

If ever there was a time for directness, it was now.

"That is, will you say why you've come, sir?" He met Rainsleigh on the walk.

Rainsleigh chuckled. "Honestly, I had not intended to stop. I've only just left my offices, returning to my hotel for the night.

Out of sheer curiosity, I bade my coachman take this street. I was puzzled, let's say, by the matter we discussed today."

Puzzled? Right, fine. Obviously, he'd seen through Trevor's ridiculous investment scheme, but why not have a laugh? Why hunt him down?

Rainsleigh continued, "Look, I don't mean to intrude. I would not have disturbed you, if I hadn't seen you cross the street. I don't typically prowl around in the dark. I can see you are occupied, and so won't detain you." He took one step back, glancing at the house.

Trevor made a command decision. What choice did he have? He'd tried to leave Piety today to meet this man for an hour, and the result was, she bloody ran away. He would not leave her again unless their lives depended on it. At the moment, the viscount was a bird in the hand.

"No, Rainsleigh—wait," he called. "Since you've come, allow me to…make a confession of sorts. I have something to give you. Normally I would not heap this sort of document on someone I've only just met, but circumstances being as they are, I have little choice. My wife has taken ill, and the fright has reordered my priorities, so to speak. I am frantic to reach her. If you'll hear my news and take what I am offering, it'll be one less thing. And I may go to her."

Rainsleigh studied him and crossed his arms over his chest. "Not gravely ill, I hope."

Trevor shook his head. Not a denial, a show of helplessness. He could not speak of it.

He climbed his front steps, unlocking the door and motioning him in. "It won't take fifteen minutes. If you have the time."

The viscount looked up and down the street, then at Trevor, and back at his carriage. After a moment, he gestured to stay the coachman and climbed the steps.

"I've no staff, save a serving boy," Trevor said, leading the way to his library. "We are very informal here. I hope you won't mind keeping your coat and hat."

"No bother," said the viscount.

Trevor looked back and saw him studying the empty rooms and bare walls.

"No furniture either," Trevor continued, "obviously. I inherited the earldom, only to discover that the previous earl had squandered the estate, much of it on costly furniture and decor. I've since sold it all, trying to dig us out of debt."

"Hmm," said Rainsleigh, "I know this predicament. It was much the same within my family, when the viscountcy came to me."

"I've sold nearly everything. I'm selling the house, too, if I can find a buyer."

"Fine property," Rainsleigh said, looking around while Trevor made for his desk. He unlocked the side drawer and tucked the damning evidence given to him by Straka in his pocket. He took a deep breath and grimaced. The viscount waited patiently across the desk.

Trevor cleared his throat. He had no real choice but to begin at the beginning. "When I left Oxford at the age of twenty-one, I went immediately to care for my gravely ill mother…"

His tedious history went on from there. The list of possible admissions was long, and personal, and strange, but nothing would make sense if he skipped any of it, and a partial truth would make the whole thing ring so very false. It was essential that Rainsleigh believe him if he intended to confide in him, if he hoped to walk away on the side of the right.

After his mother, Trevor told him about the move to Greece, his affiliation with Straka, his mother's death, and the unexpected inheritance of the earldom. Next came the arrival of Piety Grey, his courtship of her in Berkshire, their marriage.

Rainsleigh had taken a seat during the narrative, and now he leaned back in his chair and steepled his fingers. He did not interrupt. He did not scoff, thank God; and he did not call Trevor a liar—*yet*.

The only point on which Trevor did not elaborate was the faux nature of his marriage to Piety. In his mind, it was faux no more. He loved his wife, desperately so. He wanted to remain married, if she would have him.

Finally, he came to the bit that pertained to the viscount. He paused, swallowing hard, picking up a pen and then tossing it down. "On the morning after my wedding," he said, "I received an unexpected visit from my former employer, Janos Straka."

The viscount raised his eyebrows.

"He turned up in Berkshire with the sole purpose of locating me."

Another pause.

Rainsleigh prodded further. "What did he want?" It was a cautious question. He studied Trevor as he spoke. His trust was not guaranteed.

Trevor swallowed hard. "Straka 'asked,' to use the term loosely, for one, final favor. He'd made a series of bad deals and needed ready money, and lots of it, very fast. He imposed upon *me* to obtain the money for him here in England. He assumed, of course, that as earl, I had connections and access to the very rich. He assumed I would know someone like you."

The viscount cocked his head. His uncertain stare turned cold. "Someone like me?"

Trevor took a deep breath. "It was for *you*, explicitly, that he asked. Or, your money, I should say. He hoped I could find you and blackmail you for the needed funds."

Realization set on Rainsleigh's face like clay hardening in the sun. He nodded. He slapped his hands on his knees and leaned forward in his chair. When he spoke, his voice was deadly calm. "Blackmail, is it?" He rose to stand. "Valiant try, Falcondale, but I have seen far worse. I was raised by hedonists, as I'm sure your damning evidence—whatever it is—shows. After a childhood like mine, I have learned a few things abo—"

"Here are the documents," interrupted Trevor, desperately, shoving from his chair. He thrust the foolscap at Rainsleigh.

Rainsleigh stared at him, his expression so incensed, Trevor thought he would bat his hand away. Slowly, he took the extended bundle.

"That's everything I was given," said Trevor. "To be honest, I have not done more than glance at it. It's something to do with your parents and their time on holiday. In Greece."

The viscount swore and opened the papers, madly scanning the contents.

Trevor continued, "I could not, in good conscience, keep it from you. You may do with it what you will. I have mentioned it to no one except my serving boy, who I trust with my life. Even my wife does not know. I am trying to keep my former life as far from my new life as possible."

"What do you want, Falcondale?" asked the viscount, flipping pages.

"There is nothing that I want. Please understand. I am *giving them* to you. Go, and forget we ever met. I never meant to blackmail you over this—over anything at all. Our meeting today was a bit of a precursor to what I've done, just now, giving you the evidence against your family. It would have been too soon, I thought, to foist the documents on you at our first meeting. We'd meet again; I thought perhaps two or three more times. I would relate my predicament slowly, over time. But I was always going to give them to you. I've just run out of time." He raked his hand through his hair. "Forgive the unexacting nature of this plan. When my wife was injured, I..."

Rainsleigh looked up. "If you won't blackmail me, what are your plans for putting off the Greek now?"

Trevor let out a tired breath. "Honestly, I've no clue. I had hoped to figure it out before I delivered these to you, but now here we are. At the moment, the only thing I care about is reaching my wife's side, seeing her well, and keeping her safe. I have some money saved. Likely, I'll pay him off myself."

Rainsleigh studied him, stepping away from the chair and turning in a slow circle in the room. "I knew there was something off about you. Bloody well knew it. That song and dance about investing? It made no sense, but there was something more. Something intangible. Yet, I liked you. And I like very few people, I can assure you of that. It's why I had my coachman drive down this street. Instinct bade me to learn more. Never in a million years could I have guessed this."

Trevor laughed without mirth. "I can barely believe it myself."

"Where is your wife, now?" Rainsleigh asked. "In hospital?"

Trevor answered carefully. "She has arranged to be cared for in an undisclosed location. That is actually another long story, which I don't have time to tell. The good news is, Straka's spies primarily watch me. I'm careful about how I come and go. Now, you should take care, too," Trevor added, crossing to the door. "The threat of Janos Straka is very real, I'm afraid. As I said, he may be watching us, even now. I will tell him I need more time to squeeze you for the money; meanwhile I will endeavor to come up with some more permanent evasion. But just because I refused to do his dirty work does not mean someone else will. He can be very persuasive."

"I will bear that in mind," said Rainsleigh, tucking the papers in his coat. "I retain the services of some equally persuasive men for exactly this reason. I am also on excellent terms with Scotland Yard. If he threatens me, he may find himself on the inside of a Crown jail. But I do appreciate the warning. I don't suppose I owe you my gratitude for *not* blackmailing me, considering it's the decent thing to do, but I am glad about it." He followed Trevor out of the room.

"My parents were a great embarrassment to me—to everyone," the viscount continued. "I toil, daily, to live down their reputations, to pay their debts, to set the viscountcy to rights." He tapped his breast pocket. "Something like this would be a setback. I am looking to marry soon."

"Good for you," Trevor said, leading the way down the hall, "and I mean that. I would not have, ten days ago. I had no idea, but marriage suits me. Marriage to the right girl, I suppose."

"Well, I've no one in mind yet, it is simply on my list of things to do. Another step in returning the family name to respectability."

"I'm gratified that I was not another setback," Trevor said, reaching for the door. "But now you'll forgive me if I must leave you. I wish to get to my wife's bedside as soon as I can."

"Indeed. But, Falcondale?" He descended the stairs, stopping on the middle step. "I am taking you at your word. I like you. This honesty you profess does you credit." He stared Trevor in the eye. "But take heart. If I discover that this is a trick or a trap, if you are giving me only half of the damning evidence with the idea of a double-cross…"

Trevor followed him down. "I've given you all I have, my lord. The truth. The documents. My heartsick story of woe. By all means, you should employ due diligence. Have me followed, if you like." He laughed. "Your spies may join the crowd. If you need to speak to me directly, you will find me with my wife. My serving boy, Joseph, can get a message to me."

Rainsleigh stopped at the bottom of the stairs and looked up. "Will you really sell this house?"

"With any luck." Trevor sighed, rubbing his eyes with the heels of his hands. "Know anyone in the market?"

"I do, in fact," said Rainsleigh. "I would consider buying this house."

Trevor dropped his hands. "You're joking."

"No," Rainsleigh said.

"I could be persuaded to give you a very good deal—" Trevor paused, suddenly struck dumb by the weight of a very good idea. A very good, very lucky idea. While he stared at Rainsleigh, the roots of the idea spread and took hold in his brain. He took only a moment to weigh the risk of what he was about to ask. Really, what choice did he have? Desperate had become his middle bloody name. Piety's safety and their future was all that mattered. "If you would be willing to help me get the best of this Grecian thug," Trevor asked, "I could give you a very good deal, indeed." He held his breath.

The other man studied him. "I don't require a good deal, Falcondale, I have money to spare. *Trust*—trust is what seems to be in short supply."

"I've never been more honest in my life," Trevor said, his heart pounding.

Rainsleigh considered him a moment more and then gave a firm nod. He turned and headed down the walk, waving without looking back. "I will be in touch."

CHAPTER THIRTY-FIVE

Piety passed the hours in the new rented apartments in Knightsbridge in very much the same manner as she passed them in Falcondale's bedroom—fast asleep. According to the doctor, her body was conserving its energy to heal, but Piety knew that she slept for another reason altogether. To dream.

The dreams of Trevor began on the second or third night. The most glowing, wonderful dreams of her life. So wonderful, in fact, she wished, for the first time ever, that she would never awaken.

Falcondale was there, in her new room, kneeling by her bed. He held her hands and stroked her hair and whispered the most endearing words of love, and promise, and hope for a future together as husband and wife. It went on for hours, this dream, and it was so vivid, so richly detailed, she could smell the musky scent of his skin and feel the rough calluses of his hand on her cheek. Even his body felt warm beside her, staving off the usual chill that seemed to pulse from her very core.

When she awakened in early afternoon, she was alone in the room, except for Jocelyn. It surprised her, even though she knew it was foolish to think his presence had been anything more than a dream. Even if it was so colorful, so real, she had trouble shaking the feel of him, long after she was wide awake. It was as if his very spirit still loomed, leaving muddy boot tracks on the rug and heavy dents in the cushion of the chair beside the bed.

"I think I am delirious again," she told Jocelyn, looking around. The older woman raised her eyebrows and settled a tray on her lap. Taking up a spoon, she hastened to feed her a bowl of broth.

"Well," she said, "you have consented to eat without a fuss. If that is delirium, I'll take it."

Piety smiled weakly. "No, it's not that. 'Tis this dream I've had. I cannot lose the feeling of it. It's as if I'm still half asleep."

"Oh?"

Piety took the spoon from her hands and began to eat. Jocelyn gave her a skeptical look but then scooted back, watching her.

"It's silly, I know," Piety said between slow, small spoonfuls, "but I dreamed of Falcondale. He was here. In my dream. With us—with me. Kneeling right beside the bed."

"Is that so?" Jocelyn said, idly picking errant threads from her skirts.

"And now that I'm awake, it's almost as if I can sense his presence in the room. I can smell him. I can taste him."

"Well, I can assure you that we did not cook him and put him in the broth. It's lamb, my dear, and you should eat as much as you can. Will you take some bread?"

"No, thank you." Piety shook her head and felt foolish for revealing such a fanciful, intimate dream. She pushed her tray away and stretched her neck. "I…I feel like walking."

Jocelyn's head shot up. "Walk? But to where? You cannot think of going outside."

"No, no. Just a turn around the rooms. To the window. I don't care where, really, but I've been in this bed for so long, I think I've sprouted roots."

"Really, Piety." Jocelyn tsked and rose to standing, "I cannot think that is wise just yet. Let us consult with Dr. Hollingsworth when he calls in the afternoon. It worries me to see you overexert yourself so soon after we've relocated."

"But surely walking into the very next room and back is not too much." She tried to wrestle the bedclothes away. "Didn't you tell me the apartments had a sunny parlor?"

Jocelyn heaped them back around her shoulders. "You feel stronger today, and this is a praise, but let us not overdo and suffer a relapse. When you enjoy two days of strength, *and* the doctor approves, then we may venture out." Nervously, she looked over her shoulder at the door.

Piety squinted at her, annoyed and confused, but the moving beneath the weight of the coverlet drained her energy, and the sheer breath required to argue made her dizzy. Frowning, she flopped back against the pillows and allowed Jocelyn to check her bandages and hold a goblet of water to her lips.

"There, now." Jocelyn's hand soothed her brow. "Rest after your meal. I will send a boy out for the doctor and ask him to call earlier in the day, if possible. Then we may have his professional opinion about leaving the bed."

Piety refused to agree, but she did not press, and in moments, she was asleep again.

In time, the dream returned. Falcondale was with her again. This time, he seemed so close, it was almost as if he were in the bed with her. She tried to speak to him, tried to smile and call out his name, but her mouth felt dry and heavy, and he *shhhed* her gently and urged her to lie still. When she complied, he spoke, soft but clear. Assurances. Love. Words that she had longed to hear since they first met. He wept— *wept!*—and begged her to recover. Sometimes, he slept, balancing on the bed beside her, but he never left. In her dream, he was always there.

Again and again over the next three days, she experienced the dream. Each time, she awoke with a small, strange hope that it was real. Each time, she found herself alone with Jocelyn or Tiny. Still, she could not deny that the room held the vestiges of what seemed like her husband's very essence. Once, she even thought she saw his glove lying forgotten on the nightstand. She reached for it, but then Jocelyn was in the way, fussing with her bandages. When she looked again, it was gone.

It wasn't an unpleasant way to experience delirium, she thought. Eventually, God willing, she would recover, and then she would have years to truly grieve the bleak path that their doomed relationship and marriage had taken. But for now, her arm hurt like the dickens, she still had bouts of fever, and she could scarcely stay awake longer than ten minutes. Even when she was awake, her consciousness was blurry, at best. Why not indulge in the most perfect dream?

On the sixth day in her rented suite, Piety awakened in time for breakfast. It was her first morning meal in more than two weeks. Lemony morning sun coursed through the windows, brightening her groggy mood, and her stomach actually grumbled at the smell of breakfast wafting in from the next room. And for the first time, there was no dizziness when she moved. Emboldened—indeed, energized—she sat straighter, rolled her neck and shoulders, and took several deep, cleansing breaths.

She felt better.

She felt, if not good, then certainly far more like herself than she had in two weeks.

"Jocelyn! Tiny!" she called, smiling at the door to the next room. "Prepare yourselves, I'm sitting. With no discernable light-headedness. And I'm warm! Gloriously, stunningly warm. Hot, actually. Get these covers off. I think the fever may have broken."

"Wait," called Tiny, sailing in from the parlor. "You wait just a minute before you go hopping out of that bed!"

"Feel, Tiny," Piety exclaimed, slapping her hands on her own cheeks. "It's broken. The fever is gone. Ow, ow, ow!" She cringed as pain traveled down her damaged arm.

Tiny felt her head and cheeks and neck. Next she checked her eyes and pulse and bandages, gently pressing Piety back against the pillows. Piety endured it all, smiling—humming!—to herself, reveling in the first morning in more than two weeks that she felt like a functional, living human again.

"Just in time, too." Tiny helped to pull back the stack of blankets and quilts piled on Piety's bed.

"In time for what? Where is Jocelyn?"

Tiny mumbled something again, shaking her head, but then a commotion in the next room drew her attention. She heard Jocelyn's voice uncharacteristically loud and firm.

She shot Tiny a questioning look, as she craned to hear.

"I beg your pardon, madam," Jocelyn was warning, "but you may not enter the countess's sick room. Not only has she been explicit about no callers, the doctor himself has said, no guests."

"Out of my way, woman!" replied an unmistakable voice. "I have no idea who you think you may be, endeavoring to restrain me from seeing my own daughter, but you are sorely mistaken if you think you can stop me."

Idelle. Piety collapsed against the pillows.

Her mother had come. A tumble of male voices followed, along with more footsteps. All of them had come.

Piety locked eyes with Tiny. "How did they find me?" she whispered. "Why have they remained in England?"

Tiny shook her head, her expression grave. "Just showed up ten minutes ago. Miss Breedlowe has been holding them in the hall for the last ten minutes, but I guess they pushed their way through."

"But what do they want?" Piety asked. It was a stupid question; she knew the answer. There were more than a million of what they wanted, and they were all in the bank.

"Your color is good," said Tiny, pinching her cheeks and smoothing her hair. "You look like your old self. You're a countess now. Remember that."

Idelle burst into the room, and Tiny bowed her head and stepped back, leaving Piety alone on the giant bed.

Idelle gasped. "Piety, my heavens, what have you done?"

"Good morning, Mother." Piety sighed.

"Have you broken your neck?"

"I have not broken my neck. I have suffered a puncture wound to my arm."

"Boys!" Idelle called to the men in the parlor. "She is decent. You may enter."

"No," said Piety, her head throbbing at the exertion. The effort was wasted. The five brothers, led by Eli, crowded into the room behind Idelle.

"I am not well enough for visitors, Mother," Piety said emphatically. "I would ask you to leave. All of you."

"Or what?" said Edward from the back.

"Silence, Eddie!" Eli advanced on Piety's bed. "Piety wasn't threatening us." His voracious snake eyes barely blinked as he studied her.

Piety huddled deeper against the pillows, her pulse thudding in her head. If she thought they unnerved her when she was healthy and in command and surrounded by friends, she felt positively demoralized when she was sick and alone.

"But where is your husband?" Eli continued, clearly amused by her fear. "No doting earl wringing his hands beside your sick bed, *my lady*? Called away, perhaps? Pressing matters require his attention, no doubt, considering his vast new fortune."

"*Eli*, stop." Piety imbued her voice with strength she did not feel. "Not another step. You are not welcomed here."

Eli chuckled and opened his mouth to say something more but was interrupted by a scuffle in the adjoining parlor. A door slamming. A gasp and Jocelyn's hushed exclamations. A snarl of rage and—

"*Who?*" said a man's voice, speaking over Jocelyn's whispers.

Eli had the good sense to pause, take a step back, and glance over his shoulder.

The double doors to Piety's bedroom flew back against the wall.

Standing in the light of the morning sun, his face a mask of rage, was Falcondale.

"Your life is worth little as it is, Limpett," he said. "I'd step away from the bed if you value what's left."

Eli was stunned into stillness for half a second. His mouth dropped open. He backed away to the far wall.

"Get out, the rest of you," Falcondale said, striding to Piety's side.

"I will not get out," Idelle said indignantly. "My daughter is injured. How dare you think to keep her from me. I am her mother!"

"I *will* think it, and you *will* do it," he said. When he neared Piety's bed, his expression softened. It was a look of tenderness she had never known.

She looked back through the sting of tears. He was here. In flesh and blood. It had been days—weeks—since she laid eyes on him. The sight of his face caused her heart to lurch. And the tears, they couldn't be stopped.

At the foot of the bed, Idelle said, "I will not leave until I have been informed of the ailment from which she suffers and the expectations for her recovery."

"She suffers from nothing that will involve a reading of a will," Falcondale said, not taking his eyes off of Piety. "Get out."

"Your treatment of me—*of us*—is an abomination, sir. Now see here—"

Falcondale spun. "How is it that you remain in this country? We had an agreement about your immediate departure for New York. Pray, what has detained you?"

"Yes, and how did you find me?"

Before the brothers could stop him, Eddie said, "We followed Falcondale, coming and going every day."

Falcondale went still. He shot Piety a frantic look over his shoulder.

She opened her mouth, closed it, blinked. *Came and went? Every day?* Realization covered her like a cloak that someone else had whipped on her shoulders. *The dream…*

There were no words. Perhaps for the first time ever. No words.

Falcondale turned to the Limpetts. "And what did you hope to discover with your spying?" He jerked the nearest Limpett by the arm. Little Eddie stood by the door, and he yanked him with his other hand, dragging them both along through the double doors and into the parlor.

"You will secure passage on the next ship back to New York," he said. "Your ambitions here have come and gone. You may wait from now until doomsday to discover a fresh inroad into the countess's fortune, but even then, you will not find it."

Idelle allowed the brothers to be herded out while she scrambled to Piety's side. "But you did not even know he was here, did you?" She searched her daughter's face. "How curious. It causes me to wonder, why were you removed from Lord High-and-Mighty's home to begin? Propped up in a rented room across town, almost as if you had been turned out by your new husband."

Falcondale appeared behind her. "Will you go of your own accord, madam? Or shall I call the authorities?"

Idelle ignored him. "Tell me, Piety, if you're so injured then why aren't you at home in your own bed?"

"The first option is easy," Falcondale said heavily, "the second, a bother. But both are preferable to the third option, which is me removing you from the premises myself."

Idelle skittered away, hovering near the headboard, holding out a hand. "I will not be bullied from looking after my daughter's well-being!" To Piety, she insisted, "Why such surprise at finding him here?"

Piety looked from Falcondale to her mother and back again. "You were here, Trevor? In my room? You came *here*? But how did you find me?"

Falcondale ran his hand through his hair and exhaled. "We need not speak of it now. Do not exert yourself."

At the parlor door, the Limpett men had begun to edge back in, peering inside. Falcondale growled, strode to the doors, and slammed them shut.

When he walked back to the bed, he pointed at Idelle. "Here you have it, madam," he said, "although I hope that you are aware that you deserve no explanation whatsoever, and that you fool no one with your false regard for Lady Piety's health. I am well acquainted with the manner of your *motherly* concern, and it sickens me. But, just to be perfectly clear—to ensure that you may return to American with full confidence that I, alone, am now wholly responsible for Piety, that there is absolutely no cause by which you may wedge your way into her life or this marriage or her fortune, ever again—here is the situation:

"The injury your daughter suffered was a puncture to the arm. There was a collapse in her new home. I was not with her at the time, a circumstance for which I blame myself every hour."

"Of course you do," said Idelle.

Trevor sighed. "Think what you will, but a new carpenter misunderstood his duties and plastered over the foundation of the stairwell before it had been properly tied in to the structure. The oversight was grave, obviously, and he has since been let go. Piety was knocked unconscious in the collapse and took a nail through the upper arm. We were lucky that her injuries were limited only to bumps, bruises, and the puncture, but infection soon set in, and she has been fighting fever and blood poisoning for these last two weeks, although she looks bright and alert this morning." He flashed Piety a gentle smile. "Her condition has been terrifyingly grave.

"I provided her the very best comfort and medical care in my home, until she made the decision to leave and take up lodging here, so as not to be a burden on me."

Idelle drew breath to interject, but he spoke over her, "What she did not realize was that she could never, not *ever*—not in a million lifetimes—be a burden to me." He ventured a look at Piety. "She has become…She has become life itself to me, and without her—ill, fine, injured, whole—I hardly care to live at all."

He turned to Piety, speaking carefully, choosing his words. "I love you, Piety," he whispered. "I love you with an absoluteness that, likely, I will never be able to fully convey.

Please, please let me care for you. Let me love you. Give me the chance to provide for you in the same way your very existence provides for me." Tears filled his eyes. He rounded the bed and kneeled on the floor beside her.

"How wrong I've been," he continued. "How selfish. This life I thought I wanted—devoid of people, of commitment, of *you?*—you were boldly accurate about all of it. It was lunacy. All I want is you. Wherever I go. Wherever you go. We must go it together. In sickness and in health, just as the vicar said."

He put his forehead on the bed beside her.

Behind him, Piety's mother said, "Well, this is a fine operetta if ever I've seen one. Such dramatics, such—"

Trevor's head shot up. "*Get out!*" He shoved off the floor and grabbed Idelle by the arm, dragging her. She gasped and squirmed, but he did not relent. He snatched the door open and shoved her through.

"*This is* your last warning." Piety heard him shouting. "If you approach the countess again, I will not hesitate to call the authorities, after I beat the lot of you to a bloody pulp. It's over! The prospect of your daughter's fortune is gone."

"Oh, it's yours now?" Idelle said. "Because you play the lovelorn swain so well?"

"No. Because the money belongs to her!" Piety heard him jerk open the door to the hall. "She may do with it what she pleases, and the very last thing she wishes to do is to give it you. Whether she will have me as her husband remains to be seen, but I will always be her protector. From now until her dying day, which, God willing, is no time soon. Her well-being and happiness are my first concern. My only concern!"

He must have followed them into the hall. Piety heard shuffling, angry whispers, grousing.

The door slammed against the noise.

Before she was able to learn if what he'd said about her was true, or an act, or more of the same, he was gone.

Chapter Thirty-Six

Something about the deserted hallway inspired the Limpetts, finally, to fight.

They rounded on Trevor—all five of them—posturing, baring their teeth, putting up their fists. From the stairwell, Idelle urged them on with shouts and waved arms.

Trevor groaned. He hadn't the time or the energy to fight five men, hand-to-hand. Not today. Piety was a closed-door away, and he was meant to reckon with Straka in an hour. Joseph would have been useful, but he was tailing Straka, making sure he showed up for their exchange in Hampstead.

Trevor had fallen out of the habit of wearing his knife since he'd left Greece, but he'd strapped it to his belt today, in case the meet with Straka got out of hand. How convenient for this alternate purpose.

"You do not want this," he warned them, brandishing the knife with practiced ease.

The fat brother, the one with the cane launched first, swinging the cane high and bringing it down into the space where Trevor would have been. *Whoosh*. Fats staggered with the force of his missed mark. While he danced, Trevor struck, slashing his sausage arm and splitting the sleeve. The Limpett cried out, and Trevor spun and kicked. One, well-placed boot knocked the fat one's feet from beneath him. He came down with a thud. His cane rolled against the wall.

The other brothers skittered back. Trevor widened his stance, knife out.

"Who's next?" He drawled. "You want to brawl in the hallway like common criminals? I've done far worse for far less reason. Come on, then." He made a beckoning motion with his hand.

Eli was already backing away, clasping Idelle by the arm and urging her down the stairs. The small brother slunk along the wall behind them. The downed fat brother scrambled to his hands and knees. Only the bald one and the Maypole remained, heckling the others for cowardice, continuing to come.

Trevor did not make them wait. He lashed out, taking the bald one by the neck and driving him against the banister of the stairwell, leaning him over open air.

The tall one leaped to assist, pouncing on his back, but Trevor reared back and drove the knife down, lodging it into Maypole's skeletal thigh. Maypole jerked, too stunned to scream. Trevor wrenched the knife free—now the man screamed—and whipped around to hold it to the throat of the brother against the banister.

He growled in the brother's ear. "*Now*, you will go. You'll take the old woman and your brothers, collect your things, and board a ship conveying you anywhere but here. If ever you return, you will not live to tell the tale. Do you understand?"

The bald one sputtered. "You cannot mean—"

Trevor bit the knife between his teeth, looped one arm behind the other man's knees, and held him upside down from the banister.

A door open on the floor beneath them, and a young couple came to the stair railing and looked up.

Trevor ignored them. "*Do you* understand?" he repeated, louder, moving the knife from mouth to hand.

The couple below them hurried back inside.

Another brother detached from the clutch on the stairs and began to edge along the wall.

Trevor hurled the knife, planting it in the plaster, inches from the American's shoulder. He scuttled back.

"Touch that knife," Trevor said, "and three more come flying, right behind it." It was a lie, but the American went still.

He turned back to the dangler, bracing with both arms to give him a threatening shake. Suddenly, he heard footsteps from floors below. They echoed up the stairwell in a frantic clatter. There were shouts. Someone called his name.

Trevor looked down. It was Joseph. He mounted the stairs in the lobby and raced upward at a breakneck pace, taking the steps two at a time. Behind him were two men, also running. The angle was bad, and Trevor couldn't see their faces.

Something was wrong.

The plan had been for Joseph to detain Straka in Hampstead until Trevor could arrive. The exchange was set to take place there in Hampstead. Not in Knightsbridge. Not in proximity to Piety.

The Limpett brother beneath him squirmed and gave a yelp. Trevor jerked him from the banister and hauled him up, nose-to-nose.

"Go." His voice held a grave threat. "Am I clear?" The Limpett sputtered and sobbed, and Trevor tossed him to the floor.

He checked again for Joseph. The boy looked up in the same moment and shouted, "Oy, Trev! Yer lordship! He's here!"

Trevor's heart stopped.

"*Here?*"

Down the hall, an old woman opened her door and peeked out. The stricken look on Trevor's face must have been enough to frighten her back inside. She retreated and slammed the door behind her.

Joseph scrambled up another flight. "He didn't even consider going to Hampstead, Trev!"

Trevor swore viciously. He looked at Piety's door. He swore again.

Joseph called up again, "When Iros told him you came here, he struck out for Knightsbridge, too. I barely beat him here to give you two minutes' warning."

Trevor heard more scuffling—*new* scuffling—and sawing breath. He looked over the rail. Another set of boots plodded up the stairs. Slower. Heavier. A fat, hairy hand could be seen squeezing the railing.

Joseph was nearly to the top. "They are here. Behind me. Iros. Demetrios. Straka himself."

The boy careened around the final flight of stairs, running as if his life was at stake. He swore when he saw the Limpetts. "What are they doing here?"

Trevor waved the question away.

Joseph was bent over at the waist, panting. "I need a faster horse." He was proficient in Greek, but he spoke in rapid English. The Greeks would struggle to understand. "Straka came here because he thinks the viscount gave you the mo—"

Trevor cut him off with a loud cough. He shook his head with a barely perceptible jerk. *Say nothing about the money.*

Joseph fell silent and slumped forward, gasping breath, his hands on his knees. Iros and Demetrios staggered up the last few steps.

Trevor's mind spun. The exchange *could not* happen here. He would not endanger Piety.

Modify, he ordered himself. So far, everything that *could* go wrong, *had* gone wrong. But all was not lost. He could lead Straka away. He could tell him that there had been a delay in gathering the money. He would tell him he needed more time.

"*Tryphon!*" A winded bellow came from two flights below.

Trevor squinted his eyes shut. *Oh, God.* Up and down the hall, doors opened and neighbors poked their heads out. Trevor gestured wildly for them to retreat, and they complied, thank God, sliding locks noisily in place behind them.

Straka boomed again, "Your boy is loyal, but he is not so smart."

Joseph blustered, but Trevor grabbed him by the arm. "Rainsleigh must know that the exchange is no longer in Hampstead, Joseph. You'll have to go to him before he sets out and explain it, just like you've told me."

"But tell them *where?*" whispered Joseph. "Are they to come *here?*"

"No, it's too close to Piety. I'll lead him to my uncle's house. In Henrietta Place. Find Rainsleigh and tell him the plan will unfold there."

"But Trevor, they—"

"*Tell them!*" His tone was emphatic. "Please. Joe." He gave the boy a shove, sending him back to the stairs.

Joseph fled, careening past Straka as the old man rounded the topmost flight.

Straka appeared *determined*. Determined and furious. It was an unfortunate combination for the exchange they had planned. In this mood, nothing would escape his scrutiny. He might challenge the amount. He might change the deal altogether. *Bollocks!*

Trevor shot a warning look at the Limpetts who still cowered on the landing. He prayed they had the self-preservation to keep quiet and still.

"Straka," he said. It wasn't a greeting.

"The money," said Straka in Greek, heaving up the last few steps. "I have been kept waiting long enough."

Idelle Limpett chose that moment to interject. "Who are these people, Falcondale? What is this foreign tongue?"

Straka regarded her with a scowl, but he was distracted by Trevor's knife. It was still stuck in the wall, handle out. He lumbered to it and wrenched it free. "Is this the knife I gave you, Tryphon? You cannot throw it into plaster; it ruins the tip." He slid the weapon into his own belt.

"Straka," Trevor said in Greek, suddenly inspired, "would you consider the loan of your muscle? I've an errand for which I could use Iros and Demetrios."

"Eh? What errand? But where has your own boy gone?" He squinted down the stairs after Joseph.

"No, this calls for more than he can manage." He crossed his arms and pointed one finger. "I am in need of removal of this family of Americans swindlers."

Straka turned, scrutinizing the Limpetts once more.

"But what are you *saying*, Falcondale?" demanded Idelle. "Stop speaking gibberish!"

Trevor ignored her. "They've been *in my way* for quite some time. And now, I believe they have designs on your money. I was only just tossing them out. My enthusiasm made me careless with the knife."

Straka looked at him, and then back at the Americans. His face lit with delight. "Should Demetrios kill them?"

Trevor forced himself to chuckle. "Tempting, but no. What I want is to secure them on a boat, sailing away. I've impressed upon them never to return, but I haven't the time to make sure they actually set out. You and I have business, obviously, of which they are not a part."

"You want Iros and Demetrios to tie them inside a boat and set them out to sea?"

"Also tempting," said Trevor. "If my mind worked as yours does, I would never find myself in need of borrowed brawn. But, again, no. Can your men simply escort them to their lodging, expedite their packing, and see them to the port called Tilbury? Just south of London Bridge? There will be any number of ships there on which they may arrange passage. Here," he said, reaching into his purse. He removed a handful of coin. "For the hackneys or a carriage. Whatever is the most expedient."

Straka took the money and dropped it in his own pocket and then nodded to Iros and Demetrios. Without hesitation, the two beefy Greeks began herding the Limpetts down the stairs.

Trevor watched them go. "These gentleman," he called in English, "will see that you are packed and boarded on an outbound ship. I would not challenge them, if I were you."

There was the usual bluster and scuffle, but Iros did not hesitate to shove the Limpett nearest him down the next step. The brother landed on all fours with a yelp.

Idelle gasped. "I will not be subjected to abuse by a foreign thug. Do you hear me? What sorts of man consorts with people such as this?"

"I could say the same of my affiliation with you, madam."

She shouted back, "I knew you were no earl."

"Your knowledge of me is about to broaden colorfully. These men would just as soon slit your throats as bother with you, so I'd do as they say, if I were you."

To punctuate his statement, Iros drew his revolver, cocked it, and shoved the barrel between the shoulder blades of Eli Limpett.

After that, opposition ceased. They went without objection, nearly running to stay ahead.

Straka chuckled and then turned a more serious eye. "My money, Tryphon."

Trevor hedged. "I have it, but we cannot do business here. This is a building of private residences, none which I own. I'm a visitor, and we're likely to be escorted from the premises. I've just endured a noisy conflict with the Americans. I should like to remove our business elsewhere. To my house. In Mayfair."

"The money is here, Tryphon. I take it here."

"*No*," said Trevor again, an exaggeration of patience. "We make the exchange anywhere *but* here. I need only collect my things, and we can find other—"

"You *will* pay me, now, Tryphon. I've remained in your damp, frigid country long enough. The money. *Now*."

Trevor sighed. "And what if I told you the money is not here?"

"Then you would *lie*. And I would tear this building apart to find it." He looked up and down the hall. "Which door is it?" He lumbered past. "You have remained here for days. My spies have grown bored, watching this building. When you left the viscount this morning, you came *here*. Come, Tryphon. Please tell me I taught you better than this."

"Straka," Trevor said warningly, "I will not give you one gold coin in the proximity of my wife."

"So you say. Well, perhaps I will take it myself." He squinted at the door behind Trevor. He reached out.

Trevor lashed out, aiming for the old man's thick arm but catching only the billowy sleeve of his kaftan. Straka laughed and shrugged it off. He reached again for the doorknob. Trevor dropped the fabric and lunged, taking hold of his beefy shoulder instead. He was just about to haul him back, to threaten him, to increase the money, to beg him, when they heard a female voice.

"Falcondale?"

Trevor froze.

"Falcondale?"

Piety. *Oh, God, no.*

Trevor looked up. The door to her apartment was cracked, ever so slightly, and her head poked out.

"Trevor?" she called again, searching his face. Her eyes were wide and frightened. She wore a pale-pink dressing gown. The long, heavy coil of her braid swung beside her chin like a rope.

Oh, God.

Straka smiled as his greedy eyes moved up and down Piety's body. Recognition dawned. He opened his mouth to laugh—or speak or bloody sing—but Trevor would not allow him to take another step in the direction of his wife. He jabbed, sending the old man sprawling with a fist to his windpipe. It was a maneuver he learned from Janos, himself. Worked every time.

CHAPTER THIRTY-SEVEN

"Piety, get back," Trevor shouted. "Close the door and lock it behind you!"

Before him, the old man reeled and then, miraculously, regained his balance and charged with a bellow of rage.

Trevor sidestepped, evading him, but only barely. Trevor darted nearer to the door, trying to force Piety inside. Behind him, the old man drew a knife.

"Trevor!" Piety screamed. It was the last thing she managed to say before he pushed her inside, grabbed the doorknob, and slammed the door shut.

"Lock it!" She heard him shout from the hall. She blinked at the closed door.

"I'm waiting to hear you *slide the lock!*" Trevor shouted.

The two men thudded against the other side, rattling the heavy wood, and she quickly snapped the lock in place.

Tiny came up behind her. "I *warned* you not to get outta that bed. 'Don't move,' I said. 'Not one inch.' And I flat-out told you not to open that door. And what did you do?" She shook her head and held out a glass of water.

"Not now, Tiny!" Piety said. "Trevor is in a fight."

"A fight?" asked Tiny. "Eli Limpett again? He'll kill him for sure this time."

"No, no, the Limpetts are gone. It's an old man. Big and strangely dressed. He's bellowing in another language. Have you seen someone like this, Tiny? Around the building? Could he be a neighbor?"

Tiny shook her head and kept coming, trying to shoo her back in bed. Jocelyn joined the fray, willing Piety to take care, but Piety waved them both away. "Quickly," she told them. "The earl needs us. Look around the room. Let us find something that could be used as a weapon."

"A *what*?" Tiny stomped her foot. "And just what do you think you're going to do with a weapon? Mr. Trevor can take care of himself! The last thing he needs is you getting up outta that bed, trying to be part of a fight!"

"I'm not surprised," said Piety, rifling through the first drawer she came to, "that you mention what *Mr. Trevor* wants. It's how he found me, isn't it? You told him. Both of you. My whole purpose in stealing away was to be separate from him, yet here he is. He asked, and you relented."

"*Piety*," said Jocelyn, her voice fraught, "I am to blame for the earl's presence here. I…I failed you in this, and I offer no excuse. But please know that we made every effort. He would not be put off. He was desperate to find you."

Piety nodded her head but continued searching drawers and shelves for a make-shift weapon.

Jocelyn followed close behind. "But please, my lady, you must sit down. Your body has suffered too gravely for this level of exertion. Even if you were healthy, I could not agree that you should join a brawl!"

"You don't have to agree," said Piety, yanking open the door to a wardrobe. The movement shot pain down her left side, but she carried on. "I am acting of my own accord. I exonerate you from all blame."

"*Piety*," warned Tiny, "you think I'm too old to pick you up and carry you back to the bed, but you're wrong! You lost ten pounds when you were sick, and you were too skinny before that. Listen to Miss Breedlowe, and do what she says."

"Aha!" Piety came upon the sideboard beneath the window. A thick, pedestal candle on a shiny, golden candelabra flickered brightly on a doily, its oozing wax seeping heavily around the rim. Using both hands, Piety carefully picked it up.

"*Piety!*" said Jocelyn and Tiny in unison.

"Unlock the door," she ordered, making her way across the room, holding the candle steadily in front of her.

"Piety, no!" Jocelyn exclaimed.

Tiny added her voice to Jocelyn's protest. "No ma'am! *No ma'am!* You're wearing nothing but a night rail, for goodness sakes, Missy Pie. It's not even decent!"

Piety proceeded as if she had not heard. She felt her heartbeat thudding in her head, in her injured arm, in her throat. But her hands did not shake.

Jocelyn and Tiny fell into line behind her, objecting loudly, a relentless, pleading clatter. Piety ignored them. From the hall, the sounds of struggle echoed in muffled *thunks* and grunts through the door. Her strength was wavering; she was weak after so much time in bed. The candle grew too heavy, and she clunked it on the floor. She leaned against the door and listened with her hand hovering above the knob. She waited half a beat. She clicked the lock to the right. She looked over her shoulder at Tiny and Jocelyn, who were wringing their hands, stomping their feet, imploring her. She held a single finger to her lips.

She whispered calmly. "Stop. I am fine. My wound burns a little, but my fingers work. I can move it. Now, *please*. Quiet. If we can help Falcondale, we must try."

Trevor needed only four inches, perhaps five, to reach the walking cane that the fat Limpett had left behind. Straka hadn't seen it. Trevor could *barely* see it—with dark spots blurring his eyes—but still, he reached.

Straka had managed to knock his feet from beneath him and pin him down. Trevor was younger and faster, but it was a disadvantage to plant oneself in a small, tight space and refuse to move. His priority had been standing in front of his wife's door, even when Straka came at him with his own knife. Now, he was trapped beneath the giant man, flailing and wheezing. Consciousness flickered and swam.

"You *dare* to turn against me, Tryphon?" The old man raged, his spittle and sweat raining down on Trevor's face. He weighed, Trevor guessed, more than twenty stone, a punishing, immovable anvil of a man.

Trevor could barely form words. "Not, turning against... protecting... my wife." It was essential that he clarify, despite the wasted breath and exertion. If he had any hope of surviving the fight or what came next, Straka must know that he had not betrayed him.

At least, not yet.

Straka rocked forward, ignoring him, introducing even more strangling pressure to his throat, crushing him, pooling blood behind his eyes. Trevor gasped and blinked; his vision blurred. By some miracle, he remembered the cane and tried again, flinging out his hand. He grasped with fingers extended. His heels dug in. He strained; he reached.

It was no use.

The cane was inches from his hand, and he began to slip away. The world was reduced to one pinpoint of light: the fogged glass transom above Piety's door. He honed in on the light, trying to remain lucid, but it dimmed and flickered and was blotted away. Crushing, black airlessness swelled in its place, enveloping him. His hands dropped, his legs fell still, he—

"*Ooww!*"

The light returned.

Trevor's eyes shot open.

He gasped for breath, and sweet air filled his lungs.

The light became the transom; the transom took shape above the door. The floor was cold beneath him and Straka was...*off*.

Trevor whipped his head to the left. The old man had collapsed beside him, writhing, swatting at his neck and face. His wife stood over them with an upside-down candle. She had flung the hot wax of a burning candle onto the back of Straka's neck.

"Piety, no," Trevor said in a raspy voice. He reached for the forgotten cane and scrambled to his feet. "Back inside, *now!*"

"But wait, Trevor! Use this." She dropped the candle and shoved a weighty golden candelabra at his chest.

"What in God's name? This feels like it's made of lead. Your arm!" He scooped up the candelabra and rolled it through the open door.

"Thank you, but no," he told her. "The cane is better. We don't want to kill him. Yet."

Two feet away, Straka was gathering himself.

Trevor shouted again for Piety to get back.

He raised the cane, watching the old man stagger upright, waiting until he was the most top-heavy, the least stable.

Straka sidestepped to find balance, and Trevor struck, bringing the cane down hard—*whap!*—across the back of the old man's head. *Thlump.* He dropped like a felled tree.

Chapter Thirty-Eight

The task of dragging an unconscious Jonas Straka from the hallway required the combined strength of Falcondale, Miss Breedlowe, and Tiny. It was almost more work to refuse to allow Piety to help, but Trevor set her on the task of collecting Straka's kaftan, the knife, and the cane. More doors opened at the end of the hall. He saw Piety smile and wave; and he growled, dropping Straka's massive leg with a thunk, and swept her back to her own door.

"Do not be alarmed," he called to the gaping neighbors. "This man has had a nasty fall. Nothing a cup of tea won't restore. Carry on."

They were still staring when he hustled the women inside and dragged Straka behind them.

"Piety," he said, "since you appear to be well enough to be out of bed, walking and talking, saving my life, could I trouble you to locate something with which we might restrain my former associate, should he awaken?"

Wide-eyed, Piety nodded. Three minutes later, she returned from the bedroom with stockings.

"It was all I could find," she said. "I don't know where anything is. I've not been shown around the apartment yet, save the bed." She looked away. "But, I suppose you know that."

Trevor tabled, for the moment, the topic of the apartment and what either of them did or did not know. "The stockings will work nicely. Here, give them to me. I'll need to secure him by his hands and his feet, preferably to something heavy. Please stay back."

The women hovered, watching with wide, worried eyes, as he bound the unconscious man to an oak desk. Even Piety did not speak. He dared not speculate her level of resentment.

When he secured the last knot, he took a deep, uneven breath. "Miss Breedlowe? Miss Baker? May I have a few moments alone with Lady Piety?"

They nodded blankly, their fraught expressions like two defenseless captives, trying to decide which of their oppressors was the most sane.

He continued, "It's best not to leave you alone in the room with this blaggard—even bound and unconscious. I'll need to stand over him until—well, until we decide what's to be done. If Piety is well enough to sit with me on the couch," he stole a look at her, "and if she is willing to hear me, can I trouble you to wait in the bedroom?"

Miss Breedlowe cleared her throat. She looked imploringly at Piety. "My lady, would you lie down? Even on the couch?"

"I've been lying down for weeks." Piety sighed. "I'm weary of lying down. And I am fine—at the moment. Do you mind, terribly? Holing yourselves up in the bedroom?"

"Do not think of us, my lady. You are the—"

"Invalid," she cut in. "I know. But today, I feel a bit of a rally. At least long enough to learn, the identity of this dead man in our parlor."

"He's not dead," said Trevor. To the women, he said, "I will persuade her to rest. This morning has not been ideal, I know."

He exhaled wearily and stole another look at Piety. Her expression was inscrutable.

When the door clicked behind the women, Trevor drew a deep, grateful breath. The urge to scoop Piety against him was overwhelming. He fought it, determined not to rush. She had bloody *run away* to be rid of him. He might muck it up a million different, unsalvageable ways, but the one thing he could, hopefully, deliver now was restraint. The day had already been a blur of ill-timed revelations and great shock. He'd reappeared in her life only to knock a man unconscious after a brawl in her hallway. There were no guarantees.

He held out an arm, gesturing awkwardly to the couch. "Will you sit with me?"

She bowed her head and demurred, crossing whisper close beside him. He let out a breath and followed.

There was no restraint in the decision of where to sit. He could prop himself up prudently apart from her or stand. He opted for neither and settled beside her on the cushions. His leg not quite, but almost, touched hers. She did not draw away.

"Piety," he began, "how do you feel?"

She laughed. "Really, Falcondale, I've just flung hot wax on an unnamed man so you could bash him with a cane. Let us not begin with, 'How do you feel?' "

"Right," he said, "but we will return to this topic."

"Maybe we will, and maybe we will not. But first, who is that man?"

Trevor nodded. "He is called Janos Straka. I've mentioned him to you before, perhaps not by name. He is my former employer, from the years I was in Athens. He is no man you should have ever had to see. My God, the danger I've put you in. I will regret it all my life."

"I was not afraid. I only wish I'd had a more damaging weapon, but the hot wax was all I could manage. I did not want to miss. Or splatter you. And I wanted to hit bare skin, not his shirt. Or his hair."

"You did amazingly well, Piety." He chuckled grimly. "Thank God you were there. You saved my life. Again."

She blinked and looked away, staring at her knees. It was impossible to know what shocked her more, the presence of Straka or his admission that she had saved his life.

He nodded. "The whole bloody row is a surprise, I know. No one has been more appalled than me."

"But why? Why is he here?"

"It's a long story; one which I will tell you in excruciating detail, if you can bear it. But first, he must be dealt with. Regret is not strong enough a word to express how I feel about his proximity to you, especially now. But, unfortunately, we are not finished yet. Before he'll go, he and I have a transaction that we must conduct."

"A transaction? But you've just knocked him cold. You can't believe he'll be open to doing business."

"Oh, he'll be open. I've something he wants, desperately."

"What is it?"

Trevor glanced at Straka, still unconscious. "He wants money, Piety, and I have managed to sell my house. I have some to give him."

"But the money from your house, is it a loan?"

Trevor made a strangled sound—half laugh, half cough. "Ah, no. It is a payment, shall we say. The price of my freedom. After this transaction, he has vowed to not bother us ever again."

"But when did he come to you? How long have you been negotiating with him?"

"Just to be clear, I want no part of him and am, in no way, 'negotiating' of my own volition. He turned up at the wedding"—he shot her a guilty look—"and has been hounding me since."

"The wedding! But why didn't you tell—"

Trevor shook his head. "I kept the situation from you in order to keep you safe. He is a very bad man, Piety, and it goes without saying, a dangerous man. I had to know what he wanted, and how he intended to get it before I..." Trevor sighed and looked at the ceiling. To reveal it was the only way.

When he continued, the words came out hard, clipped. "I lied to you, Piety—about his presence at the wedding, about his contact with me, about the tasks he set before me. I did it to shield you, although I can see, now—considering you *bloody well ran away*—that I should have shown you the reality of the situation, no matter how bleak, rather than allowing you to assume I was still purposefully holding myself apart from you, like an idiot."

She opened her mouth to speak, but he continued on, "I knew you would offer up your own money as payout, and I could not allow that. Instead, I endeavored to figure out my own way. I kept my distance from you, emotionally and physically—as was our original agreement—because, I worried that if I showed you favor, it would give him a new pawn.

"*This* is the reason for our race back to London after the wedding. *This* is the reason I went out the night we returned. I have been very preoccupied on Straka's behalf. Unfortunately.

"Then," he continued, "the accident happened. I was forced to double down. Once I located you, I was unwilling to be away from you unless it was absolutely necessary." He quirked his eyebrow at her. "But I could not manage Straka on my own and be at your bedside at the same time. I've had to put my trust in someone else—a man I've only just met. I made a friend, of sorts—you'd be very proud. He's helped me a great deal."

"Oh, Falcondale," Piety said, dropping back against the cushions. "I wish you'd simply told me."

"I was a fool," he said. He wished, fervently, that she would call him Trevor. "But you needn't worry," he went on. "Straka wanted me to steal the money. Instead I sold my house to this man, my new friend. With *that* money, I may now send Straka packing. He has vowed, after this sum, to never intrude on me again."

"But how can this—"

Trevor shook his head. "I know, it's deuced hard to understand. There is more, much more, and I will tell you all, when you can bear it." *If you will allow it.* "In the meantime, I need to remove him as far from you and the other women as possible. Your duty, is merely to *rest*. Recover. Allow Miss Breedlowe and Miss Baker to care for you. Be sensible about your health,

Piety. Please. I'll be preoccupied with him just one more day. Perhaps less." He raised his eyebrows, imploring her.

She chewed her bottom lip, ratcheting up his temptation to reach for her. He looked away.

She began, "Can you—"

"*Eh?*" Across the room, Straka roused, snorting, groaning.

Trevor shot from the couch and stepped squarely in front Piety. "Careful, Straka," he urged in Greek. "Careful. You're all right. You've had a nasty fall."

The old man let out a string of profanity. He fought the bindings, flapping ineffectually.

"Piety," Trevor said calmly, "Please get up. Go 'round the table, keep your distance, and join the women in the other room. Lock the door."

She didn't move.

"Piety," he repeated more firmly. "It's essential that you do as I ask. Please comply with me. Just once. Please."

"I'm going," she said indignantly. "We may all assume that I have *improved*, but I cannot fly. Yet."

He turned to her, whispering apologies, helping her to her feet. It was his first time to touch her when she was not in a fevered sleep. Even with Straka threatening to erupt just feet away, he savored the warmth of her skin beneath his hands. He lingered close, his face nearly touching her hair, his hand on the small of her back.

"Go," he said gently. "Lock the door. Try not to worry."

She laughed at that, a heavy, worried sound, and picked her way around the edge of the room to the door. When she had disappeared into the bedroom and slid the lock into place, Trevor said to Straka, "I have your money, but it is not here—"

"That is a lie! Iros has followed you for days. He followed you this very morning after the meeting with the viscount. *The money is here.*"

"Take a closer look, Janos," Trevor said. "Iros is strong and loyal but hardly a logistical genius. He knows what he *believes* he saw, but there is a reason that you chose me to run your empire. Iros is a bodyguard, not a spy."

"Iros never betrayed me!" Straka strained against the bindings. His voice dropped to a deadly growl. "And if he did, he would kill me when he had the chance. His life would be worthless, if I survived. *As yours is now.*"

"Come now," said Trevor, "you cannot threaten me now. Not when I have so much lovely money for you. And why would I kill you? I don't want you dead; I merely want you away from my wife."

"Ah, yes. The wife who is not really your wife." He scoffed, then he bellowed. "Untie me!"

"Not yet. Not until you've agreed to take the money and go—agree to leave me alone forever, as you said."

"How can I take the money if it is not here? Untie me! Let us finish what we began!"

Trevor lied quickly. "Half of it is here. What Iros saw was some portion of the money to bribe the Americans. I never meant to give it to them, mind you; but they needed to see some proof." He whipped open a wardrobe and emerged with a bulging leather satchel. "Would *you* like to see it, Janos? It's your money. I have only to match it with the other half, which we can easily collect in my home, just miles from here, once you've agreed that this ugly conflict between us is over. I've blackmailed the bastard; now set me free."

"That was before you attacked me! Insulted me by tying me to the floor like a dog!"

"Agree to finish this elsewhere, then I will untie you and will fetch the other half."

Straka scowled and said nothing; Trevor dropped the money—which was, in fact, the total sum—beside his bound feet. Iros's report had been accurate, and Trevor had been careless to detour here with it instead of going straight away to Hampstead. But there had been time to look in on her, and he could not resist it.

"Here it is. We will count it together, you and I. Hopefully your Serbian debtors will accept British pounds in notes from the Bank of England. That was all he could get."

"Untie me, do you hear?" Straka roared, pulling against the bindings to peer into the satchel. "How much! How much would he give?"

"Five thousand, all told. You'll find half of it here. The balance is under lock and key at my home in Henrietta Place. Iros may be watchful, but he has not seen all of my comings and goings, not by far." The lie came more easily this time.

"Five thousand pounds," Straka said with wonder, and Trevor cursed himself for going too high. Straka continued, "Meant a lot to him, did it? Keeping all that depravity away?"

Trevor said smoothly, "He balked at the price, actually, but I held firm. Five thousand was meaningful, but not impossible. Ultimately, he saw the value in your silence."

"Untie me," Straka demanded again. "Let us finish."

"I would like to Straka, honestly I would, but I must be assured of your cooperation. We cannot fight to the death, you and I. In fact, we cannot fight at all. And we cannot remain here. My wife is ill, and we've terrified her staff. A doctor is due, soon, to call. There are neighbors. It's simply not feasible. It's why I asked to have this exchange in Hampstead. I am only here to look in on my wife. If you'd stuck to the plan, you would, perhaps, not find yourself bound."

"Fine. Untie me and let us remove ourselves from your precious wife."

Trevor crossed his hands over his chest. "Can you give me your word as a"—he made a coughing noise—"as a *man who wishes to claim five thousand pounds*, that there will be no further conflict? That we may peacefully hire some conveyance to my house and finish this?"

"Yes, yes!" Straka huffed. "Let me loose!"

"And you're aware that if you cross me, if you slit my throat and steal away with this satchel here, then you will not see the rest?"

"Is that a threat, Tryphon?"

"No, it is a fact. Joseph has very clear instructions. You saw him leave here at a fast clip. If something befalls me, he will make the rest of the money immediately unavailable to you. It goes straight to the charity box at an orphanage in Berkshire, and it will be gone from you forever. Then where will you be? You'll have the two and a half thousand pounds and the body of a dead earl, when you could have walked away with five."

"You would lecture me about sums? Untie me!"

"Give me your word, Straka! We leave here immediately! Truce?"

"Fine! Let me go!"

"One more thing, when I give you balance of the money, you leave me alone—forever. No more favors. No more spies. I walk away, as do you."

"I'll never work with you again!" Straka declared. "You're too much trouble."

He recoiled when Trevor squatted beside him, flashing his knife. It was Trevor's turn to laugh. "If I'd wanted to kill you, you would already be dead."

"Ha!" Straka scoffed, watching him slit the stockings. "You couldn't kill me. Too soft," he muttered. "Always too soft. Your thin, English blood!"

Trevor severed the stockings, but he stopped short of helping Straka to his feet. He backed away, keeping the knife handy, watching the big man lean heavily against the wall to heave to his feet. When he was up, Trevor kicked the satchel to him.

"Count it, if you like."

Straka laughed, straining low to swing the heavy bag to his shoulder. "You know I never count it until I am alone," he said. "You also know what happens if I have been—"

He was cut off by a knock on the door.

Trevor's gaze snapped to the entryway, and Janos craned around.

The knock sounded again. Louder, longer.

What now?

Trevor's gaze flicked to the old man. Iros and Demetrios? No, it was far too soon. Joseph? Please, no. It was too soon for the doctor. The maid never knocked.

The rapping sounded a third time—more of a pounding now—and Trevor stopped trying to guess. He took up the most strategic position, flat against the wall, behind the door. Janos looped the strap of the satchel diagonally across his chest and wove through furniture, making his way to the window.

"Janos," Trevor whispered. "Do not even think—"

Bam! The front door swung wide, nearly flattening Trevor, admitting a throng of uniformed policeman and Bryson Courtland, Viscount Rainsleigh.

Officers swarmed the room, filling every corner, while a sergeant barked orders. Straka bolted and was halfway to the window before they closed in and seized him. They discovered Trevor a moment later and took him up, too.

"Yes, that's right, that's them!" Rainsleigh said, striding to the center of the room. He pointed to each man in turn. "*He's* got the swag—my money in my leather satchel, just as I described. He's the Greek national, Janos Straka. Masterminded the whole thing. The other one is Falcondale, and he's the Greek's first lieutenant and chief extortionist. Arrest them both! They've just extorted me for five thousand pounds!"

CHAPTER THIRTY-NINE

It was impossible for Piety *not* to look. The shouting was too urgent and angry, the commotion too great. She unlocked the bedroom door and cracked it, ever so slightly, peeking out.

The parlor was filled with police. There was also a tall, finely dressed man. His bearing was important, and the police regarded him with deference. He crossed his arms over his chest and made small gestures in the direction of Trevor and the Greek man. The police pounced, herding them against the wall, spinning them to press their faces against the plaster and wrenching their hands behind their backs. Piety watched in horror as they clapped irons on Trevor's wrists.

She spun to Tiny and Jocelyn. "My clothes! Quickly! I must dress."

The women opened their mouths to oppose her, but something about her expression deterred them. They shared a miserable look and fled to her trunks.

Piety turned back to the door. The Greek was fighting the police, blustering, resisting. They shackled him before taking a bulging satchel from his chest. Now they were forced to unchain him and played tug o' war to untangle the bag.

Trevor appeared too stunned to fight. He craned around, as if straining to see the gentleman in the center of the room. The Greek man shouted to him in his own language, and Trevor answered.

She heard him say, "He doesn't speak English. He won't understand the charge!"

The gentleman said shortly, "Tell him it's blackmail and extortion."

Trevor translated, and there was more bluster. The policemen shouted over the angry Greek, working together to subdue him. It took four of them, but they hauled him to the door.

The gentleman shouted to Trevor over the din, "Perhaps your accomplice would go more peacefully if you explained that they will detain you separately. He is a foreigner, and you are an Englishman with a title. He needn't worry that you don't leave together. The booking procedure is not remotely the same!"

Trevor scowled at him and translated, shouting to be heard over the Greek man's tirade.

Before he'd finished the translation, they began to hustle Trevor to the door. Piety's heart seized. She spun to check the progress of a dress.

"We are looking for something that will go over your bandages!" Tiny whispered.

"It doesn't *matter*," Piety said urgently. "Anything! Hurry! The police are taking him away!"

She checked again. Trevor had finally begun to argue.

"Please, my wife! In the next room. She is not well. Pray, do not disturb her!"

The gentleman shook his head. "My accusation is not against his wife."

"My lord," a policeman said to him, "the money." He held out the leather satchel.

The gentleman rifled through it. "We'll want to count it. But it looks close to what I was ordered to place into the bag."

Trevor was nearly to the door, being shoved and pulled by two policemen. "Rainsleigh!" He finally raised his voice. "My wife! I must speak to her. Five minutes! Tell them I require five minutes. She will not understand."

The agony in his voice wrenched her heart from her chest, and she could not wait for a proper dress. "Falcondale!" she called, flinging the door open. "Wait. Please wait. I am here. Someone? Please, explain where he is being taken and why?"

Trevor craned around, fighting the hold of the officers, clawing to see her. The expression on his face was sheer panic.

"Piety! Not yet. Get back! You promised!"

Trevor squeezed his eyes shut. Of course, she would be noncompliant.

He shot a helpless glance at Rainsleigh and shoved against the policemen who held him. The viscount nodded, affected a small shrug, and ushered her back.

Good luck with that, Trevor thought, listening as Straka shouted another bright idea from the hallway.

"Bribe the police!" he said in Greek.

There was no way to finish this without terrifying her, and Trevor cursed himself for not giving her some idea of the raid. More bad timing. He hadn't managed to explain even a fraction of the necessary history before Straka came to, and then the bloody raid itself had unfolded here, in her apartment. Why had Joseph brought them *here*?

Excuses now seemed pointless. When he stole a look at her face, creased with confusion and fear, his heart found a new, more painful way to break. He refused to allow himself the unfair hope that a hysterical Piety meant a Piety who still cared, although it did cross his mind, selfish bastard that he was.

But all of this was secondary to his chief goal of resisting police with enough vigor to convince Straka. If he could do it quickly enough to not scare Piety entirely out of her wits— or beyond forgiveness—perhaps he would have managed one success for the day.

But he dare not get ahead. Now, he would pretend to fight. Two policemen hustled him near the door. He reached out and latched onto the door facing, forcing them to pry him off. He shouted and swore in Greek, matching and answering Straka's distant cries.

Behind it all, he was forced to hear the excruciating conversation Rainsleigh embarked upon with his wife.

"If you would be so kind, my lady," the viscount began.

"I would *not* be so kind!"

Trevor fought on, praying she would not wrench away, that she would not strain her bandages or pass out from the shock of the fray. He heard her whimper, and he craned, shouldering to see around the over-eager policemen. "Rainsleigh?"

"She is with me," Rainsleigh said. "She is safe with me."

It was permission enough to finish this, to finally, truly fight. The policemen wrestled him to the first landing, down two more steps, mostly carrying him while he screamed in Greek. He had the fleeting thought that, even if Piety refused to live with him as his wife, she certainly could never live here. They'd all be evicted by sundown, if not before.

Finally, the cries and bluster from Straka grew fainter, as they managed to drag him through the lobby and out the door to the street. The sergeant saw it from the window and called down with a signal. Just like that, the platoon of policemen wrestling Trevor let him go and danced back. Trevor collapsed against the wall, panting. They unlocked the irons on his wrists and he sprinted back up the steps.

"Piety, I am well. I am here. It was a charade." He grabbed the doorway, gasping for breath.

To Rainsleigh, he said, "Why the devil did you not go to Henrietta Place? Did Joseph not reach you?"

"Easy, Falcondale," said the viscount, "Joseph was convinced that the Greek would not part ways with the money for a detour to your house. We made the tactical decision to begin here. Joseph went to your house, just in case. He's run himself and his horse ragged, sprinting around town to make it right. I have apologized to Lady Piety. It was a risk, I know."

Rainsleigh looked guiltily at Piety. "I hope you'll consider blaming me and not your husband. His highest priority was that you be kept safe. I was afraid we'd miss our chance if we did not come to the last location that we knew both Straka and the earl to be, not to mention the bag of money. It was a risk, but the right one, I think." He glanced at Trevor. Falcondale shook his head slowly, feigning disgust.

Rainsleigh went on, "This bit of theatre landed your husband's tormentor in jail—hopefully forever. *And*, saved him five thousand pounds."

"But I don't understand," Piety said. She locked eyes with Trevor.

He shoved off the door and walked to her. "You look pale," he said.

"It is the color of complete and utter confusion. And fear! Please, Falcondale, tell me again. You're not being hauled to jail?"

"No, not jail." Trevor stopped in front of her. "But it was essential that Straka believe that I was going, same as he. If he ever gets out of prison, it will be safer for us this way."

Rainsleigh stepped away. "Indeed." He nodded to the policemen who still loitered in the room, and they began to file out. "The sergeant also suggests that you turn up in Scotland Yard sometime in the near future and pretend to be an outraged detainee. For the old man's benefit. It is true that they would never have held you together, and Newgate is a big place, but he might see you once or twice. Perhaps as he's dragged to interrogation? After we have rounded up his two henchmen."

Trevor sighed. "Oh, God, after an errand to Tilbury on my behalf, please."

Rainsleigh chuckled. "I'm sure that can be arranged."

The viscount put on his hat. "I've been in touch with the Foreign Office about a few of the blaggard's other schemes— fleecing the Serbians and cheating the Sultan. Apparently both factions will send their own delegation to question him. He should be locked away for a very long time—if he doesn't lose his head for the Sultan. But just in case, see it through."

Piety ignored him, searching Trevor's face. "So it's true? An act, all of it?"

He nodded. The desire to touch her was more powerful than he'd ever known. He clenched his fists at his sides. "Yes. A great fiction. My part in it, at least. I did not blackmail the viscount, but he agreed to participate in this exchange with Straka and accuse me of it in front of police. He didn't have to become involved. It was a selfless favor. He is a good man, and I owe him quite a lot."

"Do stop, Falcondale, or I may blush," the viscount said. "Take your payment. I'm very rich, or haven't you heard." He chuckled. "I hardly require the gratuity of a house." He tossed him the heavy satchel of money.

Trevor caught it and dropped it in a chair. He had no argument. In fact, there was very little he could say or do in that moment but stare at his wife. The viscount chuckled again and took up his hat and gloves. He mumbled good-bye on the way out the door but did not wait for a reply.

When they were alone, Trevor stepped in front of Piety and reached out. "*Piety*."

He ventured a touch to her cheek—one finger, tracing her profile. She did not pull away, and he delicately moved to her uninjured side, down her shoulder, down her arm. He caught her hand and held it.

"You were never meant to see any of this," he said. "It was meant to happen in Hampstead. In an abandoned bank. There was an elaborate plan."

"I…I wish I'd known. You took years off my life, Trevor. And I've only just been assured I have years left to live."

"Do not joke," he whispered. "Not about that."

She watched him, and he went on, "I wish I *had* told you. There has been so little time. The day spiraled out of control from the moment I walked in on the Limpetts. I worked as quickly as I could to make each new kink go away. I wanted you safe and peaceful and rested. Instead, you saved my life."

"You did make it go away."

"Yes, but I only lived long enough to do so because you prevented Straka from strangling me."

"I wanted to do more."

"Ah, Piety, you did exactly the right amount. As always. But now, will you indulge me? Allow me to get you back to bed? You must rest up. Who knows what wax-flinging opportunities tomorrow may bring."

Chapter Forty

Piety was exhausted, but she refused to sleep until Trevor gave some very clear, very certain sign. Something tangible and measurable that she could plan her life around. His intent. The state of their marriage. She would not descend into hazy unconsciousness again until he'd said it—whatever it was. Why he'd come. Why he'd stayed. Why his every move now seemed hemmed in by caution. Oh, how she detested caution. But now, everyone practically swam in it today.

He walked her carefully to bed, telling her how the plan evolved between him and the viscount, how the viscount bought his house, how the police were brought in to make the raid; Piety waved her hands in surrender. "Please, Falcondale," she said, climbing into bed, "if we really are safe, I cannot hear anymore. Not tonight. Later, you shall tell me each unbelievable detail. I want to hear every word, I do."

He nodded, holding back the blanket. "You've lost interest now, because no one's ordering you behind a locked door. I've seen this all before."

She laughed and realized it was her first real laugh in weeks. It felt lovely. "Not so fast, if you please." She chuckled. "Even though I don't wish to talk about the raid, I do wish to talk." He was tucking and stuffing and folding her beneath the covers like a package. She made a noise and shoved upward, sitting against the headboard.

"I must know why you came here, Trevor. Before the Limpetts. Before the Greeks. Why were you here? In my rented rooms? I left your home for a very sound reason. Why did you follow me?"

He dropped to one knee beside her and let out a surprised laugh. "Why did I follow you? Where else would I be, Piety?"

"Syria," she said. "Egypt. Peru. Tibet. China. Istanbul. The list was long. The list was a lifetime long."

"But did you hear what I said? Before, to the Limpetts and Idelle? I will not go without you. I cannot leave you ever again. I will not leave you."

"Yes, I did hear you, but forgive me if I struggle to believe. It is a complete about-face. It is exactly the sort of thing we planned to tell the Limpetts. We've lied so much, I don't know what to believe."

Tentatively, he reached under the covers and found her hand. "I will never leave, darling. I could not bear it. I couldn't bear it even before the accident, but I was only beginning to come to terms with it. That is why I kept popping up wherever you went. But no more denial." He squeezed her hand. "The prospect of losing you to some horrible accident—of losing you at all—was so terrifying to me, it stunned me into acknowledging how much I love you. How much I absolutely cannot live without you. If you will have me, and even if you will not, I am your servant, Piety." He looked away and then back at her. "My love, my only regret, *my shame*, is that I did not realize it sooner."

"But what...what about your fear of being responsible for me?" she asked softly. "What about not wanting the burden of anyone else's troubles? I have been known to embody trouble."

"What you embody, is sunlight. You solve problems; you do not create them. Never have I met anyone so capable as you. Or more spirited or willing to improve whatever task is at hand. Believe me, I will be the burden to you, not the other way around."

Unable to believe it, *afraid to believe*, Piety tried to turn away. "But my arm," she whispered, tears in her voice. "I could lose it. And then what would you think about my spirit and will? My capability? I would be the burden you fear the most."

"No. The burden I fear most is the life I would lead without you in it. Do not speak like this. If the arm goes, so be it. I will weep for your discomfort, but I will not love you any less."

"You say that," she said softly, "but I felt so helpless today. And, it is easy to love me when I am happy, and pretty, and capable, and able to make things happen."

"It is easy to love you, regardless. What it is difficult to do—what I found it impossible to do—is to *not* love you. I tried, like an idiot; you know I tried. From the moment I tackled you in my music room, I tried not to love you, but I could not. It's almost as if I was created to do only this. And I've waited my entire life merely to have you crawl through a passage into my lonely, selfish world and take up residence. Thank God. Thank God you arrived when you did."

She chuckled, wiping away her tears. "Or what?"

"Or I would have become the loneliest, most uninspired, most frightened, well-traveled architectural scholar on the earth. And all the while I would have thought I was doing myself a favor. How wrong I was." He gave a small, hopeful smile.

"Trevor, are you grinning?"

"One of the many skills I learned from you. It disarms people, and don't think I didn't notice. How friendly you come off smiling and winking, all the while you dazzle people into agreeing to things to which they otherwise never would have consented."

"I am a happy person," she said.

"That you are," he said, edging closer to her on the bed. "And you've caused me to discover happiness as well." He sighed and studied her. "Dare I... Dare I hope that you will consent to make me happy for years to come as my wife? My true-and-eternal wife? Shall we travel the world together, if you wish? Shall we have children together, if we are so blessed?"

"Oh," she said, tears in her voice again. "Is it true? Can I believe you?"

"I don't know how truer I could make it." He rose. "But I understand your hesitation, and I do not deserve an immediate affirmation. Merely allow me to be beside you for today. Then, if you're amenable, we'll do it again tomorrow. And the day after that. And the day after that. Eventually, you will see."

"And then what?" she asked, scooting up in bed.

"And then we will have a real wedding."

She laughed again. "We've already had the wedding of the year. What could be more real than two hundred revelers and a feast that lasted half the night? There was a string section."

"Ah, yes. And let us not forget a Grecian slumlord. It was a celebration to end all others. It included everything but the assurance that it was real. And every bride—and bridegroom—should have that confidence. Promises meant and promises kept."

She thought about that for a moment and then reached her arm up, her hand outstretched. "Trevor?" she asked.

He studied her hand and then took it, holding it against his chest. "Yes, Piety."

"I did think it was real. When we said the vows. And I meant every word." She gave a slight tug. He loosened his hold but she clasped his fingers and pulled him to her.

He raised his eyebrows. "So did I, Piety Rheese, Countess Falcondale. So did I."

And then, mindful of her arm, mindful of the servants in the next room, mindful of the taxing morning she'd already spent, Trevor allowed his wife to pull him completely down in bed beside her and covered her lips with a kiss.

EPILOGUE

Lord and Lady Falcondale's wedding trip was put off until Piety's arm had fully healed. In that time, she was able to see her house—now *their* house—fully restored.

"It's mighty beautiful, Missy Pie," Tiny told Piety as she gave her and the marchioness the first grand tour. "You could always see it like this. All I saw was a pile of bricks."

"We were lucky, weren't we?" Piety said thoughtfully. "I'm not sure my dream would have been realized if we hadn't moved in next to the earl."

Both the marchioness and Tiny harrumphed. "You were lucky to have the *marchioness* across the street, that is how you were lucky," said Tiny.

"Oh, of course." Piety smiled. "That goes without saying."

The marchioness cleared her throat.

Piety corrected herself. "Or perhaps it cannot be said enough."

The tour ended in the sunny rotunda, with beams of light washing the white tiles and resplendent stairwell in crisp autumn sunshine.

"Now *this* room?" said Tiny. "This room I could do without." She would barely look at the stairwell and landing that nearly took Piety's life.

"I could not agree more," said the marchioness, stomping her cane. "A bit showy, don't you think?"

Piety laughed. "But this is the heart of the house. And it's perfectly safe now. It cannot fall again."

"You won't find me ascending it, of this you can be sure," said the marchioness. "I don't care how brilliant of an architect Falcondale claims to be."

Tiny heartily agreed.

"Tiny," Piety began, looping arms with her, "I considered your aversion to the stairs, actually, when I designated your room to be here, on the ground floor. It will be easier for you to come and go." She looked at Lady Frinfrock cautiously. They had not yet broached the topic of where Tiny would reside when she and Trevor departed for their extended wedding trip.

"Egads, Tiny," said the marchioness, "you cannot mean to live *here* while the earl and countess flit across the globe. You'll be all alone while Miss Breedlowe and I fall into certain discord. What if I cannot tolerate her?"

Tiny smiled and patted Piety on the hand. "I told Piety that I'd rather stay with you, Frances, but she made me a room here, just in case. *Lord almighty.* Never in my life did I expect to have *two* fine houses to live in." She squeezed Piety's arm.

"Please do not abuse Miss Breedlowe, Lady Frinfrock," Piety implored. "If I receive a letter at some foreign port indicating that you have, er, 'fallen into discord,' then I will be forced to sail home immediately to rescue her."

"Ah, then I will abuse her immediately, just to have you back."

"Abuse who immediately?" said Trevor, clipping down the stairs. He came up behind Piety and wrapped his arms around her waist, pulling her against him. He kissed the top of her head.

"Spare us, please Falcondale," said the marchioness. "The wedding journey has not yet begun."

"Can't wait to see me sailing away, can you?" he said.

"You would take our dear Piety away for months and months—perhaps the better part of the year," complained the marchioness. "Miss Baker and I are sick about it. Positively sick. Why cannot you simply go to France for two weeks like civilized people?"

"Oh, we'll see France all right, never you fear." He kissed Piety again and she laughed. "France, Italy, the near East. My wife has generously consented to see it all."

Piety chuckled. "I haven't *consented*." She turned her face to him. "I cannot wait to see the world with you."

"You see that, my lady? She *wants* to go," said Falcondale. "But never fear; you'll have our new neighbor, Lord Rainsleigh, moving in next door to keep you occupied. His renovation of my old house will require your attention to every detail, I'm sure. Keep a watchful eye, will you? In fact, I insist that you welcome him to the street in much the same way you welcomed me."

"Devoted care and wise counsel?"

"Meddlesome attention and open scorn."

The marchioness grimaced. "So you say. I can only hope he is a better custodian of the property than you."

"Already better," said Trevor, kissing his wife again. "He's put a crew on the second floor just today, sealing up the passageway between Piety's bedroom and my old house. Nicely done, too. I've checked on the masonry myself." He stepped away, collecting the day's post from a silver tray. "Afternoon, my lady, Miss Baker."

Piety watched him go, holding her breath. She stole a look at the marchioness.

Lady Frinfrock raised one bushy eyebrow. "Did he just say *passageway*?"

ACKNOWLEDGMENTS

I would like to thank early readers of this book, in part and in whole, whose essential feedback and encouragement kept me from giving up: Janet Marlow, Barbara Taylor, Jerry and Rita Calhoon, JoLynn and Shelly McEachern, and Sarah MacLean.

I know of no author who can navigate the writing life without the patience and support of family. Thank you to my children and Mr. Michaels for realizing this dream with me.

And finally to my critique partner, Cheri Allan, whose gentle, insightful critiques, encouragement, and extensive knowledge of stair construction helped transform the manuscript into a real book.

Want more Bachelor Lords of London?

Look for Charis Michaels's next fabulous historical romance

THE VISCOUNT AND THE VIRGIN

Coming July 2016 from Avon Impulse!

An Excerpt from

THE VISCOUNT AND THE VIRGIN

She swallowed. "Lord Rainsleigh—"

He cut her off. "I beg your pardon, Lady Elisabeth, but do you know my given name?"

Bryson. Bryson Anders Courtland. Of course she knew it. She shook her head.

"May I call you Elisabeth?" he asked. "My given name is Bryson—or Bryse, as my brother calls me. I would welcome a less formal address."

She raised an eyebrow. "Will all the applicants to the prize be invited to refer to you as. . .Bryse?"

"Only the ones on which I intend to call."

Elisabeth opened her mouth. She shut it. She blinked at him. "I beg your pardon?"

He leaned forward. "Please don't think I'm being dismissive of your work—I am not. I want to know everything about your foundation and the service you provide. But I also want to know everything about you. I am very taken with you, Elisabeth. I should like to see you again. Soon."

"Oh, God."

"Have I offended you?"

"No, you've simply. . .*caught me unaware.*"

"Would you consider a courtship?"

"Courtship. . ." she repeated. She pushed from her chair and stood. "Lord Rainsleigh, we've only just met. And what of my application for the charity donation?"

He stood. They were feet apart, face to face. "My personal interest in you will be entirely separate from my involvement in the donation. I can assure you, it is only *you* who I wish to refer to me as Bryse."

She looked up at him.

He stared back, his blue eyes searching, waiting.

She sat back down. "Forgive me, my lord—er, Bryse." She spoke to her knees. "I don't know what to say, and that is a rare circumstance, indeed."

"I would also speak to your aunt. It felt appropriate to suggest the idea of a courtship to you first."

She laughed, in spite of herself. "I'd say so. Unless you wish court my aunt."

"I wish for you," he said abruptly, and Elisabeth's head shot up.

He crouched before her chair, spreading his arms and putting one hand on either side of her chair, caging her in. "How old are you?" he asked.

"How old do you think I am?" A whisper.

"Twenty-six?"

She shook her head. "No. I am the ripe, old age of thirty. Far too old to be called upon by a bachelor viscount, rolling in money."

"Or," he arched an eyebrow, "exactly the right age."

She laughed, looking away. He said nothing, and she looked back. His blue eyes were serious. Her laughter petered out. "Why me? Why pay attention to *me*?"

His voice was so low, she could barely discern the words. "Because I think you'd make an ideal viscountess."

Oh, God.

She fell back in her seat and closed her eyes but the large room still swam before them. She felt a gush of hope and joy in her chest at the same moment the bottom fell out of her stomach.

He went on, "You are mature, and intelligent, and poised. And devoted to your charity, whatever it is."

A thread of the old conversation. She clung to it. "I've just told you what it is."

"You spoke in vague generalities that could mean a great many things. I let it go, because I hope for many more opportunities to learn."

Elisabeth breathed in and out, in and out. She bit her bottom lip. She watched his gaze hone in on her mouth.

She closed her eyes again. "If your far-reaching goal is to earn an esteemed spot in London society," she peeked at him, "you're going about it entirely the wrong way. No one has ever asked to court me before. It's really not done."

"Why is that?"

Because I have been waiting for you.

The thought floated, fully formed, in her brain, and she had to work to keep her hands from her cheeks, to keep from closing her eyes again—from squinting them shut against his beautiful face, just inches from her own, his low voice, his boldness.

"I'm very busy," she heard herself declare.

"Then I will make haste."

"Is this because of last night? When I. . .challenged your dreadful neighbor?"

The corner of his mouth hitched up. "It did not hurt."

"It's very difficult for me to stand idly by when I hear a person misrepresented."

"And to think I was under the impression that you could barely abide my company. Your defense came as a great surprise."

"Oh. . .I am full of surprises."

"Is that so?" His words were a whisper. He leaned in.

She had the fleeting thought, *Oh, God. He's going to kiss me*, and then—*bam!*—the door to the library crashed open.

CHARIS MICHAELS is thrilled to be making her debut with Avon Impulse. Prior to writing romance, she studied journalism at Texas A&M and managed PR for a trade association. She has also worked as a tour guide at Disney World, harvested peaches on her family's farm, and entertained children as the "Story Godmother" at birthday parties.

She has lived in Texas, Florida, and London, England. She now makes her home in the Washington, DC-metro area. Visit Charis at www.CharisMichaels.com.

Discover great authors, exclusive offers, and more at hc.com.